'a beautiful yet unsettling story with a strong sense of place, accentuating the bond between humans and the landscapes they live in... a book to reflect on that will undoubtedly linger long after finishing.'

– Rhianon Holley, *Buzz*

'a novel that shimmers with compassion, one that crosses borders of both nations and emotions. In telling the story of a mother's love for her son and an intimate, searing portrayal of survival set amidst the Ukrainian Maidan Revolution of 2014, the author has crafted a tale that will linger longer than the half-life of many other books you will read this year. Holloway's fascination with the intersection of where history meets everyday life has given us a story told with great skill, weaving together the legacy of Chernobyl and the tragedy of human arrogance. She gives us hope that each of us can act with grace and love even in the face of overwhelming disaster and a precarious world. Sadly for us, it is even more necessary for us to hear these stories today.'

– Alex Lockwood, author of *The Chernobyl Privileges*

'A careful, tender and arresting story that explores how we're formed by the places we think we own – I was moved by this suspenseful and delicate novel.'

– Jenn Ashworth, author of *Ghosted*

'a gripping story which speaks to a universal anxiety, not just about nuclear power, but about the environment as a whole. It explores the way we respond in crisis, and the things we hold onto most when everything seems under threat. More than that, it captures the genuine love of a family who, despite their flaws, care about one another deeply. A transformative read in a time of heightened complexity and division.'

– Zoe Kramer, *Wales Arts Review*

For Mum, who taught me to read and write.

Philippa Holloway is a writer and academic. She has won prizes in literary awards including the Fish Publishing Prize, and the Writers & Artists Working Class Writer's Prize. She is co-editor of the collection *100 Words of Solitude: Global Voices in Lockdown*, and a senior lecturer in English Literature and Creative Writing at Staffordshire University.

THE HALF-LIFE
OF SNAILS

$$T\tfrac{1}{2} = 0.693/\lambda$$

Philippa Holloway

Parthian, Cardigan SA43 1ED
www.parthianbooks.com
© Philippa Holloway 2022
Paperback ISBN: 978-1-914595-52-3
Hardback ISBN: 978-1-913640-57-6
Ebook ISBN: 978-1-913640-58-3
Editor: Carly Holmes
Cover Design: Syncopated Pandemonium
Typeset by Elaine Sharples
Printed by 4edge Limited
Printed on FSC accredited paper
Published with the financial support of the Books Council of Wales
British Library Cataloguing in Publication Data
A cataloguing record for this book is available from the British Library.

Part One

α

CHAPTER ONE

He is small for his age, only a month and a half into his second year at primary, not quite six. Goose-grey eyes and jackdaw stick-nest hair that makes him look smaller. She won't cut it, no matter how many times people hint, or state bluntly, that she should. Being different will give him strength. In the long run.

He clambers over the barbed-wire topped fence, agile, careful not to catch his jeans on the rusting spikes, dashes into the field as if he is a wild animal released from a cage. An after-school ritual, necessary to rebalance him. Every weekday, as soon as they get home, he changes into jeans and sweater, hiking boots and jacket. He moves differently in his proper clothes, is less nervous, more vibrant. Once changed, they walk along the lane and spend a few moments chatting, giving him time to shake off the day's lessons and rules, and then, once they've both savoured the pause, he helps her with the last of the farm jobs. She saves the most appropriate for him, the ones he'll learn from – challenging but doable. Every day he gets a small sense of achievement, learns another vital skill.

He runs in a wide arc across the grass, head tilted to the sky as a murmuration of starlings lift, compress and dissipate before settling again in the next field. Helen watches him, her heart swelling along with the flock. Standing here, on the farm her family has owned for generations, looking out over fields of fat, pregnant ewes and wind-bent hawthorns, she can usually, even if only for a second, forget. She inhales deeply, relishes the sharp sting of cold air that floods her lungs; the rich scent of sheep droppings, the tang of sea salt from just over the horizon behind her, the brackish undertones of sodden leaves still mulching at the edge of the path. She drinks in every season, has done every year since her own childhood on the farm. It's everything she wants for Jack, all she has to offer him. He is crouching now, one small finger outstretched to investigate some hidden treasure he has spied in the longer grass near the hedge.

An only child, a single mother. The odds are stacked against them, in so many ways. They are doing okay, she thinks, as she watches him rummage, pull out his reward. He is a natural on the farm, attuned, her taidy would say. Born to it. He comes to her, beaming, his first gummy gap giving him a waif's smile.

'What did you find?'

'A tooth!'

In the centre of his mucky palm lies a sheep's molar, ridged and worn, yellowed with age.

'Good find, Jack.' She ruffles his hair and smiles. 'Will it fit in your mouth to replace the one you lost last week?'

He giggles and leans against her leg as he holds the tooth up to the light and turns it, examining every contour and tone.

'It's too big for my mouth!'

'Well,' she crouches to his level, brushes a tangle of hair off his forehead, 'we'll just have to wait for yours to grow through. Come on, we've got work to do.'

He shoves his new-found treasure into his pocket and

follows her, helps lift sacks of sheep pellets into a barrow, insists on trying to lift the handles and push it himself. She stands behind him and takes the brunt of the weight, and together they walk carefully along the lane and open the gate. The sheep know the squeal of the hinges, they bellow and start trotting towards them, their swollen sides swaying comically. Helen uses her penknife to slice the bags open, and she and Jack tip and spread the brown pellets over the close-cropped grass.

'Do you remember why we give them extra food in February?'

'For energy to grow their babies.'

'Da iawn, Jack. Here, shake the rest out over there, make sure they all get some.'

The ewes bump and shove one another, press together to get the best of the treats. She could become lost in these moments – by the rhythm of them, the realness – if the threat of losing it all wasn't a constant itch, like nettle rash, in the back of her mind. If there weren't plans for a new nuclear power station to replace the one that has dominated the coastline since before she was born; land acquisitions and groundworks already underway. She's been fighting the development from the start, tracking its growth: a steady creep towards the edge of her ancestral land, the requests to buy the family farm at more than market value. A constant worry that taints everything, bitter on the back of her tongue. She won't give in, no matter what. For his sake.

Jack has drifted, is halfway down the field, shouting to her. His voice high and half lost to the wind. She walks over, trying to shake away the constant niggling worries that line her skull.

He is jumping, pointing.

'Look Mam, she's stuck, I think.'

He's right, one of the ewes is caught in the briars that border the bottom of the field, tugging and straining then sagging back, exhausted. Helen hasn't been in this field since last night's rounds, it could have been caught for hours.

'Come on then, time to learn!' She jogs towards the sheep, slowing as she nears so as not to startle it. Jack by her side, matching her pace. Like a shadow, eager and attentive.

Helen is practical, doesn't waste time trying to settle the ewe, knows that soft words won't calm it. The best thing to do is get it free as soon as they can. She pins its head between her knees, squeezes her thighs together as it bucks, and feels it relax. Then hands the penknife to Jack.

'Wriggle in close and cut away at the bramble, Jack. Cut her fleece if you have to.'

He doesn't hesitate, and she doesn't have to tell him to be careful with the sharp blade; he's been using tools like these since he was a toddler, to her parents' and sister's horror, and has never cut himself yet. Attuned, she thinks.

Jack leans his shoulder against the swollen flank of the sheep, pulls at clumps of muddy fleece and saws away at it until, bit by bit, the ewe comes loose. Before he can finish cutting through the last knot, it gives a sudden tug backwards and slips out of Helen's grasp, then bolts. Jack staggers back, lands on his bum in the soft earth.

'Ti'n iawn?'

He nods, stands and brushes himself down, watching the ewe trot up the slope to search for any pellets left in the sparse grass. He's grinning. Tough.

'Come on, it's time to get ready,' she says, taking the knife and folding it back into her pocket. His smile disappears, and he slips his hand in hers, clings. She hopes he's tough enough. They are both nervous. They've never been apart for any longer than a school day since he was born.

Back in their barn-loft bedroom, Helen sits on her haunches while Jack brings her folded underpants and balled socks, fleece pyjamas and a tattered book for her to tuck into his rucksack. Already it holds waterproofs, a water bottle and a hand-powered torch, high-protein snacks, and a silver foil survival blanket neatly folded into a small square pouch. There is a list in carefully formed child's handwriting inside a small brown notebook, and after each item is carefully stowed he marks a tick on the page with a stubby pencil.

'Think,' she says when he's finished. 'Is there anything missing from the list?'

He sways in his big hiking boots, rotates like a miniature scarecrow in a breeze, scanning the room for anything he's missed.

Stops turning.

'Modron and Mabon.'

'Get them, then.'

He picks up a large pickle jar from the floor at the side of his mattress. It's half full of cabbage scraps and sticks, and somewhere underneath the leaves there are two large garden snails buried deep inside their shells.

'I'm ready.'

Outside, Helen pauses in the wind that cuts in off the coast and rushes over the fields, stares again over the island towards the razor-sharp teeth of Snowdonia, distant on the mainland. The sky is clear, the watery sun just on the horizon behind her. The mountains still have snow on the peaks. The fields nearby are now tinged deep blue in the fading light. She shivers.

'Did I ever tell you about the blue fields, Jack?'

He looks up at her and sighs. 'Yes. Over and over and...' Freckles on pale skin.

'Alright, no need to be cheeky.'

He carries on in a monotone, 'Taidy sprayed the fields bright blue to stop Caesar...'

'Caesium.'

'... to stop the sheep getting... dirty?' A frown. He waits to be corrected.

'Contaminated.'

Jack looks at the winter-worn fleeces and muddy underbellies of the sheep huddled against the spiky hawthorn hedge, rubs a sleeve under his runny nose. 'It didn't work, they're still dirty.'

She ruffles his hair. She wasn't much older than he is now when the first images of Chernobyl's shattered reactor flickered onto the tiny black and white portable TV in the living room. Doors and windows shut tight against the hot spring sunshine until the rooms were stuffy and her nose itched for fresh air. She remembers pressing her fingers against the cool glass of the hall window and watching her dad disappear inside the rubbery skin of a monster suit to go and check the sheep. The gritty texture of powdered milk on her tongue. There were hushed conversations in the kitchen that went quiet as soon as she or her sister walked into the room.

Enough to know that everything had changed, that they weren't safe anymore, no matter how many times they were rocked on laps and whispered reassurance. Spraying the fields years later was a game changer, Prussian blue compound to prevent the uptake of residual caesium as the flock grazed. It brought them back from the edge of bankruptcy, Helen learned. The thought of how close they came to losing everything still gives her goosebumps. Especially now.

Jack kicks pebbles into puddles while she locks up, then reaches for her hand as they walk up the lane towards her parents' farmhouse and the car her dad lets her borrow. She's late today, going over to help Ioan with his little hobby flock. Jennifer will be checking her watch.

As they walk Jack tugs at her wrist, then wriggles away and skips ahead, just out of reach. He is confident on the stony path, jumping over puddles and avoiding the peril of rocks that jut up out of the slate chips and could turn an unobservant ankle. His nerves about his first night away from her side either hidden or forgotten for a moment in the game of the journey. She can feel the tension in her shoulders, though, beneath the straps of his rucksack. Walks faster to burn up the adrenalin that floods her system whenever she thinks about the next few days. She could cancel the whole thing, of course, but what kind of message would that send him? Survival depends on identifying your weaknesses, facing them head on. She absentmindedly reaches to her side, touches the small lump on the cusp of her breast through her waterproof jacket.

He needs this. Just in case. And she does too, perhaps more.

Her sister's farmhouse isn't far. It sits right on the edge of the Anglesey coast, just a field and a sandy, root-tangled path separating the garden from black rocks and foaming sea. Wylfa Nuclear Power Station is less than a mile away, so heavy and solid it could be a castle. Except the shape is wrong. The angles are industrial, the defences military. There are no windows. It fades in and out of sight between the knotted oak trees that line the driveway, but even when she can't see it, she knows it's there.

Between the main road and Jennifer's house they pass three empty cottages, a few rubbled spaces where other homes once stood. In the last year the landscape has already been scarred beyond healing, and there are plans to strip out the hedgerows next, to relocate the wildlife. Helen has documented each change through her camera, keeps files on the plans.

As she eases the car around the potholes that lead to the farmhouse, sheep lift their noses into the wind that whips off the headland. They call out to their lambs over the threat of the engine noise.

Inside the car neither of them speak. Despite the regularity with which they come here, together, to help out with the sheep and drink tea, they both know that this time it's different. Jack is watching her through the rear-view mirror. She glances up every so often just to catch his eye, to send him a sign that it's okay. He's going to be okay. She's explained it all.

'This is a challenge, like an adventure.'

'But why do you have to go?'

'Because doing this will make us both even stronger. It's only a few days.' Holding him tight and burying her face in his tangled hair, like the first day of school, but worse.

It's a practice run, this week. A chance for him to manage without her, for a while. After all, there might be surgery, nights in hospital. Worse.

The security light comes on and half the house lights up, corners worn and lichened, the mortar receding where it shoulders the brunt of the weather. She loves this house; her grandparents used to live here, before Jack was born she even lived here for a while. Cutting her teeth as a farmer by managing the livestock, then nursing her taidy until they took him into the hospice. Remembering still makes her angry. The indignity of it. A fortnight of morphine and tubes, and people filing in and out to stare at him and cry. Everything he swore he didn't want. She'd sat with him to the last shuddering breath, using a little foam pad on the end of a plastic stick to keep his gums and lips moist while he slowly dehydrated; the sweet smell of loosening flesh under the blanket marking out his decline. They should have left him in his own bed. It would have been quicker, more humane. She already has plans for her own end, if her results are bad. There won't be any nurses to drag things out. It will be natural, quick. Easier for Jack to deal with.

She pulls on the handbrake and cuts the engine. As the wipers fall still, tiny droplets of rain bead the windscreen. Jack sits in his car seat behind her, the straps so tight they make his coat puff out in segments. He waits. The car is rocking almost imperceptibly in the wind. Jack never met his great-grandparents. By the time he was born the house had been rescued from probate by Ioan and Jen, and their fat salaries from the power station. That's the only good thing she can say about Wylfa. If it wasn't for the plant the house would

11

have gone to strangers. And now, years later, it might go to Wylfa's replacement. Apart from her parents' farm and one or two others on the other side of the site, it's the only inhabited place left. If they pursue compulsory purchase orders, everything will be lost.

Through the windscreen Helen can see the kitchen windows, steamed up from cooking. One is cracked open but not enough to clear the glass. There is movement behind the steam, blurred colours that must be Ioan and Jen, draining veg or making gravy. They fade in and out. When she unclips her seatbelt Jack copies her, and they step out of the car together, slamming their doors almost in synch. The night smells of rain and seaweed and sheep, the scent of roasting lamb just on the edge of the inhale, and then whipped away by a taut wind. She can hear waves crashing over the rocks beyond the close-cropped pasture. And a low hum. She doesn't need to look towards the floodlit glow of the power station, she feels it. A shadow or a low white noise that seeps into and colours everything around here. It vibrates.

She pulls Jack's rucksack from the boot and helps him shoulder it. It's heavy but he doesn't ask for help, just leans forward slightly to balance. He reaches back in and takes the pickle jar out of the black maw of the boot and holds it to his chest with one hand, his other hand finding hers and squeezing. She squeezes back.

'Remember what I said, it's an adventure. You'll get spoiled rotten, I'm sure.'

'Can I watch TV?' He's testing her.

'If Aunty Jennifer says so, yes. Her house, her rules, remember?'

There's no need to ring the bell. As they step into the creamy warmth of the hallway leaves blow in around their boots.

'Shoes off, Jack.' A whispered reminder, but not needed. He knows to be on his best behaviour here. He loosens his laces and shucks off the boots, then stands waiting. He's still clutching the jar.

'Hey, we're here,' Helen calls. 'Sorry we're late.'

The door to the kitchen opens and the smell of roasting meat envelops them. Jennifer comes out, wiping her hands on a tea towel. She is older than Helen, and apart from the shape of their noses, the tilt of their eyes, they could be strangers. Their hair was the same colour when they were girls: coal black, fierce. Jennifer dyed hers blonde as soon as she was allowed, turning any bullies into hopeful boyfriends. Helen had used her fists to silence them. It was quicker. The respect was worth the detention.

'Hey, come on in little man.' Jennifer kneels and hugs her nephew, pulling away when she feels the glass jar pressing on her chest. 'What have you got there?'

'My friends.'

Jennifer looks up, past his tousled head, and frowns a question mark at Helen.

'Snails.'

'Lovely.' She stands. 'Keep them in the jar, okay?' She helps Jack take off his rucksack and weighs it in her hands. 'What's in here? Bricks?'

Jack shakes his head and half smiles, and she carries on. 'You don't need to build your own house here, Jack, we've got you a room ready! Come and see while your mam goes to the field?'

Jack doesn't answer. He looks between his mam and his aunt and hugs his jar tighter.

'Do you want to come with me down to the field?'

He nods.

'Put your stuff over there then, and get your boots back on.'

He settles his snails down on the sideboard and crouches to lace his boots. Helen is proud of how deft he is – she's heard there are children in his class not yet fully toilet trained.

As they open the door again, Jennifer catches Helen's sleeve.

'Are you sure he's going to be okay here?'

'He'll be fine, he's prepared.'

They head off down the lane that slips between the garden and the orchard, Jack nimble as a goat over the roots and pebbles. He is prepared, it's just not quite time yet.

She's already done a full day's work on her parents' farm, the after-school jobs with Jack. She's tired but eager to see how Ioan's ewes are doing; they are due any time now. He meets her on the path, running to catch up. He is big; both tall and broad, a gut just the safe side of overweight. Scoops Jack up as if he weighs nothing and swings him onto his round shoulders, getting a squeal of delight for his efforts.

'How are they?' Helen asks.

'They were fine this morning, but a few seem ready to drop.' Out of breath a little.

Helen has been helping Ioan with his little flock for years, effectively managing them for him. The rest of the fields were sold off after Taid died and are now in the hands of the new project. But they'd kept a few, to keep the word 'farm' on the gatepost valid. They don't need the smallholding or the animals. Helen is pretty sure they make a loss on the livestock each year, but she's grateful there is something left. She drops in a few times a week to check things over, help with anything he still isn't sure of, or where two sets of hands are necessary.

While Ioan bounces Jack on his shoulders Helen does a quick tour of the perimeter, making sure the fence repairs from last weekend are still good, checking for any new damage.

The last group of sheep are in the barn, penned in and ready to lamb, their swollen bellies widening them out so their backs are flat as tables. Jack, finally free of Ioan's attention, scrambles high onto a stack of bales and swings his legs while the adults discuss the stock.

'You'll check them late and early? Remember, they usually labour with the rising tide.'

'Depends on my shifts, but I'll do my best.'

'There are only two that worry me.' Helen points at a pair right at the back. 'From their size, you might be looking at three, even four each.'

'Bumper crop.'

'Expect losses. You sure you don't want Ianto to come over, just in case?' A boy from Gwredog Uchaf, the other side of the lake; young and enthusiastic, skint enough to need the extra cash from overtime. Already on the books to cover her own shifts at home.

'We'll manage. I'm not useless you know.'

'I know, but…'

'If you're worried, why are you going now? Why not wait?' The edge is sharp, but she's ready for it.

'I've made provision. His number is in here.' She hands him

a thick envelope from her back pocket. 'So are the quantities for the supplements after birth, and, just in case, a list of signs and treatment for toxaemia and milk fever. They both present the same, remember? So treat for both if you see any of them go quiet and stop cudding.'

She swings a leg over a wood-pallet fence held together with twine, and squats beside a heavy-bellied ewe, running her hand along its side, pressing to feel for the hard knobbles of skulls beneath the thick, damp fleece.

'If you're worried about one, you should treat them all. But really, they should be fine. If I was worried, I wouldn't be going at all.'

She stands up and looks him straight in the eye.

'Any concerns, call Ianto. I trained him myself.'

Back at the house Ioan hoses down his wellies and slots them carefully onto a rack by the back door, while Helen and Jack take off their hiking boots in the porch.

Jennifer meets them in the back hall.

'Dinner's ready, are you staying for food or do you need to shoot off?'

'I've got time.'

They hug. Half habit, half need.

'How's Mam?'

The usual question, the heart of most of their conversations these days. The last three years have been punctuated by bad test results and hushed conversations about anti-nausea medication, hair loss and probability. Watching her shrink and blemish before their eyes. They barely talk about themselves anymore. Just Mam and the new development.

'She's fine, eating more.' She sees a softening of the shoulders beneath Jennifer's cashmere sweater. Even in her Sunday jeans and with her hair tied back she looks elegant. Helen shoves her hands into her pockets and rocks in her thick woollen socks. She's never really out of jeans. Never were two peas, but it didn't matter.

'I must get over to visit this week,' Jennifer says. She ushers them through the kitchen and into the lounge, reaches behind the sofa to pull out the basket of toys she keeps for Jack. He settles his snail jar beside him on the rug and begins removing items from the basket, lining them up in front of his crossed legs.

The lounge and dining room have been knocked into one; a big open space. A view to the garden at one end, and the field and sea at the other. Squashy sofas in pale grey are arranged around the original fireplace. A wide oak table and bookcases neatly stacked and spaced with vases marks out the dining area. Lamps everywhere. The light is soft, yellow.

There's wine on the table: white, with condensation in dewy beads on the glass. Helen paces the room, touching the things that make it her sister's: the expensive weave of the fabric covering the sofas, the silver-framed photo of her and Ioan's wedding day, a vase of shop-bought daffodils – sunshine yellow just beginning to break through the papery spathe. It's the kind of house people aspire to, a listed building tastefully renovated. An open fire, for luxury rather than necessity, has settled to an orange glow. She runs her hand over the radiator. It's warm.

Jack has lost interest in the toys already and is lying on his tummy in front of the fire, swinging his legs up over his backside. He's transfixed by the tiny world inside the pickle jar, his face close to glass. One of the snails has awakened and is gliding around its concave prison. He's had them for nearly three months now. She needs to make him release them soon, before he loses interest. She needs to make him set them free while he'll still feel the loss like a rock in his chest. He needs to own that rock.

Jennifer glides in with a carafe of water and a china gravy boat, followed by Ioan holding a serving dish heavy with the fragrant roast. There is a back and forth to the kitchen, fetching tablespoons and mint sauce, during which Helen mutters to her sister, 'This feels formal, what's going on?' and her sister replies, 'We just thought it would be nice, a proper meal together for once. I'm glad you have time.'

When they are seated around the table there is an atmosphere redolent of Christmas, of the Sunday dinners of childhood crowded around the battered kitchen table back home, their mother plump, healthy and sweating beneath her apron.

There is a pause while the feast is consumed by their eyes, laid out on platters.

'There!' Jennifer exhales. 'Lovely!'

Everything in the room is warm and yellow and creamy and soft. Light glints off the glasses like sunlight on the sea.

It doesn't take long to wreck it.

'Did you kill it?'

The gravy is still being poured and serving dishes passed around when Jack pipes up. He's watching Ioan carve the joint, the grey-pink flesh exposed and steaming.

'Kill what?'

'That.' Jack stares at the slice hanging from the fork.

'It's one of our lambs, yeah buddy.'

Jack points a delicate pink finger towards the window. Directing everyone's gaze. 'One of them?' In the field behind the house the early lambers are bleating for their babies to return, udders full and waiting for the shivering new lambs to butt their heads up under matted fleeces. Their pale shapes drift like ghosts behind the reflection of the diners in the glass. Dirty clouds in a dark sky.

'Here, have some potatoes, little man.'

Jack leans back while Jennifer tips three glistening, golden roasties onto his plate, and then looks up at Ioan again. 'How did you kill it? With a knife?'

Helen interrupts.

'Uncle Ioan doesn't kill them, he sends them to the slaughterhouse.'

Jack nods, satisfied with the answer and unaware of any discomfort he's caused. He stuffs a whole potato in his mouth, gravy running down his chin. He's a good eater, knows to pack it in when he gets chance. Helen doesn't know why he's still so small. She tears off a strip of meat and tests the flavours. It's slightly overdone, chewy.

'Did you hear James and Mererid have signed?' She hadn't planned to bring this up, not tonight, but it's said now. 'I was over there earlier. He couldn't even look me in the eye. She says they're moving to France, leasing the house back for a pound a month and renting it out to the contractors.'

'France? Sounds nice.' Jennifer gets up to pour wine and Helen sees the glance she and Ioan share. She puts a hand over her glass when the bottle is offered to her.

'They don't think the boys will want to come back here from uni.'

'She's probably right—'

'Mererid said they'd be able to pay off their fees.'

'It's a good move for them.'

'It's a greedy move. Fucking selfish.'

'Helen!' Jennifer is gesturing towards Jack with her eyes, frowning.

'He's fine, it's only a word. He's heard worse at school, I'm sure.'

'Still…'

Ioan clears his throat and Helen feels the tension in her thighs. This wouldn't be first time they've clashed over the buyouts. Ancient farmland blueprinted for car parks and containment buildings, a Soviet-style housing block looking out over the sea. Reactors and turbine halls. The argument is raging across the island. In village halls and council offices people stand over maps depicting routes for new pylons, spit biscuit crumbs and spill tea as they argue the toss between the cost of below-ground lines and the impact for tourism if the new pylons dip and strut their way across the gentle contours of the landscape. Infrastructure versus heritage. Helen has attended a few herself. So has Ioan. But tonight is not the night for arguments. She takes a long sip of water and smiles.

'Thanks, you two, for putting this on. The gravy is delicious.' Helen thinks it might be instant; there are dark clots marring the deep red-brown pools on her plate, a grainy texture on her tongue that reminds her again of powdered milk. It doesn't matter. It's food. And Ioan seems happy with the compliment. A disaster averted. The mood is almost back to the buttermilk warmth of earlier.

Then Jack spits a mouthful of lamb into his hand and holds it out towards his mam.

'I can't swallow.' It sits in his palm, a tough knot of fibre with the moisture chewed out.

'Hey buddy, don't spit at the table. It's not polite,' Ioan says.

'But I can't swallow it.' His voice is flat, stating a fact. Too often read as defiant or cheeky by everyone except Helen.

'Here, little man, I'll deal with that.' Jennifer holds out her napkin and Jack tips the wad into it. She folds it and carries on eating. Helen swallows her own forkful carefully, aware it's her mood making her own throat tight.

Jack takes another mouthful and while everyone else carries on with their dinner, Helen watches him eat. She sees his cheeks bulge and the delicate bobbing of his throat as he chews, and chews. When he taps his aunt on the arm and points at his mouth Helen has to intervene.

'Jack. You will swallow it.'

'It's okay, Helen. It's maybe a bit tough for him.'

'It doesn't matter. He's got to learn.'

Jack is sitting, one cheek bulging, between them. He looks from one to the other then moves the meat around in his mouth and tries to swallow. He almost gags. Jennifer reaches out to pat his back and Helen interrupts.

'Leave him. He's fine. He's got to learn. Jack, work up some spit in your mouth and then swallow it, okay?'

He moves his jaw carefully and everyone watches. It tightens her resolve. He will succeed. Knives and forks are paused, gravy drips from tines onto minted peas and green beans. When he finally swallows she nods and tousles his already tangled hair to let him know she's proud. He beams. They don't know how Jack works, really, what he needs. She hopes they pick it up quick.

'Good boy. Next time don't chew it for quite so long. And dip it in gravy. It's really delicious gravy.'

In the kitchen Jennifer runs water into a deep Belfast sink and Helen picks up a tea towel.

From the lounge, the violent cacophony of a cartoon. Helen usually requests the TV stays switched off if she and Jack end up staying for a panad or supper after checking the sheep, but she's deliberately being lax tonight. When she glances through to the lounge he is slack-jawed, mesmerised by the colours and fast-frame action of an animated film.

They managed to make it through the meal without any more switches being flicked. Without a meltdown. Helen is waiting for the right moment to leave; she has a long journey ahead. She twists the tea towel in her hands as the water churns the detergent into a frothy mountain in the basin. Jennifer starts scraping plates into a little compost bin that sits at the end of the counter. Moaning about how thin the biodegradable bags are that the council gives them to line these tiny brown boxes.

'All it takes is a dinner like tonight's, extra peelings and trimmings, and the whole thing will split when I try and lift it out. I just wish we'd had a garbage disposal thing fitted in the sink.'

The sound of the knife scraping on china makes Helen curl her toes inside her thick woollen socks. She grinds her jaw and hums an agreement, deciding not to remind Jennifer that she could build a proper compost heap in the garden, avoid the bags and the council recycling scheme altogether.

Jennifer begins loading the dishwasher and Helen moves aside, runs a hand across the ancient oak table in the centre of the kitchen. There are gouges from where she and Jennifer crashed their cutlery as toddlers. Others from where their dad had done the same as a kid. If she focusses hard on the table and not on the new tiles and polished worktops, she can invoke the scent and sounds of her childhood. Her taidy's pipe and the peaty smoke from the old Aga. The mewing of kittens from a box in the corner. Every spring there were kittens. 'Gotwrs, he called them. Llygotwrs. Ratters. They never had names. Why did she let Jack name the snails?

'Right, let's get these pans done and then we can relax for a bit before you go.' Jennifer has yellow rubber gloves up to her elbows, a special scourer that won't scratch the pans. Helen reaches for the first dish on the drainer. It's still hot, steaming. The bubbles slide down the edge.

'I need to ask another favour.' She might as well be blunt. She usually is.

Jennifer keeps scrubbing, but the pace has changed. Slowed. 'Okay.'

'Okay as in "yes"? Or okay as in "carry on"?'

'Both.' Jennifer positions the pan carefully on the drainer and reaches for another one – the roasting dish, thick with grease and black spikes of rosemary. She wipes the fat away with a paper towel then sinks it through the bubbles.

'I need you to keep him off school one day, midweek.'

'What for?'

'There's a school trip. I don't want him to go.'

'You know we both work, right?' She finally looks up from her task, almost sighs.

'I work too.' Helen has stepped up to manage Dad's farm while he's been nursing Mam. It's dawn till dusk, no weekends off. 'But he comes first. Always.' She nearly points out that she's never asked for a penny for her time helping Ioan. She tries to keep the irritation out of her voice. 'Look, he's at school all day. There's a breakfast club, and after-school care the rest of the week. I've booked him in so he doesn't disrupt your routine too much. It's just this one day.'

'It's not that easy, Helen. Ioan does shifts and getting cover isn't—'

'You don't.' It comes out sharper than she intended. She picks up a pan and turns away to soak up the water into the colourful cloth, softens her tone. 'You're entitled to leave, aren't you?'

'You know I've always said we can help. I mean, how many times have we offered to babysit?'

'Then help.'

'But you've gone from nothing in, what? Five years? To a whole week. And now a day off...'

'You know I wouldn't ask if I didn't need to.'

'What's the trip? Why don't you want him to go?' Jennifer abandons the dishes and dries her gloved hands.

'Wylfa.'

'Seriously?'

'I don't want him getting indoctrinated.' Helen's jaw is tight. She shouldn't have mentioned it. Should have told Jack to play sick for the day.

'Indoctrinated? They do colouring-in and make a basic light circuit!'

'It's a start.'

'Oh, for God's sake, Hel. It's not a conspiracy!'

'What's not a conspiracy?' Ioan is in the kitchen doorway, his rugby-player heft almost filling the frame. He goes to the fridge and starts browsing, picking out strips of the leftover lamb so carefully covered in cling film by Jennifer less than an hour ago.

'Helen thinks Jack is going to be "indoctrinated" on a school trip to Wylfa.'

'You're joking?' Ioan takes another beer and tosses the cap onto the counter. It bounces three times with the force, like a pebble skimming a lake.

'He's too young to be going there, getting the wrong idea.'

'Who says it's the wrong idea? You'd rather have coal mines, would you?' The beer is making him florid, his accent more fluid; a south Wales lilt.

'There are safer ways to make energy, you know that.'

'Wylfa has an amazing safety record, and *you* know *that*.' Ioan's voice booms, even though he isn't shouting.

'Nineteen ninety-three. They kept the reactor running for nine hours after that crane smashed into the core. They didn't even tell the public. They released radioactive sulphur into the atmosphere—'

'And lessons were learned! There's no way something like that would happen now.'

'The reactors are way past their sell-by date, Ioan. If you run an old car at four thousand revs for ten years straight, it doesn't matter what the safety record is. It might well blow.'

'It's not going to blow.'

'You believe. But you don't know.' She keeps her voice level. Controlled. 'And it does do damage.'

'Bull. Shit. Prove it!'

There is spittle in white webs at the corners of Ioan's mouth. Helen is prickling with heat.

'There are reports, Ioan. Some scientist has found that there is higher risk of cancer in people living downwind of Trawsfynydd.'

'Some scientist?'

'He's gone on to join a research group abroad now.'

'Wylfa is not Trawsfynydd. And you can't believe one article—'

'They both have Magnox reactors.' Helen stands firm, pressing her toes hard against wide slate floor tiles.

'The new one won't. I'm not even sure your parents' farm is downwind—'

'It's close enough...' She hasn't told them about her own potential diagnosis, not yet. Can't use it now, just to win an argument, no matter how tempting.

'Both of you, hush,' Jennifer interrupts, softly. 'Are you okay, little man?' She moves between them to the doorway, where Jack is standing, a single snail trailing across his palm.

'I've lost Mabon.'

'I'll help you find him, buddy.' Ioan rubs his mouth with the back of his hand, puts down his beer and leaves. The tension dissipates but doesn't disappear completely. Helen unwinds the tea towel and starts wiping the dishes again.

'I can ask the class teacher if he can stay behind at school, if it's a problem.'

'I just can't quite believe you are asking me to keep him away from the visitor's centre, when you're going to Chernobyl! I mean, seriously? If you're so worried about safety and cancer, why are you going?'

Helen resists the urge to cross her arms over her chest, to explain that this might be her last chance to see it, to put those demons to rest. 'The worst has already happened there. They know where it's safe to go. We've been lucky so far.'

'Look, I know Mam's health has taken its toll on you, on all of us...'

'When did you last check your boobs, Jen? How often do you check?'

Jennifer blushes, turns back to the sink.

'You need to check every month, every week is better. The nurse said...'

'That it was hereditary. That's why we check.'

'And do you?'

'Of course.'

A cry of relief seeps through from the lounge. The snail is recovered.

'I need to go. I have a long journey.'

Jennifer dries her hands and tucks a strand of hair behind her ear. 'Has he got everything?'

'He's sorted.'

'Are you leaving contact details, an itinerary?'

'It's all in the envelope I gave Ioan.'

'What if there's an emergency?'

'Jack knows what to do if there's an emergency.'

'How can he know?'

'He knows.'

'He's five!'

'He's nearly six. He's prepared.'

'Does *he* know where you're going?'

'He knows enough.'

'I'll see what I can do about a day off, but I can't promise anything.'

'Thanks.' Helen pauses at the door, then comes back into the room and hugs her sister. 'Are you going to be okay? Will you manage?'

'Of course.' Jennifer pulls away, fills the kettle and holds the cafetière up.

Helen shakes her head. 'I mean with Mam as well as Jack. And the sheep? I've told Ioan there's a lad who can help out—'

'Hel, I'm sure we'll be fine. It's only a week.'

'I know. It's just…'

'You don't have to go.'

'I need to.'

Jennifer takes her hands, and Helen feels how soft they are in her own calloused fingers. 'Why, Hel? Why now?'

'I can't…I just do.'

'Okay. But I wish you'd talk to me.'

Helen hugs her again, a tight squeeze that takes Jennifer by surprise. Fierce almost.

'I really do appreciate this, you know?' Helen mutters, letting go.

'I know. But I still think it's a mistake.'

As Helen stoops to tie her laces, her head is level with the heavy pendulum of the old grandfather clock. The motion, a regular back and forth, triggers the memory of the dream from last night, the dream she has often had these last few years. Movement, above and peripheral. A pendulum almost stopped. The smell of leather and piss. When she woke, she'd almost called the whole thing off, but her rational mind won over. It was only a dream. Unresolved and unnecessary emotion, nothing more. She closes her eyes and doesn't open them until she feels Jack beside her. She kneels up, their eyes level.

'Keep them in the jar, okay? Keep them safe.'

He follows her out onto the porch. A freezing fog has swept in off the sea, and the landscape around the house has vanished. Her nose is already feeling pinched and sore in the wind. Jack's hair moves as if it is alive, twisting and tousled.

'You've got the key.' She crouches down again and places a hand on his chest, feels the metal and looped cord beneath his jumper. Feels his heart, beating ever so slightly too fast.

He nods. Solemn. He's always had a kind of weight to him. In opposition to the lightness of his body. His physical fragility offset by a heavy soul. He's not like other kids. She can see tears welling in his eyes, and how hard he is working to keep them there.

'I'll be back soon. Remember everything we've talked about. It's just a little test. You'll be fine.'

He nods again, and she knows she's got to go before she can't. She kisses him on the nose and squeezes his shoulders. 'I love you.'

'Ditto.' His new favourite word. Whispered.

'Okay, off you go inside then.' She waits for him to walk down the softly lit corridor and into the lounge and then pulls the door shut. The sound of the lock clicking is like a rock in her chest. She needs to own it.

CHAPTER TWO

There is a pause after the door closes. Jack stands in the kitchen doorway, clutching the jar. Jennifer and Ioan glance at one another, suddenly aware they are on duty. They start talking simultaneously.

'Right, little man. Bedtime.'

'Bath time.'

'Supper?'

'Stories?'

'Hot chocolate?'

His gaze flicks between them, assessing the choices. Eyes glimmering for a second at the final offer, before remembering. 'I'm not allowed chocolate.'

Jennifer moves towards him but stops short of hugging him when he turns his slate-grey eyes on her. 'Your mam said you were allowed a few treats, so why don't you let me help you get ready for bed while Uncle Ioan makes you some hot chocolate?'

'I don't need help.'

In the guest room she watches him unpack his rucksack, arranging a book and torch on the bedside table beside the snails, then pulling out a roll of clothes that he spools out into pyjamas. While he wriggles pale, skinny shoulders into the top, she opens the bag to look for tomorrow's uniform. Black trousers, a once-white polo shirt and a red sweater, faded and wrinkled. She looks up at him, catching sight of the glint of metal on his sternum.

'What's the key for?'

He shucks the fabric over his ribs and doesn't answer.

'Is this the only set of school clothes you've got?'

He shrugs.

She digs deeper and finds another roll. Threadbare at the cuffs.

'Well, these have seen better days. What do you do at school to wear them out so quickly?' A stilted laugh.

He reaches out and fingers a tiny hole in the sleeve of the red jumper. 'Mam says they're just clothes, they don't need to be new.'

'Don't you want new ones?'

'They're just clothes.' He wriggles under the duvet and watches as she hangs the polo shirts and jumpers on wooden hangers in the wardrobe. She pulls out a pair of jeans, a long-sleeved T-shirt and a thick fleece hoodie from the bag and folds them neatly into a drawer.

When Ioan comes in, the room fills with the scent of warm, sweet chocolate. Jack drinks quickly, wiping his mouth on his sleeve. Leaving a brown smear.

'Do you want a story?'

He shakes his head. 'I just want to be alone.'

They leave the bedside lamp on and stand outside the bedroom door, dismissed. It isn't until they too are settled beneath the sheets that Jennifer realises she hasn't brushed Jack's teeth.

'Leave him now, he'll be asleep,' Ioan grunts. After a few minutes he begins to snore, something he only does after beer.

Jennifer can't get comfortable. She lies staring at the little red light on her phone charger, listening to the house creak and settle as the heating switches off for the night.

***

It's Helen's first time away from home in years. As she double-checks the panniers on her motorbike she glances over the fields, dark and familiar. She feels a heaviness deep in her thorax, as if gravity is stronger all of a sudden, or the ground itself is willing her to stay. She grinds her teeth and pulls her leathers up over her shoulders. Raises the zip, sealing herself in.

How can she tell her sister why she needs to go, even though a huge part of her doesn't really want to? She could try to explain that she's learnt how important it is to prepare Jack. She won't be around forever – a slip on the yard to crack her skull like a fallen egg, a scratch from a rusty spike of barbed wire to flood her circulatory system with poison, or more likely the pea-sized lump on the cusp of her left breast that the doctor has assured her is 'a cyst; just fluid, but best to get it biopsied as soon as possible considering the family history' – any of these could leave him orphaned. What kind of mother would she be if she didn't prepare him for losing her? She could try to explain that she just needs to see it for herself while she still has the chance. This thing that has haunted her since she was Jack's age. But they don't really talk about things like that. There is so much Jennifer doesn't know, wouldn't understand, that to try to explain now would be too difficult, risky even.

She wheels the bike along the farm track, the helmet dangling by the chinstrap from the handlebars, swinging as she navigates the potholes. She's already said goodbye to her parents; a kiss on her mam's crumpled-paper cheek, a bear hug for Dad. Promised she'll drive safe, that she's eaten, that she'll call. She could have taken a flight, arrived quicker and with a suitcase full of clean clothes and space for duty free on the way home like anyone else. But she is not like anyone else, and this is not a pleasure trip. She wants the autonomy of driving, and so she is riding her motorbike. A carefully maintained Triumph Bonneville, matte black and polished chrome. It hasn't seen nearly enough action since Jack was born.

She pauses at the junction between the farm track and the main road, glances over towards the power station. Ioan is half right, apart from the incident in the nineties Wylfa does have a good safety record. But there is no such thing as a safe nuclear power station. No matter how much training or how many policy updates are implemented, there is always the potential for accidents. She's done enough research over the last few years to know this: Mayak, Windscale, Chernobyl, Three-Mile Island. Fukushima periodically returning to the headlines as it continues to unfurl its poison into the Pacific, half-lives ticking by amid the alien sea life and fluttering water weeds.

She wavers, clutching the handlebars and calculating for the thousandth time the chances of an incident in the few days she is away. Whether Jack is ready. Whether preparing him for personal disaster outweighs the risks of industrial disaster.

Wylfa glows, floodlit on the horizon.

She can hear it humming.

She can't remember exactly when its presence switched from being nothing more than a hunkering block of sky-coloured concrete in the background into a latent bomb. Her parents told her nothing as a child, maybe even told her lies in the aftermath of Chernobyl. She relied on whispers, earwigging when they thought she was playing.

Did you hear it triggered the alarms at Wylfa? Gwyn said it was the staff going in, that it was on their clothes. All that way…

Haf and Tony are moving, said they just don't trust it anymore.

Wigley's right. It was a shambles last year. They still haven't explained what the long-term plan is.

So what is he proposing?

Evacuation plans. We have to be ready, just in case.

Whispers that lay dormant for years until the new plans reignited them, until Mam got sick and everything started to make sense. Horrible, stomach-cramping sense.

She pulls on her helmet and clips the chinstrap. Kicks the engine into life.

A few days, that's all, she tells herself. She sends up a silent prayer to any deity that might be listening and accelerates.

The first few hours of the journey are a comfortable challenge. Poor visibility across the island, the roads slicked with mud and loose gravel. The route through the foothills of Snowdonia twisting and unlit. The single headlight is a cone of light through the dark. Mountains hunker close either side. Sheep gather, skittish at the approaching roar of the bike, behind curves of tumbling stone wall. Just before Llyn Ogwen the clouds clear, and the wet road glistens like a snail trail in the moonlight, cut off by the sheer slate walls of the mountains, then appearing again. Dazzling. Dangerously beautiful. When the lake shimmies into view, a milky basin for the moonlight, she's tempted to stop.

This was always as far as she came.

Rare nights when Jack slept, dozing on his grandparents' sofa, completely unaware, and she could slip away for a few hours in the dark. Before Mam got sick and minding him was too much. Before they moved into the barn and she started spending every night going through paperwork and writing letters, researching nuclear power, corporate law and survival rates for cancer. Quelling the surging anxiety by arming herself with knowledge, making sure she was ready, just in case. That Jack was ready too.

She presses on. Trying to shed something along the way, a deliberate casting-off of duty. It is time to cut the cord; not completely, maybe, but to gnaw at it and fray it a little.

She leaves the moon caught in the lake. The novelty of the terrain beyond encompasses her, demands her attention. A flattening of the hills, a widening of the roads as they merge into motorways. She cannot think of what she is leaving behind, instead visualises the map in her head; the roads as streams and rivers leading her to the sea and the unknown body of Europe.

***

In the morning Jennifer finds Jack rummaging through the pantry.

'What are you up to, little man?' She'd thought he was still asleep, was looking forward to a quiet cup of coffee. She has her morning ritual, staring out at the bird feeder, caffeine slowly sharpening her senses. Watching the tits and finches peeking around nervously between sharp attacks on the nuts behind the wire.

'Getting food.'

'I'll make you breakfast. Sit at the table.'

She feels his eyes on her as she tidies the mess he's made in the cupboard. There are already a few empty wrappers – crisps that Ioan likes with his lunch, a small packet of shortbread she'd picked up in the coffee break at a conference a few months ago.

'Jack, can you please ask if you're hungry next time?' She watches him nod, and waits a beat for an apology, but he just stares at her with those serious eyes. 'What do you want for breakfast?'

'I don't mind.'

'Do you like toast? Jam?'

He nods again, and she drops a couple of slices in the toaster and leans against the counter while they brown. He's already dressed in his uniform, the sleeves hanging over his wrists almost to his fingers. She can't think of anything to say, wonders if she should hug him or something.

'So, what do you do about lunches at school? Do you have a dinner lady?' She glances around for a sign of the envelope with all the information Helen had promised her.

'Mam packs it.'

'Okay.' She stares into the fridge at hummus and Parma ham, feta cheese and pâté, and makes a mental note to take him shopping after she picks him up, to let him choose what he wants.

'What does she pack? Sandwiches? Crisps?'

He shrugs and waits for his toast, watching his snails crunch the edge of a fresh piece of red pepper in their jar. He's been in the fridge too.

Wylfa Nuclear Power Station is hidden behind dense rows of tall leylandii. Close up, it can't be seen at all, but there are road signs, and pairs of pylons marching out of the trees – their circumzenithal wires dipping over the road. The car park is half full already. It's windy, and the low clouds are gunmetal, bulky as ocean liners.

The car door flies open as she carefully slips out and reaches for her bag. She is normally here an hour before her official start time, enjoying the peace of the empty office to catch up on the never-ending emails. She holds her hair with one hand to stop it tangling in the wind, and half jogs in her court shoes and pencil skirt towards the office block that serves as a portal to the plant.

In the blast of dry heat in the foyer she lets her hair fall and pauses on a bright rug woven with safety slogans to pull out her pass, swiping it absently over the scanner and smiling at the Civil Nuclear Police officer while she waits for the ceiling-height metal gates to open. He smiles back, his assault rifle cradled in one arm, and taps the dosimeter at his belt.

No one is allowed past the main reception without a radiation monitor and alarm.

Jennifer has never forgotten to wear hers before; it's a part of her routine so banal, as familiar and unexceptional as putting on mascara or deodorant, that she doesn't even notice its weight at her hip during the day. She fumbles in her bag, finding the case for her reading glasses, her fingers snagging her iPhone, and finally pulls it out.

'That's not like me,' she says, clipping it to her belt.

'You're not the only one, there's always a few after the weekend. Have a good day.'

'You too.' She steps through, the metal gates gliding closed behind her. The officer watches her through the bars and she raises a hand in acknowledgement. He nods in reply, both hands back on the slick black machine gun. He's already turning towards the door and the next person, holding the gun lightly, his forefinger stretched out almost casually above the trigger, like he is pointing.

She passes posters on the wall reminding her to 'be fit for work' and to 'hold on to the handrails at all times'. She will be late for this morning's safety briefing if she doesn't hurry.

A vibration in her bag calls her attention.

how was he?

As she walks, she texts Helen back. *all okay this morning. how far did you get?*

Then again: *you never told me about lunches. what does he eat?*

By the time she exits the lift she could be in any workplace, anywhere. She walks down a long magnolia corridor, where instead of bright yellow warning signs there are framed motivational posters.

Teamwork: Individually We are One Drop, Together We Are an Ocean.

Diversity: The One Thing We All Have in Common.

Working Together: Individuals Play Games, But Teams Win Championships.

Each with a glossy photo of linked hands, climbers scaling

mountains, rowers straining against the pull of the water on oars together.

Achievement: Playing it Safe is the Riskiest Choice We Can Ever Make.

She pauses and takes a few steps back to this one. Someone has tacked a note to the glass frame. **Tell that to Fukushima...** scrawled in felt-tip.

She tilts her head, frowning, trying to identify the handwriting and failing, then snatches it off and rubs at the small greasy mark the Blu Tack has left behind.

Her phone buzzes. Another text. This time just an image.

[*Bienvenue.* White on green. Flat awning, fuel pumps. Colourful car roofs. Heavy chrome curve, handlebars.]

She's made the crossing safely then. Jennifer pushes through the door to the open-plan office, shaking her head. She should have flown.

CHAPTER THREE

She rides with purpose, to a schedule. Breaking to eat, drink and use the toilets in service stations. Europe slipping past, border controls and new languages on road signs, no reason to linger or take in the subtle shift in landscapes, the cities and villages that seem to rise up and fall away beyond the roadside. Six hours of sleep in a motel in East Germany, almost halfway, then back on the bike before dawn. At the checkpoint between Poland and Ukraine she queues, stretching out cramped muscles and pacing. The sun shimmers in the warm air rising off the queue of traffic waiting to be processed. She has time to miss Jack now, while she waits for her documents to be approved, her passport copied. She feels the pain of it in her shoulders and neck. Jack will be feeling it differently. He takes stress to his stomach. Aches and cramps, diarrhoea.

She was the same as a child.

Her first night away from home at school camp and she didn't sleep at all, just lay in the dark with the churning ache of homesickness in her belly.

She sips water from a metal canister and it's so cold it makes her teeth ache. There are no vending machines, no hot drinks on offer.

He'll be at school now.

She gazes over the lines of cars, their bonnets steaming.

Time stretches.

She looks across to where a chubby couple in a Nissan Qashqai are eating crisps, drinking Coke. There are no distractions from the inertia. She won't take out her phone and browse the news or update her blog, because she needs to save the battery. She runs through her itinerary again, but her mind wanders. How many lambs are there now? How is her dad coping? Will someone from Vista bring more paperwork while she's gone, try to persuade him to sell to make room for the new power station? She doubts he would sign anything without her, but they can be forceful: turning up in pairs, in suits, when you're not expecting them.

The queue doesn't move. A bus in the far lane hisses as its hydraulics are released, giving up hope of progress anytime soon. There is a feeling of stasis. People stand around outside their vehicles, smoking. She pulls off her glove and chews at a fingernail that has been catching the seam. There is another protest planned for March the eleventh, the anniversary of Fukushima Daiichi. They are so close, she thinks. If they can stop the new plant, and Wylfa ceases operation next year as planned, she can relax.

She has organised a group to stand with her along the back fields of the farm, wearing dust-masks and holding banners, marking the border that Vista wants to breach. There is a lot of support for her situation; the farm has become almost symbolic of the battle to stop the development. Someone has arranged for the press to attend. She feels the sting of her nail tearing, spits the fragment out. She's been to most of the protests over the last few years, taking Jack; gripping his hand so as not to lose him in the crowds, or hoisting him onto her shoulders. Finds the singing and chanting a distraction from the purpose of the protests, but knows they need numbers, bodies on the ground to have an impact. Hopes there won't be singing in her fields. Silence can be far more effective.

She looks up and notices people staring at her, at her bike. She stares back until they glance away, uncomfortable. She texts Jen again, but knows she'll be at work, that Jack will be at school. That the text is a sign of weakness.

After three hours of waiting to be called to get her passport back, she approaches the desk and asks curtly how much longer it is going to take. The woman smiles and hands her the paperwork from a pile. It might have been there for hours or minutes.

She presses on.

***

In her lunch break Jennifer searches a supermarket website for school sweaters, adds three to her online basket before pausing.

Helen might be offended.

Perhaps she can't afford new clothes, will feel the gesture as charity. She saves the items and logs out.

***

It's dusk when Helen finally reaches the small town of Ivankiv, thirty or so kilometres from the nearest checkpoint in Chernobyl's exclusion border.

She curves the bike around a large roundabout that has a giant stone egg balanced at its centre, white and hopeful amid dirty snow and dead grass. She's read about this monument, the 'Egg of Life'. Up close, while the symbolism is obvious, its size and the creeping stains of lichen seem to Helen more a grotesque reminder of the unnatural forces still permeating the area than a sign of future hope. It lies unhatched, swollen out of proportion. Reminds Helen of the bulging foreheads and mushroom features of the babies she's seen online. The nightmares she'd had while pregnant of what might be swelling inside her. The skin of her belly distended and tight.

She tightens her grip on the handlebars.

As she enters Ivankiv, she drops a gear to conform to the speed restriction within the town boundary. Feels the change in pitch from the engine through her thighs. Her visor is grubby, and she strains to see details of the town.

She passes buildings with ornate coloured tiling all over the outside, a marketplace just packing up for the day.

She shifts her weight in the saddle and slows.

Pulls over.

Her lower back is cramped from the long ride, a dull ache that echoes period pain or the early stages of labour. She eases back in the wide seat of the bike and lifts her visor, sucking in moist air. She's tired. The air smells of wood smoke, car fumes and the dank, metallic tang of old snow. She breathes it all in, huge lungfuls until her head clears. She feels the torpor lift. A leap of excitement in her gut. The journey alone is a triumph of planning, of attitude. Determination.

In no small way she's already achieved her goal.

She is parked beside a school. The kerbstones are painted in pastel shades; blue, pink, green and yellow. Pale in the fading light. There is so much colour in the town. Houses glazed in bright ceramic tiles. Whitewash stencilled with blue, pink and yellow flowers and intricate patterns. There is a cheerfulness, an optimism in the decoration. A sharp contrast to the landscape all around; the winter trees are still bare, almost black. Leaf mulch clogs the gutters and drains, muddying the snow. The sky is low and oppressive. Grey slush trampled along the pavements.

Helen takes a photo on her phone and then pulls the bike up between her legs and moves on. She's seen the school before online anyway. She wants to call Jack, to ask how his day has been. Unpick any issues and reinforce him for tomorrow.

The hotel is new, a few years old at most, and lacks the charm of the buildings she has passed to get here. There are no carved wooden panels or brightly painted facades. Red bricks and white UPVC windows could place it just as easily in a business park in Swindon or Hull. It stands between a street of detached houses with distinctive shapes to the roofs and doorways – cornices and crenulations, pillars and patterned brickwork in reds and greens and oranges – and a large block of flats whose gaudy pale blue painted window frames are peeling and mismatched. Grey walls stained with rain, sporting mycological satellite dishes in random clusters.

She kills the engine and pulls off her helmet, shaking out her hair to let the breeze in. Massages her prickling scalp. Rolls her shoulders to ease out the ache.

Three men stand by the doorway smoking. Heavy-duty trousers and identical jackets.

They stare at her.

She locks the bike and unclips the panniers, steels herself for the walk past them.

'Klasnyy mototsykl. Vin dorohyy?' one of them calls.

They nudge one another and suck on the cigarettes as she approaches.

She stops.

They are blocking the doorway.

They shuffle their feet and grin with nicotine-stained teeth.

She doesn't smile back. The trick, she has learned, is to assert your strength through body language. Even if your insides are churning. There is no need to speak or communicate in any other way. She keeps her face impassive. Tells them, with the set of her shoulders and the plant of her feet, that she is neither flattered nor flustered by the attention.

One of them offers her a cigarette and she shakes her head, gestures at the door. He steps aside to let her pass.

She doesn't look back, even when one mutters something under his breath that can only be a curse. She will look up the word 'bitch' in her phrase book later. Sound it out and see if it matches the syllables spat at her back.

She checks in with a printout of the booking, a polite smile.

'The restaurant is that way.' The girl behind the desk is young, heavily made-up and with improbably piled hair. It could be a wig. She points a carefully manicured nail towards an unlit doorway. 'Starting breakfast at six thirty. Your room is that way, number one zero five.'

As Helen reaches the double doors the men come in, laughing and joking with the girl on the desk. Helen shoulders the heavy door and inhales the bleachy scent of the corridor. Their voices fade as the door swings closed behind her.

'Jack?'

The screen is blurry, keeps freezing. Occasionally there's a distortion when he moves just as the signal drops, and his face smears.

'Look what Uncle Ioan bought me.'

Helen strains to work out what Jack is waving at the camera. It is bright toxic yellow and black, aposematic. It makes her think of wasps. Or radiation warning signs: that simple black propeller against unmissable yellow paint.

'What is it?'

Ioan leans into the frame, all wide face and florid cheeks.

'It's a digger.' Ioan pauses. Waiting for Helen's approval.

A digger. Like the JCBs ripping the foundations out of the land back home. She swallows before replying.

'Cool. So, has he behaved himself?'

Jennifer moves into the frame. 'He's been an angel. No trouble at all.'

'Can I have a few moments on my own with him?'

She can hear Jennifer giving instructions on what to do at the end of the call. *Just bring the phone to me, okay? Don't press anything.*

She waits, hoping the hotel WiFi holds up. Eventually Jack's face fills the screen. He's close enough for her to see the little scar on his top lip. Two years ago he tripped in a furrow and split his lip on the only decent-sized rock in the field. A tiny silver imperfection.

'Have they gone?'

He nods.

'You okay?'

He nods again, touches the screen leaving a smudge. She presses her finger to her own screen.

'So how has it been so far?'

'Aunty Jennifer is mad at me.' A whisper.

'Why?'

He pulls back, rubs his nose with his sleeve and frowns. 'She keeps making up new rules.' He rolls his eyes.

'What kind of rules?'

He shrugs and reaches for something off-screen. Holds up the pickle jar. 'They have to stay inside. They're bored.'

Helen laughs, and then checks herself when his brow puckers. 'This is part of the test. Follow the rules. It's only for a short time. Show her you can do it.'

'Okay.'

Helen anticipated something like this. 'Remember what I told you? You can't always make decisions for yourself.'

'But…'

'But you can keep control of the situation by doing and saying the right thing.'

'How can I?' He is wriggling, moving from the chair to the floor to lie on his stomach. The picture swirls and he's almost lost.

'By being polite. By smiling.'

He brings the phone back up to his face and nods, listening intently, leaning so close to the screen that she can see only one eye, the freckles across his nose.

'Show me your smile.'

He pulls back and smiles.

'Now as if you mean it. Come on, think of something that makes you happy and smile about it.'

'Modron and Mabon.'

'Smile at them.'

'They're snails.' He rolls his eyes again.

'I know, but smile at them.'

'But they won't know what it means. It's stupid.'

'Then smile because of them. Because of how they make you feel.'

He smiles again, less toothy, but sincerely.

'Good. Use that smile.'

He tries again but is back to the false gurning.

'How *do* they make you feel?' He shouldn't still have them. He shrugs.

'Do you feel responsible? Powerful? Because they depend on you for food and a home?'

He frowns, nods.

'Okay, so you give them things they need.'

He nods again.

'Right, and what do they give you?'

He thinks for a minute, face screwed up, then, 'I like to watch the foot on the glass.'

'Well, if you want Uncle Ioan and Aunty Jennifer to give you food and a home then you have to show them your smile. Like the snails show you the foot on the glass.'

He is concentrating, solemn again.

'Good boy. How's school?'

'Just school.'

'I love you, Jack.' She hopes he doesn't hear the catch in her throat.

'Ditto.'

'Do you like the truck?'

He shrugs. 'Mam, when are you coming home?'

When the call is over Helen slips off her leathers and pads around the room in bare feet. The carpet is thin and scratchy, a dull brown colour. She is wearing fleece-lined leggings and a long-sleeved top, but now the leathers are sloughed off like a snakeskin in the corner, she is cold. She unpacks her panniers, just the things she'll need tonight, and goes into the en suite. It's simple, functional. A plastic tub and shower, a square mirror over the sink. There is complimentary shampoo and conditioner, tiny bottles, and a paper wrap with a sliver of soap.

She runs the taps and fills a flimsy plastic cup with tepid water. She has one day in town, then the tour. She drinks another cup of the water, grimacing at the chemical tang, and strips off.

Jack is resilient, she thinks. She's made him resilient. He might be small, but he can already chop wood, light a fire, skin a rabbit, and isn't afraid to speak his mind. He's stronger than any of the other kids at his school, independent. She learned the hard way how to be tough, found out by herself that adults can be weak, other children cruel. She makes sure he doesn't have to build his own armour alone. This time apart is like an inoculation, for both of them. It might hurt, but it will make them stronger in the long run.

She pauses, one hand under the stream of water from the showerhead. This is her first time away from the farm, and her mam, and Jennifer texting to ask if she can swing by and help Ioan with something, in ages. Her first proper time away from Jack since his birth. The thought arrests her. It's nearly six years since she's only had her own needs to fulfil, longer if she counts the months of pregnancy: the changes to her diet, the abstinence from alcohol and anything else that might adversely affect his formation. The realisation is strangely liberating. Thought she'd anticipated everything, hadn't calculated feeling anything other than the pangs of missing Jack.

She slips into the underpowered spray and lets the heat of the water ease out her shoulders, exploring the curious mix of guilt and excitement this unbidden, almost unwelcome, response arouses. As the room blurs with steam she considers what to do with the unfettered hours ahead.

She hadn't expected to make such good time, had calculated for traffic problems. She should really spend the evening writing up her journal, capturing the journey before it becomes too spectral to find form on the page. She should check her email for any updates on the Fukushima protest, and Vista's website for any new information on the development. She can't let things slide just because she's away. And yet, for the first time in years she has a choice, no familial duties to timetable her evening.

She soaps herself clean, pausing at the lump on the edge of her breast to manipulate it, check if it's grown. Wonders if she should have told Jen, explained that any risks from this trip were meaningless if it was already too late. That she'd understand if she herself had a child, why protecting the farm from the developers was so important.

As she wrings the water from her hair and reaches for a towel she still can't decide what to do. The freedom isn't so much liberating, as stifling. She feels pressure to enjoy it.

There is no hairdryer in the room, but the towels are rough and get most of the moisture out. She sits on the bed and opens the last of her travel supplies – dry bread, slices of cheese sweating under cling film, salted peanuts – then peeks out the window to see if it's raining, or snowing. The trees in the parking lot are moving, but the air is clear. She decides quickly; she will find a restaurant, choose a local dish and distract herself from the swarming concerns that buzz around inside her head in the silence of her hotel room.

She wraps up in the thermal leggings, three layers of vest, long-sleeved shirt and a fleece-lined jacket, then pulls on a tight hand-knitted cap. Over the last few years she has honed useful skills; she and Jack have plenty of woollens to keep warm in winter.

She can't walk into town in her motorbike boots, but has brought an old pair of Doc Martens to wear in the Zone, discard afterwards. They've been at the back of the wardrobe in her parents' spare room for years, the leather still moulded to the shape of her teenage feet. She scans the room carefully before leaving. Her cash and passport are in a money belt against her stomach, her phone zipped into an inside pocket. Now she is moving she feels a surge of energy. This is exactly what she should be doing. She locks the door behind her and checks it, then leaves.

***

Jennifer pauses at the door, grabs her bag and phone. She's leaving Ioan in charge of dinner while she goes to check on her mam and collect extra clothes for Jack. Helen might only be gone for a week, but one pair of pyjamas and two school jumpers are woefully inadequate for a child who eats with his fingers half the time. He's still in his school clothes, muddy-kneed and grubby.

'We'll get dinner on, you go.' Ioan is piling peppers, mushrooms and tomatoes on the counter, Jack standing on a chair beside him, wearing Ioan's apron. It comes down to his feet, the belt looped around the back and tied at the front.

'Don't be long though, we can only reserve you a table at *Casa Jacques* for an hour or so.' He winks at Jack but gets nothing in return.

'Make sure he washes his hands.' He looks feral. Just before she pulls the door shut she sees his hand dash out and snatch a fat red pepper. He bites into it like an apple, the juice staining his chin.

***

It's getting dark. A crow bounces on the grass verge. It doesn't take flight as Helen walks past but skips to one side, tipping its head to watch her with its black button eye. The air is sharpening as the temperature drops. She walks carefully along the icy pavement. To slip now would be catastrophic. She has travel insurance, but with a broken clavicle or scaphoid, she'd be vulnerable. It would be difficult to ride the bike. Maybe impossible. She tests the movement of the snow beneath her boots and feels the ice forming on the surface, each step slightly crunchier than the last.

The town is shuttered. She pauses by a mural that fills a whole wall: bending wheat stems, farmers and maidens, a pair of ducks. An idealised collective community held together by domesticity and shared resources. The colours are muted in the fading light.

The first restaurant she comes to is closed. She stands in

front of the glass door and tries to decipher the opening hours, wondering if she is just too early. Perhaps the nightlife kicks off later here. Perhaps there is none.

The sign is in Cyrillic.

She has learned a few words from their shape, recognising them as symbols rather than reading them. Like Чорнобиль. *Chornobyl*. The Ukrainian spelling. She knows this matters and tries to remember to use it herself; a subtle shift towards roundness of the first vowel in her mouth when she speaks. She doesn't know the days of the week but can work out from the dash marks where opening hours should be that the restaurant is only open weekends. She won't be eating here.

She walks on, breath billowing. Dragon breath. That's what she and Jack always call it. She almost says it aloud but there's no one to hear. The tug of it hurts.

There are lights ahead. Red words over a door. Helen can hear bursts of laughter. A bar. She walks past and searches the main roads for another place to eat but there are no more restaurants. She walks back to the bar and stands outside. She had hoped for something quieter. Alcohol makes people unpredictable, more than usual, but her blood sugars are low, and her body chemistry is demanding action. She steps into the warmth and scans the room for signs they serve food.

Near the door a group of men sit playing cards, each with a cigarette dangling from their lips, despite the *No Smoking* symbols peeling off the windows. A few lean against the bar watching a small TV that is bracketed to the wall above the optics. There are no women, and no menus on the empty tables. But there are also no other options.

It's years since she's smelled the mix of cigarette smoke and beer-soaked tables blended together in a warm enclosed space. She's taken back to The Skerries in Holyhead, before the smoking ban. Sitting in the snug nursing a half. Sticky tables and pushing Andy's hand off her knee every five minutes. Watching her old college mates getting wasted, and then slipping away to ride home via Pen-Llŷn and Carreglefn just to test the bike. Perhaps it's this warped nostalgia that makes her stay, or maybe it's knowing she doesn't have to worry about Jack tonight.

She approaches the bar and the men shift away, move to a table. All except one.

The bartender tips his head, frowns a little, and then speaks.

'Shcho ya mozhu tobi kupyty? Vyno?'

Helen guesses at his question, points at the bottles of beer in the fridge behind him.

He places one on a paper disc and holds out a hand for payment. Helen pulls a roll of grivna from her pocket and passes over a few notes, calculating the exchange rate in her head.

'Tourist?' The guy next to her has turned.

'Not really.' She glances at him, sizes him up. His eyes are so dark she cannot discern a colour. Young, skinny. Straight black hair long enough to graze his eyelashes, but not styled. She sips the beer and feels the first buzz hit her legs. A sensation like the tentacles of a half-forgotten song, snatching her back through time. Before Jack. Reckless.

She takes another sip of beer. Feels her thighs relaxing.

'You ride the motorbike?'

She frowns. Apart from the buff she wears around her neck, there is nothing to give away her mode of transport.

'I heard you arrive, saw you pass.'

'What makes you think that was me?'

'People here do not ride these bikes.'

She smiles politely.

'Only old farmers have even older bikes. Not like yours. It's expensive?'

'Not especially. Cheaper than a car.'

'Looked expensive.' He isn't aggressive. It's a small town. People talk.

She turns away from him to signal the conversation is over.

'Do you serve food?'

The barman smiles and shakes his head, sweeping an arm behind him at a rack of bar snacks. She picks out spicy pork flavoured crisps, some nuts for protein. Offers out a palm full of coins for him to pick out the correct change.

'I thought smoking was banned here?' She nods towards the group of men sat by the door. The air around them is opaque. The barman shrugs and picks up a dirty towel, starts wiping glasses.

'Who is going to prosecute?' A laugh. The boy at the bar. He picks up a pack from the counter beside him and slips a cigarette between his thin lips before offering them to her. When she shakes her head, he lights up and then holds out his hand to her.

'I'm Anton.'

'Nice to meet you.' Another polite smile, but nothing offered in return. She isn't here to be hit on.

She moves to a table, scans the room again. She won't stay long and doesn't really want the beer anymore – she's a lightweight after years of abstinence – but isn't ready to go back to the cold hotel room yet. She mouths a handful of nuts and slips her phone out of her pocket, takes pictures of the room. You can learn a lot about a place from the bars. There are guns, old-style hunting rifles, hanging over the optics. The bartender is watching the TV. She takes a shot of him accepting a cigarette, then leaning on his forearms. She is trying to catch the half-smiles that flicker in the changing light of the screen as he finds whatever they are saying on the TV funny.

She is interrupted by a text message. *does Jack have any spare pyjamas?*

no, why? all ok?

fine. you?

She is just composing an answer when she feels his presence.

'I advise you to be careful.' He slides into the chair opposite. 'People here, they don't like strangers, or people taking pictures. They tolerate visitors for the money, but you might get pushed, get someone angry if you take too many.'

'I don't mean to—'

'You are here for what? For Chornobyl?'

'Does it matter?'

'People come here to work, men on contracts in the hotels. The only women who come are for the tours, the only English are for the tours.' She thinks she sees a sneer in the tightness of his lip as he looks away, back towards the TV for a second. Doesn't correct his assumption of her nationality. Close up she can see he is younger than her, but not by much. Taut, as if his whole body is wired for physicality. A sport maybe, such as swimming or gymnastics – his energy is contained in tight, jerky movements.

'And you are alone? Just be careful, okay?'

'Is that a threat?'

'No. Just a friendly warning.'

After he has gone, she waits: the phone in her hand, the screen black. This was a mistake. When she finally goes outside the temperature has dropped even further. There are hardly any streetlights. She walks slowly, her room key tucked between her fingers just in case.

***

The farmyard is wide and grey, slate chips churned into the mud under tractor wheels, mirroring the low clouds in the sky. As Jennifer pulls up to her parents' porch, Megan, the ancient Welsh Collie her father has worked for years, steps out of the barn and cocks her head, waiting to see if she should bark a warning. When she sees Jennifer she gives a half-hearted wag and limps back to her bed of old blankets.

She doesn't plan on hanging around. Once she has a few extra things for Jack she will get home, get him fed, bathed and tucked up in bed.

In the kitchen her mother is sitting at the kitchen table, a plate of half-eaten food in front of her on the tablecloth. She isn't wearing a scarf around her head and the soft skin of her scalp shows up pink and blue-veined in the light from the bulb over the table. A transparent halo of hair is just beginning to show, thin and soft as a baby's first dandelion fuzz. It's the first time Jennifer has seen her without the scarf and make-up, and she tries not to stare.

Her father stands by the range, his back to the room as he

replenishes his plate. The room is warm, hot in contrast to the toothy wind sweeping in off the coast outside. Jennifer hasn't eaten since midday, can smell bacon.

'Are you allowed to eat that?' She drops her bag by the door but stays standing.

'And hello to you too, love,' her dad says, sitting down and reaching for the brown sauce, tearing off another hunk of white bread from the ravaged loaf on the table.

'Helen said the doctor had warned against processed foods. There was a leaflet, wasn't there?'

'I know, cariad. I read it. Do you want a drink? There's tea in the pot.' Her mam indicates the huge brown teapot that has held centre stage on the table as long as Jennifer can remember.

'And the bacon and white bread?'

'She's eating what she fancies, love. She's eating is the main thing.'

Her mother pushes a piece of bacon through a smear of egg yolk, streaking the plate with a sunset. She's wearing a thick sweater that does nothing to hide the uneven contour of her chest.

'What about the antioxidants, the fibre?'

Her mam gestures to the fruit bowl, to a row of plastic bottles labelled *acai berries*, *curcumin*, *wolfberry* and *cat's claw*. She gets up and walks to the sideboard, begins to wind a silk scarf around her head, and doesn't turn back until her scalp is covered.

'What are these?'

'Your sister said they'd help.'

'Are you taking them?' Jennifer picks up a bottle and begins reading the label.

'Yes—'

'But you're still taking your proper meds?'

'Yes, cariad. She made me promise that too.'

'And eating properly? Following the advice sheet?'

'I'm just having a little treat while I can.' Her mother reaches out and takes her hand, and Jennifer can feel how delicate her skin has become, nearly pulls away, scared it might tear if she squeezes back. Her mother's suffering is horribly exposed: the purpled pockets of skin beneath her eyes, the sallowness. She should have phoned ahead, given her time to conceal her deterioration beneath silk scarves and makeup as she has for the past few years. It's like walking in on someone naked. Worse. She stares at the teapot, at the hairline crack in the glaze running from spout to base, and musters up her work voice.

'I need to get Jack more clothes, some toys.'

She catches the glance between her parents.

'Did she say you could go down there?'

'I can't get his things washed overnight and dry in time, Mam. We're both working.'

Her mam frowns, still hesitant.

'I can't send Jack into school looking like a tramp, can I? Where's the key?'

'We've got one somewhere.' Her dad gets up, groaning as if every joint has seized in the five minutes he's been sat. He starts opening drawers, rummaging through spare batteries and balls of twine.

'Cariad, you know she likes her privacy. It's important to respect that.'

'I do, but I have a duty to Jack to keep him clean and happy.'

'Here you go. Did she tell you which one is for what?' He holds out a jangling bunch on a worn wooden fob.

'I'll work it out. Thanks.'

'Jennifer,' her mother might be shrunken, but her voice still demands reverence, 'in and out, iawn?'

'Of course.'

***

Back in the hotel room Helen paces. She is still hungry, the half-empty packet of nuts spilling across the bedcovers, but she can't eat. She stops by the window again and peeks through the curtain, checking her bike is still there, still chained and untampered with.

She is angry; with the man in the bar for talking to her, with the bar for not serving food, with the whole town for not having a family restaurant open midweek. But mostly with herself.

She snatches a handful of nuts as she passes the bed and tries to chew, but ends up spitting the half-crushed kernels into her palm and then tipping them into the bin, wiping her hand on her trousers.

She should have known better. A bar! What was she thinking?

Should have come back to the room as soon as she saw the restaurant was closed. Made do with what is now strewn across the bed – nutrition and energy, regardless of flavour. She knows the value of a lockable door.

***

Jennifer slips off her work shoes in the porch and slides her feet into her mam's old wellies. Her thin tights do little to protect her from the clammy cool of the rubber, and they are loose, chafing her heels when she walks. Her nylons will be laddered. As she crosses the yard, Megan hobbles out of the barn again, ears back and tail swishing low to the ground.

'Okay, old girl?' Jennifer has never really felt an affinity with animals. She enjoyed feeding the lambs as a child, but living on a farm exposes the muck and fluids of things. She shied away from the dogs and their damp, muddied fur and rough tongues, stood on the gate and watched as her dad and Helen hauled the sheep through the trap and forced the drench gun into the sides of their mouth, plunging thick white worming medicine deep into their throats. Her dad insisted they both help with the lambing, their small hands better suited to turning tangled limbs internally, but while Helen would stay back to ensure the babies latched and fed, Jennifer would go straight to the tap to scrub her hands and wrists clean. When the fleeces were shorn and stacked, the greasy smell made her gag.

Helen embraced it all, though; early mornings spreading sheep nuts for the ewes in the week before tupping, docking the lamb tails and testicles with tight blue rubber bands. While Jennifer took the first chance she had to get off the farm, an apprenticeship at Wylfa straight from her A levels, Helen had stayed back, devoting herself to the fields and livestock.

Jennifer unhooks the gate leading out of the yard and looks at the stony path that twists away into the darkness. Megan takes a few tentative steps forward, hopeful of some company, and Jennifer pats her leg and says, 'Come on then,' only because she doesn't want to walk alone. She has a torch, but beyond the glow of light from the farmhouse windows, the path looks treacherous.

Twice she stumbles in the oversized wellies. The path is pitted, deep puddles that blind her when the flashlight catches them, reflecting the light back out. Hawthorn hedges run along one side, but the wind cuts through the bare spiky branches and screeches off over the open fields. When she moves the beam across the close-cropped grass dozens of eyes light up, pale green and fixed. Occasionally a guttural bleat is swept away by a gust of wind.

The dog has drifted away, into the field.

Twenty yards from the barn there is a gate with a heavy padlock hanging from a chain. She fumbles the keys, trying to find one that might fit, then decides to hitch up her skirt and climb over. She has the torch between her teeth and her skirt riding up when she sees the barbed wire. She wriggles the skirt back in place and goes back to the keys, trying three before finding the right one. The sound of the chain slipping away is a discordant bell, and something startles in the undergrowth, skitters off. Megan gives out a wheezy huff, tottering towards the movement. When Jennifer steps through the gate a brilliant white light floods into the lane and exposes the track and front of the barn in its harsh glare. She blinks and squints, waiting for her pupils to contract, then, relieved she will no longer have to fumble with the torch, she heads up to Helen's home.

When they were kids and free to roam the farmland, this barn had been stocked high with rolled haybales at the end of summer, their number depleting over the winter as they were shredded and scattered for the sheep in the coldest months. This is the barn they were not allowed to play in, lest the bales dislodge and crush them in a haze of dust and sweet spiky strands. This is the home Helen has never invited her to visit.

There are three more locks: an ancient mortice, a Yale, and a newer cylinder lock. The high barn door has been reinforced, an extra layer of wood added to the back, so that when she pushes it, it's heavy and no light can filter through the shrunken slats of the original panel. Inside the air is dank, cold.

She feels along the wall for a light switch, and a single bulb comes on, casting a yellowish glow over the space.

An old, dark blue Renault Clio is parked at the back of the barn, tucked in tight against one wall. Beside the door is a neat row of wellies and boots, a coat hook with overalls and waterproofs. The ground floor is open plan, basic; the concrete base stained but swept clean. There is no sign of straw or smell of animals, but it doesn't feel like a home to Jennifer, either. It certainly isn't how she would envisage a barn conversion. There are no rustic oak worktops or carefully selected industrial-style light fittings.

There are old kitchen cupboards against one wall, beige with wooden handles, held together by a run of cheap laminate worktop. A camping-gas hob and tin kettle sit neatly side by side, and at the end of the run there is a steel basin with an exposed pipe to drain away outside somewhere. There are baskets of onions and seed potatoes stacked in the darkest corner, bunches of dried herbs hanging from the walls. A seemingly homemade heart-shaped willow wreath on the back wall, now softened and bound with cobwebs.

In the far corner a section has been panelled off, and a door fixed in place. Jennifer wonders if this is the wardrobe, but when she opens the door finds it is a compost toilet, a sack of wood shavings next to the pedestal to cover the deposits. It smells faintly sweet, fertile and organic, but not offensive.

She closes the door and looks around. The space is neat and tidy, but lacks any comforts.

A small foldaway table is set against the wall, two wooden stools side by side. No fridge, no washing machine. If there is a shower or bathroom it isn't obvious.

A wide ladder stretches up to a banistered platform and another closed door. She slips off the oversized wellies and clambers up in her torn tights, finding the last key on the ring and opening the door, feeling around the door jamb for a light switch.

This room is small; half the size of the barn's footprint, it has sloping ceilings, boarded and painted but with the beams exposed, and a carpet that muffles her footsteps as she wanders around. Two mattresses lie on the floor opposite the door, either side of a round window in the end wall of the barn. One has a bright green duvet patterned with jungle animals, a crocheted blanket with each square depicting a sun or moon, a cloud or raindrop. Next to the pillow is a small pile of books, a pair of binoculars and a reading lamp. There are no teddies, but on a shelf above the bed is a neat row of hand-carved wooden farm animals. The other bed has a simple dark green cover and autumn-coloured blankets. More books stacked beside the pillow, and a flashlight.

Jennifer kneels beside them. The blankets smell frowsy, as if they haven't been changed in a while. She picks up the book on top of the pile beside Helen's bed. *The End of the World as You Know It*. At first she thinks it is a novel, but when she flicks it open the pages are tightly annotated and the chapter headings like a self-help book. Only instead of 'How to Love Yourself a Little More Each Day', she finds 'Body Disposal: Hiding and Hygiene', and 'Negotiating Rations'. She drops it and looks at Jack's pile. These look way too advanced for an early reader. *The Secret Island, The Wolf Wilder*. She stands up and looks around.

There is a trunk, wooden and scarred, under the round window. Jennifer thinks it might be their old toy chest. Behind the door there is a desk with a laptop and notebooks, a small mug full of pens and pencils, and a simple wooden stool. A shelf stacked with bulging cardboard files. Nothing else.

She opens the trunk, finding neat stacks of Helen and Jack's clothes, one side each. There isn't much, just basic items. She pulls out one extra set of school clothes, some jeans and two T-shirts for Jack, finds a hooded, woollen jumper and adds it to the pile. There are no spare pyjamas.

She looks around for toys, for any of the Christmas or birthday presents she and Ioan have bought Jack over the years, but there is nowhere they might be stored. She is just about to leave when she catches sight of the laptop again.

In and out.

Did she actually promise?

She sits on the stool and runs her fingers over the closed lid. Helen is hardly about to appear at the door and catch her. She opens it and the screen flickers to life. A screen saver. Jack wielding a small hand axe, chopping wood. Jennifer frowns at the image and taps at the enter key, expecting a password box to pop up, but instead the folders and toolbar appear, unprotected. After all the locks and chains she's had to negotiate to get in here, the lack of security on the laptop is too easy.

She shuts the lid and locks the bedroom, nearly slips on the ladder on the way down, and pauses at the big barn door before stepping out.

There is something horribly sad about the space, the sparseness of it. Everything is necessity. Apart from the crocheted blanket and books there are few signs a child lives here at all. When she steps back outside Megan is standing on the edge of the light. Her ears go back in greeting.

'Come on, old thing.'

She walks quickly up the lane, her arms full of Jack's stale smelling clothes, eager to get home and get him into a nice hot bath.

***

Helen can't settle. She's been here less than twelve hours and already feels like she's failed. Exposed herself, somehow. She needs to be more careful.

She nurses a cup of instant coffee made with the sachets and tiny pots of UHT milk, the tiny kettle on the nightstand. Wants to flush out the last of the beer. If she's honest, she never really enjoyed drinking and socialising even before Jack. Remembers the relief when she finally decided to stop going out altogether. She hadn't much in common with the other young farmers anyway, beside their time at college and farming club. And they never wanted to talk about work in the pub.

'It's down time,' Andy would say. 'Leave the beasts in the fields and relax a bit, iawn?'

She always wondered if he regretted the amount he drank: five o'clock in the morning, driving the cows into the shed for milking, hangover throbbing. Sundays aren't a day off if you have livestock.

She drains the coffee and rinses the cup in the bathroom sink. Sits with her phone on charge and checks her emails. A few more people have volunteered to mark the boundary with her in March, but a lot of the protesters want to be at the main rally point, Menai Bridge, where they will be seen and have their presence felt. A few have messaged her to say they are worried there won't be any coverage of the fields, that while they value her stance of not selling out, the protests are about the bigger picture. She replies, politely, that if Vista get their hands on her land they will have all the pieces to complete their coup. That *they* will be the bigger picture.

There are only two plots left unsold now, her parents' farm and her sister's smallholding. She goes and stands by the window, watches a few soft flurries of snow swirl in the light from the streetlamp. Her pictures of the tour will rally them to action. Remind them of what is at risk. She'll call a meeting when she gets home, she decides, tell them to their faces what's at stake.

It's late. She checks the door is locked one last time and gets into bed, pulls the covers tight around her. The blankets don't smell right. There is nothing comforting about the fluffy pillow against her cheek. She's hungry, but it's her own fault. She focusses on the ache in her stomach to make sure she'll never forget.

***

'Come on little man, time for bed.'

Jack smiles, but doesn't move.

'What's up? Are you hungry?'

A nod.

'Supper then. Yogurt?' Jennifer has stocked the fridge with fromage frais and cheese dippers, bought blueberry muffins and animal-shaped biscuits.

She waits for him to scrape the spoon around the plastic pot and ushers him upstairs to the bathroom. He brushes his own teeth.

An hour later she goes back up to check on him. He's not in bed, but sitting on the windowsill, holding the pickle jar.

'Why aren't you asleep, little man?'

'I'm not tired.' He tries to smile again, but it's more of a grimace.

CHAPTER FOUR

She wolfs down the breakfast: omelette, strong coffee, fruit. Doesn't waste time. As soon as the last morsel is inside her she heads out, straight to the supermarket. Stocks up on bottled water, individually sealed flapjacks, and packs of nuts. Some instant cup noodles in case she needs something hot. Throws in chocolate for the energy boost.

On her way back to the hotel she rounds a corner and almost collides with two women coming the other way. She steps aside, into deep snow that is banked against the fences, and the cool spike of ice water seeps into her boots through the laces. The women barely glance at her, trudge away with their shoulders stooped. They are perhaps her mother's age. Heavy bags pulling at their posture. Helen watches them go, wondering if it is only the bags weighing them down.

After the explosion in Reactor Four, she's read, Ivankiv became busy with official cars and uniforms, eventually adopting the liquidators and their families. Somewhere there is a monument to those who lost their lives. She's found little information about the town itself online, though. A few pictures, a line here and there. The town lives mainly in the reference section of the event.

She walks past the bar, closed and dark. Slows her pace almost immeasurably as she comes alongside it, her own face reflected back at her when she can't resist a glance at the window – a pale moon under the woollen cap, blank expression.

She walks on.

Kyivska Street.

Passes a market; low dark blue cabins with dark red roofs, stalls selling cheap vegetable oil in half- to ten-litre bottles. Sacks of rice and pasta. Plastic buckets and mops, rolls of vinyl tablecloths, and wooden brooms with wide brushes, the kind witches fly on in kids' stories. Wheel trims, toothpaste. There is a decent crowd, despite the biting cold.

Further on she passes more blocks of flats, neater this time. Soulless with their square structures and square windows.

She has to leave town to find the memorial. The houses become sparse and the pavement narrows, begins to crumble. Eventually she reaches the sign marking the town's limit, and the pavement stops altogether; a strip of battered Armco is the only border between the road and the trees and shrubs. She walks in the slushy snow, her socks getting wetter and her toes starting to ache. Twice cars honk their horns in warning, and she almost turns back. But then she sees it. A grey spike pointing up at the grey sky from a triangular island where the road forks. She trots over the tarmac.

The memorial is simple; a low, curved wall of black marble, not even a half circle, and a simple spear of granite encompassed, halfway up, by a ring of letters. Helen doesn't recognise the word. The wall is made of multiple tablets, each carved with the service numbers of the liquidators who went in for the clean-up. It looks like a war memorial, neat rows of numbers, but no names. She takes a few pictures and wonders why it is in such an inaccessible place. There is nowhere to park; it is essentially on a junction, surrounded by slip roads.

It starts snowing. Tiny hard pellets at first, that sting her face and make her blink too often, then soft clusters, their symmetry fragile and downy. Everything becomes blurred, blunt. Cars slow down, their tread reduced to a hush on the road. Sound is distorted, deadened. She bows her head and walks as fast as the treacherous tarmac will allow. A little further out of town there is a path which she hopes leads to the river. As soon as she is under the shelter of a large oak, she pulls out the extra layer, drinks half a bottle of water, and eats a chocolate bar to boost her metabolism and warm up. She feels more relaxed away from the town, away from people. Wishes Jack was beside her, to share the adventure.

Despite the weather she moves more confidently here, her stride adjusting instinctively to the uneven terrain, her senses attuned to the sounds of the forest. Snow sifts through the branches, and as her feet crunch on the ice a bird calls a warning, is answered from further down the path. When the route opens up she can see the river, frozen over almost, its veined grey surface already half covered by the new fall. At the deepest part, near the centre, the ice is creaking, grinding and breaking up. It moves slowly. There are bulrushes, snapped and stumpy and highlighted with snow.

She notices it through the screen on her camera first – a tiny movement on the other side, black amongst the black tree trunks. She stops taking pictures and lowers the phone. A deer maybe? It's moving parallel to her, getting nearer as the river narrows, perhaps a hundred yards away. A person? She can't be sure it's a man, but something about the movement makes her think it is: the angle of the knees, the heft of the shoulder.

She squints through the precipitation, the eddies faster, thicker, obscuring her view. It's like watching a badly tuned old TV; static and white noise. When he reaches the water's edge he stops, and they stare at each other over the ice. He doesn't wave, and neither does she. Her body responds, norepinephrine and cortisol make her heart accelerate and her glucose levels rise. She clenches and unclenches her fists, waiting.

There is something threatening in the way the figure stands, so still opposite her. He can't possibly get to her, unless he walks across the surface of the river, and she is sure that the ice isn't thick enough, that he'd sink before he reached the middle. She holds her ground. If he does try to cross and slips between the frozen sheets, she will walk away. She isn't going to risk her life for a stranger.

It becomes a game, two figures playing chicken. Who will move first?

She stamps her feet gently, wriggles her throbbing toes. The snow gets thicker. Drifts. How long should she wait before the risk of getting too cold, of getting lost, is greater than the need to win? She glances back towards the path. It's becoming vague, barely perceptible. When she looks back there is nothing opposite, and try as she might, she can't see any movement through the snow.

Back on the road she glances over her shoulder every few yards, convinced that if someone is following her she won't hear them, not with the sound so deadened. When she gets back to the hotel her nose is streaming, her feet numb. She locks herself in the room and makes a coffee with the miniature kettle on the dressing table, takes it into the en suite and runs a bath. The water hurts her skin as she eases in. Her feet are white, completely white. As she rubs the blood back into them, she begins to doubt she saw anyone out there at all.

***

'Mrs Lloyd-Jones?'

'Speaking.'

'It's Mrs Connor from Ysgol Llanfechell. I'm calling about Jack. I've got your number as a temporary contact while his mam's away?'

'Is he okay?'

'He's fine. Well, he's not hurt or anything.'

Jennifer lets her eyes flick back to the computer screen. She has a meeting in ten minutes. 'So, he's okay?'

'We need you to come and get him.'

'Why? What's happened?'

'He's being... disruptive.'

'Jack?' She half laughs.

'I think you should come.'

'I'm at work. Are you sure you've got the right Jack?'

'Yes, definitely the right one. Jack Morgan. Helen's boy.'

'I have a meeting in ten minutes, I don't think I can. What has he done? I'm sure you can handle...'

'We really need you to come, Mrs Lloyd-Jones. We wouldn't call unless we had to.'

Jack is in a tree.

Jennifer walks through Wylfa's visitor centre café towards

the outdoor seating area, through the chug of the coffee machines and fragrant steam of frying bacon, and through everyone who is staring as her nephew hisses and spits at the young woman trying to coax him down. The other children, she has been told, have gone back into the activity room to learn about different energy sources.

The woman is in her early twenties, nervous. She tucks a strand of streaked blonde hair behind her ear and pulls her cardigan closer around her shoulders. She has a nose ring.

'What happened?'

She steps away from Jack's tiny, simian protest and looks at Jennifer with tears in her eyes. 'I don't know. He's been oppositional all morning. We practically had to lift him onto the bus. As soon as we got here and tried to get him into the session he just ran. He's been up there for over an hour.'

'Oppositional?'

'You know? Defiant, uncooperative.'

'Are you his teacher?' She looks too young.

'Classroom assistant. The teacher had to go back in with the other children.'

Jennifer walks towards the tree, half furious, half sympathetic. He looks frightened, his small hands white-knuckled around the thin branches, crouching as if about to pounce.

'Hey, little man. What's the matter?'

He stares at her.

'Why don't you come down now, you can go and be with your friends.'

'No.'

'Don't you want to go and see what they're doing?'

'I want to go home.' A barely perceptible wobble in his voice.

'You can't go home, little man. Me and Uncle Ioan are at work today.'

'I want to go home.' Fiercer.

'Come on now. Come down and go into the class with your friends.'

'They're not my friends.'

'Jack, you need to do as you're told.' She hadn't wanted to lose her gentle tone, but she is now fifteen minutes late for the meeting. 'Get down now.'

'You're not my mam. I don't have to do what you say.'

'We're not allowed to, you know, pick them up or anything,' the girl with the nose ring says. Jennifer doesn't need more than this hint. She walks around behind him and reaches up, grabbing his waist firmly. As she pulls him down he howls. Twigs and last year's dried leaves shower down in fragments. He's thrashing, catches her shins and breast with his heels and elbows. 'You're not my mam, stranger, stranger!' he spits. She drops him when his teeth sink into her wrist.

'Jack! Enough now!' She's never shouted at him before. He is still, curled on the damp lawn. She looks around and sees faces pressed to the window. A colleague waves.

Her face is hot as she crouches down. 'Why are you doing this, Jack?'

'Mam said...' he wipes snot on his sleeve, sniffs hard. 'She said don't come here.' His face is pale, each freckle a hard dot. 'She said it's not safe.'

'It's perfectly safe. I come here every day.'

***

'You said you'd sort it!'

'I said I'd do my best. I never promised anything.'

'I trusted you, Jen, I don't blame him for acting up.'

'What did you say to him to make him so scared? None of the other children hid in a tree!'

'He was doing the best he could in a difficult situation. What did you do after that?'

'I ended up taking him home. It's caused a hell of a stink at work. I had meetings…'

'Is he okay?'

'He's not talking to me, but yeah, he's fine.'

'Well, the damage is done.' She's fuming. 'Let me talk to him.'

The screen blurs and then Jack's face appears. She scrutinises it for signs of damage: swollen eyes from crying, a flicker of reproach in his pupils.

'You okay?'

'No.'

Helen feels the rock in her chest swell, swallows.

'I'll be home soon, a few days now.'

He nods, withdraws. She doesn't wait for Jennifer to come back on, to say goodbye.

CHAPTER FIVE

Breakfast in the hotel restaurant. A different waiter today, a boy who can barely be out of school serves her. Another omelette, open and still runny on top, sprinkled with chives and chopped tomatoes. Helen shovels it down. It's going to be a long day, and protein will help. She pours a second cup of bitter black coffee and adds cream, treats herself to sugar. The boy comes back, polite and pimpled, skinny in his crisp shirt and black apron. She smiles warmly and says dyakuyu, when he places another plate before her, and he nods but doesn't smile back. She examines today's extra dish; small rolled pancakes stuffed with a sweet cream cheese and drizzled in chocolate sauce. Dessert after breakfast. A little too rich for the time of day, but the extra calories are welcome. As she chews she watches him, perched on a high stool behind the counter, thumbing his phone. A teenager. Gangly and uncomfortable. Jack one day. She worries for his future. He glances up and blushes.

It's still early. She can see a streetlight through the nylon net curtains at the restaurant windows. She's been up for an hour already though, dressing carefully in the clothes she has chosen for the tour – warm, old, nothing she isn't happy to seal up in bin bags and throw away on the last day. She has packed her rucksack with snacks and water bottles, a digital camera, notebook and pens, a dosimeter she bought online a few years ago, fully charged along with her phone. At the bottom there is a first-aid kit, foil survival blankets, a multitool, iodine tablets and water purifiers. It's unlikely anything will go wrong on the tour, but she needs to feel ready, just in case. Her hair is tied back, and she will pull on her hat to protect herself from any stray particles that might whip up in the wind and get caught in loose strands. She has her biker buff around her neck – it can be stretched to cover her mouth and nose when necessary, washed every evening. She's ready.

She checks her watch. Still twenty minutes before the minibus is due. She savours the last cooling dregs of the coffee and tries to imagine what Jack is doing. They are two hours behind back home. He should still be sleeping. Should be. He isn't a child with regular habits though. She never followed the parenting book routines: naps and feeds on a timetable, controlled crying, ten hours straight through. He's up late some nights, up early some mornings. It's seasonal, responsive. It's more natural. He's always followed her around the farm, up before dawn some days, and through the night for lambing. She's covered him with her coat more than once while he's slept on a hay bale and she's been wrist deep in a traumatised ewe, trying to turn a lamb so it could crown without rupturing its mother.

The boy comes back to move her plate and she resists the temptation to reach out and touch him, to feel the warmth of his hand or the immaculate cotton of his cuff.

In the street, the snow is turning to slush. The temperature has risen, cloud coming in low overnight and insulating the earth. Just a few degrees, but enough for the ice to soften and

78

turn grey underfoot. Helen stamps her feet. She has layered plastic carrier bags between two pairs of socks in the hope of keeping her feet dry, if not the boots. The Doc Martens have spent the night wedged behind the radiator, filling the room with the smell of damp, musty leather.

Perhaps that's why she had the dream again, or perhaps it's because she is here. The dream was different this time, though. Still the light in vivid, slatted stripes over a dusty floor, still the pendulum above, the slow tick back and forth and the drip, drip, drip of urine, still the inability to look up. Dust motes swirling in front of her eyes. But this time a sense that Jack was nearby. Nothing more than a sense, instinct. She could feel his panic, and her own cemented feet.

She'd woken, disorientated and tangled, and hit the wall hard with her hand while trying to find the torch she kept by her bed back home. The impact made her shout, panic more. There shouldn't be a wall there, she was boxed in, coffined.

It can't have taken long for her eyes to adjust to the dark, the glow of the streetlight permeating the curtain and showing the room in sepia, so neat and functional it could only be a hotel, but in those few, half-blind moments her own brittle physicality was spotlighted.

Slowly, she was able to pull her thoughts out of the dream-space and into the present: switching on the bedside lamp, smoothing the blanket, eventually padding to the en suite to drink water and rub her eyes in the harsh glare of the bathroom bulb. 03.23 am. Her hand automatically cupping her breast, her finger subconsciously drawn to probe the lump. Pressing until it hurt. The dreams only started when she was pregnant, only became regular after her mother's diagnosis and the plans for

Wylfa B synchronised – before this triptych of concerns, the rhythm of the seasons timetabled her priorities, kept any bad memories at bay. She needed to sleep but ended up drinking tea, the bedcovers wrapped around her shoulders, scrolling through the latest press releases on the plans for Wylfa B. She made notes in her pocketbook, a bullet-point list of issues to raise at the next Project Liaison Group meeting. Then switched off the light. An hour and a half until her alarm. Eventually she got up and packed and repacked her bag until dawn, double-checking everything until she felt calmer.

She hears the bus before she sees it, a dirty diesel rattle that vibrates through the still-empty street. Dawn is just seeping into the sky, an anaemic, dull silver. She bounces the backpack higher on her shoulder. It feels apocalyptic: the hollow town and the steel-coloured sky; the growl of the engine getting closer, the only vehicle out this early. She checks her bag for the dosimeter, even though she's already checked it three times.

The bus coughs to a stop beside her. It's old, snub-nosed, and has a yellow and black nuclear trefoil painted on the side with the slogan *Enter the Zone* in red letters beside it. The windows are steamy, but she can see the indistinct shapes of other tourists inside. A thickset man in military fatigues and boots jumps down, looks her over, and nods approvingly. He holds out a meaty hand.

'I am Sergey, your guide for the next two days. You have passport? Documents?'

She hands over the paperwork and he turns away to check her details against a printed list on his clipboard and a stack of papers in a tatty cardboard wallet.

She stamps her feet and huffs dragon breath while she waits.

She isn't allowed to board the bus until her validity is proven. She sees a sleeve wipe at the steam on the glass, and someone waves, a blurry smile. She nods back, knowing the benefit of politeness. Finally, he hands her passport back and gestures for her to climb up.

She's assaulted by the stench of the hot air being forced out of the dashboard heater and the driver's cigarette smoke. The bus seats ten people, and it's only half full, but Helen is the last to be picked up and so she has missed the chance of a window seat. There is a TV screen attached to the panel behind the driver's seat, the documentary frozen in black and white. Under this a single, side-facing seat where Sergey perches. As Helen passes he reaches out and un-pauses the programme. She recognises the grainy footage of men shovelling smouldering graphite, running, allowed only a few minutes each on top of the reactor.

Biorobota.

The real robots had malfunctioned, died. People were cheaper to replace. The images are flecked with white, like snow, but Helen knows it is the radiation damaging the camera. She's seen this documentary before.

The person who waved at her through the window is beckoning to the seat beside her. It's not like there's an empty bench, and to reject this offer would be rude. She has barely turned to sit when the bus lurches forward and she is thrown into her seat, bumping up against the girl.

'Sorry.'

'It's okay. I'm Abby, and this is my partner Jake, and Ben,' she gestures to the seats behind; two young men with woollen beanie hats pulled low over their brows. They nod and smile.

Jake is chewing on a strip of beef jerky. He offers out the pack to her, but she declines. Ben holds eye contact a fraction of a second longer than necessary. He is half turned in his seat, his back against the window so the boys can converse without twisting their necks. They all have a confident ease to their posture, American accents.

'Helen.' She shakes the gloved hand Abby holds out.

'This your first trip?'

'Yes.' She is trying to look beyond Abby at the landscape sweeping by, the fields and houses coming into focus as dawn becomes day. But the window has steamed again already, smeared where Abby ran her sleeve across the pane.

'It's our third. Ben is making a film, about the tours.'

Helen smiles and hopes this is enough. She takes out her phone, but it's still too early to text Jen, send a message for Jack. She looks around the bus at the other passengers, clearly a couple. Older, in their late forties or early fifties, with brand new walking boots and expensive winter coats. They are holding hands over the back of the seat, leaning in to mutter to each other every now and then. She thinks they are German, but it's hard to tell over the engine noise and the documentary. Abby twists in her seat towards Helen.

'It's normally packed, but people are put off by the protests. Kyiv's insane at the moment.'

'That's why I avoided it.'

'We got some good footage in the square, from a distance, you know? Long lens. Ben sent it through to the news agencies back home. Just waiting to hear now.' She checks her phone as if it might have an answer. 'You have a cute accent. Where are you from?'

'Anglesey.'

A frown and smile simultaneously. 'Where's that?'

'Wales.'

'As in dragons? Prince Charles and all that?'

'Something like that.' Easier to let it slide.

She gestures at the boys. 'New York. Last time we came it was spring, nearly summertime. Too much blossom and foliage to see anything. It was like a proper forest, cheerful, you know? It's better at this time of year, when everything is dead.' She turns and sweeps her arm against the glass again, revealing a smudged vista of frozen snow and black trees stencilled against the silvering sky. 'We're hoping to see wolves this time, not squirrels. What are you here for? Are you on your own?' She looks around as if Helen's travelling companion might have boarded unseen.

'Drove across Europe a few days ago on my bike.'

'Motorbike?'

'Yeah.'

'Cool, hey Ben?' He looks up.

Helen notes his dark eyelashes, wide jaw.

'S'up, Abs?'

'Helen here has a bike. A motorbike.' To Helen, 'Ben has a Harley.'

'What do you ride?'

Helen can't be sure he's interested, or if he's just being polite. His eyes crinkle at the edges, his smile is confident.

'A Triumph.'

'Triumph?' He frowns, trying to conjure up something to say. 'They're good rides.'

The statement could be a question, might be a question.

'They are.'

'Helen here is on her lonesome, what say we let her buddy up with us for the day, huh guys?'

Ben tilts his head, ever so slightly. Assessing. 'Sure, no problem.' He nods.

'I'm fine, you know. I got this far…'

'You'll be glad of the company when we get there. It's… overwhelming. At first, anyway.'

'Thanks.' Helen smiles, but her stomach sinks. She wants to be alone here.

At the first checkpoint they wait inside the vehicle while passports and paperwork are scrutinised. Sergey has warned them not to take pictures of the checkpoints, not to wander off when they stop to look around, not to kneel on the grass to get a better photo.

The three Americans are chatting, planning the day. The German couple look out of the window as the guards walk around the van, peering in to compare passport photos with faces. Helen sees Sergey hand over a roll of notes.

'Welcome to the Zone,' he announces as they move off.

Helen expects to feel something as they pass the red and white barrier and low, concrete block buildings. Sergey's announcement is theatrical but routine. She has prepared for a long time for this moment; now here she is, rucksack squeezed between her feet and eyes alert, and it is just the same on the other side of the barrier – snow and sleeping trees, a long tarmac road ahead.

After a few minutes Sergey begins to recite facts about the disaster, and Helen tunes out. She already knows the dates and death tolls by heart. Instead, she listens in to the conversation behind her.

'We need to get a shot of the hospital, from the inside. I want that operating theatre again only this time with the dead trees outside.'

'If they let us in.'

Helen turns and interrupts the conversation.

'Why wouldn't they let us in?'

'The buildings are old, fucked structurally. They're not supposed to give access anymore in case there's a collapse.'

'The website says we can visit the buildings, it lists them.'

The men pause and look at her as if she is being silly, and she feels unwelcome heat rush to her cheeks.

'They'll let us in.' Abby pats Helen's arm and Helen reacts automatically, pulls away. 'Without the buildings on the cards the tour is practically worthless, they know that.'

The men nod and continue their conversation. 'And we need to get the pool again, this time without any other groups in the way of the shots. And the fairground.'

'Aw, yeah. That will be awesome at this time of year.'

Helen turns back to face the front of the van, to where Sergey is sitting twisted in his seat, turned towards the German couple. They are the only ones listening. He is talking about a buried village and pointing at low humps of grassy earth between the young trees either side of the road.

'You okay? You're a little jumpy.'

'I'm fine.' Helen stares out of the window past Abby's frown, irritated.

There is, amid the raised graves of the houses and farms, a nursery still standing, and the bus pulls in to their first scheduled stop. As the group pile out Helen moves aside to let Abby through and says she'll join them in a minute. She stands on the empty bus and waits.

Abby stalls, leaning in to speak to Ben. He glances back towards the bus and shakes his head, and they walk away.

By the time Helen gets outside, the group has scattered. There are triangular yellow trefoil signs on posts at regular intervals beside the road, warning that the area is still contaminated. She treads cautiously along the path beneath the trees, forgetting to take out her camera until she sees a rusted toy truck balanced on a fence post halfway up the path.

She almost touches it.

As she moves around to find the best angle for the shot, she imagines the child who'd played with this one, Jack's age maybe, scab-kneed and buzzing with energy. A child certainly hadn't perched the toy up there; little children play on the ground, among the roots and pebbles.

As she enters the first building, water drips from a peeling ceiling and she dodges a drop, careful not to step in any of the puddles. The walls were once bright colours, lime green and sunshine yellow, and there are still hooks low down, for small coats.

**

Jennifer walks Jack in through the school gates, holding his hand despite his attempts to slip her grasp.

'You're not supposed to come in.' His voice is flat. 'Mam doesn't come in, she lets me go at the gate.'

'I just want to make sure you're safe.'

She waits while he hangs his coat on the little pegs, hooks the handle of his lunch bag over the coat's hood.

'Is everything alright?' The assistant with the nose ring. Smiling like yesterday never happened.

'Is the class teacher free? I need a quick word.'

***

Everyone is treading on things; clothes and rotting blankets. Books. Abby and the two men are staging a shot in the sick room, where a single metal bedframe sits beside a broken window and a cabinet of empty jars and bottles. Helen passes the German couple. The woman seems emotional, the man nervous. They stick close to Sergey, asking questions, pointing. Helen walks away.

In a room at the back of the building she finds rows of rusting bunk beds, a floor scattered with dead-eyed dolls and faded clothes. The thin mattresses are stained and grey. *Frozen in time*, the websites say, but there is evidence of time passing everywhere: the moulding material, the curling paint, the dried leaves heaped in the corners of the room. There are picture books propped open on desks, teddy bears arranged beside single shoes. She takes a few photos, crouching, but not kneeling, to get the best shot. The voices of the others fade in and out.

On the top of one bunk, a small white sandal is perched on the bare springs. It is identical, in Helen's memory, to a pair Jennifer had when they were small, that she was supposed to inherit. They were close, once. Shared a bedroom, shared a bath most nights.

She stares at the sandal; mucky white leather, the flower on the T-bar crushed. By the time Jennifer had grown out of them her own feet were too big. She takes a picture and looks around for the other one. There are small fuzzy slippers and enamelled chamber pots, dust and water everywhere, but the other sandal is absent.

Sergey is calling the group back with a military bark, but she needs to find it, begins to search and move things, despite being told not to touch anything before they were let off the bus, knowing not to anyway. She crouches down and looks under the bunks, aware of the weight of silence around her as the group moves down the path.

Just as the engine rumbles back to life she sees the other shoe; small, dirty, beneath the corner of a desk. She is surprised to feel a surge of relief that there is a pair after all, and almost forgives Jennifer for sending Jack on the school trip. Almost. She takes a picture and rushes out, is back at the bus and apologising before she realises she hasn't even switched her dosimeter on yet. She rubs her hands on her jeans and sits back beside Abby, who is half turned and talking animatedly to the boys. She slides the dosimeter out of her knapsack and switches it on. It purrs a slow click of background radiation. Abby turns back.

'You've got your own?'

Helen nods.

'We've never bothered. The guides know where to go. They're expensive.'

'eBay.'

'Still pricey though. You don't really need it. Just don't wander off. We just ask Sergey if we want to know the dose or get a shot of it reading high.' She resumes her debate with the boys over whether the wolves will be visible in the grey and white of the winter forest. Helen stares at the small yellow machine in her hand. She's glad she has it.

***

At her desk, Jennifer runs her fingers over the half-moon bruises on her wrist.

A handful? Boys described that way when she was at school were the big ones, the ones that swore, who snuck up behind the girls to lift their skirts or spit on them. Jack might be blunt, energetic. But he's small. Harmless.

She pulls down her sleeve to cover the marks.

***

An evacuated village. '*When the Government finally decided to evacuate, thirty-four hours and 23 minutes after the explosion, residents of Prypiat, the town built for the plant, had only two hours to pack. They were promised they could return within three days. A lie. The thirty-kilometre Zone of Exclusion was designated for evacuation almost a week after the event, and this village continued to function for those six days as buses and fire-trucks, armoured vehicles and helicopters, passed by the villagers and their grazing cattle. They weren't ready.*' Abby's voice takes on a different tone for filming; slower, cleaner.

The houses here are entangled now, in barbed-wire brambles and young, naked silver birches. It doesn't stop the group stomping through to push into one of the homes. The bright blue paint on the door is peeling off, scabbed from rain. Helen follows, letting them trample a path through, stepping in their footprints. You don't waste energy or put yourself at risk of a nasty scratch if someone else will do it for you.

'The house is basic, just two rooms. The big room has a range built into the wall; a fire and oven, a platform above,' Sergey explains, while Ben films. 'These houses had fire at the heart. This fire,' he points to the stone-cold range, where ash and half-burnt logs from thirty years ago sit, pale and soft in the hearth, 'warmed the whole house, made for cooking and hot water.' He points to the platform above, a wide shelf only a few feet from the ceiling. 'This is where the family slept in winter, to keep cold away.'

The house has been looted; furniture overturned, anything valuable missing. Perhaps by former residents sneaking back in to reclaim their possessions, perhaps by soldiers or liquidators eager to make some money from the linens, pots and pans. There is a coat, sun-bleached and dusty, hanging from a nail by the door, and shoes scattered across the floor. The odd glass bottle or jar on its side in the heaped leaves. Helen crouches to take a picture and feels someone hunker down beside her.

Ben.

His shoulder brushes hers; a prickle of something like static makes her flinch. He smells good.

'All the houses have these,' he says, pointing at a single leather boot. 'It could be a motif for the place, abandoned shoes. Reminds me of the Holocaust. Nothing left but shoes.'

She turns to him, squinting in a shaft of sunlight that is piercing the fractured shutters.

She nearly tells him about the houses back home, the evacuation there. Offers of five times market value, offers so good some of the residents living in the footprint of the proposed site took only their favourite clothes and photos and walked away. She saw it herself, visiting one of the few houses left near her sister's place to talk over plans to halt progress on the development, only to find it unlocked and silent. Half a loaf in the breadbin and crumbs on the table, a few pale patches on the walls where frames had hung, and dirty pots in the sink. A sign tacked to the gate stating a date for demolition. *Trespassers will be prosecuted*. The Vista logo.

She almost tells him, but the betrayal is still too raw. She is permeable. Needs to toughen up.

He reaches out and brushes her cheek with a finger.

'It's overwhelming, I know.'

He doesn't know anything, but he's trying.

He is there, in the background, for the rest of the morning. Giving her space, stepping in to whisper something he thinks will be interesting. His jaw has a day's fine stubble, as though he has pressed his face into damp sand and the grains have stuck. Golden.

He sits beside her on the bus, her in the window seat at last, as it coughs and splutters its way towards the town of Chernobyl, and the huge cafeteria that feeds the people living and working in the Zone, the workmen constructing the new cover for the blown reactor.

The town itself is a palimpsest; well-kept grass verges and a few functioning office buildings that only partially conceal semi-consumed wooden houses rotting into the undergrowth.

The abandonment is visible only because the foliage is skeletal in the February chill. They don't stop to explore; this is tomorrow's destination. They are here for food.

In the canteen they wash their hands and step onto the radiation monitors, placing feet carefully on the sole-shaped markers and gripping the handles, waiting for the beep that will allow them through and to lunch. They queue to be served.

Helen sits at the end of their table, a tray laden with borscht, fried chicken and boiled rice, salad made with shredded cabbage and beets, a stack of heavy brown bread and two drinks, one a fruity cordial, the other a warm amber liquid that tastes of smoke and makes her cough. She is halfway through her bowl of soup when the next table is filled by another tour group; English voices chattering. She eats quickly and listens, then stops as she sees their guide sit down with his own tray. The guy from the bar.

Anton.

He nods a greeting and takes a huge mouthful of chicken and rice, chewing slowly, while his group gossip and laugh, bonding over the novelty of the experience so far. She and Anton are the only ones not talking. He doesn't pause the rhythm of fork and mouth, is watching her every time she glances his way. He only breaks eye contact to spear the meat.

She is about to move over to his table, to ask him why he didn't tell her he was one of the tour guides, when Sergey calls their attention. He hands out maps, poor printouts in black and white, with an apology for not having them ready first thing.

'Paperwork here has hierarchy. But now you can mark where you have visited. A souvenir.' She glances at the paper

— a simple depiction of the Zone, the border thick black, the main interest points labelled: Chornobyl Town, the Reactors, Prypiat, the Red Forest. Areas of high contamination have tiny propeller signs next to them. There are empty villages listed too: Ivanovka, Yampol, Ladizhichy, Krivaya Gora. The ink is faded in stripes across the page, as if the cartridge was running out. The people at her table start sharing pens, marking out their route so far. As Ben leans over his map, she notices the slightly wavy hair that grazes his collar, the subtle flex of muscles in his neck as he talks. She hears the group behind her scrape their chairs to leave and watches Anton's tight stride as he shepherds them out, then turns back as her own group gets up. Ben stretches as he stands, a thin strip of belly exposed between his T-shirt and combats, a few curled hairs trailing downwards. She folds the map into her pocket, piles her tray with the aftermath of lunch, takes a final sniff of the smoky drink and follows him out.

They drive towards the power station. Past vast substations taking energy back onto the site instead of out. The sky is hatched with wires. They stop on a service road with the buildings in the distance and the German couple step out to take one another's photos against the iconic backdrop. There is one symmetrical set of reactors on the horizon, and one that is wounded; lopsided and scarred. Swollen with the concrete that was stacked over the exposed core, built up into a monstrous scab.

Helen expects this to be as far as they come: a chance to take pictures from a safe distance, then leave. But when they re-board the bus it draws closer and closer to the site, through a skyline tangled with power lines and chimneys, cranes and cooling towers. Her palms begin to tingle, her chest tightening as they draw nearer. Everyone has fallen silent. The first half of the New Safe Confinement structure arches in silver, like a colossal pig pen, beside the crumbling sarcophagus that has encased Reactor Four since the eighties.

They are close, and as they park they can see construction workers even closer to the cracked concrete, their hi-vis jackets and black shirts and trousers giving them the look of worker bees beside a lethal hive.

Sergey ushers them through blank corridors into a visitor's centre. It's crowded. A single room with a wall of glass, through which they can see the old sarcophagus beneath a lattice of scaffolding. It's perhaps three hundred yards away. Vast. There are printed signs on the window forbidding photography.

There must be three tour groups here. Sergey moves towards his colleagues: a plump, balding man in jeans and a bright yellow fleece bearing a tour logo, and Anton. They clasp hands, shake, then stand lined up against the back wall, watching the group. Helen moves against the adjacent wall so she can observe the room too. Her eyes repeatedly drawn to the dark shape of the sarcophagus beyond the glass.

On a large, low table there is a scale model of Reactor Four, a morbid doll's house that opens to show the layers of destruction inside, tiny model men littering the roof and damaged rooms below. *It's there*, she thinks, *buried*, glancing through the window.

The groups are mixed; she recognises the English-speaking group from lunch, some serious-looking guys with expensive waterproofs and hiking boots. A neat beard, wire-rimmed spectacles. One is making notes in a brand-new notebook. There are a couple of gamer types, in their late twenties, excited, the flash of a *Call of Duty* T-shirt between the open zip of a jacket.

The other group seem to be Russian, or perhaps Ukrainian. They are young, teenagers with trainers and lipstick, one girl in heeled boots. Bored. Being shushed and enthused in equal measure by a teacher perhaps, a woman approximately Helen's age with seemingly un-ending patience. *Grey. Concrete. Massive.*

After ten minutes of milling and chatting another woman enters. She is plump and healthy, in her fifties maybe, glasses strung around her neck from a gold chain. She goes straight to the men and accepts kisses on the cheek. Helen watches as they point out a few of the tourists, assumes they are informing her of troublemakers, special cases, vested interests. Helen isn't marked out, but Anton does acknowledge her personally with a nod. *Decaying. Concrete. Scarred.*

The woman moves to the window and raises her voice to welcome everyone, and the groups fall into the shape of an audience and quieten down. The speech has been given before, Helen can tell. The same things said many times. The woman avoids eye contact and gestures towards the sarcophagus beyond the glass without looking at it as she describes the day of the event, how the one-thousand-ton lid above the fuel elements was lifted and flipped by the blast, how the graphite ignited on contact with the oxygen that rushed in. Human error. *Buried. Concrete. Vibrating.*

Helen tears her eyes away from the window and takes in the response from the room.

There are a few mumblers near the back. One girl staring

at her phone. Helen notices the curator wince when one of the gamers says 'Cool,' for the third time.

When the talk is over the group potter around the room again, some stooping to peer inside the model, some checking their phones.

Helen waits to see what the woman will do, if she will go and stand with the tour guides, biding her time until her duty and endurance is up. She doesn't. The men are deep in conversation, and the woman stands to one side, politely smiling at no one in particular.

Helen approaches her, holds out a hand and says dyakuyu, softly. Holding eye contact. The woman blinks behind her thick spectacles, takes them off, and clasps her hand back.

'You are welcome.' Polite, but the lift of her eyebrows discloses mild surprise.

'Has no one ever thanked you before?'

'Not like that, no.'

'I don't know how you bear it. Everyone staring at it, as if it isn't real. As if it's just a movie.'

'To a lot of people it is like that, yes. Not everybody.'

'Not for me.'

The woman is still holding her hand, squeezes it slightly.

'Doesn't it make you angry, the way they react? Like it's all just been… an adventure… ?'

'They are learning. We hope they learn.'

'How do you feel? I mean, about it being like a tourist destination?'

'I work here. It is my job to help educate.' She leans in and whispers. 'But if they don't listen, if they don't look, properly look, then is all for nothing.'

'Were your family... were they evacuated?'

The woman pulls her hand back, glances over Helen's shoulder. Anton is standing apart from his friends, watching.

'Thank you for coming, for listening.' The woman smiles and turns away. Walks towards the doll house reactor and begins to point out the shattered parts to the teenagers.

In the vacuum that is left Helen feels a rising pressure. The room is noisy, humming with voices. They will be herded back onto the bus soon, whisked away to fill their eyes with more rotting buildings and remnants of homes. More photos.

She goes right up to the window, places her palms and forehead against the cold glass and stares hard at the reactor.

She wants to be alone with it, wishes the room would clear and leave her behind. She's waited years to stand here, to face up to it. She never thought she'd get this close.

Its ossuary shape is familiar, burned into her memory. A vast pile of concrete blocks, hastily erected to contain the emissions. But here, in its presence, she can see it isn't quite solid; the surface is grey and pockmarked, like a sandcastle that might collapse. Fractured. There are water stains streaking from the seams in dark tears, rusty ladders buckled against the pitted flanks. Scaffolding props up the front. Ice and snow have caused fissures, and birds nest in the cracks. And it is leaking, she knows, but there is nothing to taste, smell or feel as it does.

She presses her nose to the glass and steam forms on the pane around her face. Memories surge through her: the window at home overlooking the lawn, the cherry blossom from the tree in the centre. Exploding. Falling. Instead of playing with the petals, that spring she'd watched the blossom drift and settle. It stuck to the damp grass and eventually browned, mulched into the lawn. And Ffion. She's tried hard not to think of Ffion over the years, but now she wonders what happened to her, if she coped. They used to play together. She remembers walking across the field near the end of that long hot summer. Grass rippling in the breeze, pebbles on the track. The farmyard cracked and dry beneath her sandals and the barn door ajar. The light in slatted beams across the floor...

'Are you okay?'

She catches her breath, her fingers aching as they press the glass. It's Anton, frowning. Dark eyes and thin lips.

The room is emptying behind her.

'I'm fine.'

'You got what you came for, yes?'

She looks back at the reactor, at the men working beneath as though it is any building anywhere. At the New Safe Confinement structure, sublime in scale, waiting to be slid across. Another matryoshka doll to cover up the mess.

'I'm fine,' she repeats, but he's already moved away. 'I'm actually okay.'

It will be dark soon.

***

'She said he's scaring the other kids.'

Jennifer is unpacking shopping at the kitchen table. Two pairs of brightly coloured pyjamas covered in trucks and teddies, a packet of vests and some underpants, a stuffed toy with huge ears, its species indistinct but its formation consisting of all the cutest traits of baby mammals stitched into one. Chocolate.

'Jack? Scary?' Ioan laughs. 'Na, amhosib!'

'I know. It's ridiculous, right? But that's what she said. None of the kids will play with him.'

Ioan frowns and shakes his head. 'Scaring them how?'

'She wouldn't say. I'm not his parent or official carer so apparently she's not supposed to discuss personal issues with me. Didn't stop them calling me the other day, though.'

'She's probably overreacting. Probably just kids mucking around.'

'Probably.' Jennifer picks up the toy and walks through to the lounge where Jack is curled into a corner of the sofa, watching TV. Over the past few days both she and Ioan have been buying toys to add to the small basket of things they've always kept for him at their house. The lounge is littered with cars and crayons. An action figure lies twisted on the rug. Jack is cradling his jar of snails on his lap, his finger spiralling in his hair.

'Look what I got you, little man.' She holds out the fuzzy creature, all floppy legs and massive eyes. He looks up and blinks, as if trying to decode the offering, then takes it gently and examines it.

'What is it?'

'I thought you might like a special teddy to cuddle, while you're here.'

He frowns, stares into its glass eyes. 'Diolch.' The intonation is almost a question.

'Jack, would you like me to see if one of your friends from school wants to come over to play?'

He shakes his head and curls his finger through his fringe again. Her heart sinks, he cannot be the problem, they must be bullying him.

'Are the other children nice to you?'

'I don't like them.'

'Why? Are they mean to you?'

He frowns at her, then shakes his head. 'All they want to do is play ball or… or chase each other. They don't care about things… about things that matter.'

'And what matters to you?'

His finger returns to his hair, twirling. A little frown as he calculates. 'Sheep. Modron and Mabon. Being safe. The farm. Looking after special people.'

'Who are the special people?'

'Mam, Nainy and Taidy. You and Uncle Ioan.'

'We don't need looking after, Jack.'

'Yes, you do. Mam is always looking after you. She looks after everything.'

Jennifer doesn't know how to respond. She stares at the TV along with him for a few minutes, watching cartoon animals on an epic quest.

'Listen, little man. You don't need to worry about looking after me and Ioan. We're looking after you now, okay?'

He glances at her with cloud-grey eyes, unfathomable.

'Dinner in ten minutes, okay?'

At the door she pauses. The toy is beside him, ignored, and he has sunk back into the colourful action on the screen.

***

On the bus on the way to the hotel, they detour through a stretch of forest known to be a hunting ground for the wolves. Everyone is eager to catch a glimpse of their silvered pelts through the vertical striation of the trees.

Ben sits beside Helen, his leg against hers. She doesn't push it away.

She is filled with a sense of lightness, a euphoria and almost preternatural energy. Seeing the sarcophagus so close, acknowledging its presence as a real, solid thing rather than a mythical threat, has released her somehow. And soon it will be encased in steel, no longer leaking, and the news coverage of the New Safe Confinement being slid into place will remind people that it's not worth the risk. Perhaps even in time to halt Wylfa B. The feeling is in such direct contrast to the cautious pessimism that has become her default mindset over the last few years, it makes her reckless.

She lets her leg relax against his.

When Abby cracks a joke about using Jake's precious jerky to lure the wolf pack into sight she even laughs along with them.

They bounce through the potholes and swerve past the saplings colonising the edges of the road to varying degrees of success, and his shoulder bumps hers.

The bus stops, Sergey excitedly pointing through the window down a wide side road. The view is spectacular; the road is higher than the forest either side, and to the right the glimmer of water can be seen where the trees part. The sun is sinking, but the sky is clear, giving the scene a silver filter, making it spectral.

Everyone crowds towards Helen's side of the van, hopeful

of a glimpse of the pack. Last week, Sergey has told them, a group saw them near here. Six of them. There is talk that they paused on the road, heads lifted to scent the vehicle, ears like radars flicking from the direction of the coach to the rustlings of potential prey in the woods either side. Then they'd scent marked, and shifted in a swift, fluid movement. Gone.

Ben leans into her, one arm now across the back of the seat, resting on her shoulder. She can smell the day's sweat. He is pointing down the road.

She inhales.

She hasn't let a man this close since the night Jack was conceived. Can't remember the last time she felt this heightened sensitivity in her skin, the pleasant heaviness between her legs. There have been times when, working with Ioan in the barn in the intimacy of lambing or repairing a fence, their bodies have aligned in motion, moved together in a base, unchoreographed synchrony. The thought has crossed her mind, unwelcome, before being discarded with the shorn fleeces, castrated testicles and aborted lambs at the end of the job. If Ioan has felt it too he's never given any indication.

'Look,' Ben says, his voice a whisper, for her alone. 'What's that?'

Far down the road there is an animal, large and lumbering, crossing the tarmac. It isn't a wolf. They both lean forwards together.

'A beaver!' Sergey announces. 'These animals now move home to build on the water. This place is perfect nature reserve. You see eagles, too.'

The group settle back down. A beaver isn't as thrilling as a wolf. But Helen watches it waddle into the undergrowth, finds herself smiling. Something about the sight gives her an awkward sense of hope.

They check into the Chernobyl hotel just as the sun is drowned in a line of mackerel clouds. It's a large, prefab building. Puddles in the car park, a dim light over the door. As soon as keys are distributed, and the toilets and dining room pointed out, Helen excuses herself and locks herself in her room. She can hear the heavy thud of boots in the corridor, people shouting in English and Russian, American accents. The hotel is full despite the unrest in the capital, film-makers, tourists and writers all vying for a slice of authenticity amid the rubble.

She checks her phone, but there is no signal, and the woman who signed her group in has apologised for a lack of WiFi. The hotel is changing suppliers, she said, offering vouchers for a free drink at the bar to make up for the inconvenience.

She eases sore feet out of damp boots and shrugs off her jacket, shoving them into a plastic bag. Takes out a clean set of sweats and socks and waits outside the shared shower room for her turn. Inside she strips quickly, bagging her clothes for tomorrow, tying a tight knot in the top. In the shower she pulls the band out of her hair, washes it thoroughly. Keeps her eyes and mouth tightly closed as the suds and water run over her face.

As she washes she thinks again of Ben, runs her hands over her breasts and soaps her armpits, between her legs.

It wouldn't take much. A beer, a smile. She is tempted, lingers on the thought while the water massages her clean, eases out her shoulders and brings a flush of heat to her skin.

As she towels herself dry, her eyes scan the wall for a condom machine.

There isn't one.

There are multilingual notices advising guests what to do if they hear the contamination alarm, but no prophylactics on offer.

She ties her damp hair into a ponytail without brushing it and slips on clean pants, a tight vest, and the tracksuit.

The hotel is busy below. From her room Helen can see, in the soft orange light of the single streetlight behind the hotel, an empty road and the corner of an abandoned building across the street, half buried under brambles and trees. The black, wiry smiles of power lines hang close to the window.

***

'I've tried, little man. It isn't working.'

Jack doesn't divert his gaze. Eyes shimmering, fierce.

'Try again.'

'She probably has a poor signal. Or no WiFi. She said this might happen.'

He turns away, the seat of his pyjamas baggy, hair a mess.

***

The windows in the dining room are steamed up, the tables crowded. When she sits down, she discovers Ben has already bought her a glass of wine without asking. They are discussing the rooms; shared or private, views over the car park or the tangled woodland behind the building.

'Our last room was better. Can't believe we're stuck near the toilets this time,' Abby moans.

'Is your room any quieter?' Ben leans in. She checks her phone again, but there is still no signal. Catches sight of Anton deep in conversation with Sergey at the bar. She flicks backwards through the photos she's taken on the trip, incidentals captured when her camera was still stowed, until she finds an image of Jack. Unaware, concentrating on knotting his laces. Feels her throat tighten.

Ben's hand brushes her thigh under the table and she pulls away.

She sips water throughout the meal while the others order vodka at the bar. As they get merrier she sinks into herself, feels claustrophobic. The room is hot, the food heavy in her stomach. It takes all her energy to keep alert to the shifts in conversation as the different courses are brought out, long intervals in between. She's lost the lightness of earlier, the nascent sense of connection with the others that had emerged in the afternoon. The desire to let Ben get close, to get careless, has ebbed. She can't risk pregnancy, not again. The primal urge to protect Jack is consuming enough, loving another as much would be unbearable, surely.

Despite Ben's tentative persistence, and the echo of desire still lingering at the base of her spine, she excuses herself as soon as the last course is finished. Knows her body better than a stranger could, anyway. She'd only be disappointed. Lies in bed listening to the voices of the group in the bar below rise and fall, wondering why she feels so deflated after her earlier sense of triumph, face to face with the sarcophagus.

CHAPTER SIX

The minibus pulls up in Prypiat.

Ben grins as the door is pulled back on rusty tracks. 'The best part of the tour.'

There is already another bus here, a huge coach; tourists eager to photograph the static circle of the Ferris wheel and listing, rusting carts of the dodgems.

The sky is grey, the sun still rising behind the swollen clouds.

Helen pulls her jacket tighter as a sharp wind bites her wrists and throat. People are calling to one another, their voices sometimes clear, sometimes snatched by the breeze, as though crying out from far away. They echo and return from the empty walls of the flats and shops that stand decaying behind high, leafless trees.

Abby comes up close beside her and loops her arm through Helen's, pulling her towards the fairground.

'He likes you.'

'I guessed.'

'What happened last night? You seemed to be getting on just great yesterday.'

'I was tired.'

'You missed a good night. We hooked up with that other group. Those old guys were a hoot once they had a few vodkas in them.'

'I didn't really feel like partying. That's not why I'm here.'

'Why are you here?' Abby tilts her head, and Helen can't tell if she's genuinely interested. She deflects the question.

'If you're making a documentary, how come you're on the tour and not using permits to film?'

'It's self-funded. We're trying to get a sense of the tours for the film, keeping it real, you know.'

'So, you're just doing a hand-cam movie?'

Abby lets go of Helen's arm. 'It's a valuable perspective.' She stalks off towards Jake, who is panning the camera around to take in the tourists taking their photos. Helen hopes she isn't in too many of his valuable angles.

She walks around taking pictures for the protest back home, imagining the slogans that might be added to the websites and banners.

Don't Let Cemaes Become the Next Prypiat.

They're Evacuating Us Already.

Nuclear Power Steals our Future to Fuel our Today.

'Come on, you have to get a shot of the Ferris wheel. With a good filter it's just… you have to take this shot.' Ben. Still eager.

Her mood has been low all morning. She feels fluey, joints aching and a grittiness in her throat. Her gums are sensitive, bled when she brushed her teeth after breakfast. The rich food – sugary pancakes oozing with chocolate syrup, bread with every meal – has changed her gut flora, she thinks. Raised her sugar levels. Back home she sticks to protein and veg.

'Give me a minute,' she tells Ben. She already knows how to use a filter. Now she has decided to withdraw from the temptation of his warmth she doesn't want him around, sniffing like the dogs in the town. Abby's question still niggles. Has she already accomplished her task? The long journey alone, facing down the sarcophagus while she still can, before the New Safe Confinement Unit covers it forever? Is that why she feels so empty now? Perhaps there is nothing left to achieve here, and she is just biding her time waiting to go home.

She walks in the opposite direction to the rest of the group and takes in the town. She's seen it so many times before in photos and documentaries, it feels familiar and foreign in equal measure. She takes a few photographs of her own and compares the tiny images on the screen with the solid, scented, sensual reality around her. Bright daylight, the creak of the trees in the wind, and birdsong. She can smell damp earth and taste the defeated, almost metallic tang of melting snow where it still hunkers in less exposed corners of the wide square. The ground is hard beneath her boots.

When she turns back the road is clear. She can hear the other tourists, distant, like ghost-echoes of the people who should have enjoyed the rides and never got chance. She walks back towards them. She can see the Ferris wheel through the bare branches of the trees; each carriage stiff and rusted onto the spokes. She steps into the open square. A swing-chair ride is lopsided and rotten, the bumper cars listing on buckled boards. It should be terrifying, a warning to everyone of what can happen when you are so busy celebrating 'progress' you forget how fragile the foundations are, how uncontrollable the forces that are harnessed. But the fairground is so much smaller than the pictures she's seen online portray. She could cross it in twenty paces, and the wheel itself is now dwarfed by the trees that have grown up around it.

The buildings behind the speared branches are blank-eyed, doleful. She is struggling to get an emotional response, pulls her coat tighter. A couple crouch low in front of the Ferris wheel and use a selfie-stick to take their own picture. She looks at each person in turn, cameras pressed to eye-sockets or held up to show the view on a tiny digital screen, phones held at arm's length. No one is looking. Not really. She waits until the people move away from the wheel and gets close, stands right under that iconic symbol of a town built and then abandoned. This is what the earth will look like after we've gone, she thinks. Bright, flaking paint and earthy rust. Weeds. It's beautiful.

She looks again at it through the lens.

Breath on her neck, wide shoulders behind her. 'It's good, but try crouching down, you get a better sense of scale.'

She resists the reflex to lash back with her elbow. Ben leans in closer and reaches to point at the screen and she steps away. 'Just try the filter. Something blue-grey to make it look really apocalyptic.'

She lowers the camera.

'Can I show you something?' Ben is beckoning to her as if expecting her to step into the curve of his arm and let him lead her away.

'What?'

If she is being rude, he is too polite to comment.

'Over here,' he takes a few steps and gestures again. She follows, but at a distance.

'Look, you'll find these everywhere, if you look hard enough.'

They are standing beside the dodgems. Ben is pointing at

one of the cars. Its rubber bumper is split, falling away from the rusting chassis, and the sunshine yellow paint is freckled and bleeding rust.

'See the tag? The graffiti?'

There is a word scrawled on the side of the car in spray paint.

'Stalkers. Kids, well, adults now, but the children of the people who were displaced. They come back in and hang around, make their mark.'

He is close again, too close. She can smell the peppermint gum he is chewing.

'I think it's territorial. Like a dog pissing on its garden.' He rests a hand on her shoulder and laughs, as if he expects her to join in. She twists away.

'Why shouldn't they feel that?'

It is his turn to step back, hands raised in surrender.

'Hey, I didn't mean to offend you…'

'It's not funny, this was their home, this was…'

'It doesn't matter. I just thought you'd be interested.' Ben walks back to Jake and Abby, and Helen looks at the tag through the camera but doesn't take the shot. Instead, she caps the lens and walks away, out of the fairground, past the coaches and into the road again.

The road is pockmarked, weeds and moss splitting the tarmac. Saplings blur the stark edges of the high-rise buildings. If this happened at home would she break into the site, leave her mark on the land that used to be hers and should be Jack's? If the developers return with a compulsory purchase order would she creep under wire fences just to feel at home? Would she haunt her lost future like these stalkers?

The voices of the others are fading and she welcomes the solitude. She breathes deeply and lets the weight in her chest swell, lets it fuel her. She'll be home in a few days, ready to go to war again. Get her biopsy over with so she knows exactly what battles lie ahead.

She walks further from the group, almost reaches out to finger the hard buds of a sapling. She has to make sure Jack keeps the land, especially if it isn't just a cyst.

'Hey! Watch where you are standing!' Sergey shouts. She turns at his voice, but doesn't move, thinking at first he must be talking to someone else. But he marches over and grabs her, pulling her a few steps forwards and pointing at the ground.

'The moss holds the radiation, concentrates it. Don't step on it please.'

She rubs her arm and then pulls out her dosimeter, holding it closer to the soft, spongy moss that billows out of the cracked tarmac. The slow beeps stutter into a crescendo and then the alarm blares, the numbers flashing. She backs away, lets the machine fall quiet again and walks around, her heart rate high and her gait determined by the spread of the dark, wet growth. She is elongating her steps, cautious and agile, and it triggers a memory: the game she and her sister used to play on the walk to school. If you stepped on a crack in the pavement, on the earthy space between flagstones, you'd fall through and be lost forever.

***

'We just need a few days, love.' Dad is on the phone, apologising for calling her at work.

Jennifer sits in her office chair, staring at her desk while her father relays the conversation with the oncologist. 'We knew it might come back, and I think your mam was expecting it.'

A stapler, a jotter, a neat mug of pens bearing the Magnox logo.

Jennifer puts on her work voice. 'How's Mam taking it?'

'I think she knew already. But you know, you get your hopes up, don't you?'

'It doesn't mean she won't recover, it's just a set-back.'

But they both know she is just saying words, expected words, to dress the wound.

***

The group is assembling beside a building, and Sergey tells them it is a school, one of five in the town.

'We are no longer allowed in the buildings, because they are old and might fall. If the police find you in there you will be removed from the Zone and no more tour. If you can run,' and his eyes sparkle for a second, the shadow of a smile alighting briefly on his lips, 'then you will not get caught. I cannot stop you going in of course, but I have to warn you, it is dangerous.'

He turns his back slowly, deliberately, and Abby and the boys are off, scampering up crumbling steps into the school. The German couple follow more cautiously. Helen stands on the threshold, considering whether she might get more out of the solitude they have left behind. Curiosity wins out.

She steps into a wide hall. Broken glass tiles beneath her boots crunch like ice over frozen snow. The soft blue paint on the walls is curled and falling, and furniture is stacked, rotting, in the halls.

She can hear voices to her left and so moves up a concrete stairwell onto the first floor, stepping into the calm of a classroom with its glassless windows flung wide and a carpet of discarded textbooks, layer upon layer, soft as moss beneath her feet, but safer. She steps carefully, feeling the transgression through her boots. On the teacher's desk sits a glass jar with something inside, suspended in cloudy liquid. There is a bowl with a few damp grivna notes and some sweets, oozing sugar through the wrappers, left as if in offering. At the back of the room a set of shelves houses more jars.

Helen has always wondered how so many books ended up piled across the floor, what circumstances led to them being scattered, six or seven deep. The evacuation was messy, she knows this, but beyond the frames of the online pictures this room looks ransacked, war torn.

As voices approach in the stairwell she moves out, passes the couple who are holding hands as they pick their way through puddles and debris, and goes back down, moving around a desk positioned in the middle of the hallway with books and an inkwell ready for use, and into the main hall.

Hundreds of gas masks litter the floor, strewn, like the books upstairs, over most of the ground. A few hang from loose cables that sag like washing-lines from the ceiling, and others are arranged on the remaining desks next to carefully displayed textbooks and toys. On a chair in the corner a plastic doll sits on a broken stool, naked except for a gas mask strapped over its face and buckled behind a knot of nylon hair. Its arms are raised in supplication, or as if it wants to be lifted, held and cradled. She takes three photos, knowing they are just what the protests need. An emotional hook to make people think. This could be your child.

'The masks are not from the disaster, you know.'

Sergey has arrived beside her, silent as a cat in his heavy military boots on the dusty floor. Helen jumps, startled, then turns back to watch Jake arrange a broken TV set so that Ben can take a shot of the doll though the hole where the glass and tube once played stories.

'These are from before, for drills, for an attack from America or Europe. Gas attack, not nuclear. All children's sizes, see.' He points to the nearest mask, small and empty-eyed. 'For the children to practise. Not for an accident, there was never going to be an accident.'

Helen looks at him, trying to discern his tone.

'Good for the photographs though, yes?' He laughs and walks away. Helen kicks one of the masks, swirling dust into the room. She steps back, pulls her biker buff up to cover her mouth and nose.

'Hospital now,' Sergey shouts from the hallway. 'Good pictures there for you all.' Helen looks around at the scene, crouches low to take an identical shot to the one Ben has just taken of the doll through the shell of the TV set, then leaves the building and boards the bus with the others.

She flicks through the photos on the small screen in her hand. Dolls and gas masks and books. They had no idea, she thinks, that the threat was so close to home.

At least Jack knows, at least I've given him that.

***

Jennifer is in the toilets when the alarm goes off. Three long sounds, followed by a short blast. A nuclear incident. A drill, she's sure. She calculates the time since the last one and thinks they are due. She finishes washing her hands before reapplying powder and lipstick and leaving, checking there is no one in any of the stalls before pulling the door closed behind her.

The corridor is full of people walking towards the muster points. For a nuclear incident they do not assemble outside, they file through to the canteen and line up under lettered boards that hang from the ceiling. Stand under their surname initial and wait to be told it's over, or given further instruction.

She walks against the flow of people back to her office, grabs her phone and joins the back of the line. It's close to home time, and people are already complaining about being held up.

'It's fine for the shift workers,' someone declares, 'they've just got an extra break.'

Jennifer knows the value of the drills, regardless of time of day. It wouldn't be the first time a lockdown had led to a takeaway supper on the couch because neither she nor Ioan were home in time to cook.

They use the stairs, hands on rails, single file. Well-trained. It isn't worth wondering what the scenario is this time. The last one was a mock terrorist attack. Men dressed in black pretending to breach the perimeter. Somewhere a team will be making decisions, sweating. Life or death. Before going home to mull over any mistakes for discussion at the debrief tomorrow.

She looks out for Ioan as they near the canteen. They should be in the same queue. The people either side of her are on their phones.

'Can you get Dyl for me, Mam? No, not overtime, it's a drill. No, I'm sure it's a drill. Nothing to panic about.'

'I can't say, just ask him to let you go early, I don't want Social Services getting involved because there's no one there to pick them up again... No, I'm not being melodramatic!'

Jennifer pulls out her own phone but can't get a signal. Who would she call anyway? Ioan is in here with her, somewhere, and her parents are at the hospital.

She checks her watch. Gone five. After-school club closes at half past. Feels this new panic of responsibility spread through her system. She waves the phone in the air, pauses and gets jostled for doing so.

Nothing.

She steps out of a side door into the sunshine and takes a few steps towards the car park until the little logo tells her she's in range of the mast. Before she can scroll down to the number for the school an armoured police officer is at her side.

***

At the hospital Sergey leads them in, his previous warning about entering the buildings seemingly forgotten. He wants to show them the most radioactive item they are likely to see up close in their whole visit, a shred of clothing worn by a fireman in the days after the disaster. Helen has read all about the men brought in to put the flames out, who were among the few to die within days or weeks of the event. Before they stopped counting. The ones they couldn't deny had been directly affected.

Sergey points to a piece of dark cloth draped over the reception desk. Holds his dosimeter close. They crowd in to read the numbers as they jump, flash and scream in warning. He moves it a few inches away and the sound cools off. Someone reaches in to take a close-up and he bats their camera away, irritated. 'You will ruin your camera! The radiation can damage this audio-visual equipment.' He doesn't warn of the health risks, and perhaps there aren't any, unless the cloth is picked up, handled. Perhaps this is the most important thing, the pictures. Perhaps that's all that's left.

Helen moves away. She can feel something creeping up inside her. Disappointment? Disgust? Her own desire to photograph the site is waning. Feels ever more exploitative.

She steps into the stillness of the hospital, past offices and rows of buckled wooden benches and up onto the second floor, far enough away to get a few moments alone before the group spreads and takes hold of the building. She looks through a doorway to see rows of metal cots, weeping rust, all facing the same way, their bases angled so that the newborn babies would be tilted slightly, heads higher than their swaddled, chubby legs. In the corner more cots are stacked, tipped, a mess of sharp edges and damp mattresses.

She is about to lift her camera when she glimpses the room beyond. Moves into a tiled space, cracked and scaled with mould. There is a gurney, a large round light fitting above it with seven bulbs blown, sharp-edged. On the bed is an open medical journal. Helen goes over to it. The open textbook shows a cross-section of female genitalia; the womb, vagina and ovaries bright and red, raw in contrast to the greyscale drawing and black text on the page. Despite the passage of time the book is barely curled with damp, and only a few blooms of mould freckle the corner of the page.

She steps back, calculates the shortness of the bed. Rusting stirrups and an enamelled basin at one end. Handles either side of the headrest, to adjust the angle or to be gripped and strained against in the maelstrom agonies of childbirth.

It trips a switch in her mind.

Jack. Five weeks early, the liquid rupturing, hot and loose, between her legs. The frantic sounds of her dad on the phone to the hospital while she squatted on the bathroom floor. Rubbing his mottled blue skin with a towel snatched from the side of the bath. The heavy silence, then the bleat. His small, sticky newborn body lifted straight to her bare chest, the cord still looping down and inside her, pulsing. The immediate urge to consume him, even as the placenta was expelled.

She turns away from the bed, almost stumbles over a pile of bottles, small and medicinal in shape, that are stacked in the doorway between the delivery room and the corridor. Reaches out to steady herself and catches her hand on the rough wood of the doorway, blood rising to fill the open gash with fresh, hot fluid.

'Shit.' Her hand is trembling.

They'd sent two ambulances. One for her, and one for baby. Jack swaddled, a tiny oxygen mask obscuring his face. The doors slamming closed as they wheeled her out of the house in a folding chair, strapped in, too shocked to argue. As the breeze cut across the slate-chipped yard from the coast, she'd heard a rushing in her ears. Her own pulse or the throb of the power station? She still isn't sure. All she knows is that everything changed when he arrived. The anxieties that had grown with her bump were now released, coagulated like the blood on the bathroom floor. And the dream of the barn started again. She'd made a vow that morning, as the ambulance dipped and surged over the contours of Anglesey towards the hospital on the mainland: if he survived, she'd protect him from everything by teaching him to handle anything.

She can hear voices, echoes in the stairwell. There is a trail of scarlet drops in the dust by her feet. She squeezes the wound to flush out any toxins and reduce the chance of infection, or worse. Walks away from the noise and finds a room with just a sink and cracked toilet bowl. She manages to shrug her rucksack onto her front and pulls out the small first-aid kit stowed in the side pocket. The blood is already drying tight and sticky between her fingers.

She uses sterile wipes to clean her hand, and then tapes a large plaster over the wound. Bags the waste and seals it back into her rucksack. When she emerges from the room her fingerless gloves are covering the evidence. If Sergey were to find out about the injury there'd be forms to fill in, the day would be cut short.

Ben is in the corridor, filming the rest of the group walking towards him. Light filters in slats through the bare, black trees outside the windows. Abby is talking in her camera voice, describing the function of the hospital in the town, in the disaster.

'*There's nothing quite as creepy as an abandoned hospital, but here in Prypiat you get an extra element of fear. While this is now a popular setting for video games, the history of this building is far more unsettling in real life. It used to be a community hospital, providing routine vaccinations and treating minor injuries, but after April the twenty-sixth it became a site for treating acute radiation sickness…*'

Helen waits for the group to move into the maternity suite, invading the room with their camera. While they pause and debate a re-shoot, she slips downstairs, passes another group who are surging up towards her. Outside at last she feels the chill of fresh air ease her nausea. Finds Anton standing, smoking by the entrance.

'They'll kill you, you know.'

He startles at her voice, then frowns.

'The cigarettes. Cancer.'

He shrugs. 'I have more things to care about.'

She comes down the steps and stands beside him, glad of the distraction. 'You acting as lookout?'

'The guards aren't bothered, so long as there are dollars for them.' He flicks ash and sucks at the filter.

'Are you bothered?'

'This is most popular place after the fairground. You get good photos for your scrap book?' His eyes are almost black, his brows close beneath his fringe.

'A few.'

'Always on your own?'

'I'm not here to socialise.' She flexes her hands and feels the wound open. The blood soaks, warm and comforting, into the dressing.

'Your man, Ben, he was missing you last night.'

'He's not my man.'

Anton laughs, and licks his fingers before squeezing the end of the cigarette and tucking the butt back into the crumpled packet. He bounces on the balls of his feet.

The temperature drops as the pale sun is obscured by a heavy grey cloud.

'Why didn't you tell me, that night in the bar, that you were one of the tour guides?'

'You are nosy, Helen. You should take your pictures and go home, like the rest of them.'

'How do you know my name?'

Anton nods at the doorway, where the rest of her group are being herded out by Sergey.

Ben is grinning, slapping Sergey on the back. Later they will separate, the German couple, the film-makers, and Sergey. Any half-formed friendships will wither. She's glad she didn't waste the energy.

Walking towards the minibus she glances back once, but Anton is staring off into the undergrowth, rocking on his feet. She catches the bright orange glow of his fresh cigarette as he sucks in the smoke.

***

'You're one of our safety ambassadors.'

Jennifer sits in a high-backed chair and nods.

'Only last month you ran one of our safety briefings, on being fit for work.'

'Yes.'

'And today you decide to go outside during a nuclear event drill?'

'It was only a drill, Sir.'

'Don't call me "Sir", Jennifer. Don't get all official just because you're in trouble.'

The site manager, David Wellbeck, is a thin man. Thick hair, greyer on the left temple than the right. A pair of frameless spectacles perched on the narrow bridge of his hawkish nose. He's been to their house for dinner more than once.

He paces the room. In the uncomfortable silence, Jennifer fingers the pendant that sits at the point where her clavicles meet; a tiny gold bird.

'I couldn't get a signal on my phone. My nephew's after-school club was about to close and I needed to call them.'

'You needed to go into the cafeteria and await instruction.'

Jennifer is red-faced, almost reaches out for the sheaf of papers on the desk to fan herself. She has a headache building, pressure between her eyes.

David sits down opposite her and runs a bony hand through his hair, leaving it in comical tufts. His nickname among the senior staff is Fraggle. He's normally cheerful.

'Even if it was just a drill, you know damn well these drills have to be taken seriously. Deadly seriously. Your actions put your colleagues at risk, the guards at risk. And yourself.'

'I know. I do. I just... I was worried that Jack...'

'You said your colleagues were calling home? That's what made you realise you needed to?'

'Yes. Like I said, his mother is away at the moment,' *don't say where*, 'and he's had a tough week. I didn't want him to—'

'So you could have asked to borrow one of their phones, if you couldn't get a signal on yours?'

Jennifer stops trying to explain. Her stomach feels empty, her forehead throbbing.

'Jennifer. I don't want to do this, but the safety culture here is more important than you, or me, or anyone else.' He takes off the spectacles, rubs the bridge of his nose. 'I'm suspending you pending a full review of how and why this happened. Where our responsibilities lie, and yours. You know how important maintaining the safety culture here is. It's as much to send a message as is it to give you space to reflect.'

Jennifer feels the sting of tears. Frustration at Helen and embarrassment at her mistake compete in her chest. 'Yes, Sir.'

***

The tour is over. The ride back to Ivankiv is muted, stifling. Windows steam up and the smoke from the driver makes the air dense, gives Helen a headache. The German couple fall asleep within ten minutes of leaving the Zone; his head propped against the window, cushioned by his rolled coat, hers resting against his shoulder. Helen's eyes are drawn back again and again to the public intimacy of his slightly open mouth, the way her fingers are tucked between the buttons of his shirt.

She sits alone by the opposite window, right at the back of the bus. Jake, Abby and Ben are clustered near the front, chatting quietly to Sergey, who for the first time looks old, dark pockets beneath his eyes, bloodshot. Everyone is shattered. Setting each other off yawning.

Ben glances back a few times at Helen, but she manages to deflect, relieved he isn't being more insistent, isn't beside her. She needs the space to sink into her own thoughts, the tangle of information filling her head like brambles.

After the hospital they visited the river port: a semi-submerged boat skeletal in the mud and ice, broken vending machines and rusting tables and chairs in the café. Then back to the canteen to queue for food. Helen watched the crowds of workers and admin staff for a sign of Anton's group. She's not quite sure why she wanted to talk to him again. So far, he had shown her nothing but mild contempt, but she realised she felt disappointed when he wasn't there. She ate quickly, saving a pile of bread as instructed by Sergey for their after-dinner treat; a careful walk out onto the slippery planks of a rail bridge spanning the cooling ponds. She'd heard of the catfish that dwelt there described as 'giant' on forums and blogs, assumed it was exaggeration. Imagined 'giant' meant three-foot-long or so, not the metre-and-a-half leviathans that rose, wide mouthed and whiskered, to the surface in expectation of more food. She tossed two slices of dark bread down and watched them being swallowed as if they were goldfish pellets.

From there they spent hours walking through Chernobyl town. Formal-looking buildings, empty but carefully maintained, their exterior walls painted with vast murals depicting atomic explosions and fleeing storks. The fire station with a statue of remembrance for those on duty that night. A memorial garden with the name of each evacuated village carefully printed on signs, staked into the neat grass in two rows, a street made of grave markers. Small groups of feral dogs, possibly cross-bred with wolves and foxes, clustered around the back doors of the shop, loping after the groups of tourists in the hope of scraps. Descendants of the animals left behind in the exodus, the ones who didn't get shot anyway. A dun-coloured bitch had tracked them, tail at a low wag, until Sergey had thrown stones at it.

At every pause, photographs.

The hollowness of the space like a migraine building behind her eyes. The landscape transformed by absence, defined by it.

She too feels emptied. Considers whether it is the distance between home and here, or between the photographs and the real place that is leaving her deflated. Or perhaps the promise of sex, denied by her need for control.

She wipes her sleeve on the window and runs her tongue over fuzzy teeth, probes the ulcers and tries to focus on the discomfort. She can go home in the morning. Back to Jack, the sheep, her mother's hospital appointments and her own biopsy. The fat folder of official letters and public statements outlining plans for the new plant.

The landscape back home is already emptying; houses ripped down now the owners have left, hedgerows next on the list. Bats are being relocated, a new, purpose-built 'barn' under construction. Their old home will be made uninhabitable, slowly: noise, tiles removed one by one to let the rain and wind in, until eventually they can't bear it and settle in their new loft, nesting in timber beams that still bear the stamp of the construction company.

Helen has to protect the farm, ensure they don't do the same to her family. Already the plans show trees removed and earth banked, a contouring to prove neighbourly consideration by softening the noise, blocking the view to the new waste storage unit, the new reactors. The view right now is fields and sea, a forest where the new turbine hall will sprawl and vibrate.

The minibus pulls into a service station and people begin stretching. Helen needs to pee, spends far too long washing her hands and changing the dressing on her hand. Still gets back to her seat before the others. They stumble on, hands full of hot dogs and cardboard cups of coffee.

In Ivankiv the bus pauses only long enough for her to jump down and call thanks to Sergey. She doesn't wave them off, is already thinking of the journey home tomorrow, calculating how much sleep she'll need. She's been away too long already.

Part Two

β

CHAPTER SEVEN

Jennifer stands at the kitchen sink watching Jack through the window. It is dark outside, but the rear security light pools yellow tones into the centre of the lawn.

She is peeling potatoes for dinner, dunking them into warm water and using a sharp knife to pare off the muddied skins. Focussing on little things to stop her mind imploding: the texture of grit against her thumb, the way wine takes effect from the feet up. She hasn't told Ioan yet.

Jack is unaware he is being watched. The window is steamed at the edges inside, smeary from dried, salty rain outside, and his features are blurred.

He is stalking through the grass like an animal, hunting; slow, high steps, head tilted slightly as if listening, hands poised, ready to strike. His eyes, she is sure, are glittering with concentration.

Around him lie discarded toys. On the patio Ioan's old yellow Tonka truck rescued from the attic, rusted with age. Somewhere in the tall grass at the back of the lawn a football's pale curve, like an ostrich egg half-hidden in foliage. There are small plastic soldiers, fallen and forgotten, around the table and chairs. Jack hasn't shown interest in any of them, beyond an initial curiosity.

He is wrapped up in a new hat and coat, bright colours instead of the earth tones Helen chooses. Easier to see him.

The sky above him is indigo, the horizon bleeding behind the black spikes of bare trees.

As she rubs at the rough skin of the potato in the water Jennifer watches Jack bend, crouch and reach for something. He is utterly engaged in whatever he has in his hand, poking it gently, tilting his head to see it from every angle possible.

She dries her hands on the tea towel, leaving a faint stain in the centre of the cloth.

It's cold outside and she shivers in her short sleeves. The grass needs cutting, the leaves raking, the hedges trimming. She makes a mental list of chores, tasks to kill time.

The path is mossy, soft. The air tastes of salt and rain, and the cold catches in her lungs and makes her cough, a sharp, single bark to clear the sudden tightness in her chest.

Jack glances up and immediately lets his hand fall towards the ground, dropping whatever it was into the tall grass and sodden leaves.

'What have you got there, little man?'

'Dim byd. Dim ond ffrind.'

'Yn Saesneg, okay?'

He pauses, frowns. 'Nothing, just a friend.'

'What kind of friend?'

'A bug.'

'Why don't you show me?'

He looks at her and then glances away to the trees at the edge of the garden.

'Have you tried to make friends at school? Have you shown them your snails?'

A shrug.

'Do you like school?'

He shakes his head. 'I like it here better.'

'At our house?'

'Na, dim yn a tŷ. Yma!' He points at the ground, then swings his arm around to encompass the trees and shrubs and the bloody sunset.

***

She tries to call Jennifer, but there is no answer. Tosses the phone onto the bed and paces. She is tired. Not in the satisfied way she is after a day's work on the farm; the aches and discomfort she feels now are from sitting curled on the bus, from standing around while cameras clicked. Lumbar pain, her shoulders tight from the pull of the rucksack. She stretches and lies on the bed. Knows she needs sleep for her ride home in the morning, but her mind is buzzing.

She sits up and spends the next hour scrolling through the photos on her camera, trying to recapture the sense of the spaces they depict, and failing. Empty houses, riven space. Familiar. They look like her photos of home, of the landscape inside the boundaries sketched out by Vista; houses vacated, half demolished, gone. Nettles and grass taking over the lawns. Farms that have worked the land for generations churned up by bulldozers preparing the site for the new power station.

The hotel room is square, beige. Inert. She uploads the best images to her Cloud storage. The fish, wide mouthed and coppery. A building half consumed by barbed-wire brambles. A blank-eyed doll on a dusty floor. There are hardly any from the hospital – a badly focussed shot of an operating table, the group crowding around the reception desk, Ben's broad shoulders beneath his jacket. A string of pixels, HD. Nothing special.

She has to move, can't bear the stasis of the walls. Starts packing. It's over. She concentrates hard on the physical task of folding her clothes, laying out her equipment, writing a list of provisions to buy in the morning for the journey home. Tells herself over and over that she got what she came for: pictures for the protest, seeing the sarcophagus before it is covered forever. Jack will have learned valuable skills from her absence.

But there is something still bothering her, something intangible and needling, like she's forgotten to lock a gate or missed one of her mam's appointments. When everything is done she takes a painkiller and shrugs on her jacket, double-checking the door as she leaves. She needs to stretch out the muscles and clear her mind so she can sleep. She needs air.

She avoids the centre of town, the bar. Walks at a steady pace through the suburbs, glancing through windows where curtains are open. TV sets flickering, lamplight and dinner tables, a mother rocking a baby. The air is cold, smells almost like home. She begins to plan the days after her return, time with Jack on a full round of the fields to ensure the fences are secure, that the lambs are healthy. Time set aside to go through any new developments in the planning for the plant, any postal deadlines for formal protests.

She is calmer, her mind and muscles eased by the exercise, when she reaches the edge of the town, the end of the pavement. Feels the tarmac crumbling into the soft verge, the cushion of wet earth and sedge, and adjusts her gait to the give of the damp earth. She is near the junction where the memorial stones curve. She stops. Breathes deep. Looks around.

An owl drifts past, silent. The undergrowth exhales moths up into the halo of the streetlight. She steps tentatively across the road. Snails are traversing the wet tarmac. More than once she hears the crunch of shell beneath her feet.

She sees it as soon as she steps into the arch of the slabs. Amid the formality of the serial numbers etched into the stone there is a scar, white and ragged, still raw, where one set of digits used to be.

She crouches down and runs her finger along the wound. Fine white dust, sparkling in the moonlight. She touches her fingertip to her tongue and tastes the stone. It feels like the most authentic thing she's experienced so far.

She is nearly back at her hotel when she sees him, his tight stride crossing the road, hands deep in pockets. He steps into a dimly lit doorway in the block of water-stained flats, stabbing a key into the lock and disappearing. She pauses under a tree. Feels a pang of something, pity perhaps. The block is hopeless, depressing. The stairwells probably smell of piss, are banked with litter, she thinks. Mould clouding the bathroom ceilings. Babies crying through the walls.

She's only ever been in one apartment block, and can still remember the claustrophobia, the proximity of all those penned-in people just a plasterboard wall away from each other. Liverpool. Jack's father asking her to move in with him. Promising a new start, as if love was something that could be kindled by a change of scenery. Her deciding not to tell him after all. A high-rise was no place for a child, for her. The constant whine of traffic drowning out the birdsong. She'd atrophy.

She sees a light flick on behind a red blind two floors up and moves on. She needs to talk to Jack. More than anything, she needs to go home.

***

'He's asleep.' Jennifer rubs her eyes, reaches for the wine glass.

'Wake him up. I haven't spoken to him for two days.'

'I don't think it's a good idea, Hel, he's ratty when he doesn't sleep.'

'And you're the expert now? After less than a week?'

Jennifer closes her eyes, takes a deep breath. 'Hel, he's exhausted. He's not been sleeping well, and now finally he's settled and I just don't need the hassle. I'm tired too.'

'It's Friday night. Not like you have work in the morning.'

'Helen. He's fine. Just come home and let's get things back to normal.'

'I don't see why—'

'Why are you so angry? So oppositional?'

'Oppositional? I just want to speak to my child—'

'Listen, I've had a difficult week. Can we talk in the morning?'

The line clicks. Jennifer shakes her head and swallows the last of the wine in one gulp.

When Ioan comes into the room, a large bag of crisps and a beer in one hand, the wine bottle in the other, she doesn't refuse a second glass. When he tries to rub her feet, she pulls away.

'What's up?'

'Nothing, I'm fine.'

There is a bump from upstairs, the sound of a door opening. 'I'll go,' he says. Jennifer sips wine, her knuckles white around the stem of her glass.

CHAPTER EIGHT

Sunshine penetrates the nylon curtains, but Helen is oblivious, attention fixed on her phone, notebooks spread across the bed.

The worst of the protests are in Kyiv, but things have progressed since she planned her trip. She scrolls over a map trying to decipher the symbols that show where satellite towns have taken up the fight. Glances up at the TV set mounted on the hotel room wall. Rolling footage of Independence Square, crowds pushing against each other, testing resistance, collapsing and reforming like lava. Roadblocks and uniforms holding guns cut the screen in half. She considers the roads between here and home, her return journey. Two days in the Zone and she is out of the loop, has no idea if it will blow over in a few days to leave her free to go home, or if missiles will start flying overhead, trapping her. For a second she wonders how the others from the tour are getting on, if they are somewhere in the capital right now. But there is no point wasting energy worrying about strangers. Her eyes flick between her phone and the TV. Talk online is of state corruption, calls for the president to resign. It seems the southeast oblasts are where the major risk lies, where the worst of the clashes are played out.

Ivankiv is north of Kyiv, sits on the division between districts controlled by the people and those controlled by the pro-Russian Party of Regions. She walks to the window, pulls aside the nylon drapes. Outside the street is quiet. Birds are singing. Everything seems fine.

***

Jennifer is busy in the kitchen, emptying cupboards, scrubbing shelves and making a pile of things to donate to charity, to throw away. Anything to keep her mind busy. Jack is upstairs, quiet.

She is checking the expiry date on a packet of soup when she hears the back door slam and Ioan's heavy boots in the hall. He hollers.

'I need you, can you get your wellies on quick?'

She kicks off her slippers and meets him by the back door. He's breathless, muddied. 'What is it?' she asks, forcing her feet into cold rubber and grabbing a coat.

'One of the ewes is struggling. Helen would normally, you know… But you'll have to do.'

'Have to do what?' But she already knows. She flexes her fingers in a desperate attempt to invoke muscle memory.

They are over the first stile before Ioan stops. 'Jack! Shit, hang on.' He runs back to the house.

She is almost at the barn when Ioan catches her up, Jack balanced on his shoulders, cheeks alight with a flush of excitement and cold wind. Ioan swings him down and Jack lands on his feet and sets off running ahead, slipping into the barn before they are through the gate.

The sheep startle when they go in, jostling in their pens and bleating. The few lambs already born cry out in high, reedy voices. The ewes bellow back in deep, guttural tones. Jack has his hand through the wooden slats, scrunching his fingers into their matted, muddy fleeces. Whispering to them.

The labouring ewe is near the back. Ioan steps over the barrier and helps Jennifer climb into the pen. It tries to stand, lets out a moan. Ioan crouches by the ewe's head and wraps an arm around its neck to hold it still.

'Come on.'

Jennifer kneels carefully in the straw and shit by the back end of the animal, pulls off her coat and throws it over the barrier, then rolls up her sleeve. She doesn't want to touch it. The sweet stench of the animal's stomach and rank odour of its soiled fleece catch in her throat. The wool around its tail is cold and wet, but beneath it the heat is raw, and as Jennifer slips her hand inside she shudders involuntarily, a tremor mirrored in the trembling flank of the ewe. She tries to conjure up her father's voice as she manoeuvres her fingers around the slick knobbles of heel and tendon, folded ear and the taut, hot uterus wall.

'There are two at least, both twisted and blocking the way.'

'I can feel three feet, hang on.' She closes her eyes and tries to visualise what she is touching. Opens them again quickly.

The ewe groans and she feels muscles contract around her wrist as it tries to push her and the lambs out. She is being too gentle. She needs to push back and try to twist one of the lambs into position. Ioan holds the ewe's head tighter as she manipulates the slippery shapes into order and hooks the soft hooves between her index and middle finger and middle and ring finger before pulling, gently at first and then harder.

As the lamb breeches and then slithers out, a gush of fluid soaks though her jeans, warm and violent.

She flops the baby onto the straw and pokes her little finger into its mouth to break the hood of the birth sac. Then reaches back inside to position the twin and ease it out. The ewe is panting. Distressed. Once both are out Ioan lets her go, but she sags against a hay bale and watches as if drugged as Ioan and Jennifer lift the lambs by their back legs and swing them to clear the airways. They rub them hard with straw.

It is clear only one is alive. Jennifer rubs harder and harder and whispers to the first born, but it is limp and unresponsive. As Ioan helps the second lamb latch on to feed, she lets the first's small head drop onto the straw. Its eyes are marbled white, blind, and its front legs curved, the tendons too short to allow full extension.

'No wonder she was in a state,' says Ioan, his voice thick. He pushes it to the ewe to lick, to smell and discard. They sit side by side watching her.

Jack crouches down by the stillborn lamb.

'The baby has gone to heaven, little man.'

He looks at them, each in turn, as they speak. Assessing.

'It would've been too sick to play. It's better this way, buddy.'

'Isn't the other one sweet. Look at it feeding!'

'Are we going to eat it?' His tone is flat, practical.

'No. No, of course not.'

'Why not?'

'Because we're not, okay? We'll bury it. Say goodbye properly.'

Jack stands up and tilts his head. 'What a waste.' He wanders off towards the other end of the barn, looking in on each of the pens as he goes.

'God, where does he get this stuff from?' Jennifer rubs her forehead with her sleeve. She can't take her eyes off the white globes of the dead lamb's eyeballs.

'He's just a kid. He hasn't worked it out yet.'

'It's not that. It's Helen. He sounded just like her then.'

Ioan rubs his chin and shrugs.

'What are you going to do with it?' Jennifer asks.

'We can't bury it. Your dad's got a place for them, until they can be collected. I'll get a sack.'

He moves around the front of the barn, finds an almost empty feed sack and pours the pellets into a trough before coming back to roll the tiny body into the plastic.

Jennifer watches. 'I've been suspended.'

'What?'

'From work. A safety breach.'

'You work in an office.' Ioan is holding the sack, cradling it.

'During the drill the other day. Stupid mistake.'

'Shit, Jen. Why didn't you tell me?' He settles the bag on a bale and sits beside her, wraps his arms around her. She wants to hug him back, but her hands are caked in drying blood.

'Because I was embarrassed. Am embarrassed.'

'I'm sure it'll be okay.' Ioan squeezes her. 'Go on back to the house with Jack, I'll deal with this. Then we can have a panad and you can tell me all about it.'

Jennifer walks home with the fluid on her jeans drying hard in the breeze, Jack silent and sullen beside her. The wind carries the hum of the power plant to them as she stumbles over tree roots and rocks to get back to the warmth and order of the house. The sun has slipped behind a bank of indigo cloud and the wind off the sea is vicious. On the edge of a low rise a few fields away there is a bright yellow JCB where one of her neighbours once lived, hi-vis jackets milling around. The house has gone, foundations dug out. An open wound on the hillside.

She watches Jack, sure-footed on the path. His response to the stillbirth, practical and dismissive, leaves her chilled. Her memories of spring from childhood were softer, warmer, filled with the triumph of bouncing, bleating lambs. How many of them were born like that, lost?

***

The UK foreign travel advice website has a map. Oblasts in green and red, warnings not to visit without contacting the foreign office, or not to visit at all, depending on destination. Ivankiv is on the line where the colours meet, but there is red to the west. She'll need to detour, down, adding hours to her journey. She reconsiders the food supplies, adds extra things to the list. Her phone and camera are on charge. She leaves them there while she walks into town.

The snow has almost vanished, and sunlight illuminates the brightly painted fences and tiled doorways. Helen walks past the market, busy enough, and towards the shop. There is no sign of civil unrest.

Under the strip lights of the aisles she counts out water bottles, fills a basket with sealed packets of high-energy food. Finds a hazelnut chocolate bar with cartoon characters on the wrapper and in a moment of weakness adds it to the basket to give to Jack when she gets home. Wonders if a week at Jennifer's will have taken the novelty of chocolate away.

As she walks back towards the hotel her concerns about the trip home ease. There are people shopping, the sound of children in the local school playground. A man repairing his car at the side of the road.

When she passes the bar she slows, glances in and sees it almost empty, just a few men sitting around a table and a figure, hands thrust deep in pockets, watching the TV. She stops. Goes in.

'Still here?' Black leather jacket zipped, dark hair grazing his eyelids. He turns to the barman, buys two bottles of beer and places one on the bar in front of Helen, indicating she should join him. Takes out his cigarettes and lays the pack on the counter.

'What's this for?' She gestures to the drink.

'A thank you, for worrying about my health.' He points at the cigarettes.

'I don't drink. Sorry.'

He holds her gaze for a moment, perhaps remembering the beer she bought just a few nights ago, here. Then shrugs. Reaches and sips from her bottle. He's nervous, she can tell. Either because he fancies her, or something else. She hasn't worked it out yet.

'So, you've quit?' She rests her rucksack on a barstool.

He laughs and slips one out of the pack, lights up. 'No point. I told you, I have more things to care about.'

'Like what?'

He shrugs again, and drinks.

'I thought you'd be giving another tour.'

'They are cancelled.'

'You warned me, on my first night here, to be careful. On

142

the tour, every time we crossed paths, you watched me, as if you were waiting for something to happen. What are you waiting for?'

Anton's hand is still on the bottle. He holds her gaze and then looks away. Picking at the label, peeling the corner and rolling the paper between his finger and thumb.

'For you to go home.'

'Why?'

'This is not a place for you. Do you see any other tourists here?'

Helen looks around. The bar is almost empty, just the three men at a corner table playing durak, drunk. As she looks, a single playing card drifts to the floor and lands a good three feet away from the table. The men start arguing over who should pick it up.

'What do you think is going to happen? Are they dangerous?'

'Depends on what you do.' His eyes are back on hers, almost black beneath his fringe.

'What I do?'

'You enjoyed the tour?' he says, lighting another cigarette.

'*Enjoyed* isn't the right word.'

He shrugs. 'Most people find it interesting, exciting.'

They stand, awkwardly. He sips beer, glances back at the TV. Footage of the protests. Stubs his cigarette out, crushing the tip into a coaster until it smoulders and dies.

'You are not safe here, Helen. The safest place you have been so far is Chornobyl. Please, go home.'

He turns and strides out. She waits a few moments before following.

It has clouded over, started raining; a thin drizzle that soaks her hat and beads her eyelashes, making her blink. She sees him across the road, his hands thrust deep into his jeans' pockets, head low. He is walking fast. She shoulders the heavy rucksack and calls out to him.

'Wait!'

He pauses while she catches up. 'I saw online the protests are spreading. But here—'

'Here is like everywhere. You still plan to ride? Be careful. Roads blocks are changing all the time.'

'Can you get me through?'

'You want my help?' Almost a smile.

'It doesn't matter, I just thought—'

'Later. I have to be somewhere now.' She watches him walk away, pulling another cigarette from the pack as he goes. So long as she can get home, she doesn't care who helps.

Back in the hotel she unpacks her bags and spreads the provisions across the blankets. Assesses if she'll have enough food and water. She takes a last shower before the long ride home inside the skin of the leathers. As she is towelling her hair her phone trills. A Skype call. A swipe of her finger and Jack is there, blurry and swirling. His voice is fractured. The signal faint.

'Are y.. c...ing .ome n...'

'What? Say again?'

'..en ar. y... ..ming ba..?'

'I can't hear you. Let me ring you back.' She cancels the call and tries again, but there is no answer. She listens to the birdsong outside. Looks around at the mess on the bed. Multitool, survival bag, water sanitising tablets. If there are any issues on the way home, she can drop off grid for a while. Wait until it's safe to continue.

The phone trills again. A clear signal.

'Hi Jack.'

Jennifer's face. 'Are you on your way back?'

'I haven't left yet.'

'How long will it take to get home?'

'I don't know. I'm leaving soon, but I might be few days yet. Can you arrange for after-school club on Monday?'

'Why a few days? We need you back.'

Helen can hear the tension in her voice. 'What's happened?'

Whispers. Ioan somewhere out of sight. *Not in front of Jack.*

'I'll fill you in when you get home. Jack wants to talk.'

'Mam?'

'Hi Jack, are you okay?'

'Yeah. A lamb died. Another one.'

'It happens.'

'Its eyes were all white.'

Jennifer's voice in the background. *We've given it a nice funeral though Jack, it'll be happy in heaven.*

Helen laughs when he rolls his eyes. 'Listen, I might be a few days longer than we planned. You keep helping Uncle Ioan with the sheep for me, okay?'

Even with the poor connection, Jack's response is vivid. He doesn't protest, but the light in his eyes changes, the angle of his lips. He blinks faster.

'Ti'n iawn, Mam?'

'I'm fine. You don't worry about me.'

'Do I need to…' his hand goes to his T-shirt, to the key.

'No. No, everything is fine. Plan A, iawn? Sit tight. Love you.'

'Ditto.'

He shrinks back, fades out of shot. Jennifer moves forwards.

'Why the delay?'

'Read the news.'

After the call Helen walks to the window, stares out at the tarmac and melting snow. Realises: it is an act of violence to leave your child. The thought rises unbidden but fully formed. More than a cutting of the cord, this was an unnatural injury. She stretches and paces in the small room, feeling the pain of it in her shoulders and neck.

She considers the damage. Hell, the ferocity with which Jack clung to her after school every day for the first month. Still holds her hand all the way to the car now, small fingers gripping like claws. As if he needs to reconnect, recharge. Wonders what he's clinging to now.

But survival depends on such acts of violence, she thinks, as she moves from window to bed, from bed to en suite. Back to the window. A crow bounces on the grass verge. Her bike is chained, in sight beneath the window. She picks at the tape securing her bandage, flexes her hand to feel the tightness of the healing skin. Scar tissue is stronger than regular skin, and a healed fracture denser than un-splintered bone. Any damage to Jack is just a flesh wound, she reasons. Not fatal. It will make him stronger, in the long run. Maybe this is the real test for them all.

The TV set is silent, the images looped. She wants to go, to feel the miles between her and home disappear beneath the wheels of the bike, but is caught by indecision. If she heads off on the wrong road, her lack of local knowledge impeding the right decisions, she could be endangering herself. Better to wait, perhaps, and get home safe.

She watches the light fade through the curtain, chewing her lip. Back home decisions are easily made, the parameters known. If a storm is coming, you bring the sheep in. If a ewe is injured, you cut your losses and cull. If your child needs to crawl beneath your blankets at night to sleep, you open your arms. Even helping Mam has been a series of instinctive and logical actions. Accepting she is dying has helped her to nurse her through chemo, take up the slack on the farm so her dad can rest. Over the last few years she's taught herself to be ready for disaster, to practise overriding emotional triggers with rational thought. A calm practicality has seen her through the worse of it so far, and she has contingencies for if things deteriorate.

But here, the parameters keep shifting.

She runs through multiple scenarios in her head, drinking instant coffee and staring out of the window.

At dusk she wraps up and walks to the bar.

The atmosphere is different. She can tell from the moment she steps inside. Anton is there, among a dozen or more other men. Not sitting in groups playing cards or smoking, but crowded around the bar, around the TV set. She moves in behind them, just in time to see footage of live shots fired into the crowd.

The reaction is immediate: voices raised, a hand reaching out to snatch the remote, turn the volume up. Elbows are employed as the bodies press tighter and someone stumbles back. On the screen, soldiers in helmets and gas masks walk towards the camera under an indigo sky. The city square has become a war zone.

Anton turns, sees her and shakes his head in warning. He is trying to calm them, hands raised, repeating a phrase over and over. Two of the men bang their fists on the bar and start shouting, and one shoves Anton hard in the chest. She steps back, presses against the wall. He slips from sight, somewhere in the middle of the scrum.

She thinks of her question: *Are they dangerous?* and Anton's reply.

The primal heat of the fight fills the space, the scent of the men, sweat and vodka breath. She inches away, searching the tangle of limbs for a glimpse of Anton, for a sign he isn't consumed. On the TV Independence Square heaves with swinging batons and spitting mouths.

She is nearly by the door when more men come into the bar, blocking the entrance.

The newcomers are shouting, saliva flecking the corners of their mouths. They push past her and merge into the fray without a pause, haul Anton out just as the violence on screen ramps up. It's a live broadcast and somewhere not too far away a man is being beaten unconscious with a metal baton. She can hear sirens and isn't sure at first if it is from the TV or the street, but there is a dissipation in response to the wail.

The scrum unravels, fingers reaching to stem the blood that weeps from lips and noses. Someone spits, red and viscous, and another man laughs. Anton is walking towards her, a hand over one eye. She opens the door and glances back to check no one is following, then guides him away from the doorway, shielding him.

On the pavement she searches his face and posture for signs of damage. 'How bad are you hurt?'

He shrugs. Wipes a smear of blood from his nose across his wrist.

A noise further up the street makes them both turn. Shouting. She follows him away from the bar, down the road a little way and under a shuttered shop awning.

'Why did they attack you?'

More ruckus, the sound of a gun or firework cracking through the clear night. Anton retreats deeper into the doorway, eyes roving.

She grabs his wrist and pulls him down the street, across the tarmac and through a garden gate, drawing him under the treeline. The evening smells of November, despite the fact that spring is close; smoke and mist, the rotten mulch of leaves in rain. The faint scent of cordite. The ground is soft beneath her boots. He wipes another trickle of blood from his nostril, sniffs.

She pulls a tissue from her pocket and he presses it to his face. Through the trees they watch as a crowd passes, ten or fifteen men surging forwards, shouting. Someone is waving a flag.

'Do you know them? Are you safe?'

'No one is safe right now.' He looks nervous.

'Come on.' She leads him through the garden, keeping to the back hedge, away from the risk of a security light. At the edge she swings a leg over the low fence and encourages him to follow, loses her bearings. Anton takes over directing them. They traverse the town through gardens and alleyways, alert to lights in back windows, to the sound of the crowd. If things are this bad she needs him to help her, to navigate her through the protest zones, to translate.

They are close to the hotel when the noise changes, becomes chanting. Then gunshots that ring out in the darkness, the sound ricocheting off the buildings and merging with the cheers and shouts. Again, the sound of a siren. She fumbles in her pocket for the hotel key. Anton is breathing hard beside her, heavy and wet. She sees them surge around the corner as the lobby door yields to her shoulder; a group of men who seem to be one living organism, moving in a wave, individuals breaking off and returning, reforming.

The way they are chanting excites her; the unison, the power of many voices saying the same thing over and over. It's primitive. Terrifying. Her own body is thrumming with adrenalin.

In the hotel lobby the desk is vacant. She can hear voices in the corridors, doors slamming. If she doesn't ask now she will miss her chance.

'You said you'd help me.'

He isn't listening. She can see his eye swelling.

'I need to get out. You said you'd help.'

He frowns at her, and she wonders if he is concussed. He's no good to her injured. He moves further back, away from the glass front of the lobby, and Helen realises that here, in the harsh strip lights, they are exposed. If the men are looking for him, she has led him to a shop window and put him on display. She takes his arm and guides him down the corridor towards her room, listens to his breathing slow and relax as she unlocks the door. Inside, she leaves the main light off, pulls the cord for the little bulb over the bathroom mirror. Double-checks the door is locked.

They stand awkwardly in the artificial gloam.

Now the danger is behind brick walls, the situation feels awkward. He is glancing around, taking in the range of survivalist tools on the bed, the dosimeter charging on the bedside table. Now it is she who feels exposed. She picks up the first-aid kit and summons him to the bathroom. His eye is swelling, grazed. She tears open a sterile wipe and begins dabbing the wound.

'I need to get out, west. To Poland. I can pay you.'

'You've seen the news.' He flinches and pulls back.

'Which is why I need to leave.'

'I told you before, go home. You wait. And now...'

She drops the bloodied wipe into the toilet bowl. 'I was waiting for you. You said you'd help.'

'You should not have come here. The tour, maybe another time. But not to this place.' His eyes won't settle. He glances around: through the door to the bedroom, at her wash kit on the side of the sink, at her reflection in the mirror. Rocks on the balls of his feet, as if about to run. The en suite smells of antiseptic and shampoo. 'I will get you out. Before it becomes impossible.'

'What was the fight about? Why did they attack you?'

'Territory. Why else?'

His eyes seem to refocus. He coughs, and spits into the toilet, reaching to flush it afterwards. 'I'll be back in one hour. Be ready.' The tour guide, giving out instructions, corralling.

When he's gone she sits down with her head in her hands, wondering if he will be a liability or an asset.

***

Jennifer is still awake. The house creaks, settling into its night-time temperature; the radiators ticking, cooling. She and Ioan have spent hours online, reading about the protests, trying Helen's phone and getting voicemail. Ioan can't find the envelope Helen left, and without her sister's itinerary she has no idea how the unrest might affect her return.

Her mind flits between images of masked men throwing burning bottles into a crowd, the lamb's white eyeball, and the droop of disappointment around David Wellbeck's mouth. There hasn't been an email yet, informing her of a disciplinary hearing. There won't be one until after the weekend now. It could be weeks away. Ioan's reassurance that it was all just a show of procedure, due diligence, and she would be back in her office by the end of the next week, has only served to convince her she will be fired. Or forced to resign. A statement gesture to the rest of the team. There are consequences – life-changing, earth-shattering consequences – when you breach the safety protocols.

There are noises from down the hall. Jack going to the toilet, maybe. She pushes the duvet off, too hot, and stares at the line of light beneath the bedroom door. Left on to reassure Jack. She hears his footsteps pad across the hall, down the stairs. He must be using the downstairs toilet, perhaps as a courtesy, so as not to wake them. Her skin puckers to goose bumps and she pulls the duvet back over her legs. Shifts again, pummelling the pillow. Strains to hear the downstairs toilet flush. There are footsteps on the stairs, the sound of a door clicking shut. A scrape. A soft bump.

She gets up, tiptoes to his room and listens. He is muttering to himself. When she opens the door the light is on and he is kneeling on the floor, stuffing clothes into his rucksack.

'What are you doing, little man?'

'Getting ready.'

'What for? It's the middle of the night.'

'I know. I'm getting ready.'

For a moment Jennifer thinks he must be sleep walking, but he looks up at her, eyes fully focussed. 'What do you want?'

'What are you getting ready for?'

'To go.'

She crouches down, 'But Mammy isn't coming back yet. You're staying here a while longer.'

'Na, peidio â mynd adref.' He folds the top of the rucksack and pulls the strap tight. 'Just ready, in case.'

'In case of what?'

'In case I need to go.' He sighs, drops the bag behind the door and climbs back into bed. 'Can you turn that light off?' He points to the landing. 'It gets in my eyes and stops me sleeping.' He turns to face the wall.

***

Helen watches from the window as two boys, teenagers, examine the bike in the spotlight of the security light. They are just a few metres away. She stands motionless behind the misty swath of nylon curtain. The room light is off. They can't see her. They are wearing military-style jackets and bright trainers, and one sports the stain of a future moustache beneath his pimpled nose. Their hair is damp, or greasy, and they hop from foot to foot as they chat.

She has been waiting for Anton for hours; her bags packed, leathers on ready, bunched around her waist. She has the essentials in a belt bag clipped around her stomach: phone, passport, money for bribes, a small but powerful flashlight.

The boys might be younger than her, but they are at least as big, if not bigger. They crouch and take in the arch of the wheels, tug at the heavy lock, lean, heads together, to finger the keyhole. If they try to hotwire it, she will have to act, but for now she watches, calculating her next move.

The chest of drawers she shoved against the door shortly after Anton left is still there, but the hotel is silent. Her helmet is ready, on the end of the bed.

One of the boys swings his leg over the bike and wriggles his skinny arse in the saddle, settling onto the contours her own backside has formed since she bought it. Helen bites her lip. She feels the violation in her gut and groin, clenches her fists and watches as he runs his fingers over the dials, grips and twists the rubber handles and squeezes the fuel tank between his scrawny thighs. She knows the value of rational thoughts over emotion, though. It will be over soon.

The other boy, the one with the smear of late puberty across his upper lip, spits. They laugh and swap places, the first holding the bike steady while the other climbs on, rocks back and forwards in mimicry of motion, grinning.

Helen counts silently in her head, waiting for it to end. She can taste bile.

She is convinced, as they swagger away, glancing back and whispering, that they are planning to steal it. They are going to return with bolt cutters, wire to pick the lock. A side effect of civil unrest is a rise in crime – rape, burglary, vandalism. She knows this from news reports and survivalist guidebooks. It's one of the immediate dangers people don't usually think of, their minds on the big story. It can be the downfall of even a careful prepper. They could be back soon. With tools.

She checks her phone again for news. Dozens of police officers captured by protesters in Kyiv, transport systems halted, the UK Embassy in lockdown. The death toll rising, with protesters bussed into the capital to strengthen the rebellion. She has heard nothing in the streets below for hours, no sign that the actions of a few men in a bar have changed the world, or the town, at all. But that doesn't mean they haven't.

She needs to leave. If her bike is stolen, she is trapped. She can't wait any longer for a half-promise to materialise. She moves efficiently, has a last pee in case she hasn't the chance later, pulls the phone and charger from the socket, severing the power. Turns it off, to save the battery.

When she's ready she stands still in the middle of the room, rotates once, twice, to check she has everything. Pulls her leathers up over her shoulders and tucks the helmet under her arm. Her panniers are already packed, locked. She tucks the phone into her belt bag and zips herself into the protective cocoon of her leathers. Now she is moving she feels better, anxiety turning into action instead of festering.

In the car park she pauses in the shadow of the building, listens. Somewhere a dog is barking. A car revs in the distance. The air is sharp in her nostrils. She moves into the exposure of the security light and checks over the bike for signs of damage, notices her hand trembling slightly. Fumbles the lock and stops, telling herself to slow down. When she has stashed the chain she gently settles into the seat, checks the brakes, and walks the bike slowly to the middle of the car park before putting her helmet on. She has just revved the engine and begun to ease forwards, her mind already on which roads to take out of town, when she sees them.

It's their cocky stride that gives them away. They have changed into darker clothes, but their gait is the same. Walking towards her, from the direction she planned to take out of town. They begin to jog.

The bike is more vulnerable now; unchained, engine running. If they reach her and pull her off it is lost. She turns the other way, speeds up quickly. Grateful for the late hour, for the clear roads through town. She is breaking the law, has never driven this fast before in a residential area, but these circumstances are exceptional. She passes the bar, the market, and sweeps past the monument and away, easing into the curve of the road and away from teenagers with crowbars.

The road ahead looks clear.

There are no flashing lights behind her that might signal the police, or hazard lights ahead warning of roadblocks.

She twists into the highest gear and eases back a little in the seat, repossessing her machine. It feels good to be moving, to feel the power between her knees again. She thinks for a moment of Anton, of him coming to the hotel to find her gone. Hopes it doesn't put him in danger. Then pushes the thought out of her mind. She needs to concentrate on getting home, not worry about someone she'll never see again. As soon as she's put enough distance between herself and the town, she can stop, set the satnav, and begin the most dangerous part of the journey. Perhaps if she can make it through the occupied oblasts on back roads, the path will be clear.

It isn't until the streetlights end and the open countryside envelopes the road, that she notices the headlights behind her in her mirrors. When she does, it takes a moment for her to register the significance. She speeds up slightly, but as her distance from town increases the lights get stronger, filling the mirrors.

She accelerates again and watches the car respond. When it blasts its horn and comes up close behind, she almost fishtails. She moves in, close to the verge, in the hope the car just wants to overtake and race away, but it too slows. She speeds up again and it matches her pace. She turns, not quite last minute, down a side road. The car follows, overtakes, then brakes hard, its hazard lights on. There is movement inside the vehicle.

She doesn't stop to find out the intentions of the driver.

Swerving past, she guns the engine and pushes the bike, feeling the engine scream as she hits full throttle before changing gear, going faster than she's comfortable with. She makes random decisions at forks in the road, confident the satnav will get her back on track once she's shaken off the threat.

The roads deteriorate.

She is running on narrow farm lanes, pitted with potholes. Is forced to slow. Checks her mirrors repeatedly, her heart pounding harder every time she catches sight of the lights. The trees close in around the road. Arable farmland and fields of dozing cows, startled by the roar of her bike, are replaced with tangles of brambles like barbed wire, the occasional barn sinking back into the undergrowth. She thinks she's lost them. The condition of the tarmac is lousy, degraded. The verges encroaching, saplings where gravel should be. Each bump in the road is a jolt to the spine.

She is about to pull over when the headlights appear in the distance. The same ones, she is sure. She cuts her own lights in a bid to become invisible and navigates instead by the slats of moonlight that filter through the trees overhead. Is forced to slow further now visibility is diminished. She begins looking for a place to turn off, to kill the engine and hunker down in the hope the car passes. But the forest is too dense here and she would risk damaging the bike, plunging into a hidden ditch. The lights get closer.

She calculates the risk: there is no innocent outcome to her being caught. They are not some concerned citizen planning to tell her she has a light out and then leave. She assesses the state of the road and concludes it will slow them down too. She has more power in her bike, less weight, and can manoeuvre around the defects better. A tiny part of her is enjoying it – the thrill of using the bike for more than just pleasure, of putting her skills to the test. She's not ready to give up yet.

She accelerates. Her mind clearing, focussing only on the contours of the road. The gap between the headlights and the bike is just beginning to widen when there is a flurry of movement in the trees and shrubs to her right and the branches explode into a roiling surge of fur and hooves, muscle and movement. She sees eyes glinting in the moonlight as she brakes hard and swerves, the air around the heaving mass ballooning with hot breath distilled into cloud.

Impact.

The bike bucks sideways, unseats her. She lets it spin away, so it doesn't crush and pin her. Hits the ground hard and rolls, numb to the sharp stones and rocks that tear holes in her leathers, then slides to a stop. Hears a muffled crunch as the bike reaches the trees. She lies still, her body in a temporary state of shock. Numb. Through the mud-slicked visor, she sees something round, pink and wet press against the perspex, then a burst of mucus and steam obliterates her view.

There is a drumbeat, louder and louder, less sound than pressure.

Lights flicker in the trees, blurry behind the visor. She reaches up to loosen the chinstrap, pushes the helmet off even though it feels like her head will go with it. Tries to roll over so she can crawl away and hide and is hit by a surge of nausea and dizziness.

The beam of headlights spearing the night.

She is vomiting, strings of bile trailing like spider silk in the breeze.

Heavy breathing and a low whine of pain that could be inside her head, or coming from a short distance away.

Hands lifting her, and the liquid sensation of her knees giving way. She's laughing.

'It's okay, I got you.'

Blood.

'Dad?'

'No.'

A rhythmic hum inside her head that can only mean Wylfa is close.

Bracing herself against the back of a car seat with a hand shot through with pain, every bump like a fresh blow to the brain.

Water. She guzzles. 'Diolch, Mam.' Someone kisses her but doesn't smell right.

She laughs again though she isn't sure what she's laughing at.

Shivering, half naked, someone is holding her hair as she vomits, the water still cold as it pours out of her, each retch splitting her skull open further. She is a cantaloupe under an axe, all the juices running out.

Colours burn her eyes to black.

CHAPTER NINE

'Not at the breakfast table, little man.'

Jack slides off his chair, the snail still gliding across his palm. He walks to the windowsill where the jar is settled, the cabbage leaves wilting. Jennifer almost calls him back to finish his toast but decides to leave him. She checks the news on her phone again, but finds only information on Kyiv, on a compromise deal signed with opposition leaders by the president.

There have been no messages or updates from Helen.

When Ioan stumbles into the kitchen, rubbing the sleep from his eyes, she shakes her head gently to let him know. He makes coffee, sits beside her and takes her hand.

'What's the plan for today?'

'Try and find out what's going on.'

'How?'

'I'm going to Mam and Dad's, see if they've heard anything.'

Jack is beside her, eyes alert under a frown. 'Heard about what?' The snail is halfway up his forearm, leaving glistening loops around his wrist.

'Nothing to worry about, little man, just grown-up stuff. Do you want to go and visit Nainy and Taidy this morning?'

'Is Nainy still alive?'

'Yes, of course! What a funny thing to say. Did you think she'd died?'

'I don't know. She will. Soon, probably.' His eyes are on the snail, watching its lower tentacles feel out the skin on his arm.

'Why do you think that?'

'Because Mam said she will. And her face is going all mouldy.'

'Jack! That's a horrible thing to say!'

'But it's true. Her face is all wrinkly and bruised.'

'Well, I think the doctors are going to make her better.'

Jack plucks the snail off his elbow with a soft sucking sound, and it retreats, wetly, into its shell.

'Put it away now and go and get dressed. We'll go soon.' She watches him screw the lid on the jar and walk out of the room, bare feet and messy hair. When he's out of earshot she puts her hands up. 'I can't deal with him right now!'

'He's just being a kid, Jen. They say what they see.'

'Can you imagine if he said that to Mam?'

The weather is bright, a light breeze coming in off the sea, sunshine in bursts through sparse clouds. The snowdrops along the driveway are in full bloom, delicate white bell-heads in clusters. Ioan breaks off a damaged branch from one of the trees nearest the house, Jack watches from the doorstep.

'You don't need your rucksack, buddy. We're only going for an hour or so.'

Jack holds the straps tight and waits. His big boots laced, his new coat buttoned. Jennifer is still inside, checking her emails one last time. When she comes out, she hustles everyone into the car without noticing his bag.

As they pass the power station, she turns away, looks out

over fields and thorny hedges instead. Follows the lines of the pylons with her eyes, as they recede into the distance beyond the farmland. By the time they pull into her parents' farmyard her mind is back on Helen.

Megan totters out of the barn, tail swishing over the slate chips.

'Why don't you and Uncle Ioan take Megan for a walk, while I talk to Nainy and Taidy?'

Jack looks at her blankly.

'Go on, I bet she'd enjoy playing with you.'

'She doesn't play.'

'Well, I'm sure she'd like some company, anyway.' She looks to Ioan for assistance.

'Come on, buddy, I need some help checking the fences. Let's go.'

Jack shoulders his bag and follows Ioan across the yard. Megan follows, at a distance.

In the kitchen Jennifer puts the kettle on and calls out to her mam. Creeps upstairs to find her in bed, face sunken and head uncovered. Her skin is blotchy, discoloured.

'Mam?'

She opens her eyes and smiles. There is a smell in the room that Jennifer can't quite identify; sickly sweet, organic.

'How are you feeling today?'

'Tired, cariad. Just a bit tired.' She pushes herself up on the pillows and sighs.

'Where's Dad?'

'Out in the fields. He's got a young man helping him, with Helen gone. Busy with the lambs, you know.'

'Have you heard from Helen?'

'Not for a day or so. She'll be back soon though.'

'She's been delayed. Just wondered if you'd heard anything.' Her mam is weak, half asleep. Sharing her concern is going to worry her. 'Do you want a panad? Kettle's on.'

'Da iawn. What delay?'

'Just some traffic issues. Nothing to worry about, I'm sure. I'll bring the tea up.'

When she returns, her mam is asleep again, mouth slightly open. Jaw slack, skin like wizened fruit. The smell is subtle but clear. Decay. She closes the bedroom door softly.

Outside, Jennifer takes a deep breath to clear her nose. The first spikes of daffodils are piercing through the grass verges, dark green and firm. She goes back into the kitchen and rummages for the keys in the drawer, then strides down the rocky path towards Helen's barn. She can see Ioan and Jack halfway down the adjacent field, crouching by the fence. Further away, at the boundary to the farmland, a JCB is lifting its long neck and tipping soil from its bucket.

She swings her leg over the gate, comfortable in her jeans and trainers. In the daylight she notices the raised beds either side of the yard, a child-sized spade and garden fork leaning neatly against a wheelbarrow next to full-sized tools. The earth is partly turned, in preparation for the seed potatoes maybe. There are knotty-looking herbs at the border, grey twiggy lavender bushes. She looks at the barn. In the daylight it looks small, shabby. Lichen-stained stone and mossy slate roof. The door is solid, patched up, reinforced. She still can't see it as a home.

She unlocks the door and slips through, into a half-light. The skylights are dirty with algae. It smells fusty, unaired. She goes straight up the steep stairs to the bedroom, shutting the door behind her. The light in here is better, the round window on the far wall between the beds less mucky, streaked only with dried, salted rain. It feels damp, cold. She doesn't search around this time, just goes straight for the laptop.

The bright screen is comforting in the confines of the room. Her fingers settle easily on the keys. She starts by opening the web browser, then scans the desktop icons while it loads. Folders titled *Work*, *Personal*, *PAWB*, *Chernobyl*, *Protests*. The browser icon flashes on the toolbar at the bottom of the screen and she clicks it. Pages begin loading, refreshing themselves automatically.

She scrolls through each page. The first few are blogs: 'After the Cloud', 'PrepMommy' and 'Last One Standing'. Each one lists articles about bush-craft knives, shelter building and first aid, each has adverts down the side for equipment: sealed protein packs, crossbows, ready-packed survival rucksacks. 'PrepMommy' has a list of *Forty Survival Skills Your Child Needs NOW!* Another on how to silence children if you need to hide from danger. The first line mentions duct-tape.

She flicks away, finds herself on Wylfa's own website, familiar territory. The banner a clear image of the grey-green reactors caught between an azure sky and cobalt sea. The news pages. Links to the reactor shutdown strategy, the safety policy and waste management plan. The next tab is the replacement plant's company site, Vista. This time Wylfa is in the background, a lush field taking up most of the image, grass where the new buildings of Wylfa B will be embedded. Below are the strategic plans, links to maps showing the site and information for locals and businesses about the opportunities arising. Nothing new.

A Facebook group for anti-nuclear protesters lists upcoming events. The Fukushima anniversary is the next date. She scrolls through to see if anything is planned at Wylfa, notes that the bridge will likely be blocked to the mainland. No doubt Helen plans to stand with the crowd, banners trying to shame her colleagues as they go into work. Like last year.

The final page is a photo site, images backed up and stored on the Cloud.

She can hear voices outside, Ioan calling. She scrolls quickly through the most recent pictures.

[Broken doll, brittle leaves.]

[Gas masks scattered, dusty concrete floor. School book open.]

[Small white sandal, dirty and unpaired.]

The door below opens. She unplugs the laptop and slides it into her bag, grabs the books on the top of the piles by Helen and Jack's beds, and steps out onto the small balcony. She looks down into Jack's face, small and pale beneath his tangled hair.

'Why are you here?' he asks, his voice reedy in the hollow space.

'I'm checking something.'

His eyes dart around the barn, settle on the car, then he turns and leaves. She hears her dad outside, relief in his tone. 'Dyma chi, Jac-y-do! I thought we'd lost you!'

***

The first thing Helen is aware of is the smell.

Stale fabric.

Without opening her eyes, she knows her face is pressed against material that hasn't been washed or aired for a long time. Is under heavy blankets sour with use.

There is something else.

Smoke.

Not cigarettes or the crisp, clear scent of wood smoke, but something thicker and heavier that sticks at the back of her nose like catarrh, something embedded in the fabric and the air itself. And behind it there is something else again, the organic tang of rotting onions, of vegetal decay.

She feels sick and it isn't just the smell, it's her head. The smallest movement sends waves of nausea through her. Her head is throbbing. She tries to breathe lightly, to take in less of the odour, but it makes her panicky. When she allows one crusted eye to break its seal she lets in pain and colour. Bright blue, red and orange. She closes it.

There are sounds. A low rumble to her right, a faint scratching further away. Then the swift, soft patter of paws on wood and a second of silence before the blankets tighten ever so slightly over her legs and something curls against her. A cat. She feels the purr against her spine and drifts back to sleep.

Voices wake her, and the room must be brighter because the inside of her eyelids are lit up orange.

The cat has gone.

The voices are behind her, the clang of a kettle on a metal grate sounds like a gong, reverberating through her skull.

A low rumble reaches a crescendo.

Boiling water.

She lies still, trying to decode the input, trying to breathe without vomiting.

A man's voice, low and urgent, is interrupted by a woman. The woman has the authority. Helen hears it in the tone, the way the man's voice responds. She can't understand the words, strains to translate the sounds into words and fails. Senses they are talking about her from the whispers.

She opens her eyes again and squints at a bright blue wall, the orange and red of a thick, patterned blanket. She is weighed down with blankets. Tentatively, she stretches her legs; her hip is stiff and aching, her knee painful. She flexes her arms and feels raw skin grate against the fabric. Her shoulder is sore. The smell still chokes her but less so.

When she moves, rolling slowly onto her back until she can see the hot white ceiling peeling above her, the voices stop.

A door closes.

She is in a small room, painted white and bright blue, one window. Although a dirty net curtain is hung across the glass, the light still pierces through, hurting her eyes. Next to the window a table is piled high with clutter, and the wall behind it is decorated like a shrine: a cluster of vivid icons, draped with colourful scarves. There are mismatched chairs with clothes draped over the backs, and a sideboard laden with jars and baskets and photographs. A treadle-powered sewing machine is positioned under the window. On the floor buckets and pans overflow with sprouting seed potatoes and onions, papery skin flaking onto the floorboards.

Helen doesn't have time to process where she is before a woman is grasping her hand and kissing it, sitting on the edge of the bed to lean in close and press her wizened face into

Helen's. It must be her mam because who else could it be, but she feels detached, as if the contact is happening to someone else. The kisses are at once fierce and soft; the old woman's lips as wrinkled and velvety as dried apricots. There is a ferocious affection to the act.

Helen tenses, tries to pull away. The intimacy is too much. The woman strokes her hair and smiles down at her, and she is trapped, bears the attention out of necessity. What else can she do? Even shifting her position makes her head throb, nausea rise.

She is concussed. Vulnerable. Tired.

The woman stays on the bed beside Helen, clutching her hand and smiling. Beaming. Her steel and silver hair is almost entirely covered by a bright blue and yellow headscarf, and she has on layers of woollen cardigans and a heavy dark green skirt. Over her left breast there is a bunch of safety pins clustered like a brooch. Her face is weatherworn, sun-browned and furrowed. Not her mam. Of course not. And this isn't home, despite the familiar sight of seed potatoes stacked to be planted and dried herbs hanging on the walls.

Finally, the woman stands, limps away. Helen can see the window, the silhouette of someone beyond the grey nylon, then gone. She closes her eyes and tries to piece everything together. Remembers the protests and leaving Ivankiv, the urgency of the drive. Knows from the pain that she has had an accident, but can't recall any details. Feels a rush of panic as she recalls her bike, her supplies.

Jack.

Where is he?

She tries to get up, pushing at the heaped and heavy

blankets, breathing through her mouth to control the nausea, but the woman is back, fussing. Helen feels the nettle sting of tears as she relinquishes power to the woman, lets the fatigue take charge. Somewhere deep inside, primal instincts to get up and run are raging, but her body is betraying her.

The woman folds the blankets tight around her, fetches a small glass of thick red liquid. She gestures for Helen to drink. She takes the glass, holds it carefully and sniffs. Sweet, alcoholic. She takes a sip and gags, rolls sideways to retch so suddenly her head feels the impact again in an echo. The woman holds a steel bowl out and rubs her back until the toxic yellow bile has burned her throat and nothing more comes out. She lies back, sleeps.

***

They stop at the village shop on the way home, and Jennifer buys crisps and pasties, bottles of fruit juice and grapes. Ioan has stayed behind to help her dad, and she and Jack are alone for the rest of the day, for the first time. He trails behind her in the aisles, eyes wide as he scans the shelves of biscuits and cakes, the racks of sweets. She nearly buys him a bag of Skittles but thinks the sugar and additives might change his behaviour, and he's difficult enough as it is.

He is still wearing the rucksack.

'Can we load the picnic into your bag, little man?'

He shakes his head and looks out of the window. The checkout assistant gives her a look that's hard to read. Jennifer packs everything into a thin plastic carrier bag and they leave.

'So, while it's sunny I thought we could go to the beach.'

His eyes flicker, seagull-grey. A smile flits across his lips and is gone.

'Sound good? Come on then.' She feels a flicker of hope. If she makes more effort now, perhaps she can mitigate the upset of Helen's late return. She has to nurture a connection. As they buckle in, she realises she has no idea how.

She drives towards Cemlyn Bay, wanting novelty value for them both. Although she lives by the coast, has the bay beyond the fields, she rarely goes to the beach anymore.

By the time she's parked the car, the weather has turned. The unseasonable burst of sunshine has retreated behind a blur of cloud, and the wind is whipping up white lines on the sea. There is no one else at the beach, not even a committed dog walker. She gets out her phone to check the weather forecast, but there is no signal.

Jack is already out of his seatbelt, half standing and clinging to the back of the passenger seat waiting for her to open the door or release the child lock so he can tumble out. She scans the sky and wonders how long they'll have. She doesn't want to disappoint him now.

'We'll stay for an hour, okay?'

He nods, pulls at the door handle.

The tide is coming in. There was a time when she'd have known this without needing to Google it. When she and her sister would walk to the beach at the end of their grandfather's field and day by day know the tides, the rhythm of the waves in sight and sound and taste. They would throw their clothes in a heap of wool and denim onto sun-bleached rocks and hobble down towards the water over the smooth pebbles and sharp sticks until they could fling themselves, gasping, into the icy water. Or was it Helen who knew, and she just followed?

She looks out over this different bay. There are no diamonds dancing on the surface, just grey and white arching lines, coming closer and closer. She zips up her jacket and tells Jack to do the same, determined to stick to her word, to distract Jack, and herself, from Helen's absence. She probably hasn't called because she's travelling. She's almost certainly fine.

Within seconds of letting him out, Jack is racing towards the water. Jennifer's shouts are lost in the inshore wind. The bay curves away like a scythe, Wylfa a giant sandcastle on her right and to her left the protective shoulder of black rock that seems to embrace the beach, guarding it from the open water. She drops the bag and runs on weakening legs to grab Jack's hood, feels his little body jerk as she halts his dash towards the waves. He wriggles, but she pulls him close, trembling.

'No running, don't go near the water.' Her voice is angry.

'I want to paddle.'

'Not today, it's too cold.'

She holds his hand tightly as she marches him back towards the car to retrieve the bag. He stands quietly as she bends to lift it, and when she looks back at him she can see the clouds in his eyes. Seagulls wheel overhead, crying like hungry infants. She's already blown it.

She holds his hand tight as they walked down the rocky beach in their boots. When they reach a group of low rocks Jennifer sits and lets go. He stretches his fingers out to test their freedom and stares at her.

'You can play here, but don't go near the water, okay little man?'

'Play?'

She looks around – there is no sand to build a castle, and they haven't brought a ball. 'Why don't we collect some pretty shells?'

He tilts his head, and then nods. Crouches down and begins scouring the pebbles for yellow dog whelks and pink periwinkles. Jennifer spies the pearly inner curve of a mussel shell and holds it out to him. Catches the fleeting smile as she drops it in his palm. Maybe the afternoon is salvageable. Her phone beeps. A signal. She fumbles her coat pocket hoping it's Helen, a message to say she is on her way.

It's Ioan. *Gonna b hr a while. Bck for dinner. Takeaway?*

She hates the way he abbreviates for texts. Replies with *Okay*.

Jack is moving along the beach, a few paces, sideways. His hood catches the wind and billows out behind him.

Jennifer sends another message to Helen, and then looks out over the bay. The horizon is a straight line, grey and darker grey where the sky and sea meet. It's beautiful, even with the rapidly darkening clouds. She glances away from Jack, towards the plant. From here, the shock of its size and shape on the otherwise empty coastline is arresting. She looks away, still ashamed, vividly aware of her exclusion. Opens the internet on her phone and checks her emails in case David Wellbeck has been in touch. Isn't surprised when he hasn't. It's Sunday, she thinks, he'll be eating roast lamb somewhere. She stares at the screen and then opens Helen's photo page, the URL copied over from the laptop. She flicks through the pictures with a chilly thumb.

[Dark skies, black trees, the heavy hulk of decaying buildings.]

173

She glances across the bay at the plant, sees similar lines and angles in the grey of the reactors, the same colour as the sea and sky. Looks back at the phone and swipes her finger for the next picture.

[Motorbike, black curves like a beetle, silver trim like the edges of wings about to unfold. Panniers, shiny and bulging, engorged. Brick wall, red and beige.]

[Books, open. Pages crushed, softened with time.]

[Glass jar. Something suspended in yellowed water. Paint peeling.]

She glances at Jack as he sifts through the pebbles for shell fragments and sea-polished glass. He has his back to her.

[Windowsill. Dusty shards and curled brown leaves. A doll; dirty, matted hair, leg missing. A tiny shoe balanced on the edge. No glass. Strands of grass curl inwards, over the frame.]

Jack is moving away from her, absorbed in his search. He is making a low hum under his breath, punctuated by the wind snapping it away from her.

[Another shoe. Pale, high-heeled. Litter.]

[Wylfa.] From the other side, her side. She taps the picture to fill the screen.

[Dark low block of the turbine hall, sand-coloured sidings and slim black chimneys. Clouds low, a glow from the floodlights.]

She compares the real view with the images on the screen. Sees both sides at once. She's never really paid it any attention. It stands out in the landscape, but it has always been there. She and Helen have grown up with its solid presence behind them in childhood photographs taken on the beach or sitting smiling on tractors in the fields. They'd been on school trips and to birthday parties at the visitors' centre, had never seen the horizon behind the farm without its even edges and the evening glow of floodlights sitting between the curve of the headland and the flat line of the sea.

She lets the phone drop into her lap and looks intently at the shape of the plant, the way the colours merge with the landscape. Tries to see it as the photographer did. The mustard yellow of the turbine hall overflows into the dead bracken and grasses on the hill, foreshadows the blaze of gorse flowers about to erupt across the hillside. The dark chimneys and the base of the reactor block seep out into the black rock of the coastline, and the pale grey-greens of the reactors billow towards the sea, the sky, and seem to fall in fragments as tiny pale anemones, growing between the rocks.

She blinks in the sharp wind that races the waves, and for a moment the edge of the buildings blur and she feels something shift inside, an awareness bloom into being like the spread of lichen. The building seems to flicker, merging with the landscape one second then standing out in stark contrast the next. She's never noticed its camouflage before. She shudders and looks around for Jack. Sees the pile of shells he's tipped by her feet, but he isn't beside her.

She scans the beach, expecting to see him a few feet away, or clambering on the grassy bank that hangs over the beach in a fronded lip of sandy soil and tough sea grass. He is much further away though, with his back to her and his face to the wind. Arms outstretched for balance as he navigates the wet rocks near the headland. She calls and feels the words dissolve in a sudden gust of wind. Raindrops spike her face. He is so small, getting further out. She runs over the loose pebbles, the ground slipping away from her, feeling like she isn't moving at all. Nearly calls when she gets close, but doesn't want to startle him, make him lose his balance. Instead she hops across the wet rocks to him, reaches to sweep an arm under his and slips, her foot sliding over the weed-slicked stone and tipping her into the incoming waves.

It isn't deep, but the shock of the winter-cold water takes her breath, and she staggers when the next wave hits her thighs. Jack is standing above her, his mouth open in surprise. She gasps and reaches for him, and he takes her hand and walks back on the rocks while she pushes through the weight of the water, her jeans waterlogged and heavy. Waves pushing at the back of her knees, trying to topple her.

When they reach the pebbles beyond the foaming tide she crouches, holds tight to the front of his jacket, her face inches from his.

'Don't you dare ever do that again. Ever. Do you hear?'

He blinks. Frowns. Eyes the colour of the sea behind him.

'Do you hear me? You'll get swept away. You must never, ever go out on the rocks.' She is shaking him slightly to emphasise each word.

He nods.

She pulls him close, then. Forcing a hug so tight she feels his breath leave him.

'I can't lose you. Your mam…'

He is crying, they both are, and she rubs his tears away with her sleeve.

'Don't cry little man, I didn't mean to shout. I was just scared. You could have slipped.'

'I wouldn't. I know the rocks. I know them.'

Jennifer shakes her head. 'How can you?'

'I just do. It was you who fell. Not me.'

'Come on, home.' She takes his hand and squeezes it way too tight on the way back to the car. He keeps turning to look back, to catch a last glimpse of the huge waves now crashing closer and closer, higher and higher as the storm moves in. The wind on her wet clothes makes her quake. Her teeth are chattering. She lifts the lunch bag with numb fingers and tips the contents on the passenger seat while Jack straps in, then spreads the empty bag over her seat to protect the car from her soaked jeans. Rain spatters in squalls.

She turns the heater on full, pulls out of the car park.

The windscreen wipers smear the view, streaking the sky and sea into a blur. As they drive through the lanes the colours of the power plant rise and fall behind the treeline and hedgerows.

***

Evening, the waning light less cruel to her eyes.

When she looks over to where Jack must be still sleeping in his bed opposite her, she sees the woman, hunched in a chair, working at something with gnarly fingers. Her mind refocuses slowly.

Helen has seen this kind of room before, she's sure.

The tour.

That's what this house is like, the ones on the tour. But here is a woman, and so she isn't on the tour anymore. Must be in a rural part of Ukraine, farmland.

She watches as the woman gets up and shuffles to the door,

disappears. Waits a moment then sits slowly and pushes the blanket off all the way.

She is only in her T-shirt and pants, legs bare. She becomes distracted by her injuries: her knee is bound in rags, blood seeping through, browning at the edges. Swollen. Her hip scraped raw, deep red and purple with bruising. Someone has tended to her, brought her here. She tests her joints; nothing is broken. These are injuries from a low-speed impact, a slide. Just surface wounds. She can manage the pain if it means getting home. But the concussion is the problem. She must have hit her head as she landed. Even if her bike is parked outside she won't be able to ride it, not safely, until the headaches and dizziness subside.

She looks around at the room again, warm and cluttered. Blessedly quiet. It might be safer here, she thinks, than riding through protesting towns. But it might not.

The woman is back, covering her with blankets. Brings her tea, strong and black, with a spoonful of honey. She sips it and thinks of Jack, and her guts clench.

This is a test too far.

For both of them.

She is tired, so tired, her head fuzzy. She lies back and drifts into a half-sleep. Dreams of being consumed by brambles, of heaving flesh in the dark, steam and wet pink noses. Light in slats across the dust of the barn door, a pendulum swinging, almost stopped, the smell of leather and piss.

CHAPTER TEN

Helen is sitting up in bed, watching the cat skulk across the floor. It is tortoiseshell and white, small and stout. When she tuts, it turns wide yellow eyes on her. It's hunting. Spiders, mice maybe. She has no idea how long she has slept, but the headache has receded to a dull throb and her mouth is dry. She still feels weak and tired. From the quality of light seeping through the dull net curtain she thinks it must be at least another day since the night of the accident. She should be almost home by now.

The old woman is outside. Left twenty minutes ago with the slop bucket, her body twisted by the weight. Helen guesses she is in her late sixties, but she could be younger and just aged by hard work. She is short, and the limp pronounced, although it doesn't seem to hold her back. There is a solidity to her, a matter-of-fact acceptance of her body's state. Strength.

The cat pounces, trots out from beneath the table and crouches beneath a chair. Helen thinks she can hear a crunch as it chews. She looks around the room, still too weak to get up and search properly. She can't see any obvious sign of her belongings among the heaps of stale clothes and half-empty jars of red sauce and pickled vegetables, of icons and colourful scarfs.

She wonders if the car caught up with her, robbed her.

Half-imagined memories of headlights in the trees, of hands moving her, haunt the back of her mind. The thought that whoever was in the car has undressed her, touched her, makes her skin itch. She feels, tentatively, up the inside of her thighs for signs of bruising. Slips a shaking hand into the gusset of her pants to check for the residue of semen. Sniffs her fingers for the trace scent of lubricant and latex. There are no obvious signs of assault, no internal pelvic ache to hint she has been violated. Yet here she is, stripped down, without any possessions, and being cared for by a woman who looks as though she herself deserves care. There is no way she carried Helen here, lifted her into bed.

She has to get home.

The door creaks open, letting in a welcome gust of cold, fresh air. Helen breathes deep before it closes again, and the woman comes to the bedside, smiling and checking she is okay. Helen smiles back, her only currency, apart from the soft 'dyakuyu' each time she is offered a drink. The woman squeezes her hand, her grip strong, and hobbles back towards the range, lifting a skillet from the hook beside the fire. She rattles the pan on the grate and then slices thick white strips of fat off a hunk of half-dried meat. It hisses as it hits the pan and the smell of hot grease adds to the sour air. She reaches into the pocket of her dirty apron and pulls out, one by one, five brown eggs, which she cracks into the pan.

The smell is foul, but Helen's stomach growls. The cat has drawn close to the range, skirting around the edges of the woman's workspace, hoping for a scavenged morsel. When Helen is presented with a plate of blackened eggs and streaky fat, she doesn't hesitate to eat, nods in thanks as she licks the grease off her fingers. She is halfway through when a shadow passes the window. The door knocks.

She stops eating, drops a fried egg back into the pooled grease on her plate, and waits. The woman makes her way to the door, not in any rush, and reaches out for the person on the step, up on tiptoes to kiss them. Helen catches the flash of dark hair, a leather jacket, before he enters properly.

Anton.

She lets the plate settle on her lap, confused. He strides in, his gait nervous, glancing around. Helen waits while the woman chatters to him, while he answers in short, polite syllables. His body language is respectful, almost reverential. When she has asked him the same thing three times he nods finally, and she goes outside.

He comes straight to Helen then. Leans in, examining her with his dark eyes.

'This is what you wanted?'

'What?' Barely a whisper. Her head throbs. She catches a movement behind him. The cat. It creeps closer, belly almost grazing the ground. Anton hisses at it and waves his foot as if he might kick. It hisses back and streaks under the bed.

'I told you to wait.'

'You never came back.' Her voice is faint, raspy. She is still dehydrated, hasn't really spoken properly for days.

'I was coming back. You should have waited.' He is angry, and his sudden appearance, and attitude, make her temporarily mute. He strides once around the small room and then sits on the bed, pulling the blankets tight over Helen's legs with his weight. Nausea surges.

'You shouldn't be here. You can't be here.'

'Where even is here?'

'In the Zone. Illegally. It is top priority to get you out and away.'

'What?' It might be the concussion confusing her. She rubs her eyes.

'You are here in the Zone, without permit, without a tour.'

'How?'

'How? You rode your bike here, you—'

'What are you doing here?' She leans back into the bed, dizzy. The food forgotten on her lap.

Anton stands and paces. 'Don't play a game with me, Helen. It might not be exactly your plan, but you got what you wanted.'

'I never wanted to come back here! Why would I want to?'

'Then why did you drive here? Hey? Because I said to you it is the safest place? Is this why? Because you were scared of the protests?'

The accusation stings. 'No. I left town to go home. You were supposed to help me.'

'You went the wrong way.'

'I was being chased!'

'Chased?'

'Some boys were trying to catch me, to steal my bike and God knows what else. I didn't know where I was driving, I was just trying to get away. You said you'd help me, and then you disappeared. What was I supposed to do?'

Anton is quiet for moment. His dark brows nearly meet in the middle of his frown. He sits back down on the bed.

'How did you find me?'

He shrugs, looks towards the window. The cat has crept out from under the bed and is on the table, licking the edge of the old woman's plate. Anton grabs a piece of clothing from the pile on the bed near Helen and throws it. 'Tsssk!'

The old woman comes back in, pulls more eggs from her apron and cracks them into the skillet, busies herself slicing meat. Anton is avoiding eye contact. Helen closes her eyes and thinks. Piecing together fragments of the hour before the accident.

'Are you sleeping?'

She opens her eyes. 'It was you, wasn't it?'

'I was coming back to help. I saw the boys.'

'But it was you in the car?'

'Yes.'

'You who chased me?'

'Not chased. I was trying to catch up, to show the way out. Then I could see what you were doing, trying to get back in the Zone. I was trying to stop you.'

'You fucking idiot!' She lunges forwards and hits him, slapping his arm as hard as she can, ignoring the pain in her wrist and the way the movement feels like she's aboard a boat, tilting. He pulls back, stands up to get out of her reach. Her hair is loose and falling around her face and she brushes it back to glare at him, cradles her wrist. It isn't broken, she's almost sure, but sprained maybe. Sore.

'Where is my bike?'

'Gone.'

'Gone where?' she roars, her throat raw and voice cracking. The pain in her head crescendos. She can feel her pulse pushing at the inside of her forehead.

'It was broken. I had to hide it.'

She falls back into the musty pillows. Whispers. 'So you chase me, push me so hard I crash, and then take my bike. You are the biggest danger to me. Not some kids, not even a fucking revolution.'

'I didn't make you crash.'

'Then what did?' She senses fur and steam somewhere in her memory, but not clearly enough.

'Boar. You were driving too fast. They came out of the forest from the side, across the road. You hit one, went up and over.'

'I killed it?'

'No, you injured it. I killed it. But because of you.'

'And then you brought me here?' The hands. *I got you.*

'It was nearest safe place.'

'*You* brought me here. You.' She spits the accusation, makes clear to him his responsibility. 'Where are my things, my clothes?' She pushes the blankets away, pulls her T-shirt down to cover the paunch of skin between the hem and her pants. Catches his eyes widening at the bruises and scrapes.

'How bad are you hurt?'

'I need to get home.' She is dizzy from standing too quickly, nausea rises again, and she reaches out to steady herself on the back of a chair, bile filling her throat.

The old woman is slapping Anton now. Shooing him away from her. He raises his hands in defeat. They exchange quick words and she hears him say over and over, 'Dobre, Baba, dobre.' The eggs are burning, smoke from the pan stinging Helen's eyes. She sits back on the bed, dizzy.

The woman is pointing at the door. Before he leaves Anton stands close to the bed.

'I can't take you until you can walk. When the guards come to check on Baba Olena, you'll have to hide. Get under blankets and hope they don't hear you. You shouldn't be here.'

'Then you should have just let me go,' she whispers defiantly, as he walks to the door.

***

Still no email. Jennifer sits in the soft lamplight of the lounge staring at her laptop screen, anxiety at the digital silence squeezing her chest.

Jack is watching a movie. She glances over every so often to see his face illuminated by the glow of the TV set, his hand fingering the cord around his neck beneath his T-shirt.

Without her job she is lost. In between haunting her inbox, she has busied herself with chores; a dry-cleaning run for suits she might not get to wear again, shopping for her parents. She'd begun a thorough clean of the kitchen when the door opened and the cleaner came in.

'I'm sorry, Mrs Lloyd-Jones. Are you sick today? Do you want me to leave?'

'No, I'm just... I'm taking a few days off. It's okay, stay.' And she'd wandered into the garden to be out of the way while the cleaner hoovered and polished.

She reaches out for her mug of tea and grimaces at the first sip. Cold.

'Do you want some hot chocolate, little man?'

His eyes flick to hers and he nods, smiles. The one thing that gives her a lift. The frequency of these fleeting signs of happiness in him are increasing. He has become her challenge. She leaves the laptop and walks in thick woollen socks to the big kitchen, sets the kettle on the stove. Paces the floor while it comes to the boil. She has little experience of children, beyond Jack and her own memories of childhood, but she knows something is wrong. Dropping him off at school, without work to rush to, she waited,

185

watched him walk in, avoiding the other children who huddled together or ran around playing games. He skirted their social packs and stood, alone, under a tree at the side of the playground. Studying the bark, it seemed, intently, until the bell rang.

She mixes chocolate powder with milk while the tea steeps, pops the cup in the microwave to warm. Wonders if Helen is aware of his difficulties. She's asked Jack repeatedly for the names of his classmates, thinking she could call their parents, invite them over and nurture some sense of friendship, but he shrugs every time.

Before going back to the lounge she chops an apple into slices and scoops a dollop of peanut butter onto a saucer.

When she takes it through, Jack is lying on the floor, the movie ignored, staring through the curved glass of the jar at his sleeping snails.

'Sit up, your drink's here. And a snack.'

She settles next to him, on the floor, her knees drawn up. The room feels bigger from down here.

'Is Mam coming back, ever?' He unscrews the jar and drops a slice of apple in before he takes his own piece.

'Of course!' She hears the uncertainty in her voice. She has left more messages on Helen's voicemail, checked the news frequently for anything that might show where she is, scouring images of the riots in Kyiv for a glimpse of Helen's dark hair, pale face. Has argued with Ioan over the lost envelope of instructions, blaming him as if the demonstrations were his fault, making him search his pockets, the barn, the car, until finally giving up and apologising. She had planned to spend the day on Helen's laptop, searching through her files for any clues, but Ioan had taken her car this morning, and the laptop was still stowed in the boot.

She watches the film for a few minutes, while Jack turns the glass jar in his tiny hands, watching the snails unfurl to feast on the fresh fruit. Bambi. The mother has died, the father absent, leaving the child to adventure through the script alone, relying on an assortment of misfit friends accumulated along the way. She wonders if Jack knows anything about his own father. Helen has never told anyone who he was, just that she wanted to parent alone. Perhaps Jack's father doesn't even know about him. She changes channels, finds a children's art programme with an over-enthusiastic presenter. Glue and glitter, *here's one I made earlier*. He's not watching it anyway.

When Ioan comes in, yawning from a twelve-hour shift, she makes him a cup of tea, asks him what he wants to eat.

'I'm going to do the sheep first. Last few to lamb now. I'll grab a sandwich after.' He pours the tea into a lidded travel cup to take with him.

She follows him out, waits for him to change into wellies and disappear down the path with his powerful torch, then gets the laptop out of the boot.

In the lounge Jack is lining up toy cars in rows, focussed. She has yet to see him pretend to drive one across the carpet or make the sounds of an engine in his throat. But he seems happy enough, ordering them into neat lines. Adjusting their positions meticulously.

She settles on the table with her tea and Helen's laptop. Opens the folder titled *Chernobyl*. Lists of files clatter down the screen in alphabetical order: *Accident*, *Activism*, *Birth1*, *Chern-articles*, *Chern-tours*, right through to *Wylfa-1*, *Wylfa-2*. Jennifer scans the list, opening various files and letting them load as she moves back through the names. Most are further lists of web addresses, or downloaded PDF copies of scientific articles and reports. She opens *Birth1* expecting something similar, and thumbnails pop up and chequer the screen.

She clicks on the first one.

[Black and white. Baby's head, clean pillow. Features bulbous; one eye bulging forward, mushroom forehead.]

The next.

[Legs stretched straight, angle unnatural. Skinny. A hand on the wide dome of the head, the buttocks a bony corner of a triangle.]

The next.

[One forehead, two faces. Golden, letter-box eyes. Snowy tight curls of wool slit by two pink tongues, mid-bleat.]

There is no information about where the deformed lamb is from, whether it was a victim of the disaster in Ukraine, or a recent picture from a farm nearby, in Wales. She thinks of their dead lamb's white eyes and curved legs. Wonders if Helen took this photo herself.

She shuts the file down, and a PDF pops up to fill the screen. She feels nauseous, as though the chair were moving beneath her, cast on waves like a raft. She starts reading.

Statistics on cancer in central France, a government report.

She's seen enough. Closes down every file except the one titled *Chern-tours*. A single page spreadsheet, the rows and columns comparing prices and dates, number of days and the inclusion of insurance, airport transfers and hotel fees. There are nine companies listed, along with web addresses and contact numbers. Four have red crosses marked in a final column.

Jennifer sits up straighter in the dining chair, considering whether the crosses ruled these companies out or narrowed the search down. She scrolls up and down trying to find a clue as to which was the final choice, but there is no conclusion. She checks the date on the file. September last year. She minimises it and goes back to the desktop, searching for a more recent file, something with a booking reference or invoice attached.

Stops reading when the lights go out.

For a moment she just sits, the hidden sounds of the house suddenly amplified in the darkness; the coal settles lower in the grate, the wind bellows in the chimney, and, somewhere, the faint creak of old wood. She glances over at the sofa and sees, in the shrouded glow of the fire, the pickle jar. The fleecy blanket she'd draped over Jack's knees at the start of the film is in a crumpled heap on the floor.

'Jack?'

A spatter of rain hits the window, like gravel thrown at the glass.

She stands up. The cosy atmosphere has gone with the lamplight. The fire throws deep shadows into the corners.

'Jack?'

The sofa is empty. Jennifer runs her hand close to the TV screen and feels the static crackle and lift the tiny hairs on the back of her hand. She walks to the lounge door and listens. She can just make out a low mutter.

Jennifer fumbles the door handle. It sounds loud in the darkness. She thinks for one illogical moment that it is locked, and twists it harder, almost panicking, and then she is through and into the hall. The darkness here is solid. The door, heavy on its hinges, swings closed behind her, leaving her blind. She feels along the wall, her hands sensitive to the coolness of the old stone beneath the plaster. Her fingers register every softly ridged brushstroke in the paintwork. When she reaches a light switch, she flicks it a few times, knowing it won't work but hoping all the same. She stumbles on an abandoned shoe and kicks it away. Taps on the toilet door.

'Hey, little man? You okay?'

'Why is it dark?'

'Do you need my help?' She turns the doorknob, but it's locked.

'No. Why is it dark?' She can hear him moving around in the small room, the rustle of paper, the seat banging closed.

'It's just a power cut, okay? Shall I help you get cleaned up and out of there?'

The sound of the toilet flushing drowns out any reply.

The bolt slides back and she feels him beside her. He reaches out and puts a hand on her leg. A tiny, hot point on her thigh. She strokes his hair.

'There's nothing to be scared of. I know it was a surprise, but it's fine.'

'I'm not scared.' The tremor in his voice gives him away. 'I need my torch.'

'Let's find it then.'

'I know where it is.' He slips away, the hand gone. She hears him on the stairs. He stops halfway to slide the curtain back, letting in a scant glow from a moon half covered by cloud. Jennifer waits, listening to him moving around. The sharp beam of a torch wavers on the stairs. When he comes down he's dressed, wearing his rucksack.

'Is Mam back?'

'Not yet.'

'Uncle Ioan?'

'In the field, he'll be back soon.'

He shines the torch around, highlighting details she never usually notices: the dust in the corner of the skirting, the wonky screw on the toilet door handle. He turns the torch off.

'I can see speckles.' Jack's voice is easing into wonder, but still betrays an undercurrent of anxiety. 'Little speckles in my eyes.'

Jennifer focusses on the quality of the darkness. She too can see tiny white specks floating in her vision, like white noise on a TV screen, but fainter.

'Don't worry about it, it's normal.'

'But what is it?'

'I don't know, little man.'

They feel their way back to the lounge. The fire is low, but the glow, now their eyes have adjusted to the dark, is enough to navigate the room without Jack's torch. He moves back towards the sofa, snatches up the remote and points it at the screen.

'It won't work, little man, the power's gone.' Jennifer sits beside him and stares into the fire.

'Where's it gone?'

'What do you mean?'

'You said the power has gone. Where? Why?'

'Well, I mean the electricity has stopped coming through into the sockets and plugs.'

'But why?' He is fingering the cord beneath his shirt.

'I don't know.' She pulls him towards her, feels his resistance. 'Maybe there's a mistake in the microwave or TV.'

'What mistake?'

'Well, sometimes things go wrong and stop working. There's a special box that cuts off the power to keep us safe.'

'Where is the box?'

'Under the stairs. But that would only trip the one circuit.' She speaks her thoughts out loud, only half aware of Jack focussing on her face.

'Can you fix it?'

'If that's the problem. Maybe a naughty mouse has chewed through a wire...' Maybe she should find some candles, light up the windows to guide Ioan back home.

'Is it dangerous? Is the mouse okay?'

'There might not be a mouse. It might be a storm somewhere has knocked down one of the big wires that hang outside, or someone made a mistake at work and pressed the wrong switch.' The more she speculates the more she needs to know exactly what has happened. 'Why don't I find out, hey?'

When she stands, so does Jack, rucksack tugging at his bony shoulders.

'Stay here, I'll be back in a minute. I might be able to just flick a switch and it'll come back on.'

'Why can't I come?'

'Just stay here in the light of the fire. I'll only be a minute. Can I borrow your torch?'

He grips it tighter, then shakes his head. He probably needs it to feel safe, she thinks. She can manage.

She uses the abandoned shoe from the hall to wedge the door open so that a little light from the lounge can seep through. Jack is whispering to his snails. 'Peid â phoeni, peid â phoeni...' Don't worry.

There is no reassuring hum from the refrigerator in the kitchen, and although the windows are high and wide, any light from the moon or stars is obscured by clouds, making the room a riddle of memory. The dimensions seem to shift as Jennifer moves cautiously through the chasm between the doorframe and the wide table. She catches her shin on the corner of a chair trying to get to the second drawer down of the large Welsh dresser where the spare torches are kept.

She fumbles through a litter of batteries and string, biros and keys until she finds a small torch near the back. The rest have gone. When she presses the button a weak light makes strange shadows on the walls, and she jumps, thinking someone else is in the room with her, then laughs at her own silliness, and with relief, when she realises she is alone.

She crouches to lean into the cupboard under the stairs, where the fuse box sits with all its switches pointing upwards. Flicks them a few times just in case, but nothing happens. She is just closing the cover when she hears Ioan at the front door.

'You all okay? The whole area is out. It's black as death out there.'

'We're fine.' She eases backwards out of the cupboard, relaxing at the sound of his voice so rich and alive in the claustrophobia of the darkness.

His boots thud onto the hall floor and Jennifer hears his coat slide off the hook to join them.

The torchlight dazzles her, and he drops the beam as soon as he sees her squinting at him from her crouch on the floor.

'What are you doing?'

'Checking the fuse box.'

'No point. It's not just us, it's everyone. Where's Jack?'

'In the lounge. How far?' She stands up and stretches, lets out a breath she hadn't realised had been held tight in her chest.

'As far as I could see. It's like the Middle Ages. Night is night again.'

Jennifer moves to the window, seeking some sign of habitation beyond their borders, but there are no farmhouses left, no neighbours to put lamps in their windows. The houses are either empty or bulldozed already. The only hint at the moon is a lighter patch of swirling grey low in the sky over the invisible garden. She can just make out a low glow on the horizon from the vicinity of the plant. They have their own emergency generators. Floodlights to illuminate intruders, low level lighting for evacuations.

Ioan gives her a squeeze and then moves into the lounge, the harsh white glare of torchlight dancing on the walls then disappearing as he calls out, 'Ti'n iawn, buddy?'

Jennifer tries to light the stove to make hot tea for Ioan. The chill of his fingers still lingers on her skin beneath her shirt. The gas hisses out into the room, but the ignition fails to spark, and Jennifer realises she needs matches. She fumbles in the drawer again, finding lost things with her fingertips before catching the small box with its sandpaper side.

She can hear Jack talking, as though the darkness had amplified his voice. He is asking questions. A mixture of Welsh and English. She catches the odd word: trydan – electricity; tywyll – dark, but loses the meaning. Somehow her career path has stilled her childhood tongue, has left her translating her own language. Her eyes are adjusting to the gloom, giving her a stronger sense of the room. Things solidify.

The kettle whistles and she shuts off the gas with a snap of her wrist. Clenches the small, underpowered torch between her teeth while she makes the tea, hoping the power will come on again before the food in the fridge begins to turn and the freezer starts dripping.

She carries the tea carefully, sets the mugs down on the hearth in the lounge. Ioan has canopied Jack's blanket between the sofa back and the table, using Helen's laptop to weigh down one corner.

'Not a bad den, hey buddy?'

'It's a shelter, not a den.'

Their shadow figures grow and shrink as they move around in the strong beam of Ioan's torch. Jennifer tries to squeeze into the makeshift tent, but the space is filled with sofa cushions and Ioan's broad shoulders.

'There isn't room,' Jack states. 'Not everyone can be saved.'

'Come on, buddy. We can make room.'

'It's okay, you two play.' She retreats, stands by the window staring out into the thick inky space where she knows the garden and fields should be. It feels as though the world has gone, the house afloat in the void of a starless sky. She goes back to Helen's laptop and opens the photo site again, careful to keep the weight of the machine on the corner of the blanket.

As she scrolls though the links, she feels Ioan rubbing her leg beneath the table.

'Come and join us, Jen.'

'I will in a minute.'

'No, there's only room for two.'

'It's fine, I'm okay out here.'

[House, front torn open, grass long, dining table warping with moisture.]

[Foundation, mud, nettles.]

[Cottage, nestled between rose bushes, the rise of the power station behind.]

It takes her a moment to realise these are pictures of here, not Helen's trip. Her neighbours' farms and cottages documented in stages of abandonment and demolition. She closes the page, clicks on a link to an article from a south Wales online newspaper with the headline 'Breast Cancer rise downwind of Trawsfynydd Nuclear Power Station.'

As she reads, she reaches up and cups one of her own breasts, small and firm beneath her slim fingers. She presses into the flesh with her fingertips, palpating the tissue and searching for lumps, exploring the boundary where the curve meets her ribs, where the muscle disappears into her armpit. She swaps hands and checks the other one, automatically following the pattern the nurse had shown her shortly after her mother's diagnosis. Nothing.

She lets go, opens a new link, stares into the open wound of Chernobyl's Reactor Four. Black and white, the text describing the accident stark in contrast to the grainy photo.

Ioan's phone trills out from the hall and she jumps. As he tries to get out from the makeshift den the blanket tautens and nearly pulls the laptop off the table. She snatches it, and the blanket falls. Jack gasps, shrouded.

Ioan scrambles up and leaves the room. As Jennifer untangles Jack from the blanket she can hear him in the hall.

'Yep. Why? Iawn, wrth gwrs, I'll be there now. Deg munud.'

Jennifer is trying to fix the den when Ioan comes back in.

'I've got to go into work.'

Jennifer can't see his expression in the dim light. He is pointing the torch at the floor so as not to dazzle them.

'Why?'

'Not sure yet, but they're calling in whoever is nearest. And I'm nearest.'

'Is there a problem?'

'Must be.'

'But they didn't say what?'

'Nope.'

'Is it safe? Why didn't they say what had happened?'

Ioan looks at her, but she can't see his eyes properly. The set of his jaw, however, tells her he's worried. 'Of course it's safe. Safe as houses.'

'It is related to the power cut, though?'

'I don't know, Jen. Listen, I've got to go. You and Jack get settled and I'll call you later, as soon as I know what's going on.'

She stands in the lounge, spinning her wedding ring on her finger as Ioan disappears into the hall. The door slams. Lights flash and drift across the wall as he turns the car around. Then darkness again. A little hand taps her thigh.

'There's room for you in the shelter now.'

Jack takes her hand and pulls her under the awning of the blanket. He has arranged the cushions to make a barricade at one end, has wedged his torch in to illuminate the space. He is rooting through his rucksack, pulls out a mini packet of biscuits, the kind she's been putting in his lunch box, and divides the miniature cookies into two even piles.

'You've got to make it last. All food is rational now.'

'Do you mean rationed?' She can't help but smile, but he doesn't join in.

'When it's gone, you will die.' He takes a tiny biscuit, nibbles around the edge until it is crenulated, and puts it back on his pile. Jennifer takes a tiny bite from one of hers and puts it back too. The soft toy she'd bought him earlier in the week is lying on the edge of the den's boundary. She reaches for it.

'No!'

His voice is high, sharp.

'What's wrong, we can play Mammies and Daddies. This can be the baby.'

'Okay. But pretend the baby is sick.'

'Let's give it some medicine, then.'

He roots through his bag. This is the first time he has actually played a game since he's been here. She rocks the stuffed toy in her arms, almost enjoys it.

'No, there is no medicine.'

'So, shall we call a doctor?' She makes a phone shape with her hand: thumb to her ear, little finger close to her mouth. Starts to make a trilling sound with her tongue.

'No. The power is gone. There is no phone.'

'Can we use magic to make it better?'

'There's no such thing.' A tone of scorn.

'No need to be rude.'

Jack takes the toy and examines it, then pushes it away, out of the den.

'What are you doing?' She reaches to pick it up.

'No. It's dead. It's… dirty with Caesar rum.'

'Caesar rum?'

'The poison that killed the sheep.'

'Come on, Jack, let's play a nice game.' She picks up the toy and holds it to her, and he starts pushing her out of the den.

'Now you are dirty. Get out!' His voice is angry now. 'Get out, get out, get out!'

She crawls out, moves the laptop and pulls the blanket away, destroying the shelter. Jack is sat, panting in the middle of the cushions. Graphite-grey eyes beneath his wild hair. He looks feral.

'Enough now. Game over. It's bedtime.'

He begins to repack his rucksack, tucking the nibbled biscuits back inside the wrapper and stowing them in a side pocket. He plucks his torch from the cushions and stands, sullen. She herds him upstairs, supervises him brushing his teeth, trying not to think of where he got the ideas for the game from.

In his room, he slips the rucksack off and settles it beside the bed. She holds the torch while he gets changed.

'What's the key for?'

He clasps it in his tiny fist. 'It's mine.'

'But what's it for?'

'Emergencies. Can you get Modron and Mabon, please?' He holds out his torch.

'Will you be okay in the dark?'

He nods.

When she gets back with the snail jar he is kneeling up in bed, elbows on the windowsill, looking out over the black fields at the glow of the power station. She pulls the curtain closed and tucks him in.

'Will the light be back tomorrow?'

'The sun will be here in the morning.'

'But the power. Will it still be gone?'

'I don't know, little man.'

'And Uncle Ioan? Is he gone like Mam?'

'He'll be back, they'll both be back. Do you want me to stay with you until you fall asleep?'

He shakes his head, clutches the torch.

Jennifer sits on the landing though, until she hears him settle. Then checks he is asleep before going downstairs. Halfway down she stops and looks out of the window, staring out over a landscape made ancient by the lack of streetlights. A car moves along the main road, brilliant headlights cutting the darkness, flickering between trees. Somewhere out there Helen is trying to get home.

CHAPTER ELEVEN

She hasn't eaten for two days, not since Anton left. Drinks only tea with honey. And only because she knows dehydration will kill her if she refuses. Feels abnormally tired, dozes on and off throughout the day. Isn't sure if it is the concussion, lack of food, or if something is seeping into her.

She's getting weaker, and angrier.

He has trapped her here, left her alone in poisoned land with an old woman and no means to leave. As far as she knows he still has her clothes, her phone. She can't even call Jack and reassure him, can't get online to find a route back to him. Wonders if she'll die here, and how he'd cope.

Baba Olena fusses, cross at first, when Helen rejects the food, then worried. Tries different things. A broth made from onions and potatoes, seasoned with dried herbs pulled from a bunch hanging over the door, potatoes baked in the ash pan beneath the range. Simple meals like the ones she and Jack cook together at home, the smells teasing her homesickness. She watches Baba Olena eat, the obvious pleasure she finds in the food. Helen wants something from a packet, from her rucksack or panniers. Something clean. Every time she tries to get up, to search for her things, Baba Olena herds her back towards the bed, patting her and kissing her. If she wasn't so old, Helen would fight her off.

Sometimes she thinks she hears voices outside, catches the

shadow of someone passing the window. There could be others living here too. There are villages in the Zone with a few couples, or lone men or women, still tilling the land, sharing moonshine vodka. Fragments of community. Most of the houses decayed and overgrown, some still neat and tidy. Perhaps it is Baba Olena's neighbours checking on her, perhaps it is her imagination, or the lingering effects of her head injury playing tricks on her.

Time is blurred. She wakes in the night and can't remember where she is. Falls asleep in the afternoon while trying to strategise her way out and home. When she thinks of Jack her headaches make him spectral, a feeling rather than a real person. More than anything she craves the smell of home, the smell of the daffodils and the cold sea wind, the smell of sheep. It's stronger than hunger. Jack is part of it, but she cannot distinguish between him and the fields, the yearning is the same. A tidal swell, a belly ache, a groaning sigh.

Baba Olena is singing.

She sleeps.

When she wakes Baba Olena is gone, the room quiet.

She is worried her knee is infected, can feel heat radiating from beneath the bandage. Gets up and tests her leg. If she can get across the room, outside, she can look for her bike, get her panniers. Gorge on peanuts, on flapjacks, food not grown or harvested in the Zone. She can take the antibiotics she has stashed inside a sock, collected over the last few years from unfinished packs in her parents' and Jennifer's bathroom cabinets.

She curses Anton, again. Under her breath, then out loud.

The cat shrinks away. Helen is a prisoner. She is almost at the window when Baba Olena returns with fresh-laid eggs and a loose-necked chicken. Immediately her hands are on Helen, guiding her towards the bed, chiding her, Helen guesses from the tone of her voice. She has a firm grip, bony fingers calloused from work. A farmer's hands, like her own. Helen refuses to get back into bed, sits on the edge until her bare legs pucker with gooseflesh while Baba Olena plucks the chicken at the table, letting feathers fall for the cat to chase.

Helen doesn't eat, even though the smell makes her ravenous. The cat has learned to sit beside her, to take morsels from her hand when Baba Olena isn't looking. It's plump, greedy.

She drinks the tea and hopes the water is safe, knows that boiling it isn't enough if it is contaminated. Only distillation will help separate the heavy metal particles from the H^2O. She doubts Baba Olena has anything more than a well or pump in the yard. But she must be sensible. The water might be okay, and she won't last a week if she refuses that.

When it becomes dark, Baba Olena eases under the covers beside Helen. There is only one room, one bed. Helen shifts towards the wall, feeling claustrophobic. They sleep, the old woman soundly and with a steady snore, Helen fitfully and with long bouts of aching wakefulness. Sweating and disorientated, she lies and listens to Baba's breathing, resents the woman's robust health compared to her own mother's fragility.

Thinks of the tea and massages the lump on the edge of her breast until the tissue is sore, realises she's missed her biopsy appointment. Wonders if cancer is already annexing her organs.

She dozes. When she dreams, it is the same dream over and over, but now Jack is there. Walking across a parched field, his hand slipping from hers. A dusty pebbled yard, the sun hot on her head. Searching for him. The barn door open, light in slats across the floor. Something swinging above her head, the smell of leather and piss. Jack, gone.

***

Jennifer drinks coffee and calls the police. It's five days since Helen said she was setting off home, told them it would take a while. She's heard nothing since, and Helen isn't answering her phone. She follows the advice from the UK Government's website to call her local station first, let them deal with the Ukrainian police via Interpol. She should be home by now, something is wrong. While she waits to be put through she searches for reports of traffic accidents in Europe, wonders if Helen is safe enough in a hospital somewhere.

She has little information to share with the officer who takes the call. He promises to contact the police in Ukraine, the Embassy.

'You know the Embassy there is under siege, don't you?'

He doesn't know.

'And the police are part of the protests? Captured or rioting?'

He doesn't know this either. Tries to calm her down, to reassure her that Helen is an adult, has probably decided to stop off somewhere on the way home. When she asks to speak to someone higher up the chain of command, he promises to look into it and get someone to call her back.

She puts the phone down and watches a video on the BBC news pages in which hooded men with metal poles smash windows and throw flaming bottles into buildings. A city called Lutsk. West of Kyiv. She checks the map again to see if Helen's route would take her through it. Possibly. Checks her email for anything from David Wellbeck and sees the backlog of missives she isn't allowed to open while suspended, but not the one she's waiting for. She tries Helen's phone again but gets the same message. *The person you are calling is unavailable.*

CHAPTER TWELVE

It is late morning and she is watching Baba Olena peel potatoes when she hears the car. The engine noise clear in the quiet of the house. It gets closer, and Baba Olena stands slowly, puts the knife on the cluttered table, and peers out of the window. She shuffles over to the bed, talking excitedly, and gestures for Helen to hunker down. Pulls the blankets right over her head. Helen is stifled, feels more weight piled over her, a heap of old clothes perhaps, to conceal her shape beneath the covers.

A man's voice. Not Anton. Loud and cheerful, confident. Sound is muffled beneath the stale material, but she can tell Baba Olena is pleased to see him. She thinks she hears the chink of glass on glass. She risks moving her hand, lifts the edge to let some air in. Holds as still as she can. They are talking, fast and loud. He laughs. Baba Olena clangs the pan on the stove, and Helen hears the hiss of fat. She resigns herself to her woven cave for a while.

She drifts off, dreams of sheep. Feels the pull of the fields like a physical cord tied around her heart. Jack always on the periphery, like she's losing him. She can feel his presence, but when she turns, he's always out of sight. The sky is vast and clean. When she wakes her face is wet with tears, and Baba Olena has pulled the blanket back.

A fat, iced cake is on the table, sealed in plastic, and there are supermarket carrier bags overflowing with dark bread, tins, packet of pasta and rice. Baba Olena tears open the cake and offers a huge slice to Helen. She is tired still, dizzy from hunger. Scoops her finger through the pink icing and sucks it greedily. Eats the rest in a few mouthfuls, to Baba Olena's delight. She offers more, and Helen eats until she feels sick.

Baba Olena is singing softly, tapping her hand on her thick thigh. The visit has brought a flush to her crumpled cheeks. A shadow passes the window, a knock. Helen goes to pull the blanket back over her, but it is Anton. Stubble shadows his skin. His hair is greasy, hanging over his eyes. He asks Baba Olena a polite question and she slices bread for him, cooks him eggs. He sits at the cluttered table and eats.

'Where have you been?'

When he looks at her his eyes are haunted, dark circles making them seem deeper set.

'Busy.'

'Doing what?'

'Are you getting better?'

She pulls the blanket back enough to expose her roughly bound knee. He swallows the bread with difficulty and looks away, embarrassed. Accepts tea from Baba Olena.

'I need my things. I have medicine in my rucksack. I need clean food.'

'This food is clean,' he gestures around the room.

'This might be, but before the guard came there's been nothing but eggs, potatoes from out there.'

Anton dips bread into a broken yolk on his plate and bites it slowly. 'This place is clean. East of the accident. Inside the Zone but safe for food.' He chews and swallows, washes down the meal with the tea. 'Safe enough.'

Helen shakes her head, frustrated. 'You could have told me.'

He shrugs. 'Why, you haven't eaten?'

'Not enough.'

He leans over and gives her a chunk of dry bread. She nibbles the corner, still nauseous from the sugar rush.

'I still need my bags, the medicine.'

'Which bag has the medicine?'

'The rucksack.' He gets up. Baba Olena follows him to the door and watches. The cat sneaks in and she hisses at it, tries to shoo it out again.

Anton returns and drops her rucksack on the bed. 'Here. I have to go.'

'Where's the rest of my stuff? My phone? My clothes? Anton!'

He's on the doorstep, pauses.

'Get my things and I'll come with you now.'

'I can't take you now, it's not safe yet. Eat, get strong.' He thanks Baba Olena and she latches the door behind him, settles into a chair.

Helen rests back against the bed, supresses a scream. She should have pushed him, insisted. Baba Olena is watching her, wary. She wonders what her relationship to Anton is. Is she his grandmother? His mother? Is she doing this out of kindness or duress? Helen forces a smile, and Baba Olena smiles back, relieved. Sets the kettle on the stove again.

Helen rummages through the rucksack, finds painkillers and takes two, hoping they will quell the tidal pounding in her forehead, give a few hours' relief. She'll save the rest for the journey out.

There is no sign of the belt bag that has her phone and

passport, no chance of calling home. She pulls out her first-aid kit and folds the blanket back. It's time to assess the wounds properly. She unties and peels back the rags around her knees, breaking the seal of crusted blood. It's a deep graze, road rash, shreds of her leathers still embedded in the gravel-gouged flesh. She cleans it with sterile wipes, breathing through her teeth at the sting. Examines it carefully, searching for pus, for radiating threads of infection moving through her veins in dark lines. It is still hot and swollen, but nothing to alarm her.

Only a surface wound.

The scar tissue will be stronger than regular skin once it's healed.

She'll survive.

She dresses it in a fresh white bandage and then checks the older cut on her hand, where the dressing she'd applied in Ivankiv is filthy, frayed. That wound is sealing well. She sticks a large plaster over it, just in case. Her other injuries have scabbed over, the road rash relatively mild thanks to her leathers. The bruising is purpled, tender. Soft-tissue damage. The painkillers are already settling her head. She might have been fine to go, had Anton waited.

When she's tidied away the mess, bagged it and packed it back in her rucksack, she curses him again for keeping her at his mercy. Imagines what she'd say to Jack if she could call him. He'll be worrying. Fingers the key that hangs around her own neck and hopes that nothing has happened while she's been gone.

***

When the cleaner's key sounds in the latch Jennifer grabs the book she took from Helen's and slips out the back door, into her wellies and raincoat. Is across the garden and down the path before she can be seen.

Spring is accelerating, spearing the ground in tiny spikes of pale green, dormant buds swelling on the branch tips. The air is tangy, a hint of warmth. She walks down the path slowly, purposelessly, focussing on the feel of knotted roots and loose stones under her soles. Deliberately steps in the dried leaves banked by the wind at the side of the path, just to hear them crunch.

When she reaches the stile, she climbs up and sits on the bar. Most of the sheep and lambs have been turned out now; the ewes' heads stretched down to the grass, cropping it short, the lambs just beginning to venture from their sides. There is a small group of them near the hedge, wobbly legs already thickening. Reedy bleats, tiny pink tongues exposed with each call.

The gorse between the field and Wylfa has erupted, yolk-yellow flowers making it seem alight. The scene is idyllic, somehow, despite the solid block of the reactors just visible over the curve of the hill. But the fields around theirs are empty, the grass already lengthening without the ruminant scything of sheep to keep it short.

There are no JCBs on the land today, nothing between her and the security fences bordering the plant. She slips off the wooden step and walks the perimeter of the field, climbs the fence at the end, cautious of the barbed wire. Strikes out over land now owned by Vista, now earmarked for car parks and workers' accommodation. Six years of building-site staff, a café and shop. The grasses here are long, dampen the bottom half of her jeans as she walks. There used to be a house just at the brow of the rise and Jennifer walks towards it, finds its footprint is a muddy trench, the foundations filled with brackish rainwater. There are signs of the old garden; a different kind of grass, soft and lush green, in a perfect rectangle, gouged through with deep tread marks. Part of the garden wall remains, a gate still hanging, and she makes her way to it, stooping to pick up something shiny on the way. A marble, greenish glass with a swirl of colour through the centre. She pockets it and walks on.

Through the gate the single-track road is dashed with mud from the digger's wheels. She follows it until she reaches the next house, only half demolished. From the road she can see into the kitchen, units covered in rubble from the partially torn roof, light patches on the walls where a kitchen clock and picture once hung. She goes inside, picking her way carefully through the debris, knowing she should have a hard hat on, that if she were caught there would be no email from David, just a P45 from HR.

In the lounge, half the furniture remains. A tired-looking sofa, dark green velour. A sideboard with a cracked glass door. There is sandy soil already collecting in the corners, brought in by the wind. Water stains spreading across the magnolia walls. She settles on the sofa, pulls out Helen's book from her deep coat pocket. *The End of the World as You Know It*. There is a glossy picture of a mushroom cloud on the front cover.

The sofa smells musty, is damp. The breeze coming through the hole in the front of the house brings the scent of the gorse flowers, coconutty and fresh, with a subtle hint of plaster dust and mould beneath it. She reads the contents page, flips to the chapter on group survival after a nuclear disaster. Helen has annotated the pages in tiny writing, circled sentences, obscured the text in places. Jennifer squints to read.

How do I convince them to come with me?

Who? Jennifer thinks.

She flicks through the pages, finds a chapter on developing mental resilience. Subheadings include 'Don't be ruled by fear, use it!', 'Test yourself now so you are ready in the future', and 'Make plans, but prepare to adapt.'

In a section entitled 'Let them go', Helen has scribbled: *does love make you weak, or stronger? Develop mental control so you can help them… see list at the back…*

Better to be alone? Child = burden, emotionally and physically, unless they old enough to help? Make him strong!

Friends = burden emotionally. Focus on who matters most.

M, D, J & I – worth the risk.

There's only so much room. Not everyone can be saved! Mam? Kinder to end it?

There is a bird somewhere in the house, she hears the rush of wings, echoes in the hall. A strange whistle as the wind picks up and rushes through the gaps and wounds from the demolition.

Override emotion when necessary.

She flicks to the back of the book. A list in tiny writing. *Goals: Safeguard farm for family, optimism despite all the odds. Believe you can beat them! Do what's best for him long-term even if it hurts short-term. Test to make sure he'll manage without me.*

She stares at the bare wall opposite. There is a crack from one corner near the ceiling, widening as it creeps downwards. The cleaner should be gone by now.

CHAPTER THIRTEEN

The cat is pregnant. Helen watches from the bed as it nests, fussing over a pile of clothes in the corner of the room, pacing and agitated. Baba Olena is outside somewhere, and Helen has spent the morning pottering around the room, trying to keep her muscles loose.

She is still tired, but now she is eating her strength is improving. The headaches have faded, the nausea receded. It's as if the tide has gone out and left her mind clean and still. The clarity is like a gift.

The cat is restless, yowling. Licking itself. Helen watches as it expels the first kitten, a bulging pink sac that the cat tears open with its rough tongue, exposing a wet, dark head. There is a faint mewling. She closes her eyes for a moment, breathes deeply. It's only a cat. And Jack is fine now. Better than fine. He might not be like other kids, but that's his strength.

She needs to make a new plan. Rummages through her rucksack and pulls out her notebook. The last week has been an unexpected trial, but if she can manage this she can emerge stronger. Survivalist websites tell her that tolerating the intolerable, accepting the situation without resigning yourself to it, is the key to managing any crisis. She cannot imagine anything more intolerable than the helplessness and physical weakness she has endured since the crash. She's had no choice but to succumb. And Anton is right. To leave before she is physically capable would put them both at risk. Jen can manage, surely?

She leafs through the notebook, reminding herself of what she's accomplished so far. Acceptance without resignation. This is how she has handled her mother's illness, Vista's campaign to take the farm, and single parenthood so far. How she coped with the discovery of the terrifying little pebble under her flesh at the edge of her breast.

She counts the days, unsure if she's tallying them right. She's missed her biopsy, she knows. But appointments can be rescheduled. Optimism, she tells herself.

She gets up, limps to the window but stops herself drawing back the net. There are dead crane flies caught in the hem. She closes her eyes and visualises the slope of the fields back home, the scent of gorse that will be carried on the breeze, the mountains in the distance. She will get home. She has to believe it, has no reason not to. No matter what dreams and paranoias the concussion has inflicted on her.

She will be patient, she will build her strength slowly, she will find her bike and see if it can be fixed. If she has to, she will wait for Anton.

Be ready, she tells herself, pulling the crane flies out of the lacework, their desiccated limbs breaking between her fingers.

***

There is an email. A meeting for the next day. Jennifer paces the kitchen, relieved and anxious in equal measure. She can't bear the confines of the house much longer, the desperate attempts to fill her time with chores. On the drive to pick Jack up from school she plans what she will wear, how she will sit. Hands resting in her lap, contrite. She looks at the power station on the way past, imagines driving back down, through the checkpoint. The comfort of her office, the scent of polish on the artificial leaves of her desk plant.

She waits by the school gate for him to trail out, is used to him being last, alone. She tries to smile at the parents standing nearby, but they are in small groups and barely glance at her.

When she is the last one waiting, she goes in. The reception is closed, the hall silent. She stands, unsure of where to go. A clock on the wall ticks loudly, it's three forty already.

A door opens behind her, an older lady in a trouser suit, holding Jack's hand. She is carrying a key fob on a lanyard.

'Ah, here she is. See, I told you peid â phoeni.'

'You okay, little man? I've been here ages!' She stoops down, reaches for him. He is mucky, his sleeves chewed, his face smeared with dirt. There is a leaf caught in a curl of his hair. She reaches to pick it out and he flinches.

'He was getting a bit worked up. A difficult day.'

'Difficult how?'

'Sit here a minute, Jack, while I talk to your aunty.'

Jack perches on the edge of a bright red plastic chair, pokes at a patch of dirt on the floor with the toe of his scuffed shoe. They move away from him, into a classroom, leaving the door open so they can watch him. It smells of floor cleaner, poster paints. The walls are cluttered with laminated verbs and nouns, the names of colours under pictures of fruit and vegetables. Gwyrdd, coch, melin, glas, marwn, piws.

They talk in low voices.

'What's happened?'

'Jack has been very distracted this week, more than usual. Very resistant to joining in.'

'His mam should be home now, she's been delayed. He's just worried.'

'I understand, but it's more than that. We've had concerns about Jack for a while now. Look, we're not really supposed to do this, but can I give you these?' She hands Jennifer a sheaf of leaflets, a sealed envelope. 'Just read through them and maybe discuss it with Helen when she gets back?'

'Shouldn't you talk to her yourself?'

The teacher looks at her, as if trying to phrase her reply carefully before speaking. 'We've spoken about it numerous times already. Helen is, understandably, resistant to acknowledging Jack might need special help. It's often hard to recognise the traits when you are close to someone, a single parent. Sometimes it helps to discuss it with family before making a decision to pursue formal assessment.'

'Are you saying there's something wrong with him?'

'Not wrong, just different. We just want to help him, and without a formal diagnosis our hands are tied.'

Jennifer shoves the leaflets in her handbag and tries to take Jack's hand to lead him back to the car, but he pulls away, trails behind her. Stops to crouch and pick up a beetle that is traversing the pavement. He carries it in cupped hands until they reach the car, and then releases it into the grass verge, watching it scuttle off through the fronds and disappear.

Back home she runs him a bath, fills the soapy water with plastic toys, offers to play with him. When he refuses to undress in front of her she makes sure the bathroom door is propped open and sits on the landing, listens to him drop his clothes on the floor and slip into the water, then calls through.

'What would you like to do tonight?'

'Dw i ddim yn gwybod.'

'You must know. What do you like doing most? TV? We could play a game together.'

'Chwarae allan.'

'You can't play outside, little man, it's already getting dark.'

She listens to him splash, the soothing sound of water lapping the side of the tub. The synthetic fragrance of bubble-bath fills the landing. Lavender and camomile. When the plug gurgles she fetches a warm towel from the airing cupboard and holds it around the door for him. He comes out, wrapped and pink, still steaming. She scoops him up and carries him to his bedroom. At first he wriggles to get free, then relaxes, lets her sit beside him on the bed with an arm around him.

'She'll be back soon, I promise.'

He leans into her, ever so slightly, and she tightens her hold.

'Shall I read you a story?'

'I can read.'

'I know, but it's nice to be read to, isn't it?'

He shrugs. She looks around for books, finds his copy of *The Secret Island*, tattered and soft around the edges. When she opens it the pages are dog-eared, and there are notes in pencil in the margins, both in Helen and Jack's hand.

'What's this story about? Where have you got to?'

'There are these children, and they have to go and live with their cruel aunty and uncle. And they hate it, so they run away to live on an island.'

'On their own?'

'They take a cow.'

She flicks through the pages. Down the side of one which describes the children pilfering supplies from the larder for their escape, Helen has written *if you are on your own, think about how much you could actually carry – nothing you have to cook!* Jack has made a list beside it: *Chokolat, Crips, nuTs.* Helen has added *WATER.*

***

Helen holds onto the back of a chair and eases the weight off her injured side. Flexes her knee. The cat watches her with yellow eyes. There are three kittens and she is nursing two of them. The third is on the edge of the nest of clothes, silent.

She has taken two more painkillers, is drinking more tea to hydrate her brain. She read somewhere that concussions take roughly a week to ten days to ease properly. Not long now. She stretches her leg to its full extension and feels the tightness in her hamstrings. How quickly the body loses condition if not used.

She needs to move, to *do* something. Begins tidying, making the bed, picking through the clutter on the table. She arranges medicine bottles in a neat row, trying to decipher the contents and their use, winds loose thread back onto the reel and tucks the bobbins neatly into their box. She is sweeping the floor when she hears Baba Olena's arrhythmic shuffle in the porch. Helen tenses, realising her actions may have been intrusive.

Baba Olena stops midway into the room, looks around, as if trying to calculate what has changed. Comes to the table and moves a few things, nods, tight-lipped, then looks at Helen standing there in her pants and T-shirt holding the broom, and laughs. Is still chuckling as she rummages through the piles of stale clothes and finds Helen a loose skirt to wear, thick socks and a vast cardigan.

Helen stands, obedient, while Baba Olena pins the waistband tight around her middle to stop the skirt sliding over her hips. No shoes though. When the old woman pulls a headscarf from a bag of bright fabric Helen pauses, feels a tingling fear that to tie it over her hair is to accept her place here. The woman reaches up and folds the cloth over her hair, tying the knot beneath her chin, an expression in her eyes that Helen finds unsettling. Smiles and nods then shuffles towards the door, beckoning. The knot is tight, like the chinstrap of her helmet, makes her feel like she's choking. What if Anton doesn't come back? She tries adjusting it, then ties it again at the nape of her neck. It will keep her hair off her face at least, in the absence of her biker buff or hair tie.

The floorboards creak as Baba Olena steps out into the crisp early evening light. Helen follows. There is no sign of frost, but the air still hangs low and misty over a wide garden. Helen curls her toes on the threshold, sucking in the fresh air.

The sky has never tasted so clean.

Scrawny hens scratch at the mud and pebbles between the sodden yellowed grass stalks. Baba Olena is pointing, across the garden and towards a small field, where half the soil has been turned ready for a new crop of beets and potatoes. The sun is low, pale. A half-light blurring the view. Helen is distracted by the sound of birds chorusing in the trees that encroach on the boundaries of the little smallholding; she can pick out the songs of great tits and wood warblers, tree pipits and chaffinches. She closes her eyes for a moment and is back home; the window of the barn open, a breeze bringing the sounds of evening in. Jack beside her, where he belongs. The rock in her chest seems to grow heavier. He's probably fine, probably enjoying TV and sweets and barely thinking about her. Isn't that what she wanted? To fray the cord a little?

She opens her eyes and tries to focus on the landscape; the wide lawn, a cluster of wooden and corrugated steel outbuildings, a hefty tree branch stuck into the ground with large glass jars, enamelled buckets and aluminium pans placed upside down over the end of each uplifted offshoot, creating the impression of a cookware tree. The perimeter tangled with shrubs like barbed wire penning her in. She can't see any sign of other houses beyond the trees, any smoke rising to hint at a neighbour, but they could be there.

Baba Olena is speaking, so fast that even if Helen understood the language she'd struggle to make out the words. She clutches Helen's arm, ushers her back inside, where the smoky air chokes her and the fetid smell hits her throat like a punch.

The room feels claustrophobic after the clear air and space outside. Helen goes to another pile of clothes and starts folding them, needing something to do to stop her walking out and across the garden in the woollen socks, to stop her running. Be ready, but be patient, she tells herself. The headache is returning, and she will have to nap soon.

She glances at the cat; it is hunched over, crunching the soft bones of the stillborn kitten. Behind it the blind babies mew with open pink mouths.

***

'Any news from Helen? You said you were going to email the tour companies. Did they reply?' Ioan's head is in the fridge, his hands rooting out a post-shift snack.

'No. Well, they replied. I found the one who took her, but they just said she was dropped off. Some little town between Chernobyl and Kyiv. That's where their contract ended.'

'And the police?' He sits at the table opposite, picks at a chicken leg.

'They've filed it as a missing person case now, and alerted the police over there, but I don't think they are taking it very seriously. I mean, surely they should get the Foreign Office involved or something? A British citizen missing in a war zone? They just keep saying the same thing – she's an adult, she might just want some space.'

'Maybe she does. It's been pretty full-on with your mam and everything.'

'No, she'd never go away, not with the new plant to fight.'

'And yet she did.' Ioan gets up, fetches a beer.

'But she was coming home, Ioan. She was on her way back.'

'She did say it might take her a while.'

'Well, if she's not back by tomorrow I might call the Foreign Office myself.'

Ioan nods, licks chicken grease from his thick fingers. 'Good idea. How was Jack today? Coping?'

'Read this.' Jennifer holds out a typed page, busies herself with loading the dishwasher while he reads. By the time she's finished, he's leaning back in his chair, sipping the beer.

'You're not on shift tomorrow?'

'I am, days.'

She reaches and takes the beer from him. 'Then you shouldn't be drinking.'

'One beer is alright, Jen. I've had a long day.'

'The training says all staff must be fit for work. Not tired, hungover or distracted.'

'You been swotting up for your meeting then?' He reaches for the bottle and she lifts it higher. He laughs, raises his hands in submission. 'Chwarae teg, I'll abstain!'

'So, what do you think?' She gestures to the document lying on the table.

'All looks good, I don't see the problem.'

'Were you reading the same report as me?' She snatches it back, glances over the teacher's statements.

'What?'

'She isn't exactly happy, is she?'

'What do you mean? She says he's smart, quiet.'

'And struggles with concentration, socialising and communication.'

'It does not say that!'

'It does, just not as bluntly as I just did.'

Ioan frowns, takes the report back and scrutinises it.

'Hang on, how do you get that out of this? I thought it all sounded good.'

'Okay, when she writes "He clearly has an active imagination, we just need to bring that back into the task he's supposed to be working on", what do you see?'

'He has a great imagination.'

'Well, I see "He doesn't concentrate and is easily

distracted". It's clear he spends more time watching squirrels out of the window than focussing on his work.'

'He's only five.'

'He's nearly six.'

'Five, six, either way, I'd rather watch squirrels,' Ioan grins. 'And I've seen him concentrate fine – he helps his mam out loads, listens and follows instructions. He's capable. Much more than I was his age.' They move through to the lounge.

'Okay, but I'm more worried about the socialising.'

'Oh, I'm sure he's fine.' Ioan looks longingly at the remote control on the coffee table.

'Name one.'

'What?'

'When has he ever mentioned another kid from school?'

'He's only been there...'

'Nearly eighteen months. She said he spends most of his break times on his own, collecting pebbles or shells and arranging them in neat little lines. Not playing football. Not playing tag.'

'But you asked her if he was being bullied and she said no. He's just not one of the loud kids, not an attention seeker.'

'She said last week he was scaring the other kids. She didn't say how, but you didn't see how he was playing the night of the blackout. It was... creepy.'

'Kids play creepy games. Me and Gareth used to kill each other daily, with stick guns and stuff. It's normal.'

'She clearly thinks it isn't. That Helen should get him assessed.'

'What for?'

She waves the leaflets at him. 'Autism, ADHD, Asperger's Syndrome.'

'He doesn't need to be assessed, he's fine.'

'Is he? How are we supposed to know? We don't know what he is. We don't know who his father is, what he was like. And Helen is… different.'

'They want everyone testing these days. Normal is a relative term.'

Jennifer sighs and kneels by the fire, uses the tongs to place a few more coals in its glowing centre. 'I'm not convinced he has any of those things either. I think it's Helen.'

'Helen?'

'She isolates him, teaches him all this survival stuff. It makes it hard for him to just be a kid.'

'What survivalist stuff?'

'All kinds of stuff. Skinning rabbits, hoarding food.'

'Listen, all kids are different. So he isn't outgoing, it'll come. He's happy enough, Helen's happy enough. That's what matters.'

'Is he happy? Is she? I'm not sure either of them are.'

'Well, I know this battle with Vista is bothering her, but apart from that—'

'It isn't just the new plant. She's always been… I don't know… quiet? She didn't speak for two whole months when we were kids. Completely withdrew. She's seemed so much more in control recently. As if helping Mam and fighting Wylfa B has given her confidence somehow. But now I wonder…' She sits beside him, tucks her feet up.

'You're over thinking it, Jen.' He yawns.

'Or you're under thinking it.'

Ioan sighs and runs both hands through his hair. 'Why do you have to analyse everything? It is what it is.'

'Except we don't really know what it is. I'm worried...'

'I know you are, but don't. Not about Jack anyway. He's a kid, a boy. Skinning rabbits isn't the worst thing he could do.' He squeezes her thigh and gets up, stretches. 'I need to sleep. Are you coming up?'

'Not yet, I need to prep for tomorrow.'

He's at the door before she asks, 'Do you think we should get him a puppy? You know, something to nurture? A companion?'

Ioan pauses and rubs his stubbled chin. 'Maybe, but not without checking with Helen first.'

'What if she doesn't come back?'

'Then we'll get him a puppy. Then we'll do anything for him. But she will.' He comes back, strokes a strand of hair from her forehead and stoops to kiss her.

After he has gone she flicks through the leaflets again. There are diagnostic indicators she can match with his behaviour and the teacher's concerns, but she isn't quite convinced. Children are what you make them, she thinks. Everything they experience feeds into who they become. And Helen has been feeding him fear.

Part Three

γ

CHAPTER FOURTEEN

Helen sits by the table, skirt pulled up so she can pick at the scabs around the bandage on her knee. The kittens are fluffy, squirming. Baba Olena gives the nursing mother strips of fat, a raw egg cracked onto a saucer. Special treatment. They will be useful, ratters, when they are old enough.

Baba Olena is busy, the season demanding her time outside. At home Helen would be preparing the soil for her own potatoes, letting Jack press seeds into compost in covered trays on the windowsills. She wants to go out and work, feel the give and return of the earth beneath a spade, but there is only one pair of boots and Baba is wearing them.

Now she is feeling better they have fallen into a tentative routine. After breakfast Helen washes the dishes while Baba Olena prepares to go outside, indicates small jobs Helen might do: stitching, sweeping the floor, folding clothes. Helen paces herself. In between tasks she stands on the porch until her toes go numb with cold. Listens hard for sounds of Anton returning.

When her head demands she rest, she lies on the bright scratchy blankets of the bed decoding the old woman's life. Apart from irregular visits by the guards, the cat, and hens in the yard, Baba Olena is alone. Helen always thought she herself was adept at being solitary but compared to Baba Olena her life is a hive of negotiated relationships. Her parents,

Ioan and Jen, and Jack with her like a shadow, so serious. Even when he is at school and she is alone out in the fields, nothing but the caw of crows trailing her as she patches fences or scatters sheep nuts, her mind is always full of whose needs she must fulfil next.

Here, while Baba Olena is out tending the land, Helen feels completely alone. Severed. Wanders around the house touching things, trying to connect, but failing. This is Baba Olena's life, completely hers. Just like the barn back home is her own. She watches the old woman lifting eggs from her apron, stacking the pans after a meal, rearranging the things Helen has tidied, and sees the symbiosis of person and place from an outsider's vantage point, realises that solitude is the price the woman wilfully paid for being home, for being here. Returning to her vegetable patches and smoky stove despite the risks and warnings. She remembers reading an article on the self-settlers years ago, one of them saying that leaving was like dying. When asked if they feared radiation they replied, what is there to fear? I'd rather die slowly at home than quickly anywhere else.

Helen teases the edge of a scab, rust brown and flaking, and blood beads on her knee. She is still more tired than usual. Tomorrow she wants to find her bike, today she bides her time.

Baba Olena comes in and checks the room, gestures to Helen to move one of the stacks of clothes to another chair, then potters to the stove. Helen has started a stew of vegetables from storage crates in the porch. Baba Olena makes tea, shucks off her boots and stretches her feet towards the comfort of the fire, encourages Helen to come and help her sew. They've been doing this the last few evenings, embroidering scarves with bright stitches along the hems, darning threadbare socks until the low light and concentration have built behind her eyes and she's stopped, the yarns resting in colourful loops in her lap. The kind of jobs she is used to doing at home, on winter nights. Teaching Jack how to thread a needle, the tip of his tongue visible as he concentrates.

But now she is restless. Gestures to borrow Baba Olena's boots. Brown leather, shapeless, the soles crushed by overuse. They are still hot from her feet. Helen kisses thanks onto the woman's wind-chilled cheeks.

She gathers up a stack of dirty pots and crouches on the step in the early evening light, scrubbing pans while the old woman rests. Takes her time, trying to soothe herself with the ritual, the simplicity of it. Cook, clean, hang, sweep. Therapeutic. Like the routines at home. Building her strength for the next challenge. She uses a stained cloth to rub the last traces of an oily tomato sauce from an enamelled bowl, then shuffles across the muddy grass towards the cookware tree and hangs the pans to dry. The boots are too big, slip as she walks.

The temperature has lifted a few degrees and leaves are unfurling on the shrubs and trees beside the house. The air is moist. The house is small against the backdrop of the forest, decaying. She delays returning, rearranges some pans, her ears tuned to any sounds that might signal the guards stopping by or Anton returning. She thinks back to the night in Ivankiv, the fight. Without her phone she can't check the status of the protests, if they've escalated. He could have been beaten to death like the civilians in Independence Square. She catches her breath at the thought, surprised by an unwanted feeling of loss, grits her teeth. He's had long enough.

Her things are not in the house, but she hasn't yet explored the outbuildings. She starts with the sheds, easing back the rusty bolts and peering in.

There are tools, a woodturner, in one. Pieces of half-finished furniture in another. She makes her way in the baggy boots to the biggest barn, a low, wide construction of corrugated metal and rough planks.

At first, she can barely see in the gloom. There are two small windows of scratched and filthy perspex, but no electric bulb to illuminate the space. She can smell something raw and savoury amid the dank must of the building, and the industrial tang of petrol.

As her eyes adjust, she sees it. On the other side of the barn the carcass of the boar hangs, open and eviscerated, from a metal hook in the ceiling. Beneath there is a bucket of congealing blood. Flies. There are sections missing, hacked away.

Helen goes further in, stands beside the body. She is glad the boar wasn't wasted, left to rot beside the road. She runs a hand over the bristled flank of the animal. Tries to conjure the accident – the pitted road, a burst of energy from the side, the feeling of her bike being torn from her hands, but there is still a black hole where the memory should be. She is imagining it, that's all. And in her imagination her bike is just scratched, dented. She turns back as if she might see it now, propped in the corner, needing only a smashed headlight bulb to be replaced, or a tear in the seat to be sealed with tape. It isn't here.

She starts searching. Finds her helmet on the floor tucked amid old feed bags and rusting farm equipment, its visor cracked and smeared. Hope beating in her chest, she starts moving wooden pallets and old sacks, rolls of chicken wire and cracked sheets of corrugated plastic made opaque with thick black lichen. Finds the panniers under a workbench close to the door, and above them, among oil-stained overalls, her leathers; torn and bloodstained like the pelt of a wild animal, the collar hooked over a rusty nail. She reaches up and fingers the ragged hole in the knee, feels the sting mirrored in her own flesh. Each injury, each bruise and cut, is mapped out on the contours of the skin.

She hears Baba Olena calling her from the porch. Looks around quickly for anything else of hers and then lifts the panniers and goes out into the thin winter sunlight.

'Chashka chayu?'

Helen has picked up a few words, enough to reply.

'Ni, dyakuyu.' She doesn't want tea, or anything. She sits on porch step and opens the panniers, pulls out her clothes Anton must have shoved in there, the belt bag. Her phone. She holds it carefully, as if it is a rare egg. Presses the button on the side and Jack's face, pixelated, appears on the screen once it's loaded. There is no signal.

She closes her eyes.

The trees creak in the breeze, and birds are squabbling in the tangled undergrowth that borders the broken garden fence. The hens scratch and croon, and beneath her the wooden stoop is solid and stable. She reaches a hand up and runs it over the smooth, weatherworn timber of the rail, then heaves herself up. Walks the boundary of the garden and field, holding the phone out, trying to catch a signal from a distant transmitter.

Nothing.

She goes back to the porch and picks up her panniers and the scattered clothes. Once inside she runs the dosimeter over everything and hears only the crackle of background radiation. Gets changed into her own things, at last. In her jeans and long-sleeved T-shirt she feels stronger. She folds the borrowed skirt and cardigan carefully and lays them respectfully on the nearest pile. Stands her Doc Martens beside the door next to Baba Olena's old brown boots.

When the food is ready Baba Olena serves and they eat in silence. Side by side in front of the stove, feet stretched towards the heat.

***

[Rusty fairground. Dead trees, grey sky. Ferris wheel motionless. Cracked concrete beneath tilted dodgems. Moss oozing through, seeking sunlight.]

Jennifer sits half dressed in the bedroom, her shirt unbuttoned, her phone in her hand. Ioan is downstairs already, packing his lunch box. The kitchen radio is on, and she can hear music through the floorboards, faint. Occasionally Ioan's voice rises in volume to join it.

[Rusty sign. Toxic yellow, faded, pitted with orange and brown. Pinned to barbed wire. Black trefoil warning. Symbols, Cyrillic, separating dark earth from blue sky.]

Jennifer hears the quick, light thud of Jack's feet as he goes downstairs. She pulls the duvet across her bare legs as another spatter of rain hits the window. There is sunshine out there too. Maybe a rainbow. But the curtains are still closed.

[Building site. Curved steel arcing into sky above scaffolding. In the corner of the frame a dark smudge.]

Helen's finger? Jennifer reads the caption. *The new sarcophagus.*

The picture is dated nearly two weeks ago.

[Murky brown-green water. Fat catfish breaching the surface. Scales and whiskers, golden. Sunlight glinting in the eddies made by their tails – bright white light.]

She's seen this picture before. She's seen all of them. She presses the little button on the side of her phone to make the screen go black. Slips on smart black trousers, powders her face to cover the dark circles and applies mascara. She's barely slept.

In the kitchen Ioan is packing Jack's school bag. Jack sits at the table eating crumpets spread thickly with chocolate spread. He is swinging his legs, his foot catching the table leg.

Tock.

'Did you want some lunch, are you there all day?' Ioan asks.

Tock.

'I'm not sure. Leave it, I can nip to the canteen if I'm allowed to stay.'

Tock.

'I'll take Jack this morning, give you an extra few minutes?'

Tock.

'No. No, I want to. I'm ready.'

Tock.

'You haven't eaten anything yet.'

Tock.

'I'm not hungry. Hey, little man?'

Tock.

'Yes?'

Tock.

'Quit kicking the table, please?'

Tock.

'Okay.'

Tock.

'Now. Okay?'

'You sure you're alright? You look pale?' Ioan wipes Jack's fingers and face with the dishcloth. 'Buddy, go and brush your teeth.'

Tock.

The chair screeches across the tiles as he pushes away from the table.

'Quickly now,' Ioan calls after him. 'We're going to be late.'

'I'm fine, just a headache. Meet for lunch, if it goes well?'

'It will. Bet they've been lost without you.' He puts his bag down and holds her, kisses the top of her head. She squeezes back. 'Gotta go.'

He's nearly out the front door before Jennifer calls out.

'About the fish…'

'What fish?'

'Do you remember that guy from site management, what's his name? Seventies moustache bloke?'

'Alan?'

'Maybe, anyway, do you remember him talking about the fish near the outlet, the sea bass? He said it was the best place to fish because they were bigger and there were so many of them.'

'Vaguely, why?' Ioan zips up his jacket, one hand on the doorknob.

'I was just thinking. Is it true? Are they bigger there?'

'Probably. The water's warmer there. Do you want me to ask him?'

'No.'

'Maybe he could sell us one, for dinner.' He laughs. 'Maybe that's what's on the menu in the canteen.'

'God, I hope not.' She laughs too. 'I wouldn't eat anything he's handled.'

'So, what made you think of the fish?' He's coming back into the room, head tilted, a look of concern ruching his eyes at the corners.

'I don't know. You're going to be late. Go.' She kisses him and turns away, busying herself with her laptop bag.

When the front door finally slams, Jennifer reaches into the cupboard and takes down a packet of ibuprofen. She considers trying to wash the medicine down with water, but knows she'd end up gagging as usual, has never been able to take tablets properly. She takes two spoons from the drawer and crushes the pills into a powder, mixing the grains with a teaspoonful of chocolate spread. When she raises the spoon, she notices Jack is back from the bathroom, watching her with his mackerel-grey eyes.

'What are you doing?'

'Just having a snack.'

'You put pills in it.'

'It's just medicine.'

'Are you scared?' He fingers the frayed sleeve of his school jumper.

'No, why do you think that?'

'Because you have to go back there. Because you might die.'

Jennifer drops the spoon in the sink and screws the lid on the jar. She has no idea how to answer him.

He slips his hand into hers. 'You don't have to be scared. Everybody dies.'

'I'm not going to die, little man. I'm just going to work.' She pulls away; the intensity, the heat of his small fingers gripping her, too much. 'Come on, let's get you to school.'

In the car Jack sits in the back, strapped tightly into his child seat, swinging his feet into the back of the passenger seat.

'What kind of medicine?'

Thud.

'For a headache.'

Thud.

'Why have you got a headache? Are you sick?'

Thud.

'No, just tired. And please don't kick the seat.'

Thud.

In the rear-view mirror Jennifer sees him forming another question, puts on the CD of Disney film themes she bought for him as a distraction. He slumps back into his seat, turns away to look out of the window as the fields, hedges and stone walls merge into gardens and houses. His legs hang limp. Outside the school she forces the car door open against the wind, holding it awkwardly to prevent it being pulled from her hand and slamming shut, or being wrenched away. When they get to the school gates Jack is already drifting away, walking towards the trees at the side of the playground.

'Come back a minute.'

He turns and Jennifer sees the sky in his eyes.

'Come here a minute, little man.'

He pauses, then walks back.

'Let me say goodbye properly. I love you.' She squeezes his thin shoulders then releases him. 'Don't worry about me, okay? Don't worry about anything. Have a good day.'

'I will.' He turns away and walks through the gates, his small frame consumed by a crowd of children with similar coats and hats. He glances back once, and half waves, then is gone.

Jennifer reaches a hand up to her face to shield it from a sudden flurry of icy rain. Dashes back to the car and tries to breathe slowly behind the protective shell of the roof and windshield. Around her the surge of coats and hats and umbrellas swells as the final dash to the school gates peaks. Reds and blues and greens blur past her window through the rivulets of water sliding down the glass.

Pulling away from the school, she follows the other cars back to the main road, queuing at the junction to turn right. Her headache is still throbbing behind her brows, her eyes gritty from lack of sleep. Hands white on the wheel as she waits for a break in the traffic, for a gap big enough to accelerate into. Each time she has the chance she pauses a fraction of a second too long and misses it. Eventually the car behind sounds its horn and she jumps, blinking, and stamps her foot down, moving a few feet before the engine stalls.

Red in the face, feeling like her skin is burning, she starts the engine and lurches forward, cutting up an oncoming car and pressing hard on the pedal to move herself out of its way.

She is still trembling from the adrenalin rush when she sees the rainbow, its watercolour palette arcing in pale defiance of the rain behind her. It stretches from the plant right over the road and into a field.

The car behind overtakes her, and she pulls in, puts her hazard lights on and tries to let go of the wheel for a moment. Her fingers ache. The plant hunkers on the coastline, its colours muted and merging with the sea and sky behind the rain on the car window. It looks closed: no windows, no lights showing her where her colleagues sit checking their emails and drinking coffee. It looks like a military base.

A pylon stands beside the road, huge and armoured, its wires swooping in a circumzenithal arc above the car. Identical structures echo out across the fields to her right. She leans forwards to look up at the geometric latticework of steel, but it makes her nauseous. She looks away instead, tries to focus on the rainbow, on the message of hope it is supposed to bring. That's what she's been told since childhood, but she knows it's just an optical illusion – reflection and refraction, a dispersal of light through water droplets.

Her meeting is in fifteen minutes.

The car rocks slightly in the wind.

She closes her eyes and concentrates on what she should say and do. Sit quietly, hands resting in her lap. Contrite. The biggest risk to a nuclear power station is human error, hubris. She has read in the last few days about how the safety systems were disabled in Reactor Four before the routine test at Chernobyl, the manual disengagement of automatic shutdown mechanisms that might have prevented the explosion. Reviewed the reports acknowledging that the Fukushima disaster was foreseeable, that the company operating the plant had failed to meet basic safety requirements including adequate risk assessments, preparations to contain collateral damage, and suitable evacuation plans. Human error. Opening a door during a nuclear incident drill, letting God knows what in. But the purpose of such drills is to learn. She will agree to anything they suggest: extra training, a full safety audit, supervision. She has worked too hard scaling the ranks to give up now.

She opens her eyes and stares forwards, fixing her attention on the highest point of the rainbow as it fades out. She feels it physically, a shift in perception as if an optician has leaned in close and placed a corrective lens in front of one eye, sharpened her view for a moment; the land to her left is empty, great swathes of mud cutting through the fields where the bulldozers have been. The row of terraces on the edge of the village is a pile of bricks behind security fencing, yellow signs warning of danger flapping in the wind. If she turned, she would see her parents' farm behind her, defiant and small.

The rainbow is consumed by a bank of indigo cloud, the sunlight behind her illuminating the shining steel of the pylon in bright relief. She continues to stare straight ahead as if by doing so she might will herself to emerge from this new view of the landscape.

She focusses hard on the task ahead.

She must go into work. She must put the car into gear and pass through security and smile at her colleagues and re-check her make-up and shake David Wellbeck's hand firmly and sit in a formal room and answer questions. She must engage the gears, check the mirrors and then indicate, press her foot down incrementally on the accelerator and follow the tarmac to the car park. She must show her pass to the security guards and say hi to them over the machine guns positioned across their chests in case of terrorist attack, clip her dosimeter onto her belt or pocket and move through the steel cage turnstile that separates her job from the rest of the world. She must sip coffee and reply confidently but apologetically to the questions they ask her. She must nod and smile and ensure that if they ask her to stay she calls the after-school club to book Jack in and if Helen doesn't come home she must apply for custody, ensure he doesn't get taken into care and she realises she can't breathe out anymore, only in, and the pain in her head has spread to her chest and it feels like it's tightening and her hands prickle like she's holding a fistful of nettles and her vision is blurring until her eyes close and she is dying, dying sitting in a car five minutes from work, and home, and her dad's, and the pain in her head throbs like Jack's foot against the table leg or the back of the car seat. Tock. Thud. Tock. Thud. Tock. Thud.

The noise is outside her head.

When she opens her eyes, there is a face at the car window, a mouth shaping the words 'Are you alright?' amid a grey sheet of rain.

She can't answer, only leans back and away. Away from the concerned frown, the neat grey beard that drips so close to the glass, the woollen hat pulled down over the stranger's ears.

He reaches for the handle and her hand darts out to hit the button on the dashboard that triggers the central locking. The car beeps and the lights flash once to tell the concerned passer-by that he is not allowed in, not allowed to touch her or try to make her feel better. He raises his hands in defeat, walks away shaking his head, and when he's gone she sinks down, half lying on the passenger seat until the dizziness subsides.

She is damp with cold sweat.

Can't go into work, not like this.

After maybe ten minutes she sits up slowly and assesses the scene. The clouds part briefly, and sunlight cuts through in long, bright blades. The fields glitter, holding the rain and returning the sun. No. She is late, but not attending would be worse. She can blame the traffic. After a false start, she manages to pull the car away from the kerb and drive slowly and carefully towards the turning, dropping to ten miles an hour on the access road in line with the speed limit signs, easing the car over the speedbumps.

She checks and double-checks her dosimeter, powders her nose in the small strip of mirror behind the sun-visor. Reminds herself of the safety regulations: be fit for work at all times, walk on the left, hold the handrails on the stairs, report any trip hazards immediately, use PPE in designated areas, recalibrate the dosimeter yearly, follow all procedures to the letter.

She is smiling when she reaches the turnstile and the armed guard. He doesn't seem to notice her hand shaking as she holds out her pass for inspection.

CHAPTER FIFTEEN

She wakes early, takes painkillers with tea and sits on the step until dawn has leaked through the trees and she can hear Baba Olena busy in the kitchen. Helen fetches eggs from the nesting boxes, toasts the last of the stale bread over the grate. When they have eaten she pulls on her boots.

She packs her rucksack with bottles of water, checks there are still snacks in the side pockets. Unfolds the paper map of the Zone that Sergey gave her and shows Baba Olena. The woman squints at the faded, streaky ink. Helen points at the floor, then at the map. Raises her eyebrows in query.

Baba Olena frowns, runs a finger over the paper, then taps. There are no roads marked out, but at least she has an idea of where she is, pulls out a compass and calculates which direction Anton must have taken.

She doesn't know how to tell Baba Olena she will be back later, tries to draw on the back of the map, symbols for herself, an arrow leading away and back. The woman nods and pats Helen's shoulder. Perhaps she will be relieved to have some time alone.

At the side of the house is a faded gate, latched. She slips out, alert to the sounds of the forest. If she hears a car engine she'll have to hide. She turns the dosimeter on and clips it to her belt, decides she will only heed its chatter if the alarm sounds.

The road beside the track is overgrown. Opposite, what must have been a field or pasture is now long brown grass and young trees, buds bulging in anticipation of warmer weather, ready to erupt. She checks the compass again and strikes out, walking at a gentle pace so as not to wear herself out. Pauses as she reaches a bigger road, pitted with shallow, dirt-filled potholes. There has been no sign of any other houses, so Baba Olena's home must be at the edge of a village, the other cottages lost to the web of undergrowth beyond her garden.

She walks, her joints aching and head feeling tighter and tighter with each step. After fifteen minutes she stops and drinks, then presses on. Searching for signs of the crash: gouged gravel, bloodstains, broken branches at the side of the road. As the sun moves higher her eyes begin to hurt. The flickering light through the trees makes it feel like she's walking underwater. After an hour she wonders if this is even the right road. After two she turns around.

She eats a flapjack slowly, focussing on the sweet, heavy mash in her mouth as she chews. Slows her pace. It's fine, she thinks. I'll try again tomorrow. But disappointment sours the food.

It must be the direction she is taking. The new perspective. She catches a glint first, something bright piercing the undergrowth. Automatically squints and turns her eyes away. Two more steps and she sees a single splintered branch. Fractured but not detached. There are no signs on the road, rain must have washed away any tracks. But there is a kind of dip in the undergrowth where the grasses haven't sprung back up completely, and she steps off the road and into the ditch, treading carefully so as not to turn an ankle.

The dosimeter stutters.

She pulls away a loose tangle of branches. Sees the black curve of the fuel tank scraped, as if a wolf has clawed its flank. She can smell the tang of petrol though the wet mulch.

She squats and runs her hand over the bike, as if it is a wounded animal. Inspects it. The front wheel is buckled, the petrol tank leaked dry. The handlebars are clotted with mud.

The dosimeter purrs, chatters.

She tries to lift it and feels her lack of strength, the ache in her wrist. Her head pounds with the effort. She tries again, groaning almost loud enough to match the squeal of the alarm from the dosimeter on her belt. Drops it quick. The bike sinks lower into the brush, creaking.

What has she disturbed?

Birds shriek above as if answering the little yellow machine. She steps back a few paces and the alarm stops. A cricket chirp of static remains. She wipes sweat from her face with the headscarf and thinks. Baba Olena must have fuel in her shed, left over from farm machinery. She smelt it when she found her bags. But can she fix the buckled wheel? Patch the tank? Is it worth the risk?

She climbs back onto the road, swigs water and feels the tension ease as the dosimeter slows to background pace. At least she knows where it is.

She starts to walk away then pauses. Goes back, ties the headscarf over her mouth and nose and pulls branches over the carcass, despite the chatter from her belt. It's important to bury your dead, she thinks as she walks home.

Closure.

She can make a new plan now.

As she walks, she wonders if she would ever do what Baba Olena has done. Return to a place half toxic, needing to be home despite the abandonment all around. Anton said her place was clean, and Helen knows that there are areas outside the Zone that have higher radiation levels than some inside. Belarus took a heavy hit, but no one talks about that on the tourist sites. There are still people living in villages that should have been evacuated and weren't. But home is home. And fences can't contain contamination.

It drifts.

When she gets close to the house she runs the dosimeter over her trousers and boots, notes only a tiny jump in the reading, and turns it off, tucking it back into the side pocket of her rucksack. In the yard Baba Olena comes towards her with her hands outstretched. Pulls her in for a hug. It's as if she knows Helen has failed. Helen holds her back, wishing this was her mam: strong and solid in her arms. Then turns away and walks back outside. Rinses the headscarf carefully and hangs it to dry, then sits in the field holding her phone until the light begins to fade and her jeans are sodden at the seat from the damp earth. Watches a snail traverse a cracked plant pot, then teases its sticky foot off the ceramic rim and lets it unfurl and spiral her fingers, welcoming the solid rock of pain that fills her chest as she thinks of Jack, tries to imagine him here, beside her.

After an hour or more Baba Olena brings her tea, and when she reaches her hand up to show her the snail, the old woman plucks it off Helen's hand and drops it into the salty tub that sits beside the barn along with the other slugs and snails that risk her crops, and nods, satisfied, wiping her wizened hands on her apron. Practical.

Helen takes a deep breath and gathers her thoughts. Runs through her options: waiting for Anton, or striking out on foot, alone. Tests, briefly, the idea of staying. Letting whatever is swelling in the tissues of her chest overcome her, no longer being stretched taut by the needs of others. Perhaps Jack would be better off without her. A part of her is tempted.

***

Jennifer is on the phone when Ioan comes into the kitchen holding the lamb.

'It's been well over a week since we heard from her. No. Look I know there's a lot going on over there but surely someone can…'

'Jen, here, take this.'

'What? No, I told you already, we don't have her itinerary. The tour company dropped her off in…' She pauses to check the email on the screen in front of her. 'Ivankiv. She should have been home ages ago.'

'Jen, here.'

'No. She's never done this before. No, like I said, we've had no contact with her for… Ioan, I'm on the phone!'

Ioan thrusts a dirty towel wrapped around a tiny lamb into her arms and shrugs off his coat. He begins to strip off in the kitchen, carefully easing his bloodstained sweater over his face and then peeling off his soaked trousers, shoving it all straight into the washing machine. Jennifer holds the bundle to her chest with one hand, awkwardly.

'Okay, yes. No, I understand. I'll call back tomorrow though.' She cancels the call and tosses the phone onto the table. 'What is going on?'

The lamb wriggles in her lap, and then settles. She looks down at the blood and fluid-streaked face, the golden letter-box eyes. Feels the weight in her arms and knows, vaguely, in the back of her mind, she should feel tenderness.

'We lost a ewe. It was a fucking mess. I tried calling you to come and help, but your mobile went straight to voicemail. Didn't you hear the landline?'

'I was on the phone to the police.'

'And?' Ioan takes the lamb and begins rubbing it with the towel.

'And nothing. They say they've not had any reports of British citizens being caught up in the demonstrations, and then they gave me the same line as usual.' Unburdened of the lamb she starts pacing around the room, her hand resting briefly on pieces of furniture as she passes: the back of a chair, the edge of the dresser, the curve of the sink.

'Can you get me a box? Anything, cardboard'll do.'

'Did you hear me? She's still missing and they're not doing a thing.'

'I heard you. But there's not much we can do, is there, and right now I need a cardboard box and some clean towels or an old blanket.'

Jennifer marches out of the kitchen and down the short passageway that leads to the back door and garden. Frustration fuelling her as far as the old pig hut they use as a storage shed. She flicks on the light and surveys the scene; stacks of animal feed and old tools, the lawnmower still caked in dried brown cuttings from the last cut of autumn, a red plastic sled hanging from a hook, and beneath it all the groove in the centre of the stone floor to channel the blood from the slaughter. She shivers and starts sorting through a pile of sagging crates of drying seed potatoes and spare wellies until she finds a wooden box containing just a few dusty jam jars and spiderwebs. She lines the jars up on the windowsill and bangs the box a few times against the wall to dislodge any stubborn creatures still nesting in the corners, turns to go back to the house.

The light from the kitchen shines through the passageway across the courtyard but seems miles away. Unattainable. She needs to cross a space of about five metres. Only that. It is dark and the wind rushes in the trees. She feels her chest tighten, her breathing become sharp and quick. Only five metres, but it's getting dark.

She closes her eyes and takes in a slow breath through her nose, lets it leak out of her mouth to the count of five and then runs, leaving the pig shed door open and banging in the wind. Slams the back door closed and leans into the wall, counting, until the feeling passes.

Ioan's shape looms at the end of the short passage.

'Are you okay?'

She pushes past him into the brightness of the kitchen. 'I'm fine. I wish you'd stop asking. Here's your box.' She slams it down on the table and paces to the sink.

Ioan is bouncing the lamb gently in his arms as if it were a baby, watching her.

'What?' She challenges his gaze. 'Are you going to sort that thing out or not?'

She starts grabbing hand towels out of the kitchen drawer,

lining the box with no consideration for the quality of the cloth, no pause to select the oldest, threadbare towels. She holds out her arms for the lamb and gestures for him to pass it over, taking it and laying it carefully but clinically in the box before lifting it down and positioning it close to the Aga, so the warmth from the curved metal door of the stove can replace the heat of its dead mother's stomach.

Ioan, still in his vest and boxers, crouches to cover it with an edge of cloth. 'It needs feeding. I'll just get changed and get the colostrum powder. Can you boil the kettle for the bottle?'

His voice is low and cautious. Jennifer fills the kettle and leans back against the counter while it boils. The lamb barely stirs in the box, its thin layer of tightly curled wool drying out and fluffing. By the time Ioan returns Jennifer has made tea for them both and filled the sink with hot water to wash the bottles. A jug of water cooling on the side, ready to make the formula.

'I'm sorry.'

He strokes her hair, leans to kiss her. 'I missed you today.'

'It's just…'

'I know.'

No, you don't, she thinks. He busies himself with the task, in his pyjamas and dressing gown. Measures the powder carefully while Jennifer asks about the ewe.

'She was a mess. Must have been in labour for most of the day. Knackered. I think her uterus ruptured or something because she was barely alive when I found her, and this little fella wouldn't have made it if I'd been even ten minutes later.' He cradles the lamb on his lap, holding the bottle upside down while it suckles and pushes against the plastic teat. Thick yellowy liquid oozes out of the sides of its mouth.

'Where is she?'

'Where I found her. I'll have to get her moved tomorrow.'

'What are we going to do with the lamb? Will you take it to Dad's?'

'They've got enough on, without Helen to help. In fact, if Helen had been here—'

'Well she's not. So, what are you going to do with it?'

'How long are you off for?'

Jennifer pauses. The meeting still raw. Concerned frowns on the faces across the desk, asking if she needed more tea, some fresh air.

'They're sending a doctor around soon, so they can get their paperwork in order. But they've already decided I'm "exhausted", and that's the reason I messed up in the drill. It's the only way they can keep me on. A few months maybe? Enough time to ensure I'm "no longer a risk to myself and my colleagues".'

'Great, so you can do the day feeds, and I could do the night. When I'm not on shift.'

'Great?'

'You know what I mean. At least we have someone to keep this little fella going.' He bends his head to kiss the knobbled brow of the lamb.

'And what if I don't want to stay home and play mother to a lamb?'

'I could always take some time off.'

'They don't give out paternity leave for animals, Ioan. What excuse would you give?'

'That I'm looking after you?'

'Don't you dare! Don't make this worse than it is. I'm fine, this... excuse is just that. An excuse. A way through the red tape.'

'Yeah, well. We'll sort something out.' The lamb is full, and Ioan puts the bottle on the table. The formula runs down the side, leaving a gloopy ring around the base of the bottle. Jennifer gets him a dishcloth to wipe his hands.

'You're not staying off.'

'I could call in sick.'

'You're not sick.'

'They don't know that.'

'But I do. Be sensible, Ioan. It's only a lamb, can't we pass it on to someone else?'

Jack walks into the kitchen, rubbing his eyes. He stands, rumpled and sleep tousled, and inspects the lamb.

'What are you doing up?'

'I heard shouting.'

'No one was shouting, you must have been dreaming. Come on...' Jennifer reaches to take his hand, to guide him back towards the stairs.

'Why is it here?'

'Because its mammy... because it needs some special care. Uncle Ioan is just giving it some supper and then it's going to sleep. You too. Come on.'

'What's wrong with it?'

'Nothing, buddy.'

'What's wrong with its mam, then?'

'Nothing, little man. It's all fine.'

'Then why is it here?' His voice is rising. 'Why did you take it away from its mam if nothing is wrong?' He looks from one to the other, his little fists clenched beside him.

'It's okay, buddy. This little fella is a bit poorly. He just needs some extra care. I didn't tell you because I thought you'd worry, iawn?' Ioan settles the lamb back into the crate, beckoning Jack over. 'Now, I'm actually going to need you to help me look after it. Do you think you can do that?'

Jack nods, but his fists are still tight. He rocks on the balls of his feet.

'So, you need to go to sleep now, so you can do the first feed in the morning, iawn? Hogyn dda.'

'But if you don't tell me things, how will I know what to do?' He brushes his hair out of his eyes with one hand.

'Well, little man. Grown-ups don't tell children everything, it's to protect them.'

'That's stupid.'

'No, it means you don't have to worry. Now, back to bed.'

He is silent on the way up the stairs, still frowning when Jennifer tucks him in and leans forward to plant a kiss on his tangled head. If he were hers she'd cut his hair, give him a chance to fit in, at least.

She is almost out of the room, the light off, when he speaks. 'You're lying.'

His tone gives her goose bumps. 'What makes you say that?'

'You look at each other in a funny way.'

'We're just trying to protect you, little man. That's all.'

He rolls to face the wall. She waits in the doorway, straining to hear if he has a whispered response for her. She knows he isn't asleep, can see the tension in his tiny body, taut beneath the sheets. Eventually she closes the door with a soft click and goes back down.

Ioan has made a sandwich, ham drooping from the edges

of the bread, tomato juice running down his wrists. She hasn't eaten for hours but hasn't the stomach to join him in a late snack. The lamb sneezes, a soft, sudden exhalation. Jennifer sits in front of the laptop, opens Helen's files. She'll have to tell her parents soon, at least ask them if they've heard from Helen and then deal with any conversation that arises from the question. Her mam is too sick to deal with the worry, she thinks. Maybe she'll have to lie to her too.

CHAPTER SIXTEEN

Helen works the field beside the house, forcing a heavy, rusted spade through black slabs of clotted soil. Pacing herself. It's a kind of training, she tells herself. Building her stamina back slowly. Preparing.

Baba Olena has churned over most of the land already, and Helen is determined to finish this corner before the shadows start to stretch out over the garden. She needs this; contact with the land, the smell of the rich earth and the weight of the spade. If she can't get home yet, at least she can be useful. The rhythm of it releases something in her.

She is comfortable in her own boots. Her biker buff around her neck to keep the chill away, although she still wears the headscarf to keep her hair off her face. She has used the dosimeter to make sure the area is safe, that Anton wasn't lying just to pacify her, and this has freed her to drink the water cold, to wash without fear. Her rucksack is packed ready so that if Anton returns she is ready to go: one set of uncontaminated clothes, survival kit, rations and water, passport and money. Her phone switched off to save the battery until there is a chance of a signal. She has been working since breakfast, almost arguing with Baba Olena over the task.

Above her the sky is deep blue, the sun just over the apex. Sparrows, and occasionally a pair of jays, come to land on the ground behind her, picking out the twisting worms that the spade has exposed or sliced through. Earlier a deer stood, just beyond the field where the ground sloped away through knotted briars, and watched her work, its ear turning and flicking with each incision through the earth. Twice she was driven back into the dense air of the house by late sleet showers that stung her hands raw on the handle of the shovel and needled her face with ice.

The work allows her space to think. Now she has her things she might not need help to navigate out. She has the map Sergey handed out on the tour, and Baba Olena has already pointed to her village, helped her get her bearings. Although the bike is lost, the excursion did verify her position.

She lifts the spade for another slice, and the cat darts across her path into the long grass beside the barn. It emerges seconds later with a brindle corpse drooping from its mouth. A rat. It flashes yellow eyes at Helen and carries its bounty to the barn to feed.

She embeds the blade of the shovel in the dark soil and follows it. Baba Olena is hacking off sections of the boar with a long, curved knife, packing slabs of fat into big jars with salt and herbs, making salo. Singing. She stacks the heavy jars on the floor, where they will be cool, then shuffles out to feed the hens, patting Helen's arm on her way past.

Now Helen is no longer an invalid their dynamic has shifted. Helen contributes to the daily chores, payback of sorts for the kindness. But Baba Olena has her way of doing things. More than once now she has scolded Helen, slapping her hands when she has reached to place the jars and pans in the wrong place, becoming angry when Helen tipped a whole bucket of half-fermented potatoes into the hedge behind the house. She made Helen wash more, cutting the sprouts off with a sharp paring knife and dicing them into chunks before soaking them in warm water and sugar. Helen apologising as she worked until Baba Olena relented and squeezed her hand, showing her how to stir the mash, wrap a towel around the bucket to keep it warm.

Helen looks at the remains of the boar, bones glinting through the parted skin, the hooves and snout still caked in forest mud, the eyes marbled. She turns it on its hook, sees the marks her bike left across its side. A single piercing wound near its heart. Anton.

She should never have asked him for help, would be home now if she hadn't. She reaches out for her leathers, stiffening on the nail beside the door, and strokes the soft black contours of a sleeve, traces a finger over the silver stripe running down the seam. It would be easy to dismiss the bike as folly, to criticise herself for not giving it up as soon as she discovered she was pregnant. But she needed it more than she can even admit to herself. She feels a kind of self-indulgent grief over its loss. The issue now is getting home, back to Jack and the things that really matter. It's time to move on. She unhooks the leathers and carries them outside like an eviscerated corpse.

In the overgrown corner of the garden she cuts out square sods of grass, digs a deep, narrow pit and crouches to nestle the folded, cracking skin at the bottom before replacing the turf, stamping the earth down hard and dragging a few dead branches over the site. Then she stretches and returns to the field. Her bruises are aching, but she doesn't want to go back inside.

When she's finished turning the earth, Helen wipes the blade of the shovel clean on a tuft of wet grass and props it up just inside the door of the barn. Fetches bags of seed potatoes from last year's store and walks along the furrows dropping the wizened, sprouting tubers in and kicking earth over them, banking it with the inner curve of her boots.

She is contemplating her chances of getting out of the Zone on foot, finding a town that isn't caught up in protests, when she catches a glimpse of him, dark and skinny, emerging from the treeline. His tight stride out of synch with the stillness of the day. She lets the bag drop.

He stands at the edge of the churned field, two carrier bags in his hands.

'I could have been anyone. Why are you out here?'

'I didn't hear a car.'

'Or didn't pay attention.' He cocks his head as if they would both hear a car now if they just concentrated hard enough. There is only the sound of the wind through the trees of the forest that encroaches on the village, the distant call of a bird of prey to its mate. 'The car is a long way from here. You need to be more careful.'

'Where the hell have you been?'

'Where is Baba Olena?'

'Inside, resting. Are we leaving now?'

He steps past her, knocks and goes inside. Helen hears their voices as she tips the last of the potatoes into the furrows and hurriedly kicks the soil over them into a raised line. She takes the steps two at a time. There's no way she's letting him leave without her again.

In the porch, she slides off her boots and the woollens layered over her own clothes and hangs the cardigan on a peg. In the gloom of the house Anton is assessing the difference, noting the tidy piles of clothes, the space on the table for the bags of shopping.

Baba Olena is talking quickly, and he stops to stroke her arm. Shaking his head.

'What's wrong?'

'She thought you were going to stay.'

Helen pulls the headscarf off and hands it back to Baba Olena. 'I'm sorry,' she says, and hopes the woman understands her tone, if not her words. 'Tell her I'm sorry, Anton. Tell her I have to get back to my child. To my farm.'

Helen pulls her rucksack out from under the chair, waits as Anton explains to Baba Olena, listens to her reply. Sees her nod.

'She wants to know why you are here, alone, if you have a man and child back home.'

'I don't have a man. Tell her I'm strong, like her. I'm okay alone.'

Baba Olena grasps her arm, gestures at Anton and says something. A wicked smile in her pale blue eyes.

'What?'

Anton blushes.

'What did she say?'

'She says if you don't have a man you can have me.'

'Ni, Baba Olena.' Helen pulls away. 'Tell her I don't need a man.'

Anton puts an arm around the old woman and says something that makes her laugh.

Helen picks up her rucksack, stares at Anton expectantly.

'Are we going then? Or was that your plan all along, to be my man?'

'What? No.' Colour rushes to his throat.

Baba Olena watches, keenly. Walks over to Helen and takes her face in her strong hands, and Helen can see humour and perhaps a little pride spark in the old woman's clear blue eyes. She speaks directly to Helen, squeezing her face to emphasise each word. Then, smiling broadly, she walks away.

'What did she say?' Helen asks, her cheeks still hot from the woman's touch.

'She said of course you don't need a man. You are like her, stubborn and strong. A pain in her bottom, but that is why she hoped you would stay.'

Helen puts her rucksack down and goes over to Baba Olena, hugs her tight.

Baba Olena breaks away and starts pulling things from the carrier bags Anton brought with him, presses packets of meat and cheese into Helen's hands, stands over her until she gives in and stows them in her bag. Then fetches a jar of clear liquid from a shelf and hands it to Helen.

Anton laughs.

'What is it?'

'Vodka. Special stuff. She distils it out in the forest.'

The potatoes. 'It's safe?'

'You should drink it all,' Anton says. 'It protects you from the radiation.'

'I thought that was a myth.'

'It's whatever you choose to believe.'

Baba Olena is talking to Anton, searching through the jars on the shelf, gathering bowls and pans.

'She wants us to eat before we go. A good idea, we have a long walk to the car. Maybe a long drive.'

'But then we are going, aren't we?'

'Yes.'

'Where have you been? You left me here...' Her voice almost breaks.

'I had my friends to help. You were safe here, at least.' He looks better than the last time she saw him, clean shaven, the bruise near his eye faded.

'Have the protests stopped?'

He shakes his head. 'No, but they have moved. Ivankiv is quiet, for now.'

'And the roads?'

'Still difficult.'

'I found my bike.'

'You went out there?'

'I needed to see if I could fix it.'

He shakes his head. 'I told you it was broken. You are lucky you didn't get seen.'

'Not lucky. Careful.'

Helen sets the table while Baba Olena starts mixing flour and water, crumbling herbs. Boiling water. Anton stays standing, rocking on the balls of his feet until Baba Olena chides him, herding him to the table, Helen too. They sit opposite one another while the woman cooks. Awkward. Dust motes turn in the air between them.

'So, what's the plan?'

'I will take you as far west as I can.'

'Okay.' She wants to ask him about the protests, what he has witnessed, been party to, but it seems too personal.

'You are better?' Polite. Perhaps shy after her accusation of romantic interest.

She nods. She is a lot better, but still not herself.

'So, you have a child?' He is looking at the table, tracing his fingers along a streak of darker wood in the grain. 'I didn't know.'

She nods again.

'How old?'

'Nearly six.'

'Boy or girl?'

'Boy.'

Baba Olena sets a plate of preserved tomatoes on the table, a jar of pickled beets. There is the smell of herbs cutting through the smoky air, the sizzle of salo in the skillet.

'Is he like you, your son?'

She thinks for a moment. Is he? He has her eyes, her pale skin. But that isn't what Anton means. 'Yes, he's like me. Only stronger. I hope.'

'Where is he while you are here?'

She prickles. 'Do you ask the men who go on your tours where their children are?'

He seems startled. 'I never think of that. It's just unusual, a woman here alone.'

'He's with family.' She changes the subject. 'How long will it take to get to the car?' She is mindful of her reduced abilities. If she'd known he was coming she would have rested, maybe slept in the afternoon.

'An hour or more. Not too far.'

Baba Olena places food on the table, takes the jar of vodka and pours them each a small glass. Helen joins them in a toast, suddenly aware that her time with Baba is over. Baba Olena who has shown her everything the tour couldn't. The emotion catches her off guard. She hadn't realised there was any attachment forming, or formed, in the fortnight she's been here. Gratitude, yes. But this is something more. She sips the vodka to halt the rising tide. The liquid is sharp, heats her tongue. Won't protect her from anything.

The meat is divided onto plates, herb dumplings in a thin vegetable broth ladled out. They are eating salted boar. Fitting, Helen thinks, biting into the gamey flesh. This is the end of something after all.

***

Jennifer searches online, finds an answer. Panic attack. Easily confused with a heart attack, but temporary, a physical manifestation of anxiety. Perhaps she is exhausted. Be kind to yourself, the self-help sites say. Seek medical advice if it happens more than once, or fear of further attacks affect your day-to-day activities. There is a list of medications on the NHS website, beta-blockers, tranquilisers and anti-depressant drugs, for if it becomes a disorder. She closes the lid of her laptop and stares into the fire. The human brain is too fragile, she thinks, for the responsibilities forced upon it, or sought out. Human error is inevitable, surely.

***

'Wait.'

They are only a few feet outside Baba Olena's garden when Helen stops. It is not yet dark, but the shadows are long and the forest ahead looks impenetrable, tangled. Anton looks at the little yellow machine in Helen's hand and shakes his head.

'No point.'

'But…'

'No checkpoints, no other way out.'

Helen resists the urge to switch it on anyway, to hold it out in front of her like a torch to guide the way. Working with Baba Olena around the house and garden, she has come to feel safe. Now safety is reliant on a chance footfall or change in the breeze, on trusting Anton.

The road looks different in the fading light, softened and blurred. Evening birdsong and the damp, fecund quality of the air masquerade as old friends. She shoves the dosimeter back into her rucksack. As the village is finally consumed by trees and shadows, Helen stops glancing back. They walk side by side, Anton striding with that bouncing gait she has come to recognise, as if he is always about to run. She realises then that he reminds her of Jack; the coiled energy, the serious eyes.

'How do you know Baba Olena? Is she family?' Her voice sounds alien in the forest. He stops, not quite out of breath but close. Sweat beads around his nose.

'Not mine. But I have known her for many years.'

'From the tours?'

'No, I don't take tours to her. She is just one of the Samosely, we look out for them.'

'And there's no one else near her?'

'Not now. There was another couple, not far, but they died last year, only a few days apart.'

'Doesn't she have her own family?'

Anton walks faster, as if he's trying to get away from her questions. She pushes herself to match his pace.

'Is she completely alone?'

'They don't visit often.'

'And she…'

'She won't leave.'

Of course she won't. To leave is to die.

'Her family are in Kyiv, have a room ready for her. Every time they visit they ask her to go with them. She says they can try to take her when she is dead, but even then she will hold on so tight they will have to break her hands to move her.'

Helen laughs, believes him. Can imagine the old woman haunting the space long after her body has been interred. The laugh disappears into the trees as she imagines her situation at home, if they acquire a compulsory purchase order for the farm. Knows she will feel her own fingers breaking, will be torn and out of place.

Incomplete.

This is how she feels now, walking through the forest, so similar and yet so different from the woods between the farm and the main road, the tangled copses nearer the beach.

'She'll be okay?'

Anton shrugs, 'She knew you couldn't stay. I told her at the beginning.'

That's not what she meant, but she doesn't know how to express her question properly.

'What did she do before… you know?'

'You ask too many questions.'

She waits.

'People used to bring her clothes to mend, family, their friends. She can't quite let it go.'

They walk on in silence, Helen alert to the occasional

sounds of wildlife in the forest; mice skittering through the undergrowth. They pass the site of the accident, and Anton veers off down a smaller track, overgrown and overshadowed by trees that arch above. He could be leading her anywhere.

'How far is the car?'

'I had to hide it. Far enough to keep you safe if it was found.'

The temperature drops, and Helen zips her jacket. The trees change; conifers reach out to hold hands across the track, soft pine needles beneath their feet. Their scent rises as they crush them underfoot.

She hears the voices first. Anton is cursing under his breath as thin branches catch his jacket and scratch at his face. Helen reaches out and grabs his arm, makes him stop and listen, and they creep slowly forwards as quietly as possible until they find enough space to crouch and listen.

'What are they saying?'

'I can't hear.'

'Where is the car?'

'Not close, nearer to them.'

Helen sits back on her haunches and slides the rucksack off. It is almost dark now and despite a clean, wide moon rising, beneath the tree cover the ground is almost invisible. Anton is leaning, straining to hear, almost toppling over. The skinny muscles of his thighs tight beneath his jeans.

'They are searching. They must have found my car. Fuck, fuck, fuck.' He uncoils, moves to stand.

'Sit down!' Helen reaches for Anton and pulls him down onto the soft, damp pine needles beneath them. He holds his head in his hands and starts rocking. When he looks up she sees something close to fear in his eyes, not the anger she'd been expecting.

'What can they do?'

'They can take my car, arrest me. I lose my job and then…'

'Were you actually in the Zone, or on the edge?'

'Inside, smaller road than before but…'

'Did you see any signs? Any fences? Did you pass any old barriers or wooden beams, anything to suggest a boundary or border?'

'It was dark.'

'If it wasn't properly marked—'

'Does not make it legal.'

'Is your phone working?' She has the paper map from Sergey, but without knowing their exact location, it would be near useless. He pulls out his phone and checks, the map already loaded.

'I parked as near as I could to make the walk short.' The voices are closer, just. 'See, here.'

Helen looks at the screen, at the little blue pulse that pinpoints their location. They are a long way from the border, at their pace another hour on foot at least. She resists the temptation to ask if she can call home, hear Jack's voice for just a second. Reassure them she is safe.

'So where is your car on here?'

'Near this bend. Inside, see.'

'But if this road has no checkpoints, how could they find you?'

'Loggers, the men who manage the forest. Maybe, I don't know.'

In the distance lights flicker. The shouting is getting closer.

'They are coming.'

Helen stands and stretches out her hamstrings, expecting him to stand too. Make a decision. This is his territory. When he stays seated in the loamy mulch she bends down to him.

'Anton, what do we do? If they find us... find me...'

He stares at the floor, as if there is an answer to be found in the browned pine needles and damp earth. 'Without car it is too far. We must go back to Baba Olena.' Then he stands and starts walking the way they came.

A dog barks.

'Will it be safe there?'

'Maybe.'

The forest is deep shadow and creaking timber, smells brackish and tastes metallic, and a light breeze carries the edge of winter still. Helen breathes deep and follows Anton, supressing the sting of tears. They move away from the direction of the shouting and torch flashes, deeper into the Zone.

Clouds obscure the moon and it becomes hard to see. They walk quickly for about twenty minutes, concentrating on getting back to the house. Are making good progress when they hear the sound of an engine ahead, the slam of car doors. Anton takes her arm, veers off to the right and they stumble on for a while, half running. Helen's hip and knee throbbing with each footfall, until she has had enough, stops.

'What are we doing, Anton? This is stupid. We need to go back.'

He walks back to her. 'You have a better idea? They have my car, are at Baba's house. We need to stay away for now, go back in the morning.'

'So where are we going now?'

Anton pulls a torch from his own knapsack and they pause to shine the beam into the forest. There are no more voices. There is nothing. Their world has been reduced to thin slices of light that illuminate a pattern of branches and trunks in repeated spears. They stand close and look at the screen of Anton's phone together. They can see themselves in the pulsing blue dot, but there is just a light-green space around them, cross-hatched with pale beige lines where the roads should be, and surrounded by a jagged orange border, like the edge of a stain. Water is marked in bright blue. It looks like a map drawn in the soft pastel shades of a child's crayon set; straight lines and simple angles.

'Here.'

Anton points to a small black circle with a white arrow in the middle. A village. The blue dot pulses in time to his breathing. It is close, but not close enough to reassure as the darkness presses in around them. Anton sets off.

The ground is soft underfoot, and there are saplings and the snaking new growth of brambles to negotiate. Anton is clumsy, his jacket catching on thorns, working his frustration out by batting brushwood away with his fists. She concentrates on the task of placing her feet, of ducking beneath low branches and unsnagging her sleeves. These are movements she has made since childhood, exploring the woods back home, working on the farm.

As the darkness deepens they walk almost touching shoulders so they can both see their progress on the screen, blind to their surroundings. The torch picks out only the small space in front of them, and they keep the beam low to guide their steps. Every thought is concentrated on the game of navigation. Progress is slow, cautious.

She is beginning to feel a sense of unreality envelop her, as if time is suspended and their stumbling progress on a loop. She is almost ready to demand they stop when they emerge from a dense cluster of pines, the moon illuminating the open landscape for them. Everything is chrome, platinum, silver. Still and silent. The trees diminish in height, each a season younger than the last as the forest tumbles into the fields.

Anton is looking toward the horizon, above the treeline, to where there is a shard of curved silver light reflecting in an arc like an upturned moon. The first stage of the New Safe Confinement unit. She rests a hand on his arm. He flinches at the touch.

'Where are we?'

'We can find a place here for a rest, carry on in the morning.'

'Are there people here? Samosely?'

'No.'

The first buildings they reach are collapsed, overtaken by brambles. Helen waits while Anton searches for a place they can access. This is nothing like the tour, the villages they were driven to for photographs. This is a small settlement, seems like just a few houses, all lost long ago to the encroaching trees and vines. She finds what was perhaps once a road but is now almost covered in scrub grass and saplings.

'Here.'

She follows Anton's voice to a low barn, two sides rotted away to stumpy teeth in the prevailing weather, the roof half gone. A dinosaur of a machine hunkers, neck bent, in the exposed corner. Beside it a steel cage is threaded with last year's browned bindweed. It stands on sturdy legs, raised off the ground by at least four feet, with a ladder and a door. The floor is heavy steel, rusting but solid. Anton helps her in, wedges the door closed.

'What is this?'

'This what?'

'This cage. What's it for?'

'Gas bottles probably.'

'Why did you lock the door?'

'In case of wolves.'

She laughs, then realises he is serious. 'But they wouldn't come near us, surely?'

'Probably not, but to be safe...'

'Wolves. Nothing else?'

'Like what?'

'I was only asking.'

'You are too nosy. Always asking questions. Your nose has made this happen.' He bangs the sides of the cage hard and there is a rustle in the grass, close.

'You were the one who—'

'Who what? Who tried to warn you to leave? Who watched to make sure you got home safe at night? Who carried you when you crashed?'

'I never asked for all that—'

'You did not know you needed me, and now—'

'I didn't need you, except to navigate out. When I asked for help, offered to pay you, you left. When I didn't ask... Those boys could never keep up with the bike, those men in the bar –

if they were a problem they were my problem, not yours. If we're laying blame here, Anton, you are the reason we are here.'

They stand facing each other in the cage, eyes locked. She tries not to blink under the burn of his dark eyes.

'Was she right? Baba Olena? Did you follow me because you wanted me? Or because you didn't think a woman could manage alone?'

'I followed you to keep you safe. This is my job, to keep the tourists safe. To drive you around and make sure you don't step in the wrong place, or eat a berry, or pick up a toy. It is my job.'

'I wasn't even on your tour. It was Sergey's job. And he did it and left when it was over.'

'But you didn't.'

'I wasn't in the Zone.'

'No, but you were still in danger. Helen, these protesters aren't carrying placards and having a picnic. They are at war. And you just walked right in, taking your pictures of the town. People don't like it. They have their own fights already.'

'I'm still not your responsibility, you didn't need to—'

'I know I didn't have to, but it's what I do. I didn't want you to get hurt. You are...'

'What?' Don't say it.

'I don't know. Interesting. You remind me of myself...'

She leans against the side of the cage, stares out of the open side of the barn over the moonlit grass. There is a sound from beyond the metal mesh, a rustle of leaves and the dash of an animal across the open meadow. His anger has vented, and in its place his voice is tentative, unsure, as if he is trying to work out his motivations for the first time.

'You're not like the other tourists. You wanted something else, I think. I don't know if this is a good or bad thing. But being in Ivankiv was not a good idea.'

It isn't worth the argument.

'Are we staying in here?'

He nods.

'Then we might as well get comfortable.' She shrugs off her rucksack and pulls out her spare sweater, layers it on underneath her jacket. The wind is almost blocked by the side of the barn, but Anton is shivering. She rummages through the side pocket of her pack, pulls out the first-aid kit. Inside there is a small foil blanket, neatly folded into a plastic pouch. She unwraps it and gets him to take off his jacket, then layers it inside.

'It's only going to reflect heat,' she explains. 'Put your coat back on to protect you from the wind chill.' He zips himself to his chin and sits opposite her, his back to the wire.

When they are settled she opens her pack again and pulls out the food Baba Olena pressed her to take.

'It'll warm us up.'

He moves close as she pulls out packets of cheese, sliced meat in circles under cellophane, like salami. She hands him two slices of each, takes the same for herself. The cheese is smoky, the meat a little like venison. She squints at the packet.

'What is this?'

'Horse.'

She chews slowly. 'I've never eaten horse before.'

'It's good.' He peels a strip off his slice and drops it into his mouth.

'People have horses as pets at home. I suppose they think it would be like eating a cat.'

'I like cats. I have cat. A good cat, not like Baba Olena's. But a horse is for work, for transport. Like a car.' He peels off another slice and chews. 'So eating it is the same as eating a car.'

Helen laughs. 'You eat cars?'

'No, I mean a horse is not a pet. Don't be sad to eat it.'

Helen takes a bite of the horsemeat and cheese together. It is good. She'd eat a cat if she had to, but doesn't tell Anton. They sink into silence, each looking out around them at the wide landscape dotted with saplings and a few buildings, low and half covered in brambles and trees. They are like islands in the shifting grass. An owl hoots somewhere and they both turn to listen.

When the leftovers are packed away they sit side by side, not touching. Helen stares into the waving grass and borders of the field. The breeze is hard. The dangers invisible. She might never get home. She pulls the dosimeter back out of her bag and rests her hand on the power button.

Anton is watching her. 'Do you really want to know?'

'I don't know.'

He runs a finger down the rusting frame of the cage and holds it out to her. Particles freckle his fingerprint. He lets her look, then lifts it to his mouth and licks them off.

'You're not afraid?'

His hand is shaking, he bunches his fists and shoves them deep in his pocket.

'Why?'

'I am already full up of it, a little more won't hurt.'

'You don't have to make it worse.'

'Is it worse? Maybe this is better.'

'Better to deliberately risk getting sick?'

'You did, to come here. I have friends who do this. Who come into the Zone illegally and drink the water, eat the berries.'

'They want to reclaim it.'

'They play at being brave because there is nothing to lose.'

'And you?'

'I have lost enough already. But tonight, what choice is there? You can put the machine on and see what is the danger, but you are here already. Knowing won't change it.'

He spits, leaning close to the cage side to aim through the wire lattice.

Helen turns the machine over in her hands, runs a thumb over the blank, grey display screen. She can feel Anton trembling beside her.

'I don't need to turn it on if you don't want me to.'

'I don't want you to.'

'Are you cold?'

'Freezing.'

'Come here.' They shuffle around awkwardly until their backs are against each other. 'Now lean back, into me.'

He hesitates and then she feels his back press against hers. She tucks her hands deep into her own pockets and hunkers down in her jacket. Her phone is still cold and quiet in her pocket. She pulls it out and checks, but there is still no signal. What would she tell them anyway? The night is full of sounds; the gentle susurration of wind over the grasses, the creak of wood rubbing wood as the trees move and wear grooves in the weatherworn sides of old houses. Anton is quiet, rolls away and lies on his side.

Helen leans on the metal side of the cage. Alert to the sounds of animals in the undergrowth, to the smell of winter tipping into spring under the moonlight. A sharpness blunted by a shift in wind direction. The thaw is over. Things will accelerate now. She feels him shift against her shin.

An owl sweeps low over the meadow, white and silent. She tracks it with her eyes. A circular white face and two dark eyes, head swivelling and scanning the grasses. It tilts its wings and hovers, its dark feet bobbing up and down beneath its pale body, tail fanned and tipping for balance. She can feel Anton looking at her, his eyes hidden under the shadow of his fringe.

'Are you scared?' he asks.

She doesn't answer. The owl drops. Ascends. Something drooping in its talons.

**

Jennifer can't sleep. Is standing by the bedroom window staring out at the glow of the plant on the horizon when Ioan's alarm trills. Time for the first of the night feeds. He stirs, grumbles as he reaches for his phone to silence it.

'I'll go.' She leans to kiss him, pulls the duvet back over his broad shoulder. He's snoring again, a soft drone on the inbreath, before she has left the room.

In the kitchen she puts on the under-cupboard lights, flicks the kettle switch. The lamb is watching her from its box, ears flicking out sideways, swivelling as she moves to fetch the colostrum powder. It gives out a pathetic bleat as she passes.

She makes tea, mixes the formula. When she goes to fetch

milk for her drink she finds a sticky deposit of meconium near the fridge. Wipes it up and washes her hands.

The lamb struggles a little as she scoops it up and settles it on her knee at the kitchen table but then goes almost limp. She wonders if it's sick, struggles to get it to latch on. It sucks in bursts, slackens its mouth in between, the thick liquid oozing over her fingers. When it's had enough she sits with it curled on her lap, resting its head against her chest. She drinks her tea and tries to work out what Helen would do; if she'd be sitting up in her barn, feeding a lamb at midnight, or if she'd have let it go. Kinder that way.

CHAPTER SEVENTEEN

Birds.

Helen hears them before she is fully awake: the slow crescendo from predawn chirrups to the cacophony that rises with the sun. She is curled on her side, her good shoulder aching and stiff beneath her. She opens her eyes only when she feels the floor of the cage move, hears the rasp of rusty metal as the makeshift door catch is released.

Anton is gone. Helen rubs her eyes and looks around. He is a few metres away from the cage, his back turned, a rising spectre of steam telling her he is peeing into the dew-strung grass. He zips up and walks away, glancing around to the horizon and the forest, nosing in the hangar. A shadow of stubble across his jaw softens his features, blurs the hard lines.

Helen shifts and rolls so she can watch him. He kicks at an old tyre and something small dashes out through the scrub, making him jump back.

The sun is out, sky cloudless. She sits up, stretches. Her hip is stiff and sore from the cold, from the hard metal. She starts to fold away the foil blanket. There is no breeze, and the air is sparkling. Her breath steams.

She is sipping water, swallowing two painkillers, when he pulls out his phone and stares at the screen, jabs at it and raises it to his ear. His conversation is short and excited, and he dashes back to the cage as soon as it is over. Helen tucks loose strands of hair behind her ears and stretches out her cold muscles.

'Change of plan now.'

'Who was that?'

'A friend. We are not going back.'

Anton picks up her rucksack, eager to move. Helen eases her legs out of the cage door and sits with her feet on the top step of the ladder.

'So where are we going?'

'My friend will meet us with his car, take you to an airport.'

'There's another way in?'

'Not on this side, but Belarus, yes.'

'That's over the border. Won't we be stopped?'

'Border is inside the Zone. He knows the place. We have to go now because it is a long way.'

Anton is already striding away, using his phone to direct him.

'Wait.'

'What?'

'Can I use your phone?'

He holds it out, but she doesn't take it. What would she say? I'm alive but lost? I haven't been beaten in a riot, but I may be absorbing isotopes that will turn my own cells against me?

'You want to call home, yes?'

'Maybe later.' It would be selfish to call now, just to hear their voices, when she cannot tell them any truth that won't cause more worry. 'Go on a bit, I'll catch you up.' He pauses, and she says again, 'Go on,' waits for him to move away and then finds a dense patch of brush to squat behind.

She can see tiny insects and flies moving in the grasses

beside her. Directly in front of her a spider's web hangs between thorny branches, beaded with dew. She examines the pattern as she pees, seeking out some sign of irregularity or dysfunction. She can't fault it, but then what does she know? The spider itself might have ten legs.

She catches him up and makes him drink, shares out the last of the food. She insists.

'If we're going to hike cross country we need the energy, or we'll suffer later.'

His enthusiasm buoys her after the melancholy of the night before, but she is cautious.

'Show me the route on your phone. I need to know where we're heading.'

He points out a section where the white border of Belarus dips inside the yellow warning band of the Exclusion Zone. Doesn't give her time to assess the landscape in between. It is a swirl of green and blue. A day's hard hiking, and the terrain looks mixed. His optimism is blind. Always a mistake. She shoulders her rucksack and follows him, mentally preparing for a difficult day.

The movement eases her muscles, warms her up. By mid-morning the sun is strong, the temperature perhaps as high as twelve or fifteen degrees. Unseasonal but welcome. Helen strips away her coat and fleece. Anton keeps his jacket on but unzips it and unfastens the first few buttons of his shirt. There is the dark pink smile of a scar in the shadow of his Adam's apple. The warmth is accelerating the unfolding of the trees, the buds breaking open to seek the sun, the branches becoming blurred with a spurt of new growth.

They cross roads, pausing at the edge where dead leaves

have blown into drifts on the cracked tarmac, providing substance for the seeds to root and encroach on the old infrastructure. They look left and right, like children, before crossing quickly, wary of the logger's wagon or a search party out to track them down. The only evidence they've seen of wolves all day was a pile of scat at the edge of the village.

For most of the walk they don't talk, except to warn each other of low branches or squelchy patches of mud. Helen has time to think when the terrain isn't too hard. She doesn't have a visa and has heard of the penalties levied on people for drifting, even by accident, over the border into Belarus. Anton's plan is to cross inside the Zone and then ride in his friend's car to the capital. After that Helen is on her own. She scenarios the possibilities: the immigration office, strip searches and interviews, a hefty fine or even imprisonment. She runs over potential explanations, strategies. Her mind only breaking away from the problem when they reach a thick tangle of brush that extends as far as the eye can see both ways. A knotted reef of shrubs and trees they can't traverse without concerted effort.

Anton's face is flushed, sweaty from the hike. He looks healthier than he has for days, but it's an illusion. She's seen it in the farm hands enough summers over to know he is dehydrated. Soon the colour will drop from his cheeks and he'll begin to feel dizzy. Soon he'll be in danger, his condition a burden.

She makes use of the dense foliage as an excuse to rest. Uses the foil blanket to protect their backsides from damp, and hands Anton the water bottle. She is tempted to take out the dosimeter and check the environment but knows it won't help.

They are here. The reading won't change that. Besides, east of the plant there will still be hotspots, but nothing like the Red Forest. It is long-term exposure here that is the risk; eating the berries and mushrooms that draw caesium out of the ground and water and concentrate it as they ripen.

She asks Anton to get his phone out, calculates how far they've come, how much further is left to go.

'When is he coming?'

'Tonight.'

'What time?'

'He will pass at eleven, twelve and one. If we are not there, he will try again twelve hours later. Unless he is unable.'

They haven't enough water to last twenty-four hours. Nowhere near. She hopes the friend brings supplies, and that they don't have to drive to a town before they can slake their thirst. She starts to fantasise about the clear, cool water from the well in Baba Olena's garden. The thick, starchy mashed potatoes and crispy fried eggs. She gets up, uses a stout stick to hack away at the undergrowth, knocking a dent in the worst of it. Pulls her biker buff up over her nose as the vegetation spits up dust and dried leaf fragments with each swipe of the branch. They still struggle to move forwards; progress is slow, loud and clumsy. Birds call out warnings overhead.

When they reach easier terrain, they are both out of breath.

They keep walking, Helen glancing at Anton at intervals to ensure he isn't deteriorating.

The vegetation changes. Tough, woody shrubs replaced again by sedge and other grasses Helen is starting to recognise but has no name for. The ground becomes soft underfoot; more than just wet, it is marshy. The rise in temperature, the thaw, has saturated the land. The terrain slopes slightly. In the distance there are willows trailing skinny fingers towards the ground. Helen can smell the river before she sees it. Thirst spikes her tongue, and she feels the thickness on the roof of her mouth. She takes out plastic bags, shows Anton how to slip them on over his socks and inside his shoes to minimise the water seeping in. She leads, testing the ground carefully, stepping on tussocks and instructing Anton to place his feet where she treads.

At the bank they look across a grey marbled stretch of maybe ten metres or so, then at each other.

'I was hoping for a bridge.' Anton is quiet, shame-faced. His enthusiasm has backfired.

'We could walk along a bit, see if there are any.' A waste of energy and time.

'Which way?' Anton is frowning, looking at his phone and then swivelling his head between the up- and down-stream view. They can see a fair distance both ways before curves take the river out of sight, hiding potential crossing points.

'Are there any villages nearby? A village might mean a crossing.'

Anton looks back at his phone, jabs the screen, curses. It's dead. He flashes the blank screen at her. His eyes reveal a rising panic. A bird cries out overhead and Helen turns her face upwards, catches the pale flashes beneath the wings and tail of a large bird of prey. Huge. An eagle maybe. It circles and then drops into the grassland across the river from where they stand. After a moment it rises, talons empty. Circles again.

She pulls out her own phone, feels the weight of it in her hand; a rock, an apple, Jack's first pair of shoes. She hesitates before applying pressure to the button on the side. Knows that even if they make it across, walking in a straight line is an imprecise science without the back-up of the satnav to guide them. A slight imperfection in trajectory and they will miss their target by metres or miles.

Helen presses the power button, looks out over the water while it loads; the gentle eddies and swirls on the surface that belie a strong current beneath, the coppery tones near the edge where the smooth rocks and pebbles of the riverbed are just visible. The chirp of completion makes her jump. On the screen Jack's face beams out, unchanged and static. A little light flashes, just above the edge of the picture.

Out here, thirty kilometres or more from habitation, she has a signal. Messages. Voicemail.

They finally have their blinking blue dot back, showing their location right on the line where pastel green meets pastel blue on the map. Anton leans in, reaching over to swipe his finger on the screen and move the map around. There are no villages on this side, the only one near is the one they are heading to that is just out of sight beyond the water.

Helen lets him take it. Moves close to the edge, trying to judge the current, the depth. A light drizzle starts to fall.

'Anton, we'll just have to cross it. Here's as good as anywhere.'

They are at the widest point they can see, and Helen hopes this means the current is at its slowest. If they can wade across, bags held above their heads, then they can press on.

***

The rain is incessant. Jennifer stands by the window and watches it fall in a grey wall around the house, blurring everything into rivulets. Ioan has taken Jack to the supermarket, and all morning she has drifted between the laptop, her phone, and the window. Feeding the lamb every two hours, wiping up the yellowy mess it passes through, washing its rear end with soapy water to keep it clean. The clock on the kitchen wall measures each minute she has left before they come home, each minute lost to the walls around her.

Ioan has named the lamb Bobbins, hoping Jack will bond with it. It isn't a puppy, but it's something to care for.

Jack patiently fed it and wiped its face clean before school. Then lifted its tail and said solemnly, 'You have to put a band on its tentacles, so they fall off.' Frowned when they laughed. Went to school with a scowl. Ioan promised they'd castrate it later, together, so Jack could make sure it was done properly.

She calls her dad, ready to ask him if he's heard from Helen. When he answers, she bottles it. He has enough to worry about already.

'How's Mam doing?'

'Not good, Jen. The doctors are suggesting more chemo, but they've got that way of talking, you know? I think it's just words now.'

'Is she comfortable?'

'She's got the nurses in, you know, to wash her and everything.' His voice cracking might be interference on the line. 'I really thought she'd beat it.'

'Me too. I'll come by later, shall I?'

'Have you heard from Helen? I thought she'd be back by now.'

'She said she was visiting a few places on her way home.' The lie, no matter how honourable the reason, sticks in her throat. 'She'll be back soon.'

'I wish she were here.' His voice is tinny, fragile.

Jennifer closes her eyes. 'Why, Dad? What could she do?' Sees the words on the page: *Not everyone can be saved!*

'She's always so calm. Keeps things practical. Keeps us together.'

'I'll see you later, Dad.' Jennifer grips the phone so hard her knuckles become a small white mountain range on the receiver.

'Truth be, Jen? I'm scared.'

'Me too, Dad. Me too.'

After the call she stands at the kitchen window, watching the rain slide down and blur the garden into a swirling mess of colours. Imagining Helen holding a pillow over her mother's face. Wondering if it really would be kinder than the slow decay she is enduring.

Ioan arrives home with Jack, trailing drips across the hall carpet and leaving footprints by the door. The lamb struggles out of its box, totters on spindly legs, bleating. Jack stands under his dripping hood while Ioan stacks carrier bags on the kitchen table.

'Is it still here?'

'Yes, we're looking after it. We told you last night.' Jennifer scoops it up, holds it out for him to cuddle.

'You should find it a new mam. It needs to be a sheep.'

'Don't you want to look after it, little man?'

He shrugs, fiddling with his buttons.

'Are you going to help me feed it?'

'I want to go out to the field.'

'It's filthy out. Why not get into your play clothes and help me with Bobbins. Maybe you could make him a nicer bed.'

He tilts his head, eyes almost scornful. 'Na, diolch. I want to go to the field.'

'It's fine, Jen, I'll take him. Get your wellies on then, buddy. Don't want to ruin your shoes.'

Jack disappears into the hall and Bobbins follows, mouth open in a wavering bleat. A moment later Jack returns, carrying the lamb, dumps it in its box and sighs. Stands waiting while Ioan pulls on his raincoat. The lamb tries to follow them out, but Jack shuts the door on it. It bleats again, a high, almost silent cry, like a distant gull, and then totters back to Jennifer, nuzzling her jeans, nibbling at the fold of denim by her knee.

She carries on waiting, checking her phone, half planning dinner, listening to the rain and the clock. The weather has cut the house off from the landscape, obscured the view, muffled sounds. She feels herself detached somehow, suspended like an insect in slow moving amber. She's scared of solidifying.

The clock ticks. The rain hits the window in squalls.

The lamb is back at the kitchen door, tail flicking like a catkin in the breeze. She hears them then, back too soon. Jack crying. The torpor cracks.

'What happened?'

'He slipped. The brook has burst its banks.' Ioan sets Jack down and shrugs off his coat, splashing the walls with rainwater as he hangs it up. Jack is slicked down one side with mud, his hands black with it and a thick streak across his cheek. He stands, arms out and eyes wide, howling.

'Hey, little man. It's okay. Come on, let's get you warmed up.'

'No, I want to go back, let me go back!'

Jennifer kneels and begins to unbutton his coat, her fingers slipping in the mud. He struggles. 'Is he hurt?'

'He's okay, it was more the shock.' Ioan kicks off his boots and kneels beside Jennifer to strip Jack down. His trousers are soaked and his wellies flooded.

'Get off, get off!' He lashes out and smears mud across Jennifer's cheek.

Ioan pins his arms. 'Enough! I've said you can't go back, not like this. You'll get cold.'

His arms go limp, his bottom lip trembles, and he bites it. 'It's warm in the barn.'

'Not warm enough. Now, bath time.'

Ioan shoves the sodden clothes into the washing machine while Jennifer carries Jack upstairs in just his damp underwear, his hair plastered to his forehead on one side with mud, his eyes feral. The cord around his neck is filthy. She lets him slide to the floor and runs the taps, pours in bubbles. Doesn't give him time to protest when she slips the cord off and lifts him in. He reaches for it, but she shoves it in her pocket.

'You can have it back when you're clean, and when I've washed the mud off.'

He glowers. Sits silently while she pours warm water over his head, shielding his eyes with a face cloth, massaging shampoo into his knotted hair. She uses a handful of conditioner. Gently teases out the tangles with a comb. His cheeks go pink with the heat. He doesn't speak, is withdrawn into some internal space. She chats away to him, but he doesn't even make eye contact. When she wraps him in a towel and tries to lift him, he pushes her, leaving two small wet handprints on her jeans.

'I'm not a baby. I don't need a carry.' He holds the towel tight around himself and trails drips to the bedroom, closes the door. She decides it's better to leave him. He is embarrassed, perhaps, by the fall. She pulls the plug and goes downstairs. Ioan has gone back to finish the sheep, leaving pools of gritty water where his wellies stood. She gets a mop and cleans the hall floor, grateful for the task. The lamb follows her wherever she goes. Butts her knees gently when she stops at the sink to wash her hands.

She can hear Jack moving around upstairs, makes him hot chocolate and gets cookies from the pantry. She lets Bobbins trail behind her to the stairs, manages to hold him under one arm to help him up. She knocks on Jack's bedroom door and doesn't wait for an invitation to enter. He is dressed, in dry jeans and a T-shirt, a thick woollen sweater on the floor beside him. Standing with his back to her, leaning on the windowsill. His rucksack is propped beside the door.

'I brought you some hot chocolate, and a snack.' If anything will thaw him, it's food. Sugar.

He doesn't respond. The window is open, and a line of droplets is gathering on the sill. He is arranging empty seashells in order of size, traces a logarithmic spiral with a delicate finger. She places the warm cup next to him, the cookie beside it, and settles on the bed. Bobbins stumbles around the room, sniffing things, then curls onto Jack's discarded clothes from the day before. The lamb is weak.

She's not sure it will make it. Jack's fingers reach for the drink. He slurps and wipes his mouth with the back of his hand.

'What were you doing by the brook?'

'Looking for fish.' The sweet chocolate seems to have soothed him. He stuffs half the biscuit in his mouth.

'You know not to go near the brook, little man.'

'I wanted to see the fish.'

'It's not safe though.'

'I wanted to catch one for dinner.'

'You must stay away from the brook. Even when it's sunny. Unless you're with a grown-up.'

'Mam lets me.'

'I'm sure she wouldn't in this weather.'

'Mam says you have to learn from making mistakes. I won't fall next time.'

'Why don't you come down. You can help me feed Bobbins and we can get warm by the fire.'

'I want the key back.'

'Why? What's it for?'

'Emergencies. I need it back.' He turns his rain-grey eyes on her, holds out his hand. Palm sticky, biscuit crumbs in the creases.

'It's downstairs. You can have it back later.' She reaches past him to close the window, sees the sturdy block of Wylfa's reactors like a mirage through the downpour. They are nearly the same colour as the downpour, almost organic. She leaves him to finish his drink and goes downstairs. While she peels the vegetables for dinner she thinks of the brook, the route to the sea where the stream should drain, its banks overflowing and seeping water into the fields. She imagines the sea bass, fat and rubbery, swimming inshore, surging inside the water of the brook, luring Jack with a flash of their pewter scales. They are bigger at the outlet, near the bay.

Once the meal is simmering she goes around the house, pulling the curtains tight even though there's a few hours yet before dusk, as if this might protect them from everything out there, as if retreating can help. She sits at the kitchen table, pulls the key out of her pocket and turns it in her fingers. Then reaches for her phone.

***

'It's safe?'

'You tell me.' Helen is unlacing her boots, stripping off her boots and socks. As she unbuttons her jeans Anton turns away, embarrassed.

'I have never done this, I don't know.'

There is no point in testing the water with the dosimeter. The flow would give varied readings, unreliable. This is the most dangerous time to attempt a crossing; the river swollen from melted snow, the runoff bringing contamination from the land into the flow.

She slips off her trousers, runs her hand over her thigh. The bruise on her hipbone is green and yellow, still black in the centre. This is the first time she has seen the injuries in full light. Back in the cottage she had the filter of the dirty net curtain, the soft glow from the low-powered bulb. Her legs are so pale they seem marbled, and the cartography of her circulation system is visible in light-blue lines and tributaries beneath her skin. Her legs are unshaved, dark hairs already stiffening in the cold. Her knee is puckered and purplish around the bandage. She strips it off, revealing a twisted mouth of flesh, tight-lipped and sealed. She feels empowered by the wounds. She shoves the boots and clothes into her bag and calls to Anton.

'You need to strip down. If your jeans get wet, you'll freeze on the other side.'

His cheeks are bright pink, burning up. He glances at her and away again, quickly.

'Come on, Anton. There isn't time for this.'

'Turn your back.'

Helen turns, shouldering the rucksack and moving towards the edge of the river. Her toes sink into the silty mud, the released particles turning the water opaque. It's icy cold, and her toes ache within seconds. They will only have a few minutes to get across before the water temperature slows their joints and drags at their progress in league with the current.

She feels Anton approach, and turns to hand him a carrier bag, tells him to seal his clothes inside. He fumbles and gets the handles tied. She tightens the knot.

'We'll have to be quick. I'll go first and feel out the best route. The rocks will be slippery. Can you swim?'

He shakes his head, is either shivering or trembling.

'Okay, so tread carefully. You'll be fine.' She makes her voice sound confident, uses the tone reserved for tutoring Jack.

She steps into the water, the cold shooting pain through her ankles. The rocks are coated in a soft glaze of algae, slick beneath her soles, but she is practised in loosening her ankles just enough to let her feet slide over their surface and find the safe nook where the rocks butt against each other, wedging the sides of her feet in and stabilising her gait.

She is sure-footed and, as the water rises, leans her knees into the increasing pressure of the current to keep her balance, responding to the changing flow instinctively. Less than a third of the way across the ground falls away steeply and she almost slips, the water level rising suddenly to her hips, soaking up into the fabric of her pants. The cold is violent. She relaxes her bladder, lets the heat of urine mitigate the sting. Raises the pack higher and moves forward, ready to kick out and swim if she needs to, all the time trying not to think of how all this will feel to Anton. She feels the pressure of the water ease just after the halfway point, and the other side is shallower, the air warm on her skin after the chill of the water. There is no breeze, and the drizzle is soft.

She stands and wrings out the water from the hem of her shirt, her senses sharpened, electric after the plunge. Although she is shivering she is energised, and moves around quickly, dumping the bag away from the edge of the water and stamping to shake off the droplets that cling to her leg hair. When she has her jeans on again, she turns to Anton.

He seems small, boyish, from this side. His lithe, muscular legs look pale and skinny, and he hugs the stuffed carrier bag like a teddy bear to his chest. She shouts over to him.

'Can you throw the pack to me?'

He cups a hand around his ear and leans forwards.

'Throw the pack! Swing it over!'

He lets it drop, until he is just clinging onto one handle, and then starts to swing it, a heavy pendulum.

'Step closer, get as close as you can. Up to your ankles at least!'

He slows the rhythm and inches forward, yelps as the water creeps up his shins.

'Now, a good hard swing and let go. Aim for my head!'

She has no idea if he can make the throw, only that he needs his arms free to balance, that he'll struggle with the pack. When he does let go there is a fraction of a second where the bag seems suspended above the water, where Helen thinks it might just drop out of its arc and plummet into the depths of the pool and disappear. Then it thuds into the ground and bounces, and she scoops it up and adds it to her own, safe and dry behind her.

'You need to come on now, or you'll get too cold. Be confident, and ready for where it gets deep. Focus on me and don't think about the water.'

He nods, his eyes fixed on her, and starts walking. His feet sliding, adjusting to a terrain that shifts beneath and around him as he moves through it. Helen can see the concentration on his face, the surprise and anxiety as he negotiates the alien surface of both the rocks and the river. He is close to the drop off when her phone rings and she turns to her pack.

When she turns back to the river, Anton is gone.

The ringing silences the landscape around her, drowns out the gentle chuckle of the river in the shallows and the birdsong in the trees on the bank. It lacerates her, each shrill crescendo a physical pain running up through her wrist, out of place and harsh in this environment. She is caught between its demanding cry and the blank stare of the water.

It is the shattering force of Anton's shoulder breaching the surface, his arm thrashing like a salmon, that breaks the moment. She lurches towards the place where the water split open and his shape burst through in a shower of glistening drops and runs, ungainly and clumsily, through the shallows, reaching and pulling at the weight of the water with open hands.

The riverbed falls away beneath her and she lunges and swims, gasping as the cold water squeezes the breath out of her lungs. She feels something slither past her leg, plunges beneath the surface and opens her eyes, catches a flash of pale flesh behind the silty churn of the water and reaches out. Her fingers hook on cloth. She clenches her fist around the scrap of fabric and tugs, but the river is tugging too and she is pulled a few feet before she can brace her heels against a rock and haul her catch sideways, out of the slipstream. The tension eases and her fingers throb, readjust and tighten their grip. She moves herself carefully, drawing her prize towards her until she can slip her free hand beneath Anton's chin, dig her fingers deep into the fuzzy flesh of his jaw and raise his face out of the water. She holds him, waiting for the gasp.

He is still.

'Anton?'

She squeezes his jaw hard until his lips part, his mouth a miniature rock pool of teeth and purpling gums, full to the brim with liquid.

'Fuck, fuck, fuck.'

She takes a deep breath of her own and hauls at his weight. Buoyed by the water it moves easily at first, but as soon as the pebbles rise to meet his body she has to drag him, hands under his armpits, his head lolling back, as far as she can onto the bank. As she rolls him to drain out whatever fluid she can, his feet are still in the water, so white with cold, the blood bleached out, that he could already be dead.

She flips him onto his back and tilts his head back, almost pressing her ear against his lips to listen for breathing. The landscape is loud again: the river seeming to rush and roar, the birds shrieking, the crash of a deer through the shrubs. Everything is moving and loud except for Anton. He lies, open-mouthed and rubbery, at her knees.

She opens her own mouth wide and leans down, sealing her lips around his, awkwardly and with enough pressure to bruise them both. She pinches his nose hard and then blows, glancing out of the corner of her eye to see if his chest responds, if she has enough air for them both. Five times she forces her own frantic gasps of oxygen down into his lungs. There is still no splutter, no flicker of eyelashes.

She leans over him then, tearing his shirt open and exposing his chest, pale and almost hairless bar a whisper of dark curls on his sternum directly between his nipples. She makes a double-handed fist and leans her entire weight onto that point, forcing his ribs to bend under the pressure, counting out loud. 'One, two, three, four, five, six, seven,' the rhythm and the number something to focus on. When she gets to thirty she drops back to his mouth and forces another two breaths into him. She is on her second cycle of chest compressions when she simultaneously feels and hears something crack beneath her clasped hands. Bile rises in her throat, but she grits her teeth and continues. 'Seventeen, eighteen, nineteen.'

He coughs. It's a choking, gurgling, wet noise, like an old man with bronchitis. She stops and rolls him, holding his chin and tilting his head so the water can drain out. He is spasming, each cough a full body seizure, then violent retching that forces the swallowed water out of his stomach and throat until he is dry heaving and drooling. She wipes his mouth with her sleeve and settles him on his side, watching each rise of his ribcage as if it might be his last. Every time his chest moves she herself takes in a breath in synch, releasing the tension on the exhale and feeling it build again as she waits for his next intake of air.

He blinks, tries to move, and she shushes him, strokes his back and shoulder, and then, when his breathing regulates and she feels it is safe, she empties both packs and strips off her sodden clothes. The adrenalin is wearing off, exposing the chill. She fumbles on the clean trousers and T-shirt she was saving for once they were outside the Zone, and then piles all the dry clothes she can find on top of Anton, binding him in the foil blankets, pulling the empty rucksack up over his feet and then curling behind him. He is shaking, in shock. She hugs him tight to warm him up and calm her own shivers. Can't move him yet, not until his blood pressure stabilises. She holds him for what feels like hours, expecting any one of his shivering breaths to be his last.

They can't stay like this forever, though. Midday has long passed and the temperature will only drop lower. The drizzle has stopped, but the clothes are damp, and if they don't find shelter soon the cold will seep into their bones, dulling their brains and stiffening their muscles until they can't be bothered to move. Even if there is no frost tonight, they will die of hypothermia.

The thought of being picked apart by the carrion crows and

wolves is impetus to move. Helen helps Anton to half-sit, slowly. Supports him while she fumbles him into his trousers. He is still dazed, still trembling. When she tries to put his jacket on him, he cries out in pain, clutches his ribcage and turns even paler, a greenish tinge highlighting his upper lip. She helps him slide his arms into the sleeves and zips it up, uses a sling from her kit to secure his arm across his chest and provide support. She must have cracked a rib or two when she was pounding on his chest. A small price to pay, but another worry nonetheless. She searches the ground for any stray belongings, finds her phone on the edge of the water, half submerged, the screen black and cracked. She shoves it deep in her pocket and shoulders her rucksack. Takes out the folded map and tries to find where they are, the village they are searching for. There are no landmarks, only the curve of the river. She makes her best assessment and then helps Anton to stand, taking his weight. They stumble forward, slowly, but she is still far more confident in her stride than she is in her mind.

Now the adrenalin has worn off, she is exhausted, her own limbs so heavy that each step takes a conscious will and effort to achieve. Her only goal now is to find shelter, to warm them both up and get some real rest. Everything else can wait.

CHAPTER EIGHTEEN

'Keep him in, will you?' Jennifer picks up her car keys, 'Ioan? Please don't let him play out, not today.'

Ioan looks up from feeding the lamb, squints at the window. 'It's clearing up.'

'I know, I just think he should stay in. I won't be long.'

As the door clicks shut behind her she feels something tighten in her chest. Anxiety. She focusses hard on the feeling of solid ground beneath her feet, lists everything she can hear and see slowly and calmly, just like the websites instruct: trees, gravel, step, car, clouds, sky, wellies, pot plant.

She gets in the car and drives down the lane, easing the car around the potholes that lead to the farmhouse. Sheep lift their noses into the wind whipping off the headland.

There is little traffic. Near the turning to the plant, she indicates – habit – and lifts a hand in apology to the car behind when she accelerates and keeps going instead of turning off. She catches the shake of the driver's head, a flicker of movement in her rear-view mirror.

Megan watches with rheumy eyes from across the yard as she parks the car, pauses on the doorstep before going in. There are daffodils in pots beside the door, the yellow petals just breaking through. Her mam's wellies neatly standing to attention, where she left them last time.

The kitchen smells different. There is the lingering scent of a microwave meal, too many teacups by the sink. A stranger's handbag on the sideboard.

'Dad?' she calls upstairs, can hear voices, low and muted from her parents' room. The door opens and his head pokes out.

'What are you doing here?'

'I said I'd pop by. Remember?'

He looks confused, then disappears. Comes out a moment later, his hair uncombed, rubbing his stubble. In the kitchen he goes straight to the kettle.

'Who's up there?'

'Sarah.'

'Sarah who?'

'She's been helping your mam with... personal stuff. Showing me what to do.' He looks haunted. He has seen years' worth of births and deaths on the farm, once helped a neighbour cull their entire herd during the foot and mouth crisis, using a tractor to pile up the stiff-legged cattle into a long pyre and burn them to a raised, smoking scar on the field. Yet this – his wife needing the sheets changing, needing to be wiped clean with a flannel and rolled to prevent sores – is worse.

'Helen arranged it all, before she left. Just in case, she said. Good job she did. Panad?' He's rinsing cups, clumsy. Filling the silence.

'Let me, Dad.' She takes the tea towel out of his hands, catches the tremor. When he looks at her to say thanks she can see the exhaustion in his eyes. Red threads across his eyeballs, puffiness beneath the lids. He slumps at the table.

'She's nice, this lass they've sent. Makes your mam smile.'

'I'm glad. I'll go up in a bit.'

They sit across from one another, the table scattered with letters and forms. She sees Helen's name, the Vista logo, the calm blue Celtic knot of GIG Cymru NHS emblem.

'What's up?'

'Nothing, Dad, really.'

'Enough now. I can tell when something's bothering you. Is it your mam?'

'Always. But I'm here to help today, Dad.'

'There's something else, though, isn't there? Tell me.'

She avoids answering. Stares around the room. There are pictures of Jack in frames among the ones of her and Helen as children on the wall, a leaflet on recycling stuck to the fridge with a magnet, and a digital timer on the counter by the range. A few tiny new things. Apart from that the room looks the same as when she was a child.

'Is it Ioan?'

'No.'

'Jack?'

'No.'

'Are you sick?' He glances at her chest as if expecting to see something there, a stain or contour that would expose the problem.

She crosses her arms. 'I just miss Helen, could do with her help, that's all. Ioan's struggling with the lambing. How are you managing?'

'I've got the Parry lad covering, full time.'

'He's not at school?' Jennifer has a vague recollection of a skinny boy with gap teeth, hiding behind his fringe.

'He's eighteen.'

'We've an orphaned lamb. Needs feeding every two hours.'

'None of the others would take it then?'

'What?'

'He tried it with the other ewes and they rejected it, did they?'

'I don't think so. He came straight back with it. Is that what you usually do? We've not had a ewe die on us like this before.'

'So he didn't even try?'

'It's in a box by the Aga.'

'No wonder you're missing your sister, she'd have known. Probably too late now, but you could still try.'

They sit sipping their tea in the safety of the kitchen, until the nurse comes downstairs. She is younger than Helen expected, probably barely out of university. What can she possibly know about death, Jennifer thinks. She has a tattoo just behind one ear, a tiny bird, exposed where her hair is pulled back into a ponytail. She gives Jennifer's dad a hug on the step, promises to come back in the morning. The intimacy irritates her, the way the girl's ponytail swings behind her as she bounces to her car.

'Are you going up?'

'Not just yet, Dad. I'll let her settle. I'm going for a walk if that's okay.'

She slips out before he can answer.

***

The pace is slow, frustrating. She has to support Anton, bear the weight of the pack, and navigate without the phone.

She knows the challenge is all in her mind now, that the

rising knot of panic must be controlled. The situation is perilous, their progress potentially off the mark. And she has broken her rules. So carefully built up over the years, hardened into a way of thinking and living. The distraction of the phone was avoidable, had she kept her focus on the primary issue. Going in after Anton, that was pure folly; in direct opposition to everything she's studied about survival. With a moment's pause to think, she could have rationalised him as collateral damage. Risking her own life to save him was weakness, and now she has an injured man to look after, has lost the only form of accurate navigation.

Their feet sink into the swampy grass, and Anton groans, clutching his chest. His lips are pale, almost blue. Beads of sweat on his lip and forehead. There could still be tiny drops of water in his alveoli, mucus building up. He could drown even now, or end up with pneumonia. The sensible thing to do would be to sit him down somewhere, to save her resources and strike out alone. If she can get out, find a road, she can hitch her way into the city.

She looks at him; the long, dark eyelashes drooping, his skinny wrist at her waist. Tightens her grip on his arm and encourages him forward with soft words.

⁕⁕⁕

There are daffodils here too, all along the side of the path to Helen's barn. Dark green spearheads cracking open to reveal shards of yellow. A few have flowered fully, nodding in the breeze. Jennifer walks quickly, her hands deep in her pockets, fingers curled around the key and dirty cord. Clouds scud overhead. Lambs, already thickening around their waists and legs, cluster together, confident. Bounce for the sake of it. There is a group of five or six right by the gate, and they stretch their necks forward to bleat as she passes. As if she is an intruder and they the alarm.

In the grey gloom of the ground floor she searches for a door, a locked box or chest, opening cupboards and finding only tins and jars, the cupboards packed solid with them. Beans and tomatoes, spaghetti and soup, chickpeas and potatoes and mixed vegetables. One cupboard has bottled water, litres and litres of it.

She scales the ladder to the loft and searches there, lifting Helen's pillow to see if there is a money tin or something, rooting through the clothes in the wooden chest. Nothing. She goes back down, pulls up a chair and feels along the top of each wall cupboard, her fingers going grey with the dust, catching on spiderwebs. She washes her hands at the sink, the water gurgling in the pipe, splashing into the drain outside. She is just about to leave when she realises there is one place she hasn't looked. The car.

It hasn't been used for a while, she can tell, although the tyres look new and there is no oil staining the concrete. The grime on the roof and bonnet is dried and dusty. It is parked tight against the wall, small and quiet. She's seen it each time she's visited and not really paid any attention to it.

She leans to peer through the grimy window. The backseat is packed with sleeping bags and pillows, two rucksacks. The footwells stacked with more tins, water. In the front there is a booster seat for Jack. The keys hang from the ignition. She tries the door. It opens, releasing a warm, mildewy smell. She slides in. Looks in the glove box. A passport, the face a tiny round circle that could be any baby, Jack's name. Jennifer stares at it, trying to think of a time when Helen had ever mentioned thoughts of a holiday. Can't imagine them in a resort, by a pool. She tucks it back and keeps looking. Energy bars, two foil blankets neatly folded into plastic wrappers, a bottle of water, a phone charger and a map, a torch and spare batteries, an envelope. Jennifer feels it, slits the seal; it has a neat row of folded ten-pound notes, a hundred pounds in total. She feels under the seats, pulls out a knotted reel of rope, a folded tarp. There is nothing with a lock, nothing that would need the key.

She gets out, goes around to the boot. There is a jerry can of petrol, some waterproofs, a basic toolkit and socket set, spare oil, more food. A small motorbike helmet. She tries to imagine Jack on Helen's bike, perched behind her or tucked, perhaps, in front between her knees, escaping some terrible incident.

She lifts a black bag out and takes it to the worktop. It is a first-aid kit, bandages and tape, scissors that could cut through denim or leather. There are packets of painkillers and medicines, a bottle of TCP. She looks at the medicine, sees her own name and doctor's surgery on the label. Another has her mam's details. She drops them back in. There is a plastic box with 'Worst Case Scenario' written in permanent marker on the top. Jennifer feels sick, the contents of the car already too much to process. She opens it. Inside there are syringes, each in a sealed plastic bag. Labelled *H*, and *J*. The fluid inside is golden brown. Jennifer opens one of the bags, sniffs carefully. Detects the faintest vinegary scent and seals it away again.

She slams the boot closed. The sound seems to echo around the hollow barn. This is anxiety, she thinks. This is the problem.

CHAPTER NINETEEN

Helen sees the shape of a building in the vegetation just as dusk smudges the forest into shades of evening. Gives Anton's arm an encouraging squeeze. His breathing is wheezy, but he hasn't complained once.

As they approach, she can tell that the house is useless. The roof is sagging, the corner buckled. She can't even see the front door; there are thick brambles like razor wire woven around it, threading through the trees and shrubs to form a straitjacket around all access points.

'Come on, if there's one, there are more.' She takes Anton's hand and tugs him onwards, searching in the half-light for another structure amongst the undergrowth. Bats flit overhead, swooping low to snatch the insects drawn out by the day's warmth. Her knee aches.

The buildings get closer together as they reach the heart of the village. For a moment she dares to hope that there will be one or two houses still occupied, that she can knock on a door and present Anton, stooping but able to speak the right language, as their passport to warmth and food and a door that will close behind them, bolted. But there are no lights in any of the windows, and every patch of ground outside the houses is merely a memory of a garden; apple trees overgrown, their boughs touching the ground, fences crooked and broken as rotting teeth.

They stand on what once was the main road through town, under a defunct streetlight, and Helen surveys the options. There is a long, low official-looking structure, maybe a government office, from the time this was a collective farm. The houses either side are a little more open, accessible. She picks one, not the closest, and they wade through long grass to the side, where the door is closed.

Helen has to kick it, twice, three times, before it gives. She coughs on the dust that drifts out of the rotting doorframe. Inside it is pitch black, the shutters fastened, but she hopes this means it is protected from the wind, watertight. She flashes her torch around the room. Can see shadows of Baba Olena's house here; the same construction of fireplace with the sleeping platform above, the same solid wood floor, only this one is painted dark brown. But there are differences; instead of the clutter and colour of a home, there are empty picture frames on the walls and the table is on its side. A rusting bedframe, without a mattress or blankets, crouches in the middle of the room, and there are clothes and shoes scattered on the floor, soft underfoot.

Helen leaves Anton and peeks through a door into the back room. As her torch sweeps the boundaries something startles and flits out through a broken window. Before sealing the room off again Helen gathers the heap of material piled in the corner.

Back in the main room she rights a chair and tests its strength before beckoning to Anton.

'Come here, sit down. I'm just going to shake these outside and then we can bed down and get some rest.'

Anton sits, wincing. He is shivering.

Alone, outside, Helen pauses and lets out a deep sigh. Moonlight makes the road a pewter river. Her back aches from twisting to support Anton, her hip is throbbing. Her knee has swollen again. But they are here. Both alive.

She tests the wind direction and pulls her buff up over her nose, shakes out the material, a sheet and a thick curtain, until most of the dust has drifted away. This village is the biggest she's seen yet, and she hopes there will be a standpipe or water pump, somewhere she has a chance of getting clean water to fill their bottles.

Inside, she moves furniture and shoes, makes a space for Anton to lie, and settles him on top of the sheet and beneath the curtain. The temperature is dropping rapidly, even inside and without the wind. She rattles the fire grate and tries to peer up, seeking out a glimpse of moonlight to tell her the flue is clear. Breaks up one of the chairs and shoves the wood into the grate. There is little to use for kindling in the house, but she finds some old newspapers that will at least get the flames leaping, tries not to think of the history she will annihilate as they catch.

She is flicking sparks at it with her flint and steel when Anton laughs, a hoarse chuckle that crumbles into a cough.

'What?'

He is holding out a cigarette lighter from his pocket. The flame wavering gently. She shakes her head, strikes the flint again, and tiny sparks ignite a crumpled piece of the newspaper. The unfamiliar alphabet dissolves before her eyes.

'Where did you learn these things?' His voice is raspy.

'Growing up.' She leans to blow gently on the glowing sticks of wood. Coaxing the fire to grow. Smoke fills the fireplace.

'This is what your parents taught you? To light a fire like a caveman?'

'No, I taught myself that.'

'Why, when you can just have one of these?' He flicks the button and the flame pops up, disappears, pops up again.

'Because this lasts longer, and besides, if you rely on convenience, you're in trouble when it goes.'

The smoke spews back into the room. She pulls her biker buff up over her mouth and nose while she rattles the air feed, hopes there isn't a nest blocking the chimney. There is a clunk as she twists the small handle beneath the grate and the smoke is suddenly sucked in and away, flames leaping with the increase of oxygen. The wood spits and crackles. She leaves it and searches for more furniture to burn, smashing another chair against the wall until the pieces are small enough to fit. Anton watches her, dark eyes reflecting the yellow flames. He is still pale.

She sits beside him and roots through the rucksack. The water bottles are empty, and the last of the food long gone. She can manage without eating, but Anton needs energy, and they both need water.

When the fire is established she pulls the sodden clothes out of the pack and drapes them over the rusted bedframe to dry. Takes the water bottles and leaves Anton dozing in the dancing light while she stalks alone around the village.

The wind moves her long dark hair around her face, dry now after the slow walk, but with the coppery tang of river water still tainting each strand. Her senses are sharp to every rustle of leaves and tiny movement in the grass, to the silent shape of an owl cruising low over the fields and the distant musk of deer scat somewhere behind the treeline.

She moves quietly through tangled gardens and past empty windows searching for a well or stream. Finds a rusting tap, stationed at the point where four gardens once met, and surrounded by a swell of nettles. She tries to turn it, but it is rusted fast. Wraps her hand in her fleece, strains and feels the grating metal judder right up through her arms before it loosens, creaking and screeching, and spits out a splatter of rank water. She watches the water cough, spit, and then gush out in arterial spurts, its colour clearing.

There is no guarantee that water here isn't heavier than anything she could scoop from a stream, but she has found no streams, and they are thirsty. After ten minutes or so she fills one of the bottles and shines the torch through the plastic. The water is almost clear, a faint swirl of particles or bubbles settling in the beam. She fills the other and walks slowly, languidly, back to the house, pausing every now and then to savour the quasi-silence.

This is the furthest from civilisation she's ever been. Even in the depths of Snowdonia, on the most remote field of the farm, there are people close. Holiday cottages and ramblers, cafés and gift shops. People tipping their hats or asking directions. She can see why Baba Olena refused to leave.

***

The house is quiet when she gets back. She puts her bag on the table and calls out for Ioan. Catches sight of his shoulder as he passes the kitchen window, his arms laden with logs. She hears them clatter into the store beside the back door and sees him pass again, going to chop more.

She goes to the door and calls out.

'Is Jack with you?'

The steady thunk of the axe replies.

'Ioan! Is Jack there?'

A halt in the rhythm. Ioan's face, red and sweaty from the work, appears around the corner. 'Na, he's inside, playing with Bobbins. I found an old puppy harness in the shed, thought he could take him for a walk later.'

Halfway upstairs she stops, listening. She can't hear Jack. She moves up a step or two, identifies the drip of the dodgy faucet in the bathroom, the creak of the wind in the tree beyond the window. Then, the keening cry of the lamb. The sound is out of key with the space. It belongs in a field, echoed by the deep barking reply of a ewe's bleat.

She pushes open the bedroom door slowly. The lamb is in the harness, one leg caught and pinned back against its side where Jack hasn't fitted it properly. The leash is tied around the bed post, and the lamb is half suspended, its back legs kicking against the carpet, its front unable to reach the floor. It writhes and cries out. Jack is sitting on the floor with his back to the lamb, slowly reconstructing a jigsaw puzzle.

Jennifer kneels to free the animal. 'Hey, you can't do this, it's cruel.'

Jack doesn't look up from his task.

'Did you hear me, little man? You can't tie the lamb up. You'll hurt it.'

'I don't want it.'

'I thought you were going to look after it.'

'I think we should eat it.'

She manages to unfasten the buckle that holds the red

canvas harness around the lamb's shoulders and starts to wrestle it out. It wriggles free and bounces over to Jack, stands on the jigsaw. The tiny landscape is fractured into pieces again. He sits back on his haunches and sighs.

'I'll take it down, okay little man?' She scoops the lamb up. 'You do the puzzle again and Bobbins won't be able to accidently break it this time.'

Jack pushes the pieces into a pile, drops them one at a time into the box.

'Why can't I go outside?'

***

There are rabbits by the grass verge. The light is almost gone, but she sees their familiar shapes, hunched and soft, as they graze. They don't startle when she approaches. Back home she'd have to sit and wait, upwind, with the air rifle. They'd scatter at the first shot, and she'd walk down to finish the job, if the pellet wasn't on target. Wait another hour or more for them to come back out, cautious.

These rabbits just flick their ears towards her, sniff the air. If this area isn't part of the tours, if the loggers rarely come, they may never have seen a human in their lifetimes. She crouches, shuffles close. Reaches out a hand. The nearest animal flinches, then carries on eating. She has one chance. Lunges. Grabs. Catches the hind leg and feels it kick and strain as the others run and disappear into the bushes. It's panicking, thrashing as she readjusts her grip. She takes its hind legs firmly with one hand and makes a ring around its neck with the thumb and index finger of the other. The animal strains once more but is stretched, can't flex. With a swift jerk of her arm she presses hard with her thumb at the base of its skull, lifting the chin and pulling its back legs taut. There is a soft pop. Already the other rabbits are emerging, up on their haunches, sniffing the air. She pulls once more to be sure.

The limp body swings by her side as she makes her way back to the house. She can see the door, outlined in light, from halfway up the road, and when she pushes through, the warmth is welcoming.

Anton opens his eyes. Squints at the rabbit.

She lays it on a chair and searches the rooms for a pan or kettle to boil the water. There is nothing. The house was probably looted, anything metal taken for scrap. She takes a tiny bottle out of her rucksack, measures golden-brown drops into the water bottles. Reseals and shakes them, then lets them sit while the purifier does its work, killing microbes and bacteria. Iodine. If this were the first few hours or days after a nuclear event, the drops would also help reduce the amount of radioactive iodine absorbed into the thyroid. Prevent cancer.

While she waits for the chemical to take effect, she pulls out her multitool and makes a clean cut around the animal's ruff, teasing her fingers into the gap. The muscle is warm, taut beneath the skin. She is efficient; the pelt comes off like a glove, tears into two and hangs off the feet. She saws them off quickly, removes the head and drops the waste onto a piece of curled brown newspaper. Slits the belly from sternum to groin and guts it.

She sterilises a bent poker in the flames and spears the carcass, settling it over the edge of the fire, where the wood has burned to a low glow. Anton's cheeks are pink again, a good sign. The smell of roasting rabbit fills the room. She picks up the bottles. There is a faint deposit at the bottom, tiny particles. She kneels beside Anton, raising his head and helping him drink, carefully without disturbing the silt.

'Slowly, or you'll be sick.' His throat is exposed as he drinks, and she can clearly see the puckered curve of a scar just above his suprasternal notch. He grimaces at the taste. Water trickles down his cheek. He wipes his mouth with the back of his hand.

'Thank you.'

'You're welcome.' She takes a deep swig and tries not to think of what she might be drinking. The meat fizzes over the embers. Helen stares deep into the red glow. Anton eases himself up, tries to wrap the curtain around himself. Helen helps him remove the sling, drapes the cloth around his shoulders.

'I'm sorry.'

'What for?'

'For the river. For this.' He points at himself and then gestures to the room. 'For everything.'

She shrugs, reaches into her bag and pulls out her phone, tries the power button again. Nothing happens. The screen is cracked, the insides probably still damp. She carefully splits the case open and takes out the battery, wiping each part on her T-shirt and then propping them up as close to the fire as she can, safely. 'Hopefully it will come back to life tomorrow, once it's dried out. Then we can find your friend.'

They sit on the floor and watch the fire die down, the rabbit cooking. She turns it, gathers more wood for the fire. While they eat she throws pieces on. They need the warmth for as long as possible.

'How do you feel?' She scrutinises his face and posture. He looks okay, calmer than she's ever seen him. It might be exhaustion.

'Sore.'

'Better than dead.'

He laughs, groans at the pain.

'It's going to take a while to heal. You need to get to a hospital, get checked out.'

'Did you teach yourself that too? How to save a man's life?'

'I went on a course. It doesn't usually work, you know? Only a five per cent chance of survival.'

'Then I am lucky.'

She shakes her head. 'No, you're young. And it wasn't heart disease that stopped you breathing. I don't believe in luck.'

'Then what do you believe in?'

'Knowing my strengths and weaknesses.'

'You have weaknesses?' He smiles, the firelight bright in his eyes.

Helen thinks of Jack, his small hand clinging to hers on the walk to the school gates. Wylfa hunkered in the background. Thinks of lights in slats across a barn floor, the motion of a pendulum above her head, the smell of leather and piss. 'We all have weaknesses.'

'What are yours?'

She pauses. She's already shared too much. But here they are, outside of time and place. If they can get to the border she'll never see him again after tomorrow. 'I'll tell you, if you tell me something first.'

'Do I have a choice?'

'No.'

'Then okay.'

Helen considers her words carefully. 'The numbers, on your chest. What are they?'

Anton's eyes change, seem to shut her out. He rolls onto his back and rests a hand carefully on his breast, right over his heart. 'How did you see them?' His voice is colder, the words clipped.

Helen licks the last taste of rabbit fat off her fingers, sips water. 'When I pulled you from the river. I saw them when I was doing the chest compressions.'

Anton closes his eyes, takes a slow breath. 'I don't need you to tell me your weakness. I know it.'

Helen gives him a minute and then rests her hand near the centre of his chest, next to his, close to the point where she'd exerted so much force. He doesn't push her away, but she feels the tension threading through his body.

'Is it bruised?'

'It hurts, yes.'

'Can I see?'

He unzips his jacket. Most of the buttons of his shirt are missing from where she pulled it open; he unfastens the few that are left. Exposes a dark circle of bruising over his sternum, a purple shadow around one of his ribs, and five numbers in blue ink over his heart. For a while neither of them speak. The fire settles. Helen sips water, the bitter aftertaste of the iodine reassuring.

He strokes the tattoo, sighs, and with his eyes still closed starts talking. She watches his chest rise and fall as he speaks. 'They are my father's numbers. He was likvidator for the accident. My mother was pregnant with me when it happened, and he was fireman. My mother waited three days to see him, to find out if he was alive. He came home, got changed and went back. They told him there was no one to replace him, that he would have to carry on. He never went back to that house. My mother was evacuated to Ivankiv on day five. That's where he came to die.'

'You lived inside the Zone?'

'I didn't. I was born after.'

'But this is where your home should be?'

Anton shrugs, opens his eyes, and looks around the room. 'Somewhere like this, maybe.' He closes his eyes again. 'I have a flat now.'

'Was he one of the first?' Helen thinks about the accounts she's read of the men who attended the burning reactor; the roof sticky as tar, the glowing graphite they kicked back towards the gaping maw of fire, the flesh blistering and sliding off their bones in the days afterwards.

'No. He was called afterwards, a day or so afterwards.'

The room is cast in a bronze glow from the embers. The temperature has already dropped. Helen moves away, takes a handful of broken furniture and throws it on. Throws the rabbit bones on too. They hiss.

'You never knew him.'

'I have picture, and I met a man once who told me he knew him. Said he was taller than me, and that he told jokes even as they hosed him down in hospital. Told me he was a hero.'

'Is that why you do the tours? Because of him?'

He doesn't answer.

'I saw something at the memorial. Some of the numbers had been chipped away. Was that you?'

318

Anton's eyes open, black in the half-light. He stares at her. 'Every year I plan to leave, to go somewhere clean, somewhere safe. I have enough money. The tours pay well.' His breathing is ragged, the faint rattle of earlier on the inbreath. 'Now you see my weakness. Here, in print.'

'And the memorial…'

'So I didn't have to leave him behind. The protests have reminded people we are a borderland, two halves fighting for the same territory. Ukraine has always been this way. Ivankiv, Kyiv, are in the middle.'

'Which side are you on?'

'I am just trying to work. Like my father.'

'Will you leave?'

'I don't know, depends on what has happened. The protests were peaceful, until Yanukovych sided with Russia.' He falls silent. His chest rising and falling, fingers pressed into the numbers. Then, almost a whisper, 'My mother wanted to move back in, like Baba Olena. Blames me that she couldn't. They told her if she went back, I would be born sick, that she would miscarry. Before she died, sometimes she would look at me, and it felt like she was wondering if she made the right choice.'

'Do you have any other family?'

'Not here.'

'But you'll never leave.' It isn't a question. She knows better than him how he feels, why he will settle for the flat and the tours until he himself wears out and sinks back into the earth. She's had enough solitary hours in the sloping fields back home to have thought it through. She doesn't own the land, it owns her. And he is caught too, without knowing; the weight of personal history, of belonging, pinning him to his patch. It will take an army to detach him. Perhaps that is what will happen. Russian troops. And if he isn't killed he'll get sick, and blame the disaster when it will as much be the displacement that eats him up. For her it will be suits and hi-vis coats, company logos and paperwork.

Anton yawns. His eyes are red, from tiredness or the smoke that kicks back into the room occasionally when the wind quickens. They need to sleep. Helen rearranges the blankets, checks the clothes and finds her fleece is almost dry. She balls it to make a pillow for Anton, then lies beside him. He shifts awkwardly, pulling away at first.

'We need to stay warm, let me get closer.' She curls around him. He is thin, all muscle and sinew. Like Jack. It takes a while for him to relax. She lies, watching the firelight dancing on the curled and peeling paint. Listens to his breathing regulate, the rattle loosening. He coughs.

'You still haven't told me, about your weakness.'

She closes her eyes and feels the room sway. 'When I was small, six years old…' *Light in slats across the floor, the smell of leather and piss.* 'I watched a man die.'

Anton tries to turn, but she pushes him back, can talk to his back better than his eyes. Feels his hand take hers and hold it, comforting. She lets him, lets it pour out, verbalised for the first time.

'It was after Chernobyl, late summer. Mam and Dad were strung out, pretending everything was okay when I could tell it wasn't. It was the way they looked at each other, over our heads. Then one morning this big van came into the yard, another set of suits, blokes with posh accents and face masks wanting to do more tests. They'd already told us we couldn't sell the sheep, and the veg patch Mam had at the back of the yard was weeded over, dried up. No point watering it, is there, if you're not sure it's safe to eat.'

Each word is like a piece of armour removed, but although she feels the exposure almost physically it is also liberating.

'All the farms were being monitored. Some people were calling for culls. So, all the men get out of their van and Mam starts making tea for them, and I want to stay and see what is going on, but she tells me to go out and play. Wrapped me up in a cardigan, still worried about the exposure. Like a cardigan could save me. I walked across the fields, to my friend's place. They had the farm next to ours. Walked into her yard. It was hot, and my cardigan was itchy.'

She pauses, pulls her hand away and scratches her shoulder. She can hear Anton breathing; shallow, expectant.

'I knocked on the door, but no one came. Then I saw the barn door was open. I still don't know why I went in... Her dad was there. Just hanging there, above me. A puddle under him. He was swinging, a little bit. His legs kind of propelling him. I just stood there, like my feet were set in rock, watched his face turn purple.'

'Did you go for help?'

'No. I don't know why.' She'll never know. 'I've never told anyone.'

He reaches around, tries to take her hand again. She pulls away, eases her body from him and rolls onto her back. There is a patch of mould across the ceiling, a map of water penetration and time. Like the house is bruised.

'I could smell him. His shoes, his piss. I couldn't speak, didn't speak for weeks. It was like my own tongue had swollen up like his. Blocking my mouth. I heard Mam and Dad talking a few days later. After the disaster I started creeping out of my room to sit at the top of the stairs, listen to them in the kitchen. Talking about finances, about the monitoring. Apparently his daughter found him, later that day. Dad was angry, really angry. Kept saying "No matter how bad it gets you don't do that, you don't just give up." But he had, and his wife did too. Sold the farm and moved away.'

She pauses. The wind has picked up, and the chimney is singing; an eerie, hollow groan.

'I remember thinking, they're weak. They let it get to them.'

Anton rolls, carefully, wincing, to face her. 'You were just a child, traumatised. Violence does this, hurts your mind.'

'It made me stronger. I could have had nightmares – I do still dream about it – but it made me angry, like my dad. Not sad. You asked me, last night, if I was scared. Yes. Of everything. Of losing my home, of getting sick. Of my son not being strong enough to cope.' Her hand goes to her left breast, automatically. 'That is my weakness. A constant rock of fear right here.' She places her fist over her chest. 'But I've learned to listen to the fear. To use it.'

Anton reaches out, tentative, unfolds her fist and gently laces his fingers between hers. Rests his forehead against her shoulder. 'I'm scared too. All the time. I know your feelings.'

They lie in the darkening room. Quiet. An intimacy between them that transcends any self-imposed boundaries; that lets them both, for now at least, just touch.

***

The barn is almost empty, most of the sheep and lambs turned out already. Jack clambers onto a bale, fiddles with a trail of twine while Ioan and Jennifer work out a strategy.

'This one is a good bet,' Ioan says, pointing to an older ewe near the back. She has a single lamb, just a day old. He lowers Bobbins into the pen. They watch him totter over, bleat pathetically. He isn't putting on weight as fast as he should, is barely any bigger than the newborn. The ewe stamps her hoof, pushes him away with the hard slope of her head. He falls, wobbles to his feet and tries again.

They try three more. Each time Bobbins is butted, rejected. He doesn't smell right, isn't part of the flock anymore. On the last try he just stands near the fence, wary of approaching. His thin legs tremble.

'If we had a fresh birth we could cowl him in the sac, make him smell right.'

'But we don't.' Jennifer shoves her hands deep into her pockets. 'We should have done this straight away. It's useless.' She can feel Jack's eye on her, hard as slate. He knew.

Ioan tucks Bobbins back inside his jacket and they walk home in silence. She holds Jack's hand to stop him running off. Sends him straight to bed when they get back, checking to see the window is closed and locked, and that all the curtains in the house are closed.

Ioan settles in the kitchen, feeding the lamb and drinking tea. She sits opposite him and places the box from Helen's car onto the table.

'What's that?' Ioan picks it up, turns it in his wide hands.

'I don't know. Needles, some kind of drug.'

'You think she's on drugs?' He opens the box and lifts one

of the bags. The amber liquid glows in the light from the kitchen bulb.

'They're labelled, one each.'

Ioan lets out a sigh and the lamb shifts on his lap, its golden eyes unblinking.

'I don't think he's safe. Not with her.'

'What do you mean?'

She explains about the car, the notebooks. 'She's ready to leave, everything packed, passports, the lot.'

'Why would she go? She's so determined to keep the farm going.'

'I don't think she wants to go, she's just ready in case something happens. A meltdown, a leak. An explosion.'

'So what do you think this is for?' Ioan points at the box. An old takeaway container, the syringes capped. 'It might be medicine, iodine or something to add to their food? Looks like iodine.' He lifts the bag again and holds it to the light; tiny grains swirl in the solution.

'I think it's a suicide kit. For if something happens and she can't get them out. She reads all this stuff about survival. It's extreme. Here, listen...' She opens her laptop and reads a section from the PrepMommy site. '*If you can't guarantee their safety, or if the worst has happened and they are already suffering a slow and distressing death, you should have a plan to make the end as gentle as possible. Hot chocolate, cuddles. A sedative to ease them into sleep. Make sure they are gone before either moving on or dealing with yourself.*'

'Shit. She wouldn't do that though.'

She gets up and paces. 'Maybe you're right. Maybe it's iodine... but maybe it's something else.' It could just be theoretical, a safety net never intended for use. 'Maybe it's time we got advice. All this fear and paranoia. It's borderline abusive, isn't it?'

'Jen, once you get people involved there's no going back.'

'Then what do we do? Wait for her to come back? To keep filling his head with all this... this nonsense?' She thinks of Wylfa, the risk of human error. How easy it is to make mistakes. Sits down again, and stares at the box. Feels her chest tightening. Her mam is only a mile or so away – soiling herself, sipping Complan, in pain. Is Helen planning something for her? Would it be so bad if she were?

'She's a good mam, she loves him.'

'I never said she didn't, Ioan. I don't know what to do. I'm scared is all. For him.'

CHAPTER TWENTY

'She's not coming back, is she?' Jack is sitting at the kitchen table, feeding greens to his snails. She has bought him a new school uniform, combed his hair. He looks almost kempt. He screws the lid on the jar and watches as Modron and Mabon emerge slowly from their shells, test the new vegetation with stretched necks and wavering eyes.

'She's just been delayed, she'll be back.'

He watches her turn out pockets on jeans and work trousers, place the loose change, spare keys and hairgrips on the worktop before loading the washing machine.

'Please can I have a drink?' He half smiles at her.

'Of course, milk?'

'Yes, diolch.'

When she turns back from the fridge he's across the room, looking out of the window. She puts the milk on the table and scooches him out of the way while she finishes loading the machine. He sips, leaves most of it.

'Come on, let's get your shoes on.' New shoes too, not yet creased. She babies him, bending to tie the laces. He needs babying, needs to be treated like a child. His school bag leans against the wall. It has become routine, almost normal. Where is my sister? she thinks. Who is she? And then, as she stands and reaches for the car keys: if Helen doesn't come back will this be my life; the school run, packing biscuit bars and crisps into a satchel?

He gazes up at her from underneath his dark, curled hair. Wide eyes.

'I feel sick.'

She drops to her knees again, places a hand on his forehead. His face is warm but not hot. She has nothing to guide her. He has no spots, no snot or rashes.

'Like you're going to be sick, or just a bit queasy?'

'I don't know. My head hurts.'

She feels lost for a moment – to send him in sick would be cruel, and yet she senses he is malingering. In the end she feels she can't risk it. He needs looking after.

'Okay, then. Back to bed. I'll bring you some water in a minute.'

He scampers upstairs, a little too energetically. If he doesn't pick up by lunchtime she'll call Helen's GP, get him checked over. She has already planned to look into the legalities of requesting a care order or some kind of temporary custody later. If Helen doesn't come back she will have to make the arrangement formal. The police have no information on her whereabouts, are hampered by the ongoing political situation in Ukraine, and there is no sign of order being restored anytime soon.

When Jack is settled in bed with water and his book, she loads the dishwasher and wipes the tops down. She has told the cleaner not to come, given her full pay to stay away until she's back at work. Jennifer needs something to occupy her time while she waits for her penance to be served. The company doctor is coming late morning, might give her a return date. The thought lifts her. Perhaps she was tired, is tired still.

When the washing machine is finished she pulls the tangle

of clothes out into the basket and stands it on the worktop. Looks out of the window. Heavy clouds are scudding across the sky. She can hang it out later, if it clears.

She flicks the TV on while she tidies the lounge, a 24-hour news channel. Half listens to reports on Russia's annexing of Crimea, a teenager from Leicestershire being tried for planning a terrorist attack, and the response to the Budget. She is wiping down the mantelpiece, collecting dust and a dead fly into the soft yellow of the cloth, when she feels Jack standing behind her.

'What's up, little man?'

'I want to go outside, but the door is locked.'

'You said you were poorly, you can't go outside.'

'I need some fresh air. It's not raining.' He goes to the window. Bright sunshine and trees just budding with pale pink blossom. Above it all the sky is a vast, blank cyanotype.

'I said no. Go back to bed. If you feel better later, I'll take you and Bobbins for a walk.'

'I want to go now, on my own.'

'I don't feel comfortable with you outside on your own, so play inside.'

'But I always play in the garden without a grown-up.'

'Not anymore.' She clutches the cloth and feels the body of the fly crumble between her fingers. He goes back upstairs.

She starts hoovering, moving furniture and trying to second guess what the doctor will ask. If she rests, is fit for work, she won't make any more mistakes. She changes the end of the hoover pipe, attaches a nozzle to fit into the corners. Tries not to think about whether any of today's engineers had a bad night's sleep, or a glass of wine before bed. There are enough safeguards, she thinks, for such things to be mediated. The human brain may be fragile, but there are systems in place, procedures to prevent one mistake bringing the whole thing down. She takes her time, sucking crumbs from between the sofa cushions, diverting energy from the anxiety into the task.

By the time the doctor arrives the house is immaculate, and she has showered, applied subtle make-up: projecting a healthy glow. She offers tea and they sit in the lounge, a plate of biscuits neatly arranged on the coffee table.

'I'm fine, really. I'm sure they told you this is just procedural.'

'I'm not here for them, I'm here for you.' The woman is older than Jennifer, her mascara already smudged a little beneath her eyes. She wears soft grey chinos and a blouse that gapes slightly at the bust.

'I'm fine, really. I had a busy week and made a silly mistake. I've had a good rest now and am ready to go back.'

'Tell me a little bit about that week. What made it busier than any other week?'

'I'm looking after my sister's little boy, he doesn't sleep well. I'm not used to having my routine changed. I guess I wasn't sleeping enough.'

'Is routine important to you?' Her voice is soft, but not unnaturally so. She isn't local; Jennifer detects a hint of the Midlands in her flat vowels. A blow-in, moved here for the beaches and forests maybe, a semi-retirement. She sips her tea and waits.

'Yes, I suppose so. I mean, it keeps things working, doesn't it?' There is a bump, the sound of feet on the stairs. 'Just a moment, he's off school today, feeling poorly.'

In the kitchen Jack is rooting through the pantry, stuffing his pockets with muesli bars and school snacks.

'What are you doing?'

'I'm hungry.'

'You said you felt sick.'

He doesn't respond, is caught, and he knows it.

'Go back to bed and once this lady has gone you can go to school for the afternoon, if you feel better.' She ushers him out of the room, up the stairs. In the lounge she apologises. The woman smiles sympathetically.

'How old is he?'

'Six soon, in a few weeks. His mam's never left him before.'

'And how are you finding it, looking after him?'

Jennifer thinks of the barn, the car, and the bruises on her wrists from pulling him down from the tree. Now is her chance to ask for advice.

'It's fine. Nice to have some quality time with him. Another biscuit?'

***

The car is small, old. A Lada from the eighties maybe, from the Soviet era.

Helen and Anton stand back from the road, in the long grass at the edge of the forest, watch as it approaches. Anton is unsure at first, then steps forward, waves carefully. When the vehicle slows he turns to her and grins.

'It is him.'

Relief they have made it to the right area gives them a final push of energy to walk up the slight embankment towards the road. Her phone is still dead, but her compass and the map at least kept them from veering miles off course.

Anton is opening the passenger door, beckoning to her.

Helen approaches the car cautiously. It is square and boxy, the blue paintwork faded, patched up in parts and not sprayed over. Gives the impression of being a car-shaped globe, small maps of foreign islands marked out in filler and rust over the wheel arches and beside the bonnet. Anton leans in and slap hands with the driver, who cranes his neck to look at her around Anton's chatter. She is excluded by their shared language, the outsider again. As she moves away from the trees and towards the car she feels the power balance shift, becomes guarded.

The young man in the car is skinny, dressed in combat trousers and a black T-shirt. His head is shaved so close to his skull that his scalp shows pale blue through the stubble. A cigarette bounces on his lips as he grins, a roll-up as skinny and tatty as himself.

'Helen, this is my friend, Maksim.'

She smiles and nods, assessing his stature and attitude. Maksim's grin widens, shows teeth that are small and rounded, browned at the gums from tobacco or too much coffee. He lounges in the driver's seat proprietorially. She can sense his enjoyment of the situation, the novelty of it fuelling him. It puts her on edge. He exudes the scent of unpredictability.

Anton is weak, the long hike has depleted any reserves of energy from before the incident at the river, and his breathing comes in short, painful gasps, even when resting. He coughs frequently, painfully. She hopes it isn't the early signs of pneumonia from the river water, or a perforated lung from the fracture. Infection, sepsis. He isn't feverish but could burn up any minute.

There is a struggle to get the passenger seat to tilt forward, and Helen steps in, helps him manoeuvre carefully onto the backseat. He eases into the corner, one arm across his chest. Closes his eyes. This is the risk – now they have overcome the main obstacle he will relax, give in to it, believing that it is over. She lets the front seat fall into place with a clunk, shoves the rucksack into a footwell already brimming with fast-food wrappers and empty bottles, oily rags and newspaper.

'First stop – food!' Maksim revs the engine and pulls out, too quickly. There is no other traffic on this bleak back road and he drives with abandon. Helen grips the door handle and waits until they are travelling at a steady pace before fumbling for the seatbelt.

'Is broken,' Maksim grins, his sidelong glance taking in more than her startled reaction. 'You don't need it. I don't need mine.' He rubs a hand down his unrestrained chest. Helen twists to see Anton – slumped, pale. He doesn't have a belt on either.

The scenery that flickers past is almost identical to the landscape around Ivankiv; pine trees and deciduous forests, split apart by tracts of open farmland. Only now everything is thickening, fuzzy around the edges with new growth. Spring is forcing its way out through the mulch of winter – thin spikes of green stripe the black, churned fields, small flowers spill over the sides of the road, and every tree is unfurling pale green tongues towards the sunlight.

For the first time she feels a flicker of hope for the future pushing through the leaden anxiety, a nascent belief she can win. But she needs to change tactics. Opening up to Anton was like a slow release of pressure, as if surfacing from a deep lake. Empowering. As the farms and forests flash by she begins to strategise her next move: she can't do it all alone anymore. She will talk to Jen properly, and Ioan too. Explain everything and get them onside against Wylfa B. Once the plans are halted she can focus on Jack. He is struggling with school, just like she did at his age, but he'll be fine so long as they can keep the farm. That's where he can be himself, where he learns the most. But he also needs to learn how to work with others. She should give him something to love and share his life with. Not a sibling, she's sure of that, but perhaps a puppy. He's shown a kind of affection for the snails, so maybe he's ready.

'How long until we get there?' she asks Maksim.

'Maybe... four hours?'

She knows she should try to sleep, recharge, but there's little chance of that with Maksim's erratic driving. She braces her feet against the footwell and watches him shift gear, the engine whining. At least there isn't much traffic around.

***

Two months. In the first instance. She feels the hollowness of the time stretch out ahead.

'I'm concerned you rely too heavily on the structures of work, and haven't given enough time over to your family, to nurturing the relationships that will support you when you need them,' the woman said, folding her notebook back into her bag and standing up. 'Spend this time resting, going out for walks, cooking. Reconnect with your family. You'll need time and space to cope with your mother's situation. The job isn't going anywhere. Find strength in those around you, and you'll come back fortified.' She'd written a prescription for Diazepam, 'to take the edge off'.

Jennifer had let her out, shaken hands on the doorstep and thanked the woman for her time. Then closed the door and wandered into the kitchen, furious. Time is the last thing she needs.

She sits at the table and makes a list of everything she can do to keep busy. Tax returns. She could do them herself this year instead of turning over their payslips and profit and loss accounts from the farm to the accountant. A holiday, maybe. Repairs on the house. Guttering and pointing to fix the storm damage of the winter and prevent further costs.

Jack is quiet upstairs. The lamb's box is empty, the towel rumpled and stained. She can hear the drone of a fly in the window. Sunlight penetrates the glass.

Time to hang the washing out.

She makes it as far as the kitchen door before her chest tightens. The smell of detergent fills her head. Flowers, or a version of them, orchids maybe. She rubs her nose and looks out of the window beside the door. Real flowers press their petals against the salt-smeared pane. Beyond, Jack is walking down the path, away from her. His dark hair defying the sunlight as his legs disappear into the long grass at the end of the garden. Above him the washing line is an empty thread.

She knocks on the window to get his attention, to beckon him back in, but he is lost in the dappled light beneath the apple tree. She takes a deep breath and picks up the basket of laundry, gets to the end of the passage and places it on the floor.

A fly is dying slowly on the windowsill, its wings picking up dust as it struggles on its back. There are hours to fill before Ioan is due home from work. She imagines him in his overalls and mask, maybe behind the heavy respirator, sweating inside the protective suit, alien and safe. Swigging PowerAde on his break to replenish lost body salts, showering quickly before dressing for home.

She looks outside again, at the empty washing line cutting through the sky, disappearing into the leaves of the apple tree. Opens the back door and smells the sea on the wind. On the doorstep there is a large pickle jar, empty. Cabbage scraps shrivelling on the path.

**

'So, you are the girl who plays in the Zone, yes?'

'I don't play.'

'But you like to take risks.'

Helen looks at him. His eyes are on the road, but his grin is wide, and he is nodding to himself.

'Did you eat anything there? Drink the water?'

Helen twists in her seat again to check on Anton, wondering what he has told his friend. His eyes are closed, although she is sure he isn't asleep. 'Are you okay?' She reaches around to squeeze his knee. He smiles ever so slightly and nods, doesn't open his eyes.

Maksim lets go of the steering wheel with one hand and pulls down the front of his T-shirt. 'Look.' He twists and the car swerves slightly on the road. 'They already have my thyroid, so when I go in there, I eat and drink and nothing happens.'

There is a curved scar just below his Adam's apple, resting on the jutting shelf of his clavicle. He smiles as she leans in to look closer. 'They call these Chornobyl necklaces.'

'I've seen pictures.' She thinks of Anton, neck exposed. The puckered pink wound.

'Is better in real life, yes?'

He grins wider. Helen thinks that if he became any more pleased with the situation his face might split. The scar on his throat is like a second, permanent grin.

'Anton, vona myla!' he calls back, through the rear-view mirror.

'Vidchepys, Maksim.' It's barely more than a whisper.

Helen sits on the periphery, tense. The sense of comradeship with Anton fading.

'Vona tvoya? Mozhna ya yiyi viz'mu?'

'Vona nalezhyt' sama sobi.'

'Ya vse zh mozhu sprobuvaty.' Helen sees him wink at Anton through the mirror. She doesn't like the way their conversation makes her feel, the automatic exclusion of their shared language.

Anton sits up and leans forward, supporting himself on the backs of the front seats and hovering in the space between Helen and Maksim. 'Ty b ne vyzhyv!'

Maksim explodes with laughter, his body seeming to crumple and fold as he howls and slaps his thigh. 'This man, here,' he waves towards Anton's face with a loose wrist, 'he thinks a lot of you!'

'I should think so, I brought him back from the dead.'

'Fuck me!' Maksim exclaims. He runs a hand over the stubble of his head. 'I want to hear it all. All.'

The farms and villages are slipping away. Maksim pulls over into a service station and they climb out. The strip lights are dazzling, harsh, and Helen goes straight to the toilets to relieve herself and wash. She can let out nothing more than a trickle of orange fluid. Her kidneys ache. She strips off her clothes and changes into the fleece-lined leggings and long-sleeved top she wore under her leathers to travel in all that time ago. Crams the contaminated clothes into a plastic bag and shoves them deep into the sanitary waste bin. Soaks some paper towels and scrubs her boots, running the muddied soles under the tap until they are clean. Finally, she stands at the sink and lets the hot water redden her hands raw, washes her face over and over. Drinks, the tap water cupped in her palms. It tastes of chemicals.

When she goes back out into the shop area Anton and Maksim are standing near the counter, wolfing down hot dogs. Maksim pauses mid-chew to look her up and down. Anton hands a hot dog to her.

'Horse meat?'

'Probably.' Anton smiles around the processed bun. He looks better, a little. If he can eat he's probably okay.

She sinks her teeth into the spongy bread and barely chews, but is already on the next bite, ravenous. The cheap processed food might give her stomach ache, but refuelling is vital. Maksim is queuing again, his skinny arms piled with bottles of soft drinks and bars of chocolate, a huge bag of crisps. He has tattoos peeking out from beneath his sleeves. Helen tries to see what they depict, but it's more a swirl of blue than a distinct part of something.

When they get back into the car the bounty is shared out. Helen sips at a fizzy drink, the bubbles making it hard to slake her thirst fast enough. She belches and Maksim laughs, nodding again to affirm her actions as pleasing to him. The bag of crisps is passed around, salty and moreish. She takes a handful and shoves them in three and four at a time. Her fingers are greasy. She licks them and wipes them on her legs, uncomfortable with the fullness of her stomach.

'So, in the Zone, what did you do to this man?' Maksim waggles his eyebrows suggestively. Licks the salt off his lips.

'I drowned him, then broke his ribs.'

The grin drops. 'Why? What did he do?'

'He tried to kill me, chased me into the forest on my motorbike and straight into a pack of wild boar.'

Maksim looks from one to the other, his mouth loose; the newly rolled cigarette he has just placed there hangs, the paper caught on the moisture inside his lower lip.

She looks at Anton and they both start laughing. Him clutching his chest and crying out a little as he does so. Helen feels something, a smouldering affection maybe. Their conversation of the night before still lingers, unspoken but binding.

Maksim tries to replace his smile and join in. 'You are joking. It's a joke!'

Anton opens his shirt and shows his friend the bruising. Maksim looks at Helen and nods solemnly. She straightens her spine, accepts the praise.

To Anton he says, 'Ya ne dumayu shcho ya budu tsym ryzykuvatyy.'

'What are you talking about?' Helen gazes directly at Maksim. She won't let him exclude her anymore.

'The Zone will be busy soon.' He lights the roll-up and starts the engine. Pulls out of the parking area with a jolt.

'What day is it?'

'Thursday.'

'I mean the date.'

'Fourteen.'

'Of April?' Helen has lost track of the days since the end of the tour but can't have lost this much time.

'March. Next month is anniversary. But it gets busy in the weeks before, lots of tourists remember, and the festival of Radunitsa. It is already on the news.' Maksim smirks. 'Every year it is a celebrity again, and I can show off my necklace for the news cameras.'

'Maybe people won't come this year,' Anton says. 'They will be told not to travel.'

The night in Ivankiv has faded behind the bike accident and the journey through the Zone.

'What has happened? Are the protests still going?' Helen asks.

Maksim looks at her, amazed, then grins, nodding again. She wants to reach out and use her hands as a vice, to hold his skull still while he talks.

Anton is hanging between the seats. Helen imagines what will happen if they crash, the force of sudden deceleration making his body a missile. He'll be through the windscreen in an instant. She reaches for the seatbelt socket beside her and holds it tight.

'Riots. The protests against the government spread from Kyiv. You know about the protests?'

Helen considers his words, thinking of the last few weeks. 'So now the whole country is rioting?' World War Three could be underway and they wouldn't know.

'Yanukovych is gone.'

'Gone?' Anton leans forwards.

'I saw on the news, they went to his house and found it empty, abandoned. His offices too.'

'So, Putin has his chance to step in?' The question is anxious, peppered with coughs.

'Anton, he's taken Crimea.'

Anton sits back as though he's been kicked in the chest. Helen turns to him, watches his mouth open and close, but no words come out. Maksim chatters on, detailing everything his friend Anton has missed while in the forest.

'He's raised the flag and called a referendum. The Party of Regions is hoping for a new Soviet Union.'

'And the rest of the country?'

'My Babushka says the country will split; the East will go to Russia and the West to Europe. The middle will be battlefield.' The smile has gone from Maksim's face, and Helen sees a weight in his eyes.

'How does this affect you?' she asks.

'Whatever happens there affects here, and he's my friend.' He taps his scar. 'My brother. It's only you who will go home to a place where there are no wars over territory.'

They each sink back into their seats, processing the information as the fields become villages and the villages become suburbs and the city grows out of the ground in stone and concrete and streetlights. It isn't on the same scale, she thinks, but it is a war, nonetheless. Fields, hedgerows, the contours of the land. Territory.

CHAPTER TWENTY-ONE

His rucksack is gone, most of his clothes. His school uniform discarded on the floor like a shed skin. Jennifer searches the house first, knowing it is futile. In the pantry there are half-empty boxes of muesli bars and mini-biscuit packs. His wellies and school shoes are still in the porch, but his hiking boots are missing. She searches through the jackets and coats, through the ones that have slipped into a heap on the floor. His new, bright coat is there, but not the sour-smelling old one he arrived in.

By the time Ioan gets home she is halfway to the field, tripping on the roots in her haste, visualising him tucked up on top of a hay bale, playing at survival. The tightness in her chest has a focus now. She calls to him from the field, searching the boundary with her eyes as she approaches the barn. Barbed wire and brambles.

The warmth of the barn is tinged with sheep shit, sweet hay; it smells like home. He'll be here she thinks, calling again. The ewes bellow back, hollow barking calls repeated in treble by their lambs. They watch her as she searches, clambers on bales, moves pallets to find a den or hidey-hole where he might be crouched, nibbling biscuits, making them last.

On her way back she racks her brains for where else he might be. Dusk is leeching sunlight from the sky, a band of cloud flat on the horizon like a tidal wave. She stops and scans the terrain.

To one side the slope of the empty field towards rocks and roiling sea, to the other a scarred landscape. Empty and half-demolished houses, any one a potential hideout. Dangerous and crumbling. The wind whips her hair into her mouth, over her eyes. Could he have tried to make his way home, to the barn? She looks at the most direct route; more barbed wire and brambles, gorse bushes, the solid block of the reactors behind ten-foot-high security fencing. CCTV. Men with machine guns patrolling the perimeter. He'd never make it through.

Ioan is eating cold cuts from the fridge when she gets back, his purple Magnox fleece still on, his eyes tired from a twelve-hour shift. He stops chewing as she tells him.

'Have you called the police?'

'No, I wanted to look first, to see if he was down in the barn. We should check Mam and Dad's too.'

'Could he have gotten that far?'

'I don't know.'

She fumbles her pockets, goes to the washing basket still sitting, damp and tangled by the back door. Turns out the pockets of her wet jeans. 'He's got the key.'

'What key?'

'That thing he had around his neck, on the cord. For emergencies, he kept saying. Must've taken it this morning while I...' She groans. 'He's planned this.'

'What are you talking about, Jen, planned what?'

'This morning, he didn't want to go into school, said he felt sick. He's been planning this.'

'Jen, you're not making sense. He's five. He's probably playing somewhere. Camping out.' They both know, from the tone of Ioan's voice, that he's wrong.

'No, you don't get it, Ioan. She's been training him for this for years. He's out there somewhere, playing something, yes. But it isn't just camping. He thinks she isn't coming home.'

***

The city is noisy. Even with the windows closed Helen can smell exhaust fumes, food, rain-soaked tarmac. The noise has crept up on her, become almost unbearable.

'Stop the car, Maksim.'

'We are nearly there, don't worry.' That grin. She could slap him.

'Please, just find a quiet street and pull over.' Her tone gives no option for discussion.

Maksim nods and swerves away from the main thoroughfare. The sound of horns blaring fades as they move towards a residential area, big houses set back from the road, architecture to die for. He pulls over near a small park. Helen can see people walking little dogs, pushing prams. It could be Manchester, Liverpool, anywhere.

She opens the door and gets out, sucking in the wet green air from the park. Walks away from the car. After a few moments Anton joins her, takes her hand.

'What's wrong?'

'How do you feel?'

'Okay. Tired. Why?'

'I just...' She can't explain, isn't sure herself. If she questions it, she knows some deeply held belief will fissure. Over his shoulder she can see Maksim smiling, hoping to catch

343

them kissing, maybe. She gently extracts her fingers from his hold, resets his drooping sling. 'Can you walk a little?'

He nods. They go a little way into the park, away from the car. She has no idea what the Embassy will say when she walks in, how much trouble she'll be in. They have decided she should say she was fleeing the protests, got lost, deny any knowledge of the Exclusion Zone and their route into Belarus. She will tell them she hitched a lift into the city after her bike broke down. Deny she knows the names of the strangers who picked her up.

When they are a reasonable distance away from the road, partly obscured by ornamental shrubs, and it is only the occasional disapproving glances of the mothers with their expensive pushchairs that intrude on the moment, she stops.

'Promise me you'll go straight to a hospital.'

'I promise.'

There is an awkward silence. They are barrelling towards an end, and she's not sure what is ending. There is a pressure to say something, coming from within. Somewhere deep. But she hasn't come this far to let herself be swept away by transient, misguided feelings. That Anton has breached her defences in some small and indefinable way doesn't give her the excuse to cling onto him.

Anton follows her gaze across the grass. There are children on swings, a young couple walking and stopping to kiss every few yards, an old man in an oversized coat slouching alone on a bench. Anton rocks on the balls of his feet, coughs and winces. Shoves his free fist deep into his pocket. The air smells of blossom and traffic fumes, and there are birds singing. The city provides a background hum of industry and commerce.

He pulls his hand out and unfurls his fingers.

'I want you to have this.'

'What is it?' Helen leans close and looks down at the bright red and green ribbon in his hand. A red, enamelled cross hangs from it, a pale blue circle with a drop of bright blood at the centre, dotted lines branching through it and out. The Greek symbols for Alpha, Beta and Gamma are in gold beside each route.

'It is his medal. For being Likvidator.'

'I can't take this.'

'You are not taking it; you are receiving it.'

She places a finger on the drop of enamel blood, the lines of gold that represent the different kinds of radiation that penetrate it.

'You earned it, in there. You saved my life, you got us out. Here.' He pushes it into her hand and folds her fingers over it. 'You will keep it safe, yes?'

She squeezes it until she can feel the imprint of the metal in her flesh, then pushes it deep into her pocket before pulling off her biker buff and sliding it over his head. The Welsh flag is bright against his skin.

'It's not the same, not as important. But it's all I have really.'

'You have already given me enough.'

Helen frowns, unsure if he's being sentimental, uneasy if he is.

'Like my broken rib, like my bruise…'

She laughs and slaps him gently on the arm.

'But you are not having this back. I like the dragon. Fierce, like you.'

'It's in my blood.' She immediately regrets the quip, but Anton smiles. She takes out her multitool and opens the blade.

Anton's eyes widen. 'Why the knife? You want to make another scar on me?'

'No, I want you to cut my hair.' She pulls her long, tangled hair into a rope and holds it out.

'Why? It is beautiful, part of you.'

She must be careful, if he does have feelings for her, that he doesn't get the chance to express them. Better things go unsaid than regretted.

'I don't want to set off the radiation alarms at the airport, make any more trouble for myself.'

'You have checked?'

'I want it gone to be sure.'

Anton looks at the knife in his hand. 'Here? Now?'

'Yes.' Helen turns away from him and tips her head back. He is tentative at first, taking small sections and sawing through them carefully with the blade, but it is taking too long. 'Don't worry, Anton, it doesn't hurt. Just hack it off.'

He takes a bigger handful and Helen feels the blade close to her scalp, the pressure and then release of the hair shearing away. Most of the clumps fall around her shoulders and onto the grass, but smaller strands are caught on the wind and float away, catching on the shrubs or drifting off across the park.

When her head is close-cropped, and she feels the chill of the spring air on her scalp between the uneven tufts, she collects as much of the offcuts as she can, shoving the tangles deep into a litter bin.

They climb back into the car. Maksim can't keep his eyes off Helen's face and head. She runs a hand over her scalp and feels the sharpness of the stubble, the rough cut. Sticks out her chin and looks Maksim right in the eyes.

'I liked your hair so much I wanted the same look.'

Maksim runs a palm over his own buzz cut, then his hand moves around and settles on his throat. 'You look like one of us now.' The smile has slipped again, and she sees the same look in his eyes that Anton has. The performance is over.

***

The kitchen is busy; two uniforms sipping tea, pacing. Radios crackling. Jennifer keeps mixing up their names, apologising. Ioan has joined the search, grabbing the big torch and pulling a woollen hat low over his ears. He's called on distant neighbours too, mates from work. The security guards at the plant have been notified, are patrolling the perimeter, checking CCTV footage for a shape that might be a small boy with a big rucksack moving through the long grasses and rocks.

'Where did you say his mam was again?' one of the uniforms asks. They've taken off their yellow coats and hung them over the kitchen chairs, are leaning on the worktops, conferring.

'Ukraine.' She puts the kettle on again. No one has finished their tea yet.

'And you found these, where?' The box with the syringes is in a sealed plastic bag, labelled and dated. An incident number scrawled in permanent marker on the side.

'In her car, at her house. She isn't... she doesn't...'

They glance at one another.

'How long have you been worried about him, your nephew?'

An impossible question. If she'd said something earlier, to

the doctor, would Jack be in bed now? Or in a Social Services assessment centre, safe but locked in?

'Can I get some air, please?'

'Of course.' One of the officers follows her into the garden, as if she too might abscond into the emptied landscape. She goes to stand at the far end of the lawn, leans on the dry-stone walls. There is damp moss beneath her hands, the rush of the sea in her ears, and something else behind it: the low roar of the plant, turbines and generators. A throb. She looks over, towards its glowing outline. The space between her and the reactors is cut through with torch beams, thin strips of lights wavering and dipping, as the search party moves through the gorse and over the rocks towards the churning sea. Beyond the bay there is a steep incline, sheer rocks, and beyond that the outlet, where the fish grow fat in the warm water.

**

Ten minutes in the car, and they are in the heart of Minsk. Maksim pulls over again and points to a tall, pale stucco building, one of many similar structures on a wide busy street. There is no space to park and he is bouncing in his seat, looking around for police.

There isn't time for a proper goodbye, just rushed thanks: an unguarded moment where Helen feels an overwhelming gratitude to Maksim for his unquestioning help and leans over to peck him lightly on the cheek, laughing at his nodding enthusiasm and wide smile in response.

Then she is standing on the pavement, her rucksack strap clutched in her fist, looking at Anton through the grubby window. He mouths something as the car pulls away, but she can't make out the words. She raises her hand and watches the car merge into traffic, watches until it is gone, and she is alone on the wide flagstones, surrounded by people rushing past.

She shoulders the bag, sucks in the city air and steps up to the door. There is an intercom, a camera. She is asked to show her passport through the lens and then buzzed in. At reception she has to hand over her bag, her broken phone and answer questions on why she has a dosimeter. She tells the truth.

'I was in Ivankiv, I went on a tour of Chernobyl.'

'Why?'

'Just to take some photographs.'

The security guard nods as if this is the same as going to Disneyland. 'I went once, hell of a creepy place.'

She doesn't have an appointment and will have to wait. Her situation needs consultation. The right person needs to be available.

For an hour or more she sits on a fabric-covered chair and acclimatises. On the wall beside her a section of the Union Jack is painted, floor to ceiling. A pot plant sits on a side table, the tips of its long fronds browned and curling. There are no magazines to read, and the wall-mounted television is switched off, reflecting an obsidian mirror image of the room. She stares at her reflection and doesn't recognise it. Sees what could be a boy, a cancer patient, a holocaust survivor, a soldier.

The receptionist comes out from behind her protective glass window, apologises for the delay and switches the TV on. BBC news.

'Would you like a hot drink?'

Helen nods, knowing her face is surly, her haircut

aggressive. She should play vulnerable here, get on the right side of them, but she is frustrated at the wait, at the rushed drop off and now the delay to get home.

'Tea?' If the woman is cautious in any way because of the dishevelled person sitting, legs sprawled and boots splayed, in her waiting area, she doesn't give it away. Probably has pepper spray in her pocket, Helen thinks. Good on her if she has. No doubt there are more armed security guards somewhere behind the glass, waiting for something to happen, a call to action.

'Coffee if you have any. Please.' Helen smiles, lets her face soften.

The woman smiles back. 'Of course.'

Helen watches the screen while she waits, absently at first, while two newsreaders debate the Budget. Footage of the Prime Minister giving a statement, promising a referendum if he wins the general election, on whether the UK should stay in the European Union or split and become independent. I will let the people decide, he says, but let me negotiate first. He uses Ukraine as an example of how the nations are stronger together. How the EU is supporting the west of the country against Putin.

'It will never happen,' the receptionist says, handing Helen a white mug with the UK Embassy logo in silver on the side. 'Everyone knows leaving would be catastrophic for the economy. He just wants to stay in power.' She pats Helen on the arm, as if it is the intangible promise of a vote somewhere in the future causing her brow to crease. Disappears behind her bullet-proof perspex. Helen realises she could have asked to use the phone, but she is too tired to get out of the chair.

She pulls her knees up and stares at the TV, sipping the coffee. It's weak, too milky, but somehow reassuring.

The report moves to the unrest in Ukraine, the 'Euromaidan Revolution', according to the tickertape. There are death tolls rolling past. Images of protesters burning alive in Independence Square, caught in the crossfire of Molotov cocktails. As Helen cradles the cup a photograph fills the screen.

Slightly wavy hair grazing his collar, stubble on a smiling jaw; fine, as though he'd pressed his face into damp sand and the grains had stuck, golden.

Ben.

The newsreader is listing the foreign casualties of the protests. The picture changes to an older man in a suit, at some kind of formal ceremony. Glass of champagne in hand. Helen leans forward to listen. Five foreign nationals have lost their lives in the last fortnight. Two journalists, a photographer and two tourists. There is no information on how, or what has happened to their friends and colleagues.

Helen closes her eyes as the story moves on, leans her head back into the wall behind her. She can almost smell him: fresh sweat, toothpaste on his breath. Flinches when someone touches her arm.

'Are you okay?' The receptionist. 'They're ready for you now.'

'I'm fine.' She downs the last of the coffee and hands the mug back, follows the woman through into an interview room. She's glad they never slept together. Glad it wasn't Anton on the screen. She files away the ache for later, won't forget.

CHAPTER TWENTY-TWO

The taxi driver won't shut up. Asks questions and doesn't seem to mind that she doesn't answer. She is in the back, desperate for silence after the long, early morning train ride from Liverpool, sick to her stomach from the smell of the pine-tree-shaped air-freshener that swings from the rear-view mirror. Just after Llanrhyddlad she asks him to pull over, needs to feel the ground beneath her feet.

There is no pavement, and her hip is stiff from being seated for so long. She sips water from her bottle and starts to walk, inhaling the landscape; farmland, a hint of salt, the coconut fragrance of gorse just beginning to flower. Daffodils cluster in the verge, like beacons.

Home.

She feels it like a rock in her chest. Owns it.

She finds her stride, anticipates the weight of Jack against her chest, the wriggle of his bony ribcage as she squeezes him. It's a weekday, he'll be at school. She has already run through the pros and cons of turning up at the gates, demanding they let her take him home. Has decided, against the urgent need to hold him, that it is better if she waits. She will get herself thoroughly clean and unpacked before waiting at the school gates at three, avoid an argument with the teachers.

She's missed the turn from winter to spring but can smell the chill of the night lingering on the periphery of her senses.

The hedgerows might be thick, the sky low and pillowed, but there are still small patches of frost in the shadows under the trees, delicate crystals highlighting the grass. She passes stone-walled farms, wheelie bins at the end of tracks, slanted trees stunted by the wind. Cows and sheep graze, together, in the fields; the lambs bold and vocal, the heifers rotund and ready to calf. There is a pylon beside a long hangar, the wires dipping over the road. Their route is straight, marching over farmland: bases sunk deep in beds of nettles and barbed wire, yellow signs warning of electrical danger. The road curves past gateposts and neat cottages, gardens just coming into flower.

There is a row of dark trees on the near horizon, the cusp of a slight incline. Beyond it the shell of a farmhouse behind security fencing. Helen walks to the top of the rise, pauses. Beyond the wreck there are empty fields, bulldozers. She can see the sea, silver shards, where the land dips, and then Wylfa: rock black, sky grey, gorse yellow. A modernist sculpture on the coast. Sublime.

She sets her teeth. This view she can cope with, and when the last reactor is brought down the building can stay forever for all she cares. Can slowly erode and take on the lichens and rust of the landscape until, like the buildings in the Zone, it is consumed. But she will do everything she can to keep the rest as it is. Grass, rocks, anemones, bats.

She turns back, a few hundred yards downhill, a gradient just enough to set her knee singing. Takes the short track into her parents' yard, intending to check on her mam before stripping and showering, going home to her own barn.

Ioan's car is parked beside her dad's. He must be on a late

shift, or a day off, helping her dad. As she nears the house Megan barks, a weak warning cough. The haircut has changed her silhouette enough to confuse a rheumy-eyed dog. She's a threat now.

'It's me, silly,' Helen says, and the dog's ears go back, tail low, wagging. She scratches her scruff, scans the land beyond the house for signs of activity. Lambs bleat beyond the hedge, and the horizon is hazy – like a chalk drawing. She could cry with relief at the sight.

She shrugs off her rucksack and leaves it on the step then goes inside. The kitchen is cold, the Aga unlit. Helen can smell the grease in the unwashed frying pan on the hob, the sickly scent of potpourri from a bowl on the sideboard. Everything feels wrong.

'Mam?' The house is quiet. The clock ticks.

She fills the kettle, thinking she can take her mam a panad, say a quick hello before scrubbing herself clean in their shower. Sets out two mugs and wonders if while she's been away Jack has been allowed to go out after school with Ioan and her dad, helping. Thinking of him in the fields, doing what he loves best, fills her chest with pride. She can't wait to trade stories with him later, curled up under their blankets in the attic of the barn.

While the water boils she files through the mail stacked on the table. There are eleven letters addressed to her and her dad, all bearing the Vista logo. Three from the hospital.

She slits open letters from Vista with her thumb, scans the notices.

'Bastards!'

There are deadlines for oppositions to be lodged. She

checks the calendar on the wall. She has two days. A new plan for the border at the edge of their land. A ten-foot-high concrete wall where the hedgerows sprawl. Noise mitigation, security. An application to relocate adders from the site, and a request to rent fields from her dad to re-home them – no mention of an anti-venom strategy for if their sudden concentration in a new habitat and proximity to cattle leads to bites. A fold-out plan of the new areas now owned, the site swelling, borders spreading like a water stain across the map. It's happening again, Helen thinks. Just like the villages flooded for reservoirs, mountains sold for profit.

'If you steal a sheep they hang you, if you steal a mountain they make you a lord,' she mutters, spreading the letters and plans out over the table. 'He's probably after a knighthood.'

The kettle crescendos and switches itself off. She flicks through the rest of the letters, tallying the workload. Realises her plan to spend the afternoon with Jack is scuppered. Instead she'll have to read through everything again, then begin the letters. She can contact the press over the snakes. She chews her lip. Feels the pressure build. Goes outside and stuffs the stack of letters into her bag to deal with later. She is just about to go back inside and check on her mam when she hears a call.

'Hey!'

Jennifer is running down the lane towards her, hair scraped back, eyes red. No make-up. She looks old.

'Hey you!' Jennifer is out of breath. Stops a few paces away, scowling. 'What do you want?'

'It's me.'

Jennifer squints, rubs her eyes. Steps forwards slowly.

Recognition unfolds her face, is replaced quickly enough by a sob. 'Helen?'

Helen runs her hand over her shorn scalp. 'Yeah.'

'Where have you been?'

'I tried to call, there was no answer so I—'

Jennifer pushes past her, into the kitchen. Helen follows, stands by the cold Aga while Jennifer slumps in a chair, her head in her hands. Hair a mess. Helen can see her leg trembling.

'What's the matter, Jen? Is it Mam?' The nagging feeling that things aren't quite right surges. She should have gone straight up.

Jennifer is shaking her head, slowly.

'What then?' Unease spreads through her stomach, turning it liquid.

Jennifer is staring at her, lines either side of her mouth as if she has been folded somehow, become smaller. 'Where have you been?'

'It's a long story. Has Jack been okay?'

Jennifer seems to erupt, standing so quick her chair topples backwards, cracks loudly against the tiles. 'Helen! Where the *fuck* have you been?' Then she is lashing out, slapping and shoving. Backs Helen into a corner.

Helen takes the first few blows out of shock, and then raises her arms in defence, pushes back. Jennifer's attack fizzles out quickly. Helen holds her wrists, feels her sag, breathing hard. Pulls her in for a tight hug, sweeps strands of loose blonde hair from her eyes. She knew her extended absence would be a worry but hadn't calculated on this response from her sister.

'It's okay, I'm here now.' Jennifer's body feels fragile in

Helen's arms. She's shaking slightly with each trembling sob, her hands curled inwards against Helen's chest, like a child. Helen pats her back gently, unsure of what else to do. An awkward intimacy.

After a moment Jennifer pulls away, still shaking. This is more than concern about her absence, Helen thinks. Her sister might have worried, been angry, even, at the extended responsibility, but here she is, crumpled and pale. Thinner.

'Jen, what is it? Are *you* ill?' She props Jennifer against the worktop and reaches automatically for the lump on the curve of her own breast, searching Jennifer's chest as if she might see in X-ray vision any similar anomalies. 'Have you found something?'

Jennifer shakes her head, wipes her nose with a tissue from her pocket.

'Then what is it?' Her tongue is sharp and her head feels like it's full of bees. Images swarm in her skull: her dad injured in a field, Ioan poisoned by a radiation leak, the farm lost to developers. Behind them all the ice-clad fear that it is something far worse. 'Is it Jack?'

The front door bangs, her dad shuffling in, nose red from the wind and padded shirt buttoned high. Ioan is behind him, face grey, stubble weathering his cheeks and chin. They both gawk at her.

'What happened to your hair?'

The question hangs, unanswered and abstract between them. Jennifer sniffs.

'What's going on? Where's Jack?' He's at school, she thinks. Someone just tell me he's at school.

Ioan pulls out his phone, walks to the window. Asks for

someone by name. Mandy or Mary perhaps. Her dad hugs her, an encompassing hold that immediately feels as if it's for his benefit, not hers. She bears it, then extracts herself.

'The police need to talk to you, Hel, and Social Services. Jack's been—'

'He's gone.' Ioan has finished on the phone, is rubbing his jaw. 'He's gone, Helen. Three days now. We've searched and the police have been out. They're still looking – they've got people checking the port, the station.'

Helen remembers her arrival in Holyhead, the hi-vis jackets and radio static at the turnstile. She hadn't been there for years, thought it was normal to have guards at the entrance.

'Where have they looked?'

'Everywhere.'

'What happened? Why did he go?'

'You tell us, Hel. Tell us why he'd rather set off with a rucksack full of biscuits than stay with us?'

Instead of answering she runs upstairs, gently pushes into her mam's room. The woman in the bed is barely there; sunken and hollowed out. The room smells like her taidy's did those last few days in the hospital. She bends to kiss the soft, loose skin on her forehead.

'Ddrwg gen'i, Mam. I had a plan but... things have changed. Caru chdi.'

Her mam barely stirs.

Downstairs Ioan has lined up more cups on the worktop, is dropping teabags in. 'They'll be here in about half an hour, forty minutes.'

Helen doesn't even pause to listen. Grabs her rucksack from the step and is halfway across the yard when Jennifer shouts.

'Don't you want to know what's happened since you left?'

Helen doesn't break stride, marches to the barn, ignoring the hop and bleat of the lambs. It's unlocked, gaping. Inside she scans the ground floor. The car has been searched, doors and boot open, black metallic fingerprint dust over the handles and doorframes. Her stuff has either been taken or unpacked, sleeping bags unravelled and spilling over the seats like discarded cocoons. She climbs the ladder and finds the bedroom similarly ransacked. Her laptop gone.

The police. Social Services. Because he's missing? She isn't stupid, knows they'll question her lifestyle, listen to the teachers' opinions over hers. She looks at the set-up from their point of view – a child sleeping in the roof space of a barn with his mam at nearly six, on the floor. A child using knives and rabbit traps from toddlerhood. A child without toys, without friends. They won't get it. They don't know him, what he needs. Would they take him?

She grabs the last few things of use she can find in the kitchen – a bottle of water, a roll of twine and a small tarp, shoving them deep in her bag. As she leaves she can hear voices on the path, Ioan bellowing her name. She ducks beside the barn, slips through a fence and behind the hawthorn. The buds here are still tightly coiled, like little fists. The bark brown-grey, knotted and fissured. She catches her cheek on a thorn as she pushes through, sees the minutiae of life amid the spiny twigs; spiderwebs, shrivelled haws, last year's nests unravelling, wisps of fleece. Beyond, the land opens up; a slope on one side leading towards the coast, a rise obscuring the farmland from the road on the other. Wylfa behind, humming. She hugs the hedgerow, walks in the ditch. Reaches a stream under a low coppice of alders and wades through, following it towards the sea. Feels her heart stutter. If Jack is gone…

The landscape here is too dense and uneven for hiking routes. She skirts the edges of Ffion's old farm, on the market again – empty for years – until she reaches a rocky area, thick gorse bushes, an empty cottage buried deep in saplings. The land is uncultivated. If anyone cared to check they'd find her name on the land registry, but she's told no one.

Two and a half acres of overgrown woodland, rocks and crevices, a house that teenagers don't even bother to explore or use as base for tentative sex and graffiti.

A forgotten patch. Her back-up plan.

She doesn't waste time on the cottage. It is a single-storey stone building, two rooms, no water. The whitewash has long since peeled away, exposing the solid stone beneath. Inside there is nothing but broken remnants of furniture and weather-torn curtains, spiders and mice. The windows are boarded.

She slips between rocks, into a hollow. Nettles and thistles rise up and the sound is dulled beneath the undergrowth. A blackbird startles, rustles through dead leaves before breaking out. She can hear its warning call. At the heart of the thicket she pauses, listens. The wind is a soft susurration in the leaves. She pushes aside a tangled thatch of dead branches, then slips her hand down the neck of her T-shirt. Pulls out a dirty cord, a key like a pendant. The entrance to the bunker is slightly raised on a concrete block barnacled with lichen and moss. Cut into the rock, a tiny door. She stoops to enter.

Two wide eyes, black in the crepuscular gloom, pupils dilated.

'It's me. Mam.'

They blink.

The floor is littered with crisp packets, biscuit wrappers. There is a small lamp on an old wooden crate beside the nest of sleeping bags and blankets. Water bottles lined up along a wall. A camping stove and gas bottles in another corner. A further door, iron-studded, in one corner.

'Did I do it right, Mam?'

She glances around. The room is like a cell. Dank and grey. He has carefully portioned food into piles. Not touched the stove. A sickly-sweet smell catches her throat.

'I've been going outside to the tŷ bach, like you showed me. At night.'

She drops to her knees, reaches for him. He slips into her arms, small and fragile; all bones and hair and thick fleecy jumper. She feels the urge to consume him then, to protect him. Like a hare will eat its own leverets when threatened. He wriggles, but she barely loosens her grip.

'And I didn't eat everything. Look.' He relaxes the clawed grip on her arm, and points at the muesli bars and popcorn bags he's squirrelled away.

The smell, now the door has swung almost closed behind her, is thick: not like the stench of Baba Olena's home, but putrid and dangerous.

'You did great, Jack.' She kisses the top of his hair. Buries her face in the greasy, animal tang of it. Closes her eyes against the desperation of the room around her. Unnecessary. Why did he feel the need to come here? No windows, stale air. This is for dire emergencies only. But it shows he's learned, is capable. She swells a little, with pride, even as shame seeps in.

She lets him go. Sits on her haunches. He rubs her head,

little fingers through the tufted, stubbled cut. 'Can you do mine like yours?'

'Maybe.'

'I missed you.'

'Ditto,' she whispers, knowing there isn't a word big enough to describe how much.

He fetches her a bottle of water, some food. Divides a small packet of miniature cookies into two and places the little discs in her palm. Sits beside her, nibbling. As though it's a game. The weight of him resting against her thigh chokes her. She gets up to prop the door open with a rock, sees dust swirl in the green light that filters in. The room is even worse in the light; cracked walls and filthy floor, rusting brackets bleeding trails down the concrete. On the bundle of sour bedding there is a shape, curled and pale. She leans forward to inspect. A lamb, dead. This is where the smell is coming from.

'I was going to eat it.'

She scoops it up in the blanket, damp and bloated. Takes it outside to the edge of the thicket. Its eyes are open, marbled white in death.

Three days, Ioan had said. Three days in there with a dead lamb.

'I was going to make a fire and cook it, but you said smoke might make people come, so I waited.'

She smiles at him, but her throat is too tight to answer. He is frowning, looking up at her with those unfathomable eyes. She holds him again, and he wriggles onto her lap. Curls into her like he's always been there. They'll take him. She knows this, and knows too, that she must decide on her next move soon. It will take a while for them to search, and if they haven't found him yet, haven't come this far with dogs or whatever they used, then they probably won't find them now. But she can't take that risk.

And yet she is paralysed.

She can hear the hiss of the wind in the trees beyond the bunker door, smell the mulch of last year's leaves and the fresh green promise of the new growth. Jack is settled, curling his fingers in the tangled knot of his fringe, calm. She could stay here forever.

After hours or minutes, Jack moves; slips off her knee and sits in the doorway, watches a wren hop through the lowest branches of the hawthorn. She moves too. Starts to go through their supplies, checking on water and food stocks. There's enough here to last months; the room below, behind the steel door, is stacked with provisions. They have two big rucksacks, could strike out and see how far they might get.

She starts repacking her bags and finds the stack of letters from Vista. Spreads them out before her. The new map of requisitioned land unfolds, colour-coded and lined. The land is sectioned, shaded, the borders angular and encompassing. Her parents' farm is a concave bite out of the confirmed perimeter, sits inside the proposed site map. She scans over to the other side where the lines butt up against Cemaes. Stops. Double-checks. Her sister's place is inside the border, the fields and footprint of the house all showing up as owned by the company. She searches the key at the side of the map again, must have made a mistake. Jack shuffles close on his knees, leans in to look.

'Where are we, Mam?'

She points to a spot on the concrete floor, beyond the edge of the page, safe.

There is no mistake; the property is consumed, inside the development zone. Her grandparents' house. Her heritage. She checks the date on the document, a few days after she left. Then the decision must have been made months ago, to show up here.

They signed.

She folds the map, stacks the letters and tucks them into her rucksack. 'Come on, time to go.'

'Home?'

'Na, we can't go home, not yet.' She crouches in front of him. 'But we can't stay here.'

He packs his own bag, tucking snacks in every pocket, rolling his sleeping bag like a pro. Manages to get it on his back without help.

'Where are your snails?'

'I let them go.'

'Hogyn dda!'

He beams.

She locks the bunker and covers the door with brushwood, kicks dried leaves against the pile. They squeeze out of the copse, through the rocks.

'Are we going on an adventure?'

'Kind of.'

She starts walking, Jack at her side. His hand reaches up, gripping hers like a tiny claw. She squeezes back. The clouds are low, gunmetal heavy. The wind has picked up, sweeps through the long grass making it seem like the surface of a lake. She thinks of that night with Anton, the Exclusion Zone open to them alone.

'While I was away I camped out in the forest,' she says,

smiling down at him. He looks up at her with wide eyes, wolf-grey. 'The radioactive forest.'

'Really?' Doubt and awe in his voice.

'Yes.'

'Were you scared?'

'No.'

'I wouldn't be scared either, would I, Mam?'

Back past Ffion's farm, the ground overgrown and neglected. Wild. A gate somewhere banging in the wind, moss on the roof.

'Why are we going this way, you said we couldn't go home?'

'Because Mam has some work to do.'

When they reach the stream she lifts him, carries him clinging like a monkey to her shoulders, her arms tucked tight under his skinny rump. Eases him down on the other side. When they near the thick hawthorn she leads him through. He pulls back, straining against her hand. 'Why can't we just go? Like we always played?'

'Because running away would only make things worse, in the long run.'

There is a car parked in the gateway to the farmyard, its nose poking through onto the track. Ioan and Jen are talking to two people in dark coats. Pointing. Jack's hand grips tighter.

'Did I fail, Mam? Did I fail the test?'

She crouches to face him. 'No, you passed the test, Jack. You did it perfectly. I'm so proud of you.'

He grins, touches her face.

'But now we have a bigger test, and I know you're ready.'

'You're not going again, are you?'

'No, I'm not going anywhere.'

She leads him slowly up the track. He is sure-footed, agile. But doesn't let go of her hand. There is a woman in a dark blue coat, sensible shoes, a man in uniform. She recognises him, was in the same year as him at high school. Robert Jones. Bobby. He looks embarrassed. Smart and tidy in his hat and hi-vis, radio sputtering at his belt. She runs a hand through her shorn hair and sets her jaw.

The woman, Mary or Mandy, reaches for Jack's other hand. 'Come on, dyn bach,' she smiles. 'Let's go and get some lunch, hey? You hungry?'

He looks up at his mam, clutches her hand tighter. 'It's okay, come on.' Helen walks him towards the car, but the woman stops.

'Let me, iawn? PC Jones needs a quick word.'

Helen stoops to Jack, gives him a kiss. Untwines his fingers from hers. 'I'll be there now, iawn? You go on.'

He twists, looks over his shoulder as he's led to the car. Stumbles on a root and is steadied by the stranger's hand.

The wind picks up, coats flap and the trees beside the barn roar. Car doors slam and the engine turns over. Bobby Jones steps forwards, awkward. Coughs.

'You need to come with me, Mrs Morgan.'

'It's not *Mrs* Morgan,' Helen retorts, 'and I'm not going with you, I'm going with him.' She steps towards the car, reaches for the door handle just as it pulls away. Feels hands on her arm, dragging her back. She resists, tries to struggle free, but the hands squeeze tighter.

Jack's face is a small circle behind the car window, his hair a jackdaw's stick-nest tangle. He is mouthing something, but she can't make out the words.

'Let me go!' She twists and escapes the grasp of Bobby Jones, staggers back, panting.

The car bumps over rocks, bounces in potholes and is gone.

Jennifer is leaning into Ioan's arm, tears on her eyelashes. She moves towards Helen and Ioan puts out a hand, pulls her back.

Bobby Jones mumbles into his radio, keeping one eye on her.

Helen digs her hands deep into her pockets, finds the medal Anton gave her, the sheep's molar from Jack. She squeezes them hard in her fist until it hurts, focusses on the pain as she tries to think of what to do.

'Ms Morgan?'

Helen turns her back on them, looks out over the fields. The sheep are scattered, the lambs fat and audacious. She scans the landscape. Beyond the farm there is a JCB, its neck curved and black over the warning yellow of its body. It is tearing up a hedgerow. If she listens hard she might hear the branches screeching as they rend and fracture. She holds the medal and the tooth, stroking the smooth red enamel, running her finger over the worn ridges. Breathes in: sheep shit, sea salt, daffodils. She's ready.

DISCLAIMER

The Half-life of Snails is a work of fiction. While some real locations and historical facts are depicted here – to the best of my intentions accurately and based on extensive research – the characters, characters' homes and storylines are entirely fictitious. This novel in no way represents any real people or their situations, and any resemblance to real people or experiences is entirely accidental.

ACKNOWLEDGEMENTS

Thanks go, first and always, to my husband Simon and son Xandr, whose patience and support has carried me forwards and still does. I couldn't have done this without you. Mum, you taught me words and the confidence to use them. You made me a writer. This is for you. Beyond this, my entire family for making me the bloody-minded, determined, strong woman I am today. I love the bones of you all.

I am grateful to Edge Hill University for the funding to undertake the Doctoral research and visit to Chernobyl that made this novel possible, and to my friends and colleagues there for support and encouragement along the way, especially Leon and Craig.

I am indebted to Maxim Krygin for ensuring I was safe inside Chernobyl's Exclusion Zone, and for taking me off the tourist track where possible. Also for ensuring my spelling of names, places and villages was accurate. A special thanks goes to Maria Adamovna Uropa and Hanna Zavorotnya for welcoming me into their homes, and especially to Hanna whose hospitality was overwhelming. Similarly, I'm humbled by the hospitality and openness of Richard and Gwenda Jones of Caerdegog Uchaf Farm, for sharing their real story with me and discussing my fictional one with such generosity.

Thanks are also due to Darron Hodges, site manager of Wylfa B, for the tour of the proposed site and answering a million questions, and to John Greenbank for the tour inside Heysham Nuclear Power Station and answering a million more.

Kim Plaister, Kirsty Williams, Sarah Adams, Jessica Rowlands and Andrew Blankley ensured my Welsh dialogue was right. As a blow-in, Welsh is my second language and therefore sometimes weirdly formal, so these good friends have kept me on track. Diolch yn fawr iawn!

Jonathon Turnbull and Karolina Uskakovych generously translated the Ukrainian dialogue for me, ensuring it was as spoken and local, dyakuyu!

Lucy Siebert, Director of Hack Green Secret Nuclear Bunker, has been an amazing friend and ally, thank you for all the end-of-the-world and prepper chats!

The team at Parthian are amazing to work with, especially my editor Carly Holmes, whose enthusiasm for the novel and professional advice have made the whole process a pleasure throughout. It's a wonderful feeling when your book finds its home…

An extra special thank you to the X-10 Pŵer yn y Tir/Power in the Land artists, especially Helen Grove-White, whose support, encouragement, and generous loan of her house for a writing retreat at Brynddu gave me new insights into the landscape and nuclear issues I was researching, and space to think.

And G… without you I'd never have learnt the 'two-wheeled cornering' approach to writing. Cheers mate.

PARTHIAN

Fiction

Figurehead

CARLY HOLMES
ISBN 978-1-914595-05-9
£10.00 • Paperback

"Carly Holmes is a bewitching writer, and *Figurehead* is a book that's as full of eeriness and enchantment as one could ever wish for." Buzz Magazine

The Incandescent Threads

RICHARD ZIMLER
ISBN 978-1-913640-64-4
£20.00 • Hardback

THE FIFTH NOVEL IN
THE INTERNATIONALLY
BESTSELLING *SEPHARDIC CYCLE*

"Zimler is an honest, powerful writer."
The Guardian

PARTHIAN

Fiction

The Lake

BIANCA BELLOV[A]

Translated by Alex Zu[cker]

£10.00 • Paperba[ck]

ISBN 978-1-913640-[...]

WINNER OF THE E[U PRIZE]

FOR LITER[ATURE]

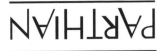

Fear of Barbarians

PETAR ANDONOVSKI

Translated by
Christina E. Kramer

£9.00 • Paperback
ISBN 978-1-913640-19-4

**WINNER OF THE EU PRIZE
FOR LITERATURE**

The Cormorant

STEPHEN GREGORY
ISBN 978-1-912681-69-3
£8.99 • Paperback

'A first-class terror story with a relentless focus
that would have made Edgar Allan Poe proud.'
New York Times

Revenant

TRISTAN HUGHES
ISBN 978-1-912681-66-2
£9.99 • Paperback

'...ccomplished ... Hughes' prose is
...ng and luminous.'
...ncial Times

The Levels

HELEN PENDRY
ISBN 978-1-912109-40-1
£8.99 • Paperback

'...stounding debut... an elegant, wise and warm
...that stays with you long after finishing it.'
Mike Parker

...on

...CONRAN
...0901-23-6
...erback

'...a great new talent.'
...nd